25 Days in December

Poppy Alexander wrote her first book when she was five. There was a long gap in her writing career while she was at school, and after studying classical music at university, she decided the world of music was better off without her and took up public relations, campaigning, political lobbying and a bit of journalism instead. She takes an anthropological interest in family, friends and life in her West Sussex village (think *The Archers* crossed with *Twin Peaks*) where she lives with her husband, children and various other pets.

25 Days in December

Poppy Alexander

ORION

An Orion paperback

First published in eBook in Great Britain in 2018
by Orion Fiction as *25 Days 'til Christmas*
This paperback edition published in 2019
by Orion Fiction
an imprint of The Orion Publishing Group Ltd
Carmelite House, 50 Victoria Embankment
London EC4Y 0DZ

An Hachette UK Company

1 3 5 7 9 10 8 6 4 2

A CIP catalogue record for this book is
available from the British Library.

ISBN (Mass Market Paperback) 978 1 4091 8153 8
ISBN (eBook) 978 1 4091 8154 5

Typeset by Born Group

Printed and bound in Great Britain by Clays Ltd, Elcograf S.p.A.

www.orionbooks.co.uk

For Jonathan

Daniel

He looked at the calendar as he shrugged on his coat. Nearly December. He still found it strange how time kept passing, the earth kept turning on its axis, each day taking him further away from that awful moment ten months ago. The moment she left him.

People say death is a shock, even when it's expected, and they are right. He had been astonished. And that was the easy part, the disbelief. The hard graft was the bit that followed, the grief that came in waves, each first anniversary painfully borne . . . her birthday, his birthday, and now the big one. Christmas.

He wondered if the Christmas Tree Girl would be in her usual spot. This would have been the fourth year, long enough to call it a tradition, him walking past her twice a day, smiling sometimes and catching her eye. Most days she had been preoccupied, busy with other customers, so he would end up passing unacknowledged, creating an odd sense of disappointment which hung over his entire day. Then – on a Saturday in early December – there would be the ceremonial 'making the visit to buy the tree'. Zoe would always argue for the first Saturday in December and Daniel would want the second, worried the tree would be dead and bare by Christmas Day. The good-natured discussions would start at the end of November and Zoe would generally win. Last year, he had had to bring her in her wheelchair, wrapped up against the cold because her circulation was so very poor. Her lips had been permanently blue, as if she had been eating blackberries, her cheeks flushed in a parody of good health; but by then her movements were slow and her voice weak.

The Christmas Tree Girl had still greeted Zoe as if nothing had changed, teasing her about her hat, ignoring the wheelchair but unselfconsciously hunkering down on her haunches to be on the same level, straining to hear her whispered words and making a joke of her own stupidity when she had to ask her to repeat herself. The Christmas Tree Girl never pretended to understand when she didn't. Not like other people, people who were embarrassed and dismissed her with an exaggerated smile and a nod. Zoe thought they were idiots and Daniel agreed. No, the Christmas Tree Girl had been different.

As always, last year, the intensely difficult question of which tree to choose had been fully engaged in. An unlimited number of trees had been examined and their form, height, bushiness and general appearance thoroughly explored. A shortlist would be drawn up and judging would be repeated until – at last – a selection could be made, and Daniel could lift the tree onto his shoulder and heft it back to the car. Last year, the Christmas Tree Girl had quickly packed up her money tin, slipped on her rucksack and taken the handles of the wheelchair. By the time Daniel had the tree properly balanced on his shoulder she had been ready to go.

'Where's the car?' she asked.

'You can't . . . what about the trees?'

'They'll be fine. You can't manage on your own.'

They walked the short distance back to his parked car talking about nothing in particular. He wished it were further. There was that awkward moment when she turned to leave.

'Merry Christmas,' she said, giving Zoe a wave through the window as the girl settled herself inside the car.

'Merry Christmas,' he replied, wanting desperately to kiss her on the cheek. Stopping himself, he held out his hand instead. 'Merry Christmas,' he said again, feeling like a complete tool. She shook it, grinning that grin where her mouth went up further on the right than the left – but her eyes still looked sad.

He blinked hard, dismissing the memory. He didn't need to make the Saturday visit this year. He wouldn't need a tree . . . but he desperately wanted to tell the Christmas Tree Girl why. He wanted to tell her – this woman whose name he didn't even know – that he had lost Zoe, that she was gone for ever and he couldn't bear it. He wanted to tell her because he had looked into her eyes and he had seen something he now saw in his own reflection.

The Christmas Tree Girl knew about loss.

Kate

'We're all very excited about it,' finished Mr Wilkins, straightening his unforgivably awful tie and giving Kate a smug grin.

'So,' she said, dragging her mind reluctantly back into the tired little beige-carpeted space off the stock rooms where Mr Wilkins had created himself a domain, 'what you're saying is – despite promising last year was the last time – you want me to stand outside the shop and sell the Christmas trees again.'

'We do! Your talent and enthusiasm for the task in the previous three years has been noted within the Portman Brothers' senior management team,' he said, clearly expecting her to be fawning with gratitude. 'And this year is the most satisfying challenge ever. With a bigger-than-ever stock of six foot premium blue Norwegian firs – at a higher-than-ever retail price, I might add – we are aiming for our best year yet.'

'Am I on a bonus?'

'No.'

'Do I have to work extra hours?'

'Yes.'

'Do I get overtime?'

'No.'

'Is there marketing support?'

'Yes.'

'And do you mean actual marketing support, or do you mean me wearing a sexy elf costume with curly slippers and a crotch-length tunic in the freezing cold? Again?'

'Yes.' Mr Wilkins paused. 'The second one,' he added. 'You'll have to get yourself some fur-lined knickers,' he suggested with an unattractive leer.

He wasn't wrong, thought Kate. The wind whistled straight up the High Street from the river and it didn't bother going around anyone in its path. She felt the cold in her bones. In previous years she had genuinely worried about getting hypothermia.

'Is there a budget for fur-lined pants?' she asked, without optimism.

'No. Non-uniform attire will be provided at the expense of the individual employee.'

I bet it will, she thought glumly. 'So,' she said, 'with no sales-related bonus and no other perks, what is my motivation for saying yes, exactly?'

'I think,' said Mr Wilkins, with barely concealed malice, 'all staff on contracts which are expiring in January would be well served to ask themselves not what Portman Brothers can do for them but what they can do for Portman Brothers.'

'My contract is ending?'

'The thirty-first of December,' confirmed Mr Wilkins. 'How time flies when you're having fun . . . You are, as you will doubtless remember, on a rolling contract which renews in line with the business year end, regardless of start date. It's all in there. Do you not recall?'

'Well, yes,' said Kate, because she did vaguely remember something about it. The contract terms had been generally poor, she definitely remembered that much, with the bare minimum wage, holidays and benefits, but she had needed a job as a stopgap, not imagining she would still be there. 'But it's just continued every year. I didn't think . . .'

'That's because it's been rolling,' he explained patiently. 'But now it's been getting on for four years – can you believe? – since I interviewed you for the post. You brought Max, I recall. He was only, what, three?'

'Two,' said Kate, faintly. 'He was two. And he's called Jack.'

'Yes, well, anyway,' he said, losing interest. 'Like I said, four years down the line, belts tightening, cutbacks, same old, same old . . . Always wise to make a good impression, don't you think? Don't want to find yourself starting the new year at a loose end, especially with a little lad to support.'

Helen opened the door of the bright pink terraced house with a broad smile on her face.

'Sorry, sorry,' said Kate. 'I had a meeting after work. I thought about calling when I got out but I decided to just get here asap.'

'No problem,' said Helen, who was sunny by nature but was also smiling for a reason; she made a penalty charge of fifteen pounds for all parents collecting after her seven o'clock cut-off point and the minute hand was now firmly south of ten past.

She had earned it fair and square, thought Kate without rancour, although it was money she could ill afford to lose. That said, Helen was a rock without whom Kate would not be able to work at all, and she owed the older woman for far too many kindnesses over the years to begrudge the little boost to her income.

'He's been fine,' said Helen. 'Done his homework, eaten a good tea; getting a bit tired now though. Mrs Chandler said to tell you she wanted a word when you take him in

6

tomorrow. Jack'll tell you why,' she said, pulling a face. 'At least he'll tell you his version.'

'Fighting!' said Kate once she had Jack in the car. 'What have I said to you about fighting?'

'Dad did fighting as an actual job,' he said sulkily. 'And Uncle Stuart said he was a "bloody hero".'

'Don't swear. And that's not the point. Dad was a soldier. It's not the same. Anyhow, what was the fight about?'

'Lucas and Krishna said Father Christmas only comes if you've got a dad.'

'Well, how the heck do you work that one out?'

Jack sighed. 'It's simple,' he said. 'You know Father Christmas can't get to all the houses in the world in one night, right?'

Kate blinked. 'He can't?' she asked, playing for time.

'Obviously not,' said Jack, with heavy patience. 'That's not real, is it? So, he has to do a thing where he uses the daddies, see? So, it's – kind of – a thing where it's him but not him, right? The dads . . .' he cast around for logic, 'they help. See?'

'Oookay,' said Kate, 'but that's fine, because you have got a daddy, haven't you?'

'Yeah, but he's just a stupid star now isn't he?' said Jack, pointing at the sky through the car windscreen. 'How's he going to help Father Christmas bring me presents from there?'

By then, they had arrived back home. Miraculously there was a parking space just outside the launderette and Kate nipped in quickly before it was taken by someone else. She checked her watch. They had arrived home in the sweet spot between daytime parking charges and night-time visitors. She and Jack lived in Stokes Croft, the edgy, 'up and coming' area that never seemed to quite come up. The architecture was mainly late Victorian houses – now largely flat conversions – interspersed with brutalist sixties architecture replacing what had been flattened by stray wartime bombs meant for the docks. It was the only place near the centre of the city – and therefore work – that wasn't stupidly expensive. That was one of the reasons why Kate had been so pleased to find the nearly affordable little flat above the launderette. The comforting smells of soap powder and hot laundry floating up the stairs to their front door, accessible only via the launderette itself, were another plus.

'Time for bed,' she said, noticing the little boy rubbing his eyes as she opened the flat door, nudging him ahead of her as she came in behind him, carrying their bags.

'Can we have hot chocolate?'

She thought quickly. There was barely any milk, but enough for one mug, providing she gave him toast not cereal for breakfast and drank her tea black tomorrow morning. ''Course you can,' she said, with a smile.

'Don't you want any?' he asked, as she measured out the last of the milk and put the mug into the microwave.

'Not for me, thanks lovely, I'm fine.'

'Can I have marshmallows?'

'None left,' she admitted, 'but I'll get some more as soon as I get paid.'

'Yay! I love marshmallows . . . But I love hot chocolate without them too,' Jack added, hastily, noticing the sadness on his mum's face.

By the time he was in his pyjamas, hot chocolate drunk, face washed and teeth thoroughly brushed under Kate's supervision, he was dragging his feet and yawning noisily. She chivvied him into his bedroom that wasn't a bedroom and encouraged him into bed. Kate had been amazed to see a two-bed flat to rent in her price range but when she came to view it, the reason for the low rent was obvious; the so-called 'second bedroom' was – technically – a cupboard, or at least an internal space carved out of the main bedroom by a flimsy partition wall. It had its own door from the little hallway but no outside wall and consequently no window of its own. Kate worried about Jack being in there without direct access to daylight or ventilation, but she had made it cosy with a little chest of drawers, a narrow single bed with a bright, space-themed duvet cover, and lots of bookshelves, piled high with children's books, mainly bought second-hand from charity shops.

That night, Kate had barely started to read when Jack's eyelids drooped and then fluttered closed. She continued for a few minutes more, lowering her voice gradually to a whisper before closing the book, but as she stood up his eyes flew open again.

'I need a colander,' he announced, suddenly wide awake.

'A colander?' she said, sitting back down and tucking a lock of his hair out of his eyes. She needed to get it cut. 'Any particular sort of colander?'

'A vent colander.'

'For vegetables?'

'Noooo . . .' he said, in frustration. 'Not vegetables,' he pulled a face. 'A *vent colander* . . . so we can tell when Christmas is.'

'Ah!' said Kate, as the penny dropped. 'An advent calendar.'

'Yep. One of them,' Jack agreed with relief, 'I think there are chocolate ones,' he added hopefully.

'So I've heard,' smiled Kate. 'I'll have to see what I can do.'

*

In the flat's mean little sitting room, with its dingy furnishings and a basic kitchen arranged along one wall, she moved around quietly, tidying Jack's possessions with nothing but the yellow light from the street lamp outside to guide her. She needed to get things sorted and then settle down to at least a couple of hours of jewellery making. It wasn't a hobby. The craft, which she had been doing since Jack was tiny, had turned into a useful way of making extra money, but after an already busy day it was hard to find the motivation to do it.

Folding his discarded school jumper, she gazed out of the tiny square window at the night sky. The glass was veiled with dirt, not on the inside, but on the outside from the traffic fumes and the dust from the street. The sky was clear though; Kate could see the moon and even some of the brightest stars.

Had she been wrong to tell Jack that his father was looking down on him from the sky? It had seemed a comfort to tell him something – perhaps she even believed it herself – but now, gazing out at the white pinpricks of light, so many millions of light years away from the earth, she wondered . . . could Tom really be there with them in any way at all? Was he sorry to have left them alone – a widow at twenty-six and Jack at just two? She pressed her forehead against the cold glass. She hated this time of year. The knock at the door had come days before Christmas four years ago. She had assumed it was one of the other wives from the army base, coming for a coffee, to borrow some milk or just for a gossip. But when she saw the two officers there in dress uniform, caps tucked under their arms and gloves in their hands, she knew.

Initially, the Army had been more than kind, inviting her to stay in her quarters for 'as long as she needed'. But just weeks later one of the other men – Tom's comrade – had become a nuisance, making it clear he was all too happy to 'comfort' her in her grief. The support from the other wives had fallen away pretty rapidly then. Sympathy had been replaced by beady looks as they jealously defended their men from the pretty young widow. Kate had taken the hint. The army pension wasn't much and it had been swallowed up supplementing the fees of the good but expensive care home where Tom's grandmother Maureen – who had raised him – had been put within months of his death. Grief had accelerated the dementia that had been nibbling at the edges of Maureen's mind for years. Kate still took Jack to see her occasionally, but it was a long journey and she didn't recognise either of them any more. She kept thinking Jack was Tom as a boy, which frightened and confused him.

Kate had picked herself up, moved to Bristol, found a rubbish job and put a roof over their heads. The daily grind of living had occupied her mind and kept her going. Since Tom's death, Christmas had brought on a particularly strong urge to disappear under the duvet and come out when it was over. Instead she steeled herself to make sure Jack had a good time on Christmas Day. But this year he was older and more aware so he knew much earlier that Christmas was coming. It was going to be December tomorrow. The anticipation was building, and Kate was going to have to stifle the duvet urge for a whole month. She groaned aloud at the thought.

Was this really all life held for them both now? The poverty, the fatigue, the lack of joy . . .? She had adored Christmas before Tom died. He had laughed at her rituals, her plans – starting in October with the present lists, the stirring of the pudding in November, dancing around the kitchen to the cheesy Christmas songs playlist on the iPad:

Slade, George Michael, Mariah Carey . . . where had that old Kate gone? She gazed out of the window at the sky. This was her, now.

She was a star too; cold, remote, distant and lonely.

Jack had already lost one parent. He couldn't afford to lose the other. She needed to share the joy of Christmas with her son: to be his mother properly, to be there . . . He deserved nothing less, but where would she find the strength to do it?

She needed a Christmas miracle.

1st December

The rushed visit to the pound shop, on the way to work, had not been a success. There were advent calendars, but they weren't chocolate ones. They were flimsy, and the designs were uninspiring. Plus, she had twelve pounds and twenty pence to last her until Friday and it was only Monday. At least four pounds of that was going to be needed to keep the gas and electricity on in the little flat; another four pounds for the bus, and then the rest for suppers all week. It was pasta with tinned tomatoes and cheese all too often, because it was cheap. There was always the food bank at the church up the road, of course. She had not yet resorted to that. Not yet. She had managed her meagre resources so far with steely resolve and relentless planning.

And on that note, the whole advent calendar thing was impossible. There was no point at all looking at the advent calendars in the store itself: even with her staff discount they were well beyond her reach. The big, three-dimensional cardboard creations were for the rich kids. There were even some versions for grown-ups, with hand-made chocolates and beauty products for the women, posh shower gel and miniatures of whisky for the men.

Jack had mentioned it again pointedly that morning – it was December now – and Kate had fobbed him off, saying she had always opened her advent calendar in the evening so maybe he should wait until tonight and see what happened.

And now it looked like there would be nothing happening, thought Kate in despair.

'You all right love?' asked Pat, as Kate came exhausted into the staffroom to have her twenty-minute break. 'Cuppa?'

She nodded, wordlessly sagging down onto the hard, plastic chair, closing her eyes for a moment. Then, as if it weighed a ton, she dragged her head up to meet the older woman's eye.

'Hi Pat. Yes please, tea would be amazing, sorry.'

'S'all right,' said Pat, sliding a mug towards her. 'Strong and sweet, just like you.'

'I'm definitely going to be strong by Christmas,' agreed Kate. 'The trees are huge. The trunks are like – well – tree trunks.'

'You shouldn't be hauling that sort of thing around. You're only little. It's not right. What about health and safety?'

'I'm not that small,' said Kate, with a spark of energy driven by indignation.

'Yeah you are,' said Wayne, joining them and occupying one entire side of the table by spreading his legs wide, a huge hand curving around his cup of instant coffee, which was in a mug urging them all to *Keep Calm and Drink Coffee*. 'You're tiny.'

'Only next to you. Everyone looks small next to you: you're like King Kong.'

'All muscle, darlin',' agreed Wayne.

'So why aren't you shifting those trees for Kate then?' said Pat, with spirit. 'Compared with Kate's five foot nothing, you'd do it in twenty minutes.'

'Doing the lights though, ain't I? Highly skilled job, that. Not everyone can do the Christmas lights, mate. They have to be done in a very special way,' he said portentously, tapping the side of his nose. 'Plus, I can't imagine Mr Wilkins would want to see me in that elf costume of yours.'

'Nor do we,' Pat assured him promptly.

'I don't see what's so hard about sticking a plug in a socket,' teased Kate, but she mustered a smile as she said it. Wayne was a dull-witted but kind young man, who coached Jack at football most Saturdays, and would do anything for anyone, once they got past the initial attitude.

'You were late this morning,' said Pat to Kate, without judgement. 'I told Mr Wilkins you were here but had gone to the loo. I hinted at girlie stuff. Sorry.'

Wayne shuffled awkwardly and cleared his throat. Girlie stuff was definitely not his thing.

Kate gave him an amused but understanding look and explained wearily about the advent calendar issue.

'Well, there's a thing,' Pat said triumphantly. 'What a bit of luck! Hang on . . .' She jumped up as fast as her arthritic knees would allow and went to rummage in her locker.

'Now, I nearly didn't bring it in this morning, but then I thought, well, chances are I'll be going straight there . . .' She chatted on, the words inaudible from the cupboard; '. . . would want it for the beginning of December,' she finished as she emerged triumphant.

She patted down her hair with one hand whilst holding a paper bag with a string handle in the other. She plonked it on the table and pushed it over to Kate.

'You'll probably hate it. Not exactly the kind of thing you're after, but still, it might do if you're desperate . . . I won't be offended . . .'

Kate plunged her hand into the bag and pulled out a mass of green, white and red knitting, all rolled up like a Swiss roll, with what looked like a piece of bamboo in the middle. Unravelled, it revealed a large oblong of red hanging from the horizontal bamboo handle. It was scattered with embroidered white snowflakes, but what caught the eye was the rows of knitted pockets, five across and five down, twenty-five in all, each with a number painstakingly embroidered onto the front, along with a little Christmas motif – a reindeer on one, a candle on another, a Christmas wreath on another. The pocket for Christmas Day had no number on it, just a big, elaborately embroidered star, shimmering with transluscent beads and sequins.

'It's an advent calendar,' exclaimed Kate. 'Oh, my goodness, tell me you didn't knit it. It's amazing!'

Pat blushed and ducked her head: 'I get bored,' she admitted. 'I made a couple last year and they seemed to go down all right. Mind you, the Christmas Fair was earlier last year. This year I can't see them selling. Too late, like I said.'

'But this isn't something you would use just for one year,' said Kate, examining it wonderingly.

'We're in a disposable society now, but – no – I would hope it would become a tradition,' admitted Pat, her face lighting up at her friend's obvious approval. 'Obviously you pop new things in the pockets each year . . .'

'There's something in them already,' noticed Kate, seeing for the first time that the little pockets each had a discreet bulge.

'Just chocolate,' admitted Pat. 'Not very original. I had some chocolate coins . . .'

'That's exactly what he wanted,' beamed Kate, sagging in her chair again but this time with relief. 'I must give you something for it. You were going to raise money for charity with it. I can't not.'

Pat waved her away. 'Don't be silly. Charity begins at home. The Christian Mission would be very happy to know it was going to such a lovely little boy. Entirely appropriate.'

'Thank you,' said Kate, but it came out on a little sob. She wiped away a tear, laughing at herself.

This was all too much for Wayne. 'Mate . . . knitting, girlie stuff and crying,' he muttered to himself as he got up. 'I'm off.'

'Right,' said Kate, shaking herself into a more positive mood. 'That's solved one problem. On with the next.'

Spending a year stuffed in a carrier bag in a corner of the vast store cupboard in the staffroom had not done the elf costume any favours. Kate was desperate to get a thermal vest and leggings to wear underneath it, but that was all money she could be spending on presents for Jack. Dressing quickly, in case Wayne came back and had the shock of seeing her in her underwear – or, God forbid, Malcolm Wilkins walked in and got a thrill – she layered two old T-shirts under the green tunic instead and put on an extra pair of tights, making sure the ones with holes were underneath. As first days went, she was lucky: the weather was still mild.

'It's a shame you having to work so hard in December,' said Pat as she finished off her tea. 'All the extra hours, what with your little lad.'

'Jack loves being with Helen, though,' replied Kate, doing up the belt on her tunic. 'I think they're making salt dough Christmas decorations today. She's really good at them.' Kate refrained from adding that she had struggled to get a childminder who was prepared to work evenings and weekends. Most wouldn't. For Saturday care, Helen charged a premium which nearly wiped out the benefit of Kate working. But management had made clear that if she valued her job, Saturday working was a 'must'.

'You're not on a rolling contract too, are you?' Kate asked Pat, her worrying conversation with Mr Wilkins coming back to her.

'Am I what, dear?'

'On a rolling employment contract? Does your contract come to an end at the end of this year too?'

'Goodness, I hope not,' said Pat, her forehead crinkling with worry. 'Why on earth do you say that?'

'Nothing, nothing . . . I've got one because it's all I was offered at the time, and I signed but I wish I hadn't now. You've been here for years, it's probably different.' She explained briefly her conversation with Malcolm Wilkins.

'Oh dear,' Pat said, in dismay. 'I think that's terrible.' She paused, clearly considering whether to say something. 'I did hear . . .'

'Go on.'

'I heard things weren't good,' Pat admitted. 'Trade hasn't been what the directors would like. I gather this Christmas is critical. If it doesn't go well, apparently there might be, well, redundancies.'

Kate swallowed. 'Redundancies,' she said. 'I don't know how it works and I couldn't find the paperwork at home last night, but if I'm really on a rolling contract, they'll be able to chuck me out without paying anything. I'll be the first to go.' She felt sick. The cheese sandwich she had brought from home for lunch sat in her stomach like a boulder.

'It won't come to that,' said Pat kindly, placing a reassuring hand over Kate's. 'But you might want to have a word with HR,' she added, her brow knitting again in concern. 'Just to see what the situation really is.'

'You worry too much,' Tom had always said. She wished hard, causing a physical ache in her chest, that he was there to tell her that now, to hold her against him, to warm her and comfort her in the way he always did, his chin resting on the top of her head. A tear leaked out as she leaned her head against the bus window. She straightened, wiped it away and sniffed hard. I worry too much, she told herself, making a pledge to go to the HR department during her first break tomorrow. Better to know the truth than immediately fear the worst.

'They're not out yet,' said Seema, as Kate skidded to a halt beside her. 'Catch your breath, you're fine.'

Kate shot her friend a grateful look. 'How was your day?'

'Got up, shouted at children and husband, brought children here, shouted at them again in public, went to work, got home, picked up smelly socks, threw away fresh veg I was going to use for a stir-fry, called Anil and asked him to get a takeaway for dinner again, decided not to walk the dog – again – came here again, just waiting to resume child-shouting activities. You?'

Kate smiled. Seema was ridiculously elegant and poised with her immaculately draped saris and her impeccable eye make-up. She was beautiful. Kate couldn't imagine her shouting at anyone. She worked part-time at the registry office so she could fit it in with Krishna's school days. She constantly told Kate she should get a job with the council too, because they were so child-friendly. Kate had kept an eye on the recruitment pages for a time but had got out of the habit after months. Nothing had come up that she had the right experience for. She wasn't really qualified to do anything, that was the problem. The only skill she had that made her different from every other mum looking for working hours that suited the school run was her ability to make jewellery. It was a hobby, but Tom had encouraged her. She was going to have a little workshop at their next army quarters. A spare room. It was all part of the plan. And then the plan – the plans – had all disappeared in a puff of smoke . . .

'Uh-oh,' Seema added, grabbing Kate's arm and talking through the corner of her mouth. 'Incoming at three o'clock.'

The queen bee, PTA Chairperson Anastasia Green, who always arrived half an hour early so she could park her people-carrier right outside the school gates and catch up with her text messages. Having checked her make-up in the drivers' mirror, she had now climbed gracefully out and was sauntering their way. She was wearing designer gym gear, as she usually did, its figure-hugging nature showing off her tight, gym-honed figure.

'God, I just always love your beautiful traditional dress,' she gushed to Seema, who smiled tightly at her in reply. Kate – who knew what Seema thought of Anastasia – dug her friend in the ribs and settled into trying to disturb Seema's carefully poised facade by making her laugh.

'God, yah,' Anastasia went on, oblivious, 'it just looks so elegant . . . I wonder if I could get away with one.' She looked down at her perfectly toned body. 'Not sure I could carry it off like you do.'

'I'd suggest we should swap,' said Seema, giving Kate a quelling look, 'but I don't think anyone wants to see me in your gym stuff, to be honest.'

Anastasia tossed her head, pleased with the compliment. 'I do have to send away for it,' she said with false modesty. 'I'm annoyingly tiny and the normal gear just hangs off me. So frustrating. I'm sure you find the same, don't you Kate?'

'What with us both being short, you mean?' she asked, for unnecessary clarification. 'Nah, what I do,' she confided, leaning in as if imparting a valuable secret, 'is make sure to eat lots of cake. That way, though I'm little I'm also quite squat, so I can still fit into normal sizes, providing I take up the trouser hems. Think of the money I save.' She nodded emphatically. 'Think less "Kylie" and more "garden gnome",' she added. Seema snorted inelegantly, and Anastasia grinned a ghastly grin, not sure whether she was being teased or not.

'Anyway,' said Seema composing herself and looking at her watch. She glanced at the school's main entrance, which was sure to be flooded with a mass of blue-clad primary school children at any moment, 'what can we do you for?'

'Well,' said Anastasia gazing heavenward as she ticked a list of tasks off her fingers, 'the whole PTA committee is just massively overcommitted already, up to our eyes, and we've still not got the tombola, present wrapping, Santa's Grotto, lucky dip or whack a rat covered for the Christmas Fair,' she looked at them both accusingly. 'And the thing is, girls, we are all just getting a teensy bit fed up of making up for the other mums. I know what you're going to say,' she said, holding up her hand to stem a flow of words which neither Seema nor Kate were actually contemplating, 'you working mums are too busy for all this stuff, but I'm busy too, you know, and there are other ways . . .' she added, darkly.

'Like . . .?' Kate ventured, nervously.

'Well, Kai's mum's really high powered in the City and she got one of her high-net-worth clients to donate a helicopter ride for a raffle prize. Just an example.'

'I don't think many of my customers are "high net worth",' muttered Kate, thinking of her typical customer, who tended to be a woman of a certain age looking for flesh-coloured control pants or a nice, sensible navy-blue cardie.

'And I'm pretty sure asking for a present from people coming in to register a death is sort of frowned upon,' said Seema, a smile still playing mischievously at the corners of her mouth.

'Yes, well, not exactly that, obviously,' said Anastasia crossly. 'But what about you, Kate, you were seen selling

Christmas trees today outside Portman Brothers, I gather,' her mouth twisted into a fleeting expression of disapproval, 'I am sure the department store would be delighted to donate a tree for the school hall.'

Kate was sure they would not. 'I'll ask,' she said, shuffling her feet.

'Fine,' snapped Anastasia, 'if you would.' At that, she turned sharply on her heel and shimmied off, glancing up under her eyelashes at one of the dads who, caught looking admiringly, blushed and looked away rapidly.

'Phew,' said Seema, wiping her brow theatrically. 'I thought she was going to make us actually do something then. I might have had to go in with my nuclear excuse.'

'Which is?'

'We're flipping Hindus, aren't we?'

'God, yes, that's brilliant!' said Kate, genuinely impressed. 'I wish I could say that. She couldn't make a fuss: it would be culturally insensitive.' She paused. 'Hang on a minute, you guys do Christmas, you definitely do . . .'

''Course we do,' said Seema. 'You don't think Krishna would let us miss out on that? We looove your quaint little rampantly consumerist traditions. And anyway, "when in Rome . . ." and all that. Anyhow, what are you two doing now? Do you want to come back with us for a bit?'

'Could do,' said Kate, brightening. 'We were just going home, that's all.'

Krishna had a new DVD and the two boys were soon happily ensconced in front of the television. As Seema bustled about the little kitchen making them both a cup of tea, Kate had a look through Jack's school bag, taking the opportunity to throw away a blackened banana skin with a shudder of disgust.

'What's this?' she asked, extracting a crumpled piece of yellow A4 paper. The school used different colours for different communications and yellow was a letter from the headteacher's office. Never a good sign. 'Jack's been put in some extra literacy class thingie on Thursdays,' she said, reading. 'Has Krish had one of these?'

Seema peered over Kate's shoulder. 'Don't think so.' Seeing her friend's concern, she added, 'But that's good isn't it? Glad to see the school is earning its money and differentiating its teaching.'

'Yeah, but why does Jack need differentiated teaching?' insisted Kate.

Seema said nothing, just giving her friend a sympathetic look.

'Do you think Jack's okay?'

Seema snorted. 'Of course he's okay. What do you mean?'

'Sometimes I just think . . .'

'Listen,' said Seema firmly, 'All our kids are completely different. They are different to each other, to their brothers and sisters, to everyone. They are who they are,' she explained. 'And they're all "okay",' she added with weight, putting her arm around Kate's shoulder. 'Don't worry.'

'Sometimes I feel like I don't notice things I ought to notice, with Jack.'

'How can you not notice what you haven't noticed?' asked Seema with irreproachable logic.

Kate tutted. 'You know what I mean . . . I just worry that sometimes, with everything going around my head – I'm so wrapped up in myself, I'm not seeing stuff that's obvious to other people. Important stuff,' she admitted. 'Being a rubbish mum, basically, and now it's nearly Christmas . . .' She explained her thoughts of the previous evening to Seema, and her ambition to make Jack's Christmas amazing this year.

'That's brilliant,' said Seema. She gave her friend an encouraging smile. 'I've been waiting for you to say that. What we need is a cunning plan.'

'What? I didn't mean now,' said Kate, wearily. She was leaning heavily against the kitchen worktop, cradling her tea mug in both hands, her eyelids drooping with fatigue.

'Why not now?' said Seema. 'Hang on.'

She disappeared into the cupboard under the stairs and came out carrying an armful of stationery.

'Right,' she said, dumping it on the kitchen table. 'Sit down.'

Kate sat.

'Pick a colour,' Seema ordered, fanning out a fistful of colourful card for her to choose from.

'Erm, why?'

'Planning. Planning always involves stationery. This is something I know. And I happen to be well equipped with the stuff.'

'You're not kidding. Does Krishna use any of this?'

'On pain of death, certainly not. This is *my* stuff.'

'Then I am honoured,' said Kate, pulling a piece of red card out from the selection Seema was holding.

'Good choice. Now,' said Seema, selecting a silver pen. 'First, the heading.'

Quickly, Seema had marked out a series of lines on the card in pencil, and was now working on an elaborate calligraphic header with a pen that produced a thick, flowing line of silver.

'*Jack and Kate's Christmas Miracle*,' Kate read out as Seema swiftly and expertly created the words.

'You are so good at this.' Kate marvelled. 'I was thinking about doing something like this, but – well – I didn't have all the gear, for one thing.'

'I know. Now, we just need . . .' She started another line and – using a gold pen this time – she continued, with the words, *In 25 Easy Steps*. 'And then we've got these,' she said waving a set of oblong stickers. 'These are for the daily things.'

'So, what are they?'

'What are what?'

'The twenty-five easy steps. Come on, you were saying about going to see the Christmas lights? That can be one of them.' She grabbed a pen and wrote it on a sticker. 'What else?'

'I dunno, the nativity play at school, for example?'

'Perfect,' said Seema, writing it in and putting it on the red sheet.

'Is that the right date?'

''Course.'

Kate was in awe of Seema's organisational skills. If she had been asked, she might have been able to hazard that the nativity would be during the school term – probably this side of Christmas – but that would have been about it.

'What else?'

'It's a big ask – a return to life,' explained Kate to her friend, desperate for her to understand. 'I'm not even sure what I mean. But achieving it – well, it's little stuff isn't it? Just things that are happy, joyful . . .' She grabbed a pen and wrote, jotted a few down, some of the daft things she used to do with Tom or when she was a child. She put in serious things, stuff that they had to do anyway but was about Christmas: the chores, the silliness, all the things that were not part of the daily grind. A little parcel of joy – one thing for each day, counting down to Christmas Day where she simply wrote two words: *Be happy*.

Seema was looking over her shoulder as she scribbled. 'Nice,' she said. 'You need more. What about snowball fights, sledging, maybe?'

'We'd be lucky,' said Kate. 'In Bristol? We haven't had snow for years. Not proper snow.'

'It might happen. Put them in,' said Seema. 'You can just pick from the list, look, they just peel off.' Her voice cracked.

Kate looked up at her friend sharply and was touched to see she had a strange smile on her face and tears in her eyes.

'I can't tell you how long I have been waiting for you to see these things,' she said, her voice wobbling with emotion. 'Since I met you – it's been nearly four years you realise? – I've been waiting.'

'For what? For me to do what?'

'To . . .' Seema waved her arms, searching for the words, 'to stop shutting yourself off. You've been focusing on Jack and not allowing yourself to feel anything. Him? He's fine, other than having to make do with just a tiny part of you. You're half alive, Kate. It's time to come back.'

Kate blinked. She didn't know what to say, so Seema went on: 'This Tom – I think I would have loved him if I'd known him – he would hate to see you doing this to yourself – to both of you.' Seema took a deep breath, considering her friend carefully. 'Look,' she said, 'you know the safety instructions when you get on a plane?'

'Yes. What's that got to do with anything?'

'When the oxygen masks come down from the ceiling you've got to put your own one on first, haven't you? That's what they tell you. Before you can do anything to save your loved ones, right?'

'Okay, I get it,' muttered Kate. 'A bit of a tortured analogy, but fair enough. I get it. To help Jack I have to help myself be well first. What's your point in connection with this though? I'm doing Christmas cards with Jack, outings, shopping, carols . . . that's me doing it too.' It felt her friend was criticising and she had never experienced that from Seema before. It hurt. 'I'm trying, Seema,' she said.

'You are,' Seema reassured her, sitting back down at the table and grabbing a pen. 'Very trying. Now pour us a glass of wine. Tea's not good enough for this job and you've got some important gaps to fill in your miracle plan.'

Holding two large glasses of Pinot Grigio from her friend's well-stocked fridge, because Seema insisted Prosecco was for weekend nights only, Kate stood at her shoulder and peered at what she had added.

'I'm not doing that,' she complained, spilling the wine as she gestured at one of the stickers Seema had written.

'Ohmigod, I'm *definitely* not doing that,' she exclaimed, pointing at a slip of paper. 'You lot are too mental for me.' Seema and her gaggle of friends had a tradition of going 'out, out' which meant pre-loading at one of their houses, massively glam clothes and make up, cocktails, nightclubs and mayhem which generally didn't end until someone cried, someone else threw up and they all got a taxi back in the early hours of the morning.

'Shh,' said Seema dismissively, 'You absolutely should do a "going out, out" night. Anil will babysit. Jack can come here. Now, am I in charge or not?'

'Not, actually,' said Kate, but she was genuinely rattled, her heart pounding and palms sweating.

Seema put a hand on her arm. 'Be brave,' she said.

'But this is all stuff I don't . . .' She stopped, pressing her hand to her mouth.

'It's all stuff that's outside your comfort zone, yeah.'

'Well, maybe not the drinking mulled wine, I'm quite good at that,' she joked weakly.

Seema ignored it. 'It's all stuff that's difficult because change is difficult. This isn't about finding twenty-five mildly fun things to do between now and Christmas, this is about changing your life – changing Jack's life – for the better.'

'I know,' said Kate. 'It was my idea,' she insisted, but then sagged slightly. She was tired. This was hard. 'So when do I have to do this "going out on the pull" thing,' she asked, with resignation.

'Before Christmas, obviously,' said Seema, 'but it's the pinnacle really, I want you to do the other stuff first. Building up to it.'

'Like the beauty spa thing? The hair? The manicure? That's a bit ambitious. I don't have any money.'

'Don't worry,' said Seema, who was the queen of the spa treatment and fully intended to sort Kate out herself. 'I have a cunning plan.'

'Oh dear,' said Kate. Now she was very worried indeed.

'Finished!' claimed Jack loudly, holding up his plate for Kate to see. 'Can I have my advent calendar now?'

'You've eaten the skin too, good boy,' said Kate, giving him a smile. She had taught him not to waste food. They didn't have the money for that. 'Go on then, where's number one?' She had managed to get the first Christmas Miracle note into the pocket while he was eating.

'There!' he said, reaching to his full height to slip his little hand inside. 'Yay!' he said, pulling out the bright gold coin and trying to pick the foil off. Failing, he went to bite it instead.

'Let me,' said Kate, taking it from him and popping it off, first one side then the other. 'What else is in there? Can you feel all the way to the bottom?'

Jack delved back into the pocket and pulled out the sticky note..

'What does it say?'

'Argh,' he complained. 'I've done my reading already today,' but he opened the scrap of paper and frowned at it. 'See – the – Ch . . . Ch . . .'

'Christmas,' prompted Kate, quietly.

'Oh yeah, "See the Christmas – licked . . . lig . . ."'

'You can do it, we've done the "gh" sound haven't we?'

'I can't remember,' said Jack, on the edge of a wail.

Kate relented. 'It says "See the Christmas Lights",' she said, hugging him to her side as he held the paper, his mouth full of chocolate. 'It's Tuesday tomorrow and you go to Helen's after school don't you? So, I could collect you from there and I thought we would go back into town and see the Christmas lights go on,' she said. 'Would that be fun? That bloke who plays a doctor on the telly is pushing the button, I think, and there'll be a big countdown, and then the whole street will be lit up ready for Christmas shopping.'

'Are we going to be out late? Will it be dark?'

Kate nodded.

'Cooool!' said Jack.

'So,' she said, 'given that we're out late tomorrow, I think it's bedtime, don't you?'

And that was just day one, thought Kate as she supervised tooth brushing and face washing. Twenty-four days to go until Christmas Day and she had a plan. She was determined, every day in the lead up to Christmas this year, they would do something Christmassy. It would be a mini-celebration of life, the universe and everything. Miracles happened, but not often. It helped if you could give things a nudge in the right direction. She was determined that was what she was going to do.

2nd December

The bus from work had been held up by a stand-up row between a taxi driver and a cyclist, an amusement and irritation to passengers and passers-by. In the end there had been quite a crowd, cheering, barracking, offering their views, shouting at whichever protagonist they felt was most in the wrong. The delay had set Kate's heart rate soaring. She had had to clench her fists to avoid jumping out of the bus and knocking their heads together. Too often recently she had been charged the extra fifteen pounds for being late to collect Jack from Helen.

By the time Kate had jumped off and jogged to Helen's house, she was sweating, her hair was sticking to her forehead, and her face was beetroot.

'It's brilliant,' she exclaimed, as Jack proudly showed her his salt dough decoration, which was resting on a baking tray in Helen's kitchen.

'He has to dry out,' Jack explained. 'And then I can paint him next week, can't I Helen?'

'You can,' she said, ruffling his hair. 'Now run and get your stuff,' she told him, 'so your poor mum can go home and have a rest.' She turned to Kate. 'He's been fine. A bit tired.'

'Him and me, both,' admitted Kate, wondering whether the Christmas lights plan was a good idea. 'Father Christmas or snowman?' she hissed under her breath, gesturing towards the baking tray once she was sure Jack couldn't hear.

'Hard to know at this stage,' whispered Helen. 'Painting should clarify things.'

'Can we hang him on our tree, Mum,' Jack asked as he came back in, dragging his rucksack on the floor.

'Don't drag,' said Kate, automatically, picking the rucksack up and slinging it over her own shoulder. 'I'm sure we can find a really good place for him.'

'He has to go on a tree,' insisted Jack. 'We've got to have one. We are going to have a tree, aren't we, Mum?'

Kate looked at Helen in desperation but got just amused sympathy.

'People don't have to have Christmas trees,' she ventured. 'Our living room's not very big, is it? We might be better off with, maybe, a branch with some decorations on it?' she said hopefully. 'That can look really pretty.'

'A tree, a tree,' wailed Jack, instantly plunged into despair.

'We'll see,' said Kate. 'Let's just . . .' She threw her hands up. 'We'll see.'

Jack was tired and whiney. She wondered again about the plan to see the switching on of the Christmas lights, but when she suggested they go straight home, he was furious.

'Okay, okay,' she said, 'keep your cool, monkey boy, but early night tomorrow for both of us, I think.'

On the bus, he slumped against her side and even had a little nap on the journey, lulled by the warmth and the motion of the bus. Waking just before their stop, he looked out of the window, gleefully pointing out some of the shops' Christmas window displays. Kate was glad they had come. So what if he was tired and grumpy this evening? It was Christmas, and he was only six years old. If he wasn't on top form at school tomorrow, so what? At his age, he wasn't taking life-altering exams or anything. The only compulsory exams were tests to see whether the teachers were any good, and Kate firmly resisted any attempts to pressure him with those.

The town centre was packed. Office workers had clearly decided to stay and enjoy the show, delaying the usual rush hour. Ironically, Kate and Jack ended up standing on the little bit of pavement outside Portman Brothers where she sold her trees.

Waiting for the local minor celebrity, who starred in a long-running soap filmed in Bristol, she wondered, standing there with Jack pressed to her side, whether she would see the man with the woman in the wheelchair this year. The man with the eyes that turned up at the corners and twinkled when he smiled. Would the young woman be even more unwell? Would she even be there? From tomorrow she would start looking out for him when she was at work. He must work near here. In previous years she had seen him most mornings and evenings but not every day. Sometimes they even exchanged a smile. But what if he was gone? What if they had both gone? Changed jobs, moved away . . . or worse?

At the thought, Kate's stomach gave a lurch of loss that she didn't quite understand, and she tried to push the thought of the twinkly-eyed man and his poorly sister out of her mind so she could focus on making sure that Jack enjoyed the show.

As always, the build-up was huge, and the moment itself was an anti-climax. The crowd cooperated gamely with the countdown and when they got to 'one' the soap opera doctor made a big deal of flicking the switch, and the same old decorations they had every year flickered into life; tiny pinpricks of green, white and red light, picking out Christmassy designs on the gantries that ran overhead down the street – a Santa's sleigh, a snowflake, a pair of bells . . . Kate had had plenty of time to study them from her freezing vantage point on the pavement over the previous three years, and they had little charm left for her now. But Jack oohed and aahed, and she was glad she had brought him even though, as always, being surrounded by the more conventional, happy families made her feel bitter and inadequate.

How could she compete? Gazing over the crowds of excited children with their parents and grandparents, she saw a mother with twins of perhaps four years old. She wasn't stressed, as Kate would have been. She held the hand of one while the other took a turn on her father's shoulders, grabbing his ears with no fear of falling, his hands reaching up to hold her steady as she giggled and bounced. She imagined Tom being with them, as he should have been, holding Jack up so he could see, backing her up with the unpopular 'mum' stuff like insisting he wore his hat, having silly in-jokes with him that no-one else got. Tom had been a great dad. They were lost without him. Kate was lost without him.

The crowd was starting to move, to disperse, and she became aware she was being jostled from all sides. She looked around. It was nothing in particular, she quickly realised, just sheer weight of numbers as people started to leave, but she glanced down at Jack anxiously. He didn't like being touched. His happiness at being there, out late on a school night, had kept him going, but now Kate saw the usual, worrying signs. He had shrunk into himself, his little face blank and pale.

'Jack?'

Nothing. His eyes were glazed, he hunched over slightly, his hands coming up to cover his ears.

'Jack?' she said again, more urgently, putting a reassuring hand on his arm, pulling him to her. Their eyes met briefly. She held his gaze. 'You're fine, monkey boy. You're fine.'

She had him. She would get him home. He needed to be out of there, and fast.

Then, a burly man, pushing a path through the crowd, barged Jack and tripped, landing heavily against him, nearly knocking him to the ground.

'Sorry, laddie,' he said, but Jack was lost. He inhaled for what felt – to Kate – like a hundred years. Then, after hovering on the brink, he unleashed a thin, piercing, scream. It poured out of his tiny body like an unearthly and never-ending siren, rising effortlessly above the noise of the crowd. The jostling around Jack stopped. Despite the crush, a space cleared around him, as if the scream itself had created a force-field.

Kate knew all too well the only solution was to physically remove his rigid little body from the circumstances that had caused his distress. She grabbed him around his skinny body and lifted him up. The crowd parted around her as she made her way to the bus, with Jack still screaming, his eyes and fists screwed tight shut. 'Oh, bless,' she heard from one woman as she passed. 'Special needs . . .' came another phrase, floating into her ear as she passed. 'Childen with no manners . . .' said an older woman, with a mean face.

Kate didn't care.

3rd December

It was going to be impossible to afford a real tree this year. The quality of the trees from Portman Brothers was great – Malcolm Wilkins wasn't wrong. The store was selling top-notch Nordman firs – six feet tall for sixty quid and eight feet tall for a massive eighty pounds. Even with her measly ten per cent staff discount, Kate was not going to be able to do anything about Jack's desperate longing for a real Christmas tree.

Tears pricked at her eyes. He only wanted a Christmas tree, for goodness sake, and he was like his dad in insisting only a real one would do – the smell, the look, a plastic one was a pointless compromise – and Kate agreed . . . but fifty-four pounds represented two weeks of food and dinner money, or a month of electricity if she was careful with the heating and barely used the immersion heater. It just wasn't a goer. The beautiful wide, blue-green needles were supposed to be extra-long-lasting too, which was a shame as they would be dumped at the local municipal tip within weeks regardless.

Astonishingly enough, despite the high price, Kate had sold three of the taller ones already this morning and five of the shorter ones. She wondered at how much disposable income people seemed to have. One tall, grumpy grey-haired man, whose heavy, dark eyebrows gave him a pronounced scowl, had come along and bought two eight-foot trees.

'The wife can't decide whether to put it in the dining room or the sitting room. This solves that bloody problem,' he grumbled, peeling off twenty-pound notes from a wad in his pocket. As he handed over the money he gave Kate a piercing look. 'This is a bloody awful job they've got you doing, standing out here in the cold. I hope they're paying you enough.'

Kate smiled and said nothing.

'My daughter's about your age. I'd like to see her working as hard as you. Doesn't know she's born.' He looked embarrassed. 'Here,' he said, pushing two tenners at her, 'a bit extra to help you along, eh?'

She shook her head. 'Frowned upon,' she explained, with a smile, wishing that wasn't the case. An extra bit of cash that week would be a godsend.

'Mmm . . . pity . . . well . . . look after yourself,' he said, pushing the money back into his wallet. He tucked a tree under each arm and, despite the weight, strode off determinedly, turning briefly back to look at her, his expression fierce, but his eyes kind, soft with genuine concern.

Kate blinked back tears. It would be nice to have a father like that, she thought, complaining but caring, nagging . . . looking out for her. It wasn't that she didn't have parents, it was just that she might as well not have them. Always formally distant, they had politely brought her up at arms' length and now suited themselves by travelling the world in a boat they had bought after selling the family home without consulting her, buying rental properties for income to sustain their itinerant lifestyle. It didn't occur to them that Kate and Jack might need moral or practical support and it certainly didn't occur to them to give it. Instead, they turned up every ten months or so, for lunch and a catch up, exclaiming over Jack's extraordinary increase in height, before moving on, restlessly, to their next adventure.

She was so preoccupied with the older man she didn't see who was approaching her until he was just a couple of yards away. He wore the same overcoat as last year, but it was hanging differently now. He had lost weight and looked older – gaunt, even. With a sinking feeling she registered he didn't have the woman with him. Kate dreaded the worst, but then she remembered it was a weekday. The girl was only ever with him at the weekends, of course. Here he was, on his way to work; a clever, professional job, she imagined, based in one of the plush, modern office buildings off Cabot Circus, towards the docks. He might be an architect, or a lawyer.

She realised she was staring and she looked away. When she glanced back, she met his eyes and then she saw . . . what was it? He looked so different this year, his eyes blank with suppressed pain. She looked away again, frowning, feeling her gaze was an intrusion when all he was doing was casually catching her eye, as anyone might who suddenly encountered a small, blonde woman dressed as a Christmas elf as they strolled by on their way to work. Why was she even assuming he remembered her from previous years, just because she remembered him? He was handsome. It must happen to him all the time.

Just then, a woman in an extraordinarily awful multi-coloured coat pulled at her arm.

'Are you serving?' she demanded. 'I've been standing here . . .'

'Sorry,' said Kate quickly. 'How can I help?'

She answered a string of imperiously posed questions and then the woman went away without buying a tree, announcing to no one in particular, 'I may as well go to the garden centre. At least one can park the car.'

Free at last, Kate looked around her but the man had gone. If it was like last year, he would have gone past and turned right, and would not pass her again until at least six o'clock that evening. She looked at her watch. It was past ten o'clock in the morning. He had been late – perhaps a breakfast meeting before the office; he looked as if he was the kind of man who had breakfast meetings. She sighed and noticed she was smiling. It was an alien feeling to be finding a smile on her face rather than deliberately putting it there – a good feeling.

Daniel groaned aloud as he hung up his coat. What a plank, he thought as he replayed their encounter in his head. First, she catches him out staring fixedly at her as she serves that old man, then she sees him looking at her as if he knows her – which must throw her a bit, as there is not the slightest reason for her to remember they've ever met before. That said, he told himself, sighing as he sank into his chair, there's a chance she would remember Zoe: his sister had a way of making an impression on people.

Out of sheer masochism, he replayed in his mind the bit that morning when their eyes locked. Time seemed to stand still, for him at least; for her it must have felt like an eternity being glared at by this random bloke. No wonder she had looked away with that puzzled expression. He had almost been glad of that woman in the mad coat, distracting her so he could slip away before he did anything else to make a tit of himself.

He sighed and swigged the coffee his friend Paul had left on his desk. Thankfully it contained a triple shot. He needed it.

'Tough night?'

'Just a bit,' Daniel admitted.

'What was it this time?'

'A few calls,' he said, staring out of the window, 'just your normal stuff – loneliness, bereavement, existential angst . . .'

He paused, taking another gulp. *Thank God for caffeine.*

'Anything in particular?' Paul knew his friend and he knew that look. He was relentless.

'A young lad,' Daniel admitted. 'Only sixteen it turns out . . . but he's lived through more than your average teenager, and not in a good way . . .'

Paul nodded. The people whom Daniel ended up supporting in the middle of the night, all night, usually, had generally had a lot of 'life' thrown at them and rarely 'in a good way'.

'So . . .?'

'Yeah, so . . . turns out he's in foster care because his single mum's too busy taking drugs to bring him up, and he's had this girlfriend for the last couple of years only she's in care too, and the social workers in their wisdom have decided to move her to a new placement in Leeds. So . . . he's alone again, hates the children's home, he's being chucked out soon anyway . . .'

'What? At sixteen?'

'Yep. And it took me five hours on the phone with him, persuading him not to check out completely but to send a text to this key worker he apparently gets on with, but who's been told to hand his case file to someone else because of some ridiculous restructuring nonsense.'

'Check out? You mean he was going to kill himself?'

Daniel nodded. 'Razor blade at the ready.'

'Mate,' said Paul. 'I seriously don't know how you do it.'

Daniel shrugged and chucked the empty coffee cup in the recycling. 'Thanks for that. I needed it.'

'And I don't know *why* you do it either,' Paul added quietly as Daniel walked away, rubbing his face. But he did know why. His friend had been taking every shift offered, working through the night for two, three, even four nights a week, listening to other people's misery . . . Basically, he was doing anything to avoid being home alone and having to think about his own sadness. Something was going to have to change. And soon.

Kate and Jack thought their Christmas biscuits were brilliant. The whole flat was filled with a delicious fug of hot butter and cinnamon. The reindeer-shaped ones were fiddly, and the legs tended to break off when they prised them off the baking tray, but the bell-shaped ones and the stars turned out pretty well.

'We have to ice them too,' explained Kate, 'and then thread string through the holes so we can hang them up.'

'On the tree,' said Jack doggedly, shooting his mother a look. 'We've got to get it soon,' he pressed. 'It's been December for aaages . . .'

Kate laughed and ruffled his hair. 'It's been December for precisely three days,' she said. 'When I was a little girl, we would always put the tree up on Christmas Eve, not before. We've got a long time to see what we can do in between. There's the list. We've got your nativity play, haven't we? And mince pies, and the Christmas market . . . Now listen, stop eating them all,' she warned. 'We need some left over to ice and put on strings tomorrow. Also, I'm not sure you're going to have room for tea at this rate.'

Luckily Seema had given her the heads-up at the school gate that the class's Secret Santa names were going to be handed out the following day. As Jack was finishing his tea, Kate slipped a bit of paper into the advent calendar promising this as his 'Christmas' activity for the following day.

'Yay!' he said, once he had haltingly read it aloud. 'I wonder who's going to get me.'

'Never mind you,' laughed Kate. 'The important thing is to see who *you* have to do a present for, and get them something really good that they'll like.'

There was a five-pound limit on the present value, thankfully, but she had been racking her brains to think of something that Jack would approve of which wouldn't need any money to be spent at all. Maybe seeing who it was would inspire them both when she collected him from school tomorrow.

First, though, she had a worrying meeting to get through. Pat's comments on the possible redundancies, along with this ridiculous 'rolling contract' thing that Malcolm Wilkins had announced she was on, had made her decide to find out her exact position at Portman Brothers. Tom had always said that you should 'know your enemy'. He didn't shy away from finding out the truth, even when it was unwelcome, and he had always encouraged her to fight her corner too, although it had been a damned sight easier to do that knowing there was a pair of strong arms to hold her and warm her when life got challenging.

Just then, Jack threw his arms around her thighs and gave her a hug. 'I love Christmas,' he said, dreamily. 'It's just like real life . . . only more exciting.'

4th December

'I can see you are an exemplary employee,' said Sarah, the Human Resources manager, across a large desk. Kate had been put in a disconcertingly low chair, making her feel like a naughty child pulled into the headteacher's office.

'You've met all your targets,' Sarah mused, tip-tapping the immaculate red nails of her left hand on the desk as she shuffled through the papers in the file with her right. 'It appears your appraisal last January was excellent, and that you are a valuable contributor within your team.'

'Good-o,' said Kate, sourly. 'The thing I didn't know at my appraisal last January was that I was a fag paper's breadth away from losing my job. No one mentioned that.'

'But you didn't lose your job,' said Sarah, leaning forward slightly and giving Kate a reassuring smile. 'You were retained on payroll for another year and – from what I can see – you have continued to be an asset to Portman Brothers. The lingerie department has met all its sales targets throughout the year.'

'But what's going to happen at my appraisal this New Year,' pressed Kate. 'I've heard they'll be letting people go.' What a ridiculous phrase, she thought, as soon as she had said it – like people were pining to be released from slavery, rather than hanging onto their pay packets for grim death.

'I can't comment on that,' said Sarah, the warmth immediately dissipating and the shutters coming down.

'But,' Kate swallowed and pressed her hands together, 'it would be last in, first out, wouldn't it? And, technically – from what you're saying – I've only been employed for a year, haven't I? Not that I had a lot of choice at the time, of course. It was take it or leave it and Mr Wilkins knew I was desperate for work. I just never thought it would be used to crap on me from a great height. I should have known it would, of course.' She also hadn't imagined, at that point, Kate remembered, that she would be doing a rubbish job for so long. The jewellery-making had been her original and best idea, but making it come to fruition was harder than she thought. And there she was, more than three years later. Sarah pursed her lips, sitting back in her chair and crossing her arms. She looked embarrassed, thought Kate in mitigation.

She remembered being told the whole 'last in, first out' principle wasn't based on morality, but on cost-effectiveness. The shorter time an employee had been there – at least technically – the cheaper they were to sack.

'So, what would I get?'

Sarah raised a questioning eyebrow. 'In what sense?'

'Redundancy. Pay-off. What would I get. If it was me?'

'There is no statutory redundancy pay for employees with less than two years' employment. But as I said, I couldn't possibly comment on whether there will be redundancies in the new year.'

'But I've been here for four, nearly.'

'Mmm, but technically . . .' Sarah said, waving her hand at Kate's contract.

'That's not fair.'

'You may very well say that. I couldn't possibly comment.'

'Sure, I know – but, basically, my best outcome would be another one-year contract?' pressed Kate.

'A zero hours contract is more likely, at best,' admitted Sarah.

'What's that?'

'A contract which allows Portman Brothers to rota you for as few or as many hours as they require on a weekly basis. These are the terms I have been asked to set up as standard for newer employees.'

Kate felt the blood drain from her face. 'But that would be a disaster,' she whispered. 'Not knowing how much I was going to make each week, not knowing what childcare I need to book . . .'

'It's the gig economy. That's what the world has become. A job for life with a yearly bonus and a gold clock on retirement is just not a thing nowadays,' explained Sarah. 'I'm sorry. It's hard, I know.'

'I bet you don't know,' said Kate, angrily, getting to her feet. 'I bet you've got a gold-plated deal yourself. They need you, don't they? They need you to do their sacking for them, and to offer these contracts that ruin people's lives. I don't know how you sleep at night.'

As soon as she left, she kicked herself for the outburst. Her head was pounding. It was expanding with rage, concern, a feeling of desperate powerlessness . . . but the only thing she had achieved with her temper was to make things worse. Great.

Daniel was also concerned about how he came across. 'Be cool, be cool, be cool,' he was muttering to himself, as he walked down the street towards the store. Then it occurred to him that being caught talking to himself was not going to persuade her he wasn't a weirdo. He clamped his mouth shut and shoved his hands deep into the pockets of his coat. Catching sight of his reflection in a shop window, he realised that looking grim-faced and tense wouldn't help either. The woman – what was her name; he couldn't call her 'Christmas Tree Girl' for ever – was hardly going to want to acknowledge a bloke who looked like he was just off to murder someone.

He consciously relaxed, dropping his shoulders and taking a deep breath. She was just a girl. A woman. And he was just going to give her a smile, maybe say hello – actually not 'hello', maybe 'hi' or something. If it went well, he might comment on the weather too . . . but let's not get ahead of ourselves, he told himself sternly. He could see her from a hundred yards away, but this time he didn't stare fixedly – that was something he was keen to avoid doing again – so instead he found himself looking at anything but her, swivelling his head like a loon, checking out the shop windows and even staring at the sky, as if that held the answer . . .

Suddenly, there she was, just six feet away. His eyes locked onto hers. She had a bemused smile on her face as she looked at him.

'Good day,' he said, and brought his hand to his forehead, as if he was going to remove a hat he wasn't wearing. He hesitated briefly, breaking his stride, then he accelerated away, leaving Kate smiling after him.

'Idiot, idiot, idiot.' he chanted under his breath as he turned the corner to his street. 'Did I really say, "Good day"? What the hell was that? I sounded like my dad. My grandad. And the hand thing for God's sake . . . Did I seriously just salute an elf? A hot elf?' He struck his forehead with the palm of his hand. A gaggle of teenagers walking towards him looked at each other nervously.

'Sorry girls,' he said, giving them an engaging smile. 'I'm fine.'

*

'Ask her out, for heaven's sake,' said Paul, when Daniel got to the office.

'God no, I couldn't. She thinks I'm an axe murderer.'

'Then I'll ask her out for you.'

'Great. Then she'll think I'm an axe murderer who still lives with his mum and collects action figures.'

'Okay, yeah, that would be bad . . . In that case you're just going to have to get over yourself. It's time.'

'I know,' said Daniel. But it didn't feel like it was time. Not for that. Instead, since Zoe died, it had felt like time stood still, like life had frozen at that point and he couldn't ever imagine moving forward, or even wanting to, loathing the sense that he would be moving further away from his life with her towards a future he couldn't imagine and wasn't sure he even wanted.

'Plus,' Paul went on, relentlessly, 'let's face it, you're not getting any younger . . .'

'What? I'm thirty-two! And you're older than me, remember.'

'Yeah, but I've got Cara, haven't I? We've done two years. We're engaged, the wedding's in the diary. I'm on it, mate. You? You're just not putting the effort in. I'm not sure I've ever seen you get beyond the second date.'

'When I need your help I'll let you know,' said Daniel, laughing reluctantly. 'Now, isn't there somewhere – anywhere – you should be? Other than here, obviously.'

Paul closed the door exaggeratedly quietly after himself and Daniel sighed in relief.

'I just want to tell her,' he said to the empty room. 'I just want to tell her what happened to us. To me. Because it's happened to her too. I know it. She will understand.'

*

46

'It's Lily,' Jack told Kate doubtfully.

'You're Lily's Secret Santa? That's good, isn't it? You went to her birthday party last term didn't you? She seems lovely . . . don't you think?'

'Ye-es,' admitted Jack, 'but she's a girl.'

'Hmm. She is definitely a girl,' agreed Kate, stifling a smile. 'Do you have any idea what she'd like?'

'Well, no, because it's going to be girl stuff, isn't it?' said Jack with heavy patience. 'I dunno, do I?'

'She's just a girl, darling, she's not from outer space.'

'Kate!' called a voice, as they both turned away from the school gate.

'I was hoping to catch you,' said Anastasia, who had broken into a trot but slowed to a saunter once she had Kate's attention. Kate glanced at her watch anxiously. They could end up waiting a while for a bus if they missed the one at half past three.

'I seriously think I might book you for a jewellery sale,' said Anastasia, when she arrived. 'I know you could do with the opportunity . . .'

'I'd be delighted . . .' said Kate, gritting her teeth at Anastasia's patronising tone.

'Yes, I know. So, shall we say the week before Christmas at my house? Not sure what day . . . I'll let you know, if you can stay available. I've got six or seven girls who will come, nothing elaborate, but I could do some nibbles. Can I rely on you to bring some wine?'

Kate recoiled. 'I don't usually,' she said. 'Normally the host . . .'

'Oh, really?' said Anastasia, her manner suddenly cooling. 'I naturally thought, since I'm providing the venue and the audience . . .'

'That's fine,' said Kate quickly. 'I can bring a few bottles.'

Anastasia smiled, her approval returning in an instant. 'That's good. Make it a case. I am sure it will be worth your while. Bring lots of stock, won't you? I'm sure the girls will appreciate a good choice.'

'Darlin' boy,' said Mrs Akintola when they went into the laundry to get to the flat. 'You gettin' sooo tall! You be taller than your Mammy by New Year.' She was folding towels with great deftness and speed as she spoke, not stopping for a moment.

'That's silly,' said Jack, grinning. 'Mum's really old and I'm only six so far.'

Kate pulled a face. 'Damned by my own son,' she said. 'I hope I'm not completely over the hill.'

'You too grown up for a young girl. How old are you? Not even thirty? I hope you got some good parties to go to this Christmas,' the older woman said. 'You know I'll babysit anytime . . . You need to put on your dancin' shoes.'

'Not sure I've got any,' said Kate, 'but you're not the only one to say so.' She hoped Seema's insistence on the girls' night really was going to include babysitting. If not, Mrs Akintola was going to have to step up then too. 'Thank you. I do need to ask you about babysitting actually, there's definitely one night coming up and there might be two.'

'A party?' said Mrs Akintola hopefully.

'Sort of. I've been invited to do a jewellery sale at a friend's house.'

'Extra money for Christmas?'

'Hope so . . . and also, I need to book you for my staff Christmas party too if that's okay?'

'Good,' said Mrs Akintola. 'Just write down the dates for me. I'll bring DVDs and popcorn,' she said to Jack. 'I've got some new ones I got for my grandchildren. We can have a movie night.'

'Cool!' said Jack. He liked Mrs Akintola.

As landladies went, Mrs Akintola was an angel from heaven, thought Kate. The rent was affordable, and repairs were quickly dealt with by one of her several handsome sons, two of whom were single, triggering much far-from-subtle matchmaking on their mother's part.

Jack was soon happily absorbed, messily piping white icing onto the biscuits which had survived the cooking and eating of the night before.

'Maybe Lily's present could be a box of these biscuits,' suggested Kate hopefully. She was sitting next to Jack at the breakfast bar which separated the lounge from the kitchen and where they ate all their meals. She was fiddling with her jewellery supplies which were at high risk of getting covered in icing.

'I could pipe her name onto them,' said Jack. 'That would be cool.'

'Excellent idea. Look, here's a box,' said Kate, emptying out the cardboard box her silver jewellery wire came in. It was nearly empty anyway. 'We could cover it in Christmas paper and draw her name on the top too.'

'Brilliant,' said Jack.

'Brilliant,' thought Kate, silently. Five pounds saved. With luck her jewellery sale would go well. There would be a few late nights before next week, and having to take wine along was going to have a big impact on her profits, which were on a narrower margin than Anastasia appreciated, or cared about. She might bung up her prices a bit. Tom had always said they were too low – that she should value her stuff more highly – but raising prices risked selling less, which would be an even bigger disaster than denting profits with wine. As well as being bad for morale.

When Jack had done his advent calendar (Christmas movie night tomorrow) and gone to bed, she cleaned down the breakfast bar thoroughly and spread out her materials. She already had some large, quite complex necklaces which she could sell for a good price, but experience told her these parties just before Christmas were more about lower value items to be bought as presents. Some simple bracelets could do well and the long chains with a pendant could be produced cheaply and priced reasonably. Earrings were more risky – not everyone had pierced ears, but dangly ones were fashionable this year, so Kate decided to make sure she produced some of her more popular designs. She worked in silver wire and glass beads mainly, buying semi-precious stones when she could. Lacking equipment and space limited her and she pined for a proper, equipped workspace. She had so many cool designs in her head. A good evening, with enough wine, could make her a couple of hundred pounds. That kind of money was worth working for.

5th December

'Hurry up Mummy, it's starting,' said Jack.

'Just putting the marshmallows on,' Kate reassured him.

'Lots please!'

'The exact right amount, cheeky,' she smiled, as she brought the two mugs of hot chocolate over to him. 'Budge up.'

Jack scooted over on the settee, so Kate could sit down, just as the opening credits finished.

'What's it about?' asked Jack, as she tucked the duvet around them both. The flat was cold, as usual, but she was reluctant to put the heating up any more.

'You'll see . . .' said Kate. 'I used to watch this with my mum when I was your age.'

'Wow, so it's really old.'

'Yeah,' said Kate, dryly. 'But it's a classic. *A Wonderful Life*, it's called. Just watch, look, we're missing it.'

Within minutes, Jack was entranced, sipping his hot chocolate automatically as he stared, unblinking at the little screen. Kate had watched it every year for as long as she could remember and had been scrutinising the television listings looking for when it might be on. She could have bought it on DVD, of course, but that would have been spending, which was always best avoided if there was a free alternative.

While the comfortingly familiar story played itself out, Kate's mind wandered and all her thoughts were negative ones: the scary prospect of losing her job, the impossibility of affording new school shoes, and the Christmas presents she would like to get Jack. She fretted about the limitations of her jewellery sales, mainly because she couldn't afford to buy the raw materials she would like . . . She was desperately missing Tom, the companionship, the cuddles, the endless positivity to balance her own pessimism, and – let's face it – the marital benefits . . . Then, there was the inadequacy of the flat – when would she ever be able to afford a garden for Jack to play in? Would he look back on his childhood and remember the deprivation? The poverty? Would it even be a contrast to his adult life? Probably not . . . the chances were, she was condemning him to a lifetime of failure and low expectations anyway. Statistically, he didn't have a prayer. Her thoughts were so bleak she couldn't even cry. Instead she felt a dark space inside herself, a bottomless void which threatened to suck her into an underworld she doubted her ability to escape.

The film had ended a little late and despite such a long tough week, she summoned a weak smile when tucking Jack into bed.

'Night, night monkey boy,' she said.

'I'm not a monkey,' he said sleepily. 'But I am a boy . . . Oh, actually,' the thought struck him, 'I'm going to be a camel.'

'Oo-kay, and when is this unlikely transformation going to take place?' asked Kate, a real smile replacing the forced one.

'Me and Krish,' murmured Jack, his eyes closing against his will. 'For the Tivity.'

'Great,' said Kate, tucking his duvet tightly under his chin to keep out the cold draught.

She went back into the lounge and texted Seema: *Are they really going to be camels?*

Yep. I'm afraid so, came the reply, swiftly. *Dreading the costumes. Let's make a plan.*

And that was another challenge to add to the list, thought Kate as she glanced at the clock and settled down to her jewellery making. It was going to be a late one.

Daniel had also been watching television that evening. He had been flicking idly through the channels, looking for a diversion to pass the time before the whisky kicked in and made him drunk enough to get some sleep. The film, on the tiny TV in the corner of the boat's small lounge area, was already halfway through, but that didn't matter. He had watched it with Zoe often enough to know the plot backwards. He even remembered it being part of the Christmas ritual when his parents were still alive.

'Come on boy,' Zoe had chivvied imperiously last year, 'it's on. Where's my cup of tea.' He had brought two mugs and sat with her as she watched, mopping her tears at the end, teasing her because she always cried, and to hide his anxiety that her crying made her fragile breathing even worse. It would be the last time they performed this particular ritual. He had known that even then. And now, it was another anniversary to be borne.

'I'll be your guardian angel,' Zoe had said, at the end of the film. 'When I'm dead, I'll come and look after you and stop you jumping off Clifton Suspension Bridge.'

'Nah you won't,' he had told her. 'You'll be in heaven with Mum and Dad having a great time. You're not going to bother to come and rescue me from my own idiocy.'

They had never shirked away from the death thing as a family. When Zoe was born, the heart issues were even more obvious than her Down's syndrome. She was blue and too weak to feed. Daniel's mum spent hours patiently dripping expressed milk into her mouth, only to have her regurgitate the whole lot minutes later because of her reflux problems. The paediatric consultant gave her months to live – a couple of years at best. And then she proved him wrong. She kept proving him wrong as time went on, but the prognosis remained sombre. Zoe didn't know she wasn't supposed to be able to do things. If she wanted to do something badly enough, she did it. Eventually. It took her nearly two years to learn to ride a bike but, with Daniel's patient input, she succeeded. It was a tricycle, because her balance was poor, but – even though peddling from the house to the park and back left her exhausted, her triumphant expression was an inspiration.

Zoe also knew her heart was poorly and that, one day, it would stop working. She had no fear of death. Daniel, on the other hand, had dreaded her leaving him for years, especially after both their parents died within six months of each other. His father had apologised for leaving him with responsibility for his sister. 'It was never the plan . . .' he had said, days before his own death. 'The last thing we wanted . . . leaving you with Zoe, you should have your own life.'

He had not wanted his own life. This was his life. The last thing he wanted was what he had now. The loss of his mother, father and then sister, within two years of each other. He would do anything to have family again. To have Zoe with him. He sloshed another inch of Scotch into the glass and climbed up the narrow wooden stairs to the little deck area, gazing up at the tall, warehouse buildings – mostly converted now – from his mooring right in the heart of the city.

'Cool . . .' Zoe had said, when she first saw his little houseboat, a million miles from the Victorian villa they had grown up in and where Zoe had lived with their parents until they died. She visited often and then, when her father's death left her alone at home, she moved in with Daniel full time. He gave up his bedroom in the prow of the boat, sleeping instead on the sofa-bed pull-out mattress in the lounge area. It was cramped but Zoe pronounced it perfect, despite the inconvenience of having to leave her wheelchair in his car and have him bring it to her when they went out. The boat was small enough for her to get around it without needing wheels. Too weak to get out much, she had never tired of watching the river, the changing light, the weather, the seasons and the pulsing life of the city. The view provided a vibrant backdrop to a life that was closing in on her as it drew to an end.

6th December

'Nooo,' Jack murmured as Kate gently tried to shake him awake.

'Come on, sleepy-head. Time to get up. It's Saturday and I've got to get to work.'

'Tired . . .' he complained, turning onto his tummy and burying his head in his pillow.

'I know, darling . . . but I've got to get you to Helen's. You've football this morning. You like football.'

'Don't want to do football.'

Kate paused. Even when he was shattered, Jack always wanted to play football. His Saturday morning coaching sessions were the highlight of his week, which was just as well given the number of Saturdays Kate had to work. She felt his forehead with a practised hand. Cool and dry.

'You'll be all right when you get going,' she chivvied gently, pulling the duvet off.

'Brr, it's cold, Mummy, don't do that.'

She relented, putting it back over him. He was right. The flat was really chilly. 'Come on darling, your clothes are right here on the end of the bed. Pop them on, then you can come and eat your porridge. That'll warm you up.'

'Don't like porridge.'

'Bad luck, monkey boy,' she said. 'Pancakes soon, but not today.'

*

'When are you picking me up from Helen's?' said Jack, with a slight whine in his voice, as he spooned his liberally syruped porridge into his mouth.

'Right after lunch,' said Kate brightly. 'Just a half day at work today. And then, do you remember what we're doing? What did the advent calendar say?'

Jack thought for a moment and then his face lit up. 'Christmas Steps!'

'Yay! That's right.' Christmas window-shopping at Christmas Steps was what the little slip of paper she slipped into his calendar had said the previous night.

'Can we go to the Oldie Sweetie Shoppie?'

'Of course. If you're good,' said Kate.

By the time she had dropped Jack off at Helen's, he had perked up. She felt lousy having to give up precious time with him when he wasn't at school, but she had no chance of getting any Saturdays off between now and Christmas. The tree sales were going well, and she hoped her success was doing a little to secure her employment prospects. As she smiled, chatted and heaved Christmas trees around, she was ever aware it was Saturdays that *he* was most likely to arrive with the woman who had looked so sick last year.

He didn't appear. She left it until the very last minute to leave, fussing around until Wayne, who was taking over the stand for the afternoon, told her to get lost.

It was nearly three o'clock by the time she and Jack got to Christmas Steps, and the daylight was fading fast on a now dull, rainy day.

'We should be getting you a new coat,' she fussed, pulling the zip on his hoody right up to his chin and pulling the hood up over his head.

He immediately pushed it off again. 'I'm fine, Mummy,' he said. 'Can we go to the sweet shop first? Can I have liquorice?'

'Let's take our time,' said Kate, 'look at those amazing baubles!'

'For our Christmas tree?' asked Jack, immediately making Kate regret the diversion she had chosen.

'At fifteen quid each, I think not,' she said faintly, spotting the price tags. But they were beautiful. Blown glass, with swirls and streaks of gold, each one had a feather inside like it had fallen from an angel's wing. While Tom was still around, she had tried to start a tradition of buying new decorations each Christmas, just one or two special ones, and – with his army salary to rely on – she would not have ruled out buying one. That kind of expenditure was out of the question now.

'Okay,' she gave in. 'Let's hit the sweet shop and then we can work our way back slowly. Just window-shopping, mind . . .'

'Windows? Boring . . .'

'Not actual windows, you twit,' she teased, pretending to clip him on the ear.

'It's gone, Mummy!' Jack's cry of anguish was heartbreaking. He turned back to her and pointed up ahead.

'What's gone?' she said, catching him up and putting her hand on his shoulder. And then she saw . . . the fantastic little sweet shop, hunched low, halfway up the worn, stone steps, with its bow window, like something out of *The Old Curiosity Shop*, the ox-eye glass-paned space crammed with big jars of old-fashioned sweets – was devastatingly altered. The glass panes were opaque like cataracts, obscured with a streaky layer of whitewash. The shop sign in the glass window of the door was turned drunkenly to *Closed* and below it, obscuring the rest of the window, was a large green and blue estate agent's sign.

To Let, it declared, with a telephone number for enquiries.

'Oh, that's such a shame. I wonder . . .' Kate said, looking everywhere for a sign saying where they had moved to. 'Perhaps they moved to a bigger shop,' she murmured, but there was nothing, just the telephone number of the estate agent.

'What a pity,' she said, trying to sound brisk, but feeling inescapably sad. They had come here often – including once with Tom, before he died. It was on a day trip to Bristol from the army base and, even though Jack hadn't been old enough to remember it, Kate had told him the story on subsequent visits as a way of mentioning him. 'What a missed opportunity to close down just before Christmas,' she said, more to herself than Jack. 'You'd think they would want the benefit of the Christmas rush.'

Jack couldn't have cared less about the micro-economics of the situation. 'My sweets!' he wailed, nearly in danger of losing it. 'We were going to get liquorice. And fudge.'

'I'm not sure we were going to get both,' corrected Kate, gently. 'Tell you what, let's go and see what they have in the newsagent. I'm pretty sure they could do us a sherbet fountain at the very least.'

Disaster was averted with a sherbet fountain for Kate, most of which went to Jack, and a small packet of Haribos as his own official choice. He was persuaded to let her lead him back to Christmas Steps. Despite the Christmas carols playing and the lights twinkling above and around the little shops as well as inside them, Kate could see the signs of economic distress. A couple of other shops – not nearly as well placed as Jack's 'Oldie Sweetie Shoppie' had also closed down since Kate had last been there. The sweet shop had been in a prime location. Placed halfway up, it was prominent and visible. She allowed herself a daydream of telling Malcolm Wilkins to stuff his job and setting up a little shop to sell her jewellery. She could have a workspace in the shop, with proper equipment so she could do more designing and real silverwork, she could take commissions . . . She brought herself up sharply. It was ridiculous. There would be no workshop. Not in her life now, not without Tom.

It turned out Christmas shopping without money was not as amusing as she thought. It was cold, too, and Jack was soon complaining and dragging his feet. Finding her last fiver, she waved it at him. 'Hot chocolate?' she bribed.

'Yay!' said Jack. 'Yes please.'

Jack's hot chocolate, with everything on it, ate up a big chunk of the fiver, so Kate chose a cup of tea. It was cheaper than a latte.

They could see the sweet shop from the café window, a dark, forlorn space in the row of brightly lit shops, standing out like a missing tooth.

Almost before she knew what she was doing, Kate found herself dialling the number on the estate agent's board. It was an agent specialising in commercial properties so – she glanced at her watch – she wasn't really expecting an answer, late on a Saturday afternoon.

'Hello, James speaking?'

'Oo, sorry,' said Kate, slightly breathless, 'I was expecting to leave a message.'

'You can if you like,' came the brusque reply. 'But I'm here. How can I help?'

Kate briefly explained, feeling like a fraud for wasting his time. She should ask about the rent. She was sure that would be the end of it. Something stopped her, and James didn't volunteer the information.

'Why don't I show you around?'
'I . . . are you sure?'
'Twenty minutes?'

'You're getting unfit, mate,' said Paul dispassionately, watching Daniel leaning forward to catch his breath, his hand resting on Paul's garden wall.

'Thanks.'

'Too many takeaways. You should come for supper. A proper meal. I've persuaded Cara off the vegetarian stuff – some of the time at least. I've been cooking steaks for her and she loves them. If I say so myself, the grub's not half bad sometimes.'

'That'd be nice,' Daniel gasped, wiping his brow. 'We've just knocked ten minutes off the usual circuit; though, to be fair, it's more like you're getting fitter rather than I'm losing it.'

'Yeah, yeah . . . whatever. Fancy a beer? Seeing as you're here?'

'You should ask her out,' said Cara as they all leaned against the kitchen work surfaces, their hands cupping mugs of tea. Daniel had said it was too early for beer, and anyway he was still recovering from all the whisky he had drunk the night before.

'Ask her out?' he repeated, looking enquiringly at Paul. 'Amazing. I didn't even see your lips move.'

'We talk,' said Cara, without rancour. 'And anyway, you should definitely ask someone out. Tell me about her. What does she look like?'

'She looks like an elf. She's a Christmas elf, that's the thing.'

'No, I mean, how does she look?'

'Cold,' said Daniel. 'She looks cold, whenever I see her. It's the elf costume, it's not exactly . . .'

'God, you're hard work . . .' said Cara, taking a deep breath and trying a different tack. 'What's her name?'

'"Christmas Tree Girl",' admitted Daniel, flinching exaggeratedly as Cara raised a hand in frustration, 'Okay, look, I just don't know anything about her. She's . . . I dunno . . . I don't even know . . . I mean, she could be married, even.'

'Ask her, for the love of God,' said Paul. 'And then we can all stop worrying about you quite so much. Ask her to come to supper with us.'

'No thanks,' said Daniel. 'Talk about chucking someone in at the deep end.' He looked at his friend, who looked back with concern in his eyes. 'All right, I will. Probably. Possibly. Eventually.'

'Well you've only got 'til Christmas,' Cara reminded him, 'so you'd better step on it. Anyhow, talking about my amazing matchmaking skills . . .'

'Were we?'

'We were . . . I take it you're still on for this evening?'

'This evening . . .?'

'Supper. Here. Seven o'clock. Don't be late. Never mind Tree Girl, I've got a friend I want you to meet.'

'Did I agree to this?' Daniel turned in an air of slight desperation to Paul.

'Not even sure *I* agreed to this,' said Paul and then caught sight of Cara's face. 'Yeah mate, you agreed, I definitely said something about it a few days ago and you made a noise.'

'I made a noise?'

'It was a *yes*-y sort of noise,' said Paul, with a hint of pleading in his voice.

Daniel sighed. 'What shall I bring?'

'Beer, mate. We're going to need it.'

*

Kate and Jack hovered in the café until they saw a man in a suit with a scrubbed, pink face and a short back and sides, who looked very much like he might be an estate agent called James. As they approached, a woman in vertiginous heels, very tight jeans and a waist length fur jacket was walking down the steps towards them from the opposite direction. She was wearing sunglasses despite the fading light and was carrying what Kate guessed was a very expensive handbag in the crook of her left arm.

'Are you James?' the woman said as she arrived. 'Let's get this over with, shall we? I've got a launch party to get to . . .'

The woman waited, tapping her heel impatiently until poor James had wrestled the door open. She didn't seem to have seen Kate and Jack at all.

James held the door open and met Kate's eye.

'You're the other one?' he said.

She nodded apologetically and slipped into the shop behind him.

The woman was poking around the gloomy little space disdainfully. The floor was just dusty planks. The little bow window which made the frontage so charming still had some shelves in place, which would be handy with a thorough clean down, but clearly they were not to the woman's taste. Kate had a peek through the door at the back, which revealed a tiny storeroom, a sink and plug for a kettle, and a dark, slightly smelly toilet. It was unappealing, but she could see the potential. The storeroom would clean up and make a perfectly good workshop area. She didn't need a huge amount of space, just a bench, a stool, some shelves and a power socket. There was a window badly in need of a clean and she definitely needed a desk lamp with a powerful bulb as well, which was no problem. Jewellery was small. It didn't need space. As for the shop itself, again, space was not a big requirement – just as well . . . but what was the point of thinking about it? The whole plan was impossible.

'What is the annual rent?' she asked, hesitantly.

James turned to her in surprise and gave her a figure which made her recoil. 'And rates are on top of that, of course,' he said mentioning another staggering but not quite so huge figure. 'As you will gather from that, the landlord is looking for a rent below the current rateable value, which means the unit represents excellent value for its size and location.'

Jack was watching the other woman with his mouth open. Her face was compelling viewing. She was clearly older than she had first appeared. Her forehead was glassy smooth and her lips were so plumped up she had a permanent pout that looked as if she was just about to kiss someone. Her manner suggested otherwise though.

'I would need a big skip and some industrial cleaners before I did the fit out,' the woman was saying to James. 'It's going to take six weeks minimum to get it up to scratch. I hope the landlord won't expect me to be paying rent for that.'

'I am sure my client is open to fair proposals, but I would counsel you not to play too hard to get. There are,' he paused and looked emphatically at Kate, 'other people interested.'

The woman, looking at Kate for the first time, gave her a crushing scowl which looked odd on a face which was largely immobile.

Ah, thought Kate. That's what we are here for, pressuring the real clients into thinking there's competition . . . Fair enough; I was wasting his time too.

'Thank you,' she said to James, giving him a half wave and nudging Jack to stop staring, close his mouth and leave. 'We've seen what we need to see. I'll be in touch.'

Or not, she thought, as she hustled Jack up the steep steps to the street.

'Getting dark, darling, we need to get home,' she said, and then she broke her stride, stopping abruptly, making Jack cannon into her.

'Sorry Mummy, what is it?'

'That, my son, is a camel costume,' said Kate, who was now outside the charity shop just yards from the bus stop.

'We won't miss our bus, will we, Mummy?'

'Nope. This'll just take a mo . . .'

Kate and Jack traipsed in and she took a cursory look at some books and old china to mask her true intentions. Then, she moved in for the kill.

'How much for this?' she asked the elderly lady behind the counter who came out to greet them – or stop them stealing, judging by her forbidding expression. For the second time in just a few minutes Jack was struck dumb in awe. The lady was clearly a keen purchaser in charity shops herself – presumably this one. She was wearing an eclectic mix of paste jewellery, including some striking shoulder-length diamanté earrings which made an interesting pairing with her sensible twinset and tweed skirt.

Kate was holding up a heavy, beige wool man's coat with a leather collar and horn buttons.

'That's pure wool, that,' said the lady. 'Nice quality. Going to have to be a tenner, I'm afraid.'

'Really,' said Kate, meeting her steely gaze with one of her own. 'There's moth damage on the sleeve.'

'There is?' The lady went to look. 'What a shame, just a little hole.'

'A couple of holes . . . and here too, look,' said Kate. 'It's no good to me as a coat, I'm cutting it up to make it into a camel costume.'

At this, the lady's expression softened. 'For the little one?' she said, looking at Jack. 'He's just like my grandson, Charlie, only five, but tall for his age, just like his Dad.'

'I'm six,' said Jack, giving the woman a beady look.

'And you're going to be a camel?' she said, undaunted, bending down to him.

'Yeah . . .' he replied, uncertainly. 'And Krishna, me and Krish are both camels. We are for the three kings . . . they've only got two camels though,' he said, spotting the oversight for the first time.

'So actually, I need to get two costumes out of this,' said Kate, holding it up thoughtfully.

'No problem,' said the lady, now enthused at the challenge. 'Each sleeve can be the camel's neck so that's two. There's plenty in the body to make the head. Do they need whole body suits? I would just get them to wear brown trousers and T-shirts . . .'

'Great, good idea, you've got something, haven't you Jack?'

'Am I going to wear a camel head? Cool . . .'

The lady was now on a mission, rummaging in a box of fabrics.

'Aha!' she said, emerging looking a little ruffled. 'Black felt. I knew I'd seen some. And look, a couple of belts, you could make bridles and reins?'

'That's all lovely,' said Kate regretfully, 'but I need to keep the cost down . . . I'm sure I can manage with the coat, somehow,' she said, holding it up again.

'Let's call it a fiver for the lot, lovie,' said the lady quietly, looking over her shoulder. 'Don't tell anyone. Our manager will have my guts for garters. You'd think we were Portman Brothers, the airs and graces she puts on.'

Kate was happy to help support someone over a workplace power struggle and handed over the fiver before the lady changed her mind.

'Come and show me,' the lady called after them as they left.

'People are nice, aren't they Mummy?' said Jack sleepily, leaning against Kate as they travelled over to Seema's house.

'They are, darling. Mostly, if you give them a chance, they are.' He was right, of course. Out of the mouths of babes . . . it was something she had always loved about Tom, too, his gift for seeing the best in people, despite doing a job that brought him into contact with some of the most evil people in existence. His stories, when he came home each time, had centred on how the lads had been able to help repair a road, or take a child to hospital, acts of heroism and kindness, not annihilation and death. It had been like his brain was programmed to focus on the good. His son was the same. She was glad.

Daniel had been working Crisisline shifts most weekends. It had kept him from thinking he had nothing to do on a Saturday night, which he didn't and this – as a single guy in his early thirties – was a bit lame. That was probably why the phonelines were so busy on a Saturday night – all those other lost souls who didn't have anywhere to go.

Not only was Seema's husband Anil looking after Jack, Krishna and Krishna's older brother Sohail for the night, Seema had invited the girls they were going out with over to hers to pre-load and get ready. Going out on the town was the very last thing Kate felt like doing, but she had to admire Seema's energy and enthusiasm. They were a group of four; Kate, Seema and two other mums who had six-year-old daughters, Amy and Karen. They were pleasant, fun-loving women whom Kate knew vaguely.

Seema was much better at the friend groups than Kate was. It was partly because Jack was already two when they moved to Bristol and mums who had had their babies at the same time had already formed their little tribes. Amy and Karen were friendly and sweet though, not cliquey, and Kate had enjoyed their company well enough in the past. But they were morbidly fascinated by Kate's widowed status, and wanted to talk about Tom in hushed tones, which Kate found a bit wearing after a while.

There was much drink being taken as they got ready, painting each others' nails, trying out dramatic eye make-up on each other and – in Kate's case – schushing up her classic black dress to make it a bit more sexy, something Kate wasn't entirely sure she wanted it to be. She also wasn't a massive drinker nowadays, as it just made her parenting and work obligations even harder to meet. She envied the other women having husbands to take noisy children away somewhere the following day, so they could have the luxury of recovering from their hangovers in peace.

Daniel wasn't a big drinker either, but he felt he needed a stiffener before he braved Cara and Paul's blatant match-making attempts. Fond as he was of them both, he wished they wouldn't. What he wouldn't do to be volunteering at Crisisline instead. Barbara had refused him permission to give up another Saturday night, though, insisting he must have better things to do.

He really didn't.

He sat at the bar, cradling a double Scotch on the rocks and idly gazed into the smoked mirror wall behind the shelves in the bar. It allowed him a glimpse of the door and he could watch the crowds of people slowly filling the bar, idly checking out the women with their unlikely winter tans, bare legs under short skirts and elaborate eye make-up. False lashes were mandatory, it seemed. The thick, heavy spiders glued to their real lashes weighed down the eyelids so much the girls had sultry, come-to-bed expressions simply because they could not open their eyes very far. Several seemed to have actual feathers coming out a couple of inches from where the eyelashes would normally end. A couple had tiny sequins attached too. There was an outbreak of Christmas deely bopper headbands with Santa heads and reindeer antlers, even though there were still nearly three weeks to go.

A gaggle of four noisy women bundled in through the door, laughing. A beautiful dark-skinned woman was clearly the leader and she quickly got them organised on a table near Daniel's barstool, ordering Negronis all round from an appreciative barman. The blonde woman, last through the door and more reserved than the others, caught his eye.

Christmas Tree Girl. She hadn't seen him. Discovering he was sitting there several minutes in would have been weird, but just as he was about to turn around, catch her eye and acknowledge the acquaintance, a very drunk man with a tight grey suit and greased back hair lurched over to them.

'Laydeez,' he said, loudly, 'looking for some fun?'

The Indian woman was still at the bar. The two other women looked at each other and burst out laughing but Christmas Tree Girl just looked uncomfortable, staring at the table and flinching away from him.

'So what are you lovely milfs doing without a man to service your every need tonight,' he went on, and before any of them had time to answer he made a grab for Christmas Tree Girl. 'You especially,' he said, 'sad-faced girl, you look

69

like you especially need to be shown a good time.' He did a hip thrust in her general direction that nearly unbalanced him completely, making him put all his weight on the hand he had on her arm. She winced under the weight.

Daniel had seen enough.

'You've failed to make a favourable impression mate,' he said, laying his hand heavily on the man's shoulder and pulling him backwards so he would release his grip.

'And who the hell are you?' he reeled around angrily.

'I'm your guardian angel, mate,' said Daniel, 'here to stop you getting yourself into a situation you can't get out of. Now bugger off and bother someone else.'

For a moment, the whole room held its breath. The only sound, within twenty feet of them, was the thudding background music, as everyone waited for the fight to erupt. The man gave Daniel a furious look, curling his lip and looking him up and down. Daniel waited patiently for the appraisal to be complete and then gave the man a shove.

Shrugging off Daniel's hand, the man turned and slunk away, cursing as he went.

'What's a milf?' Kate asked Amy and Karen.

'Us,' giggled Karen, partly in relief at the positive end to the encounter. 'Mother's they'd like to – you know . . . and I wouldn't mind a bit if he thought so,' she said, gesturing at Daniel who was watching the man depart, making damned sure he left completely. The barman was of the same mind, gesturing to the bouncer on the door to extract him and evict him from the premises.

'Are you all right?' asked Daniel. It was Kate he was looking at.

'Thank you, yes, I'm fine,' said Kate. 'He wasn't exactly my type,' she added.

'I should hope not. Big night planned?'

'Probably,' she said, smiling at Seema who was just coming back from the bar with a tray of drinks, oblivious to what had just happened. 'Unfortunately,' she added.

'Be safe,' said Daniel, draining his drink and shrugging on his coat.

'I will,' said Kate quietly to his departing figure.

'So, you nearly pulled then,' Seema said, when she had been filled in on the excitement by Karen and Amy.

'The greasy-haired bloke? Yeah, the one that got away,' joked Kate.

'Actually, I meant him,' said Seema, nodding her head at Daniel. 'He's lush. Do you know each other?'

'Not really.'

'Shame.'

'Hang on,' protested Kate. 'That's not on the list. I do not need a man to achieve my Christmas miracle.' She meant it. It felt critically important to her that she and Jack had to find their own way, find their feet. If, after that, another relationship presented itself then she wasn't entirely uninterested.

'Fair enough,' said Seema. She knew when she was beaten. 'Seriously nice arse though.'

As he opened the gate to the garden of Paul and Cara's little terraced house he dearly wished he was manning the phone lines instead.

The woman Cara had lined up for him was already there. Introducing herself as Hayley and planting a kiss on his cheek in greeting, she was plump, blonde and loud. Cara had clearly given her a briefing and Daniel could see she was bursting to mention 'the thing'. Idly, he watched the clock and made bets with himself how long she would take to bring it up.

'So, Daniel,' she breathed, after the briefest of conversations about the weather. She pushed her breasts forward as she leaned in towards him, a large glass of Prosecco in her hand. 'I'm so sorry to hear about your sister. She was a Downs wasn't she?'

He looked at the clock. One and a half minutes, he reckoned. That was better than he'd thought, if he was honest. She must have tied herself up in knots managing to go that long without drawing attention to the thing that marked him out and made him different to the other young men. It was almost like a smell, an aura, that women could discern in him. Some of them seemed to like it on the whole. Unfortunately, those women tended to be the wrong ones.

'She was a young woman,' said Daniel, 'not "a Downs",' but then, as her face fell, he smiled at her. 'It's fine, it's just that – well – if you'd met her, it would have taken five minutes and the last thing you would have been thinking about was how she was born with Down's syndrome.'

'Yeah, but it must have been awful . . .' she pressed. 'And to die so young from it. I can't imagine . . . Such a tragedy.'

'Down's syndrome isn't a disease.'

'But she died of it,' said Hayley, perplexed. 'At least . . .' she looked uncertainly at Cara, who was busy bossing Paul around in the kitchen end of the room.

'She died of a congenital heart defect,' he explained as they sat at the long dining table crammed into the other end of the room, where he and Hayley had been banished. 'She was born with it. They,' he hesitated, even though he had trotted this out a thousand times, 'they didn't fix it when she was a baby, so it became unfixable. As she grew it got worse and, well, eventually she just couldn't survive it.' He bowed his head, and Hayley pressed her hand onto his arm sympathetically.

He couldn't dislike this ignorant woman. She was kind, but simple, and Cara had done her best. With a supreme effort, he raised his head and smiled.

'She was twenty-two,' he said, 'which was actually amazing. When she was born we were told she had no chance of becoming an adult.'

'Sooo sad,' said Hayley, seeming grateful for the smile. 'And you're how old?'

'Thirty-two,' said Daniel, making a rueful face. 'Really old.'

'And you're . . . single?'

She clearly already knew he was.

'I've been looking after Zoe,' he explained. 'Our parents died so, obviously . . .'

'And now you're free.'

Daniel wasn't at all sure he would look at it that way. 'I'm alone,' he offered instead.

'You don't have to be,' she said, her perfume and her winey breath surrounding him like a fog.

'How's it going, mate,' murmured Paul when Daniel escaped to the fridge to get the Prosecco bottle out. As far as he could see, it was only Hayley drinking it, but the level was going down pretty fast.

'She's, erm . . . very sweet.'

'Not the sharpest tool in the box?'

'Yeah, but nice, erm . . .' Daniel searched for something positive to say.

'Nice tits?'

'I was going to say, "nice smile".'

'Yeah.' Paul thought for a moment. 'Nice tits too though.'

'Shut up, you prat. She's fine, but don't expect me to take her home.'

At least he would get a good supper, because Cara was a fine cook, Daniel reminded himself as Hayley told him all about her nail bar business. She showed off her own, extraordinary nails – each one a different sign of the zodiac with two on each thumbnail – and explained how the future was in false nails, fake eyelashes and also brow tattooing, in which she was going to be trained.

'I'm ambitious, Daniel,' she explained earnestly. 'I want to do stuff with my life. I don't just want a man to support me like some girls do . . .'

He had nodded and smiled and nodded and smiled until he thought his face was going to fall off. At the end of the night, by which time Hayley had polished off two bottles of Prosecco and a large Bailey's, she was tearful at Daniel's bereavement again, holding his face in both hands and weeping. 'She was so young – and a disabled too . . . it's so sad.'

He got Cara to tell him where Hayley lived and called a taxi.

By the time he had manoeuvred her into her coat and found her bag – a gargantuan challenge as she needed holding steady at all times – Paul was standing back laughing behind his hand.

'I think she's a bit far gone,' Cara had added, in a whisper. 'You should make sure she gets home safe but you probably wouldn't want to . . . you know . . . best not to take advantage.'

Daniel gave her a look of stark disbelief, and turned back to getting Hayley out of the door without falling down the steps.

To his relief, she fell asleep in the taxi, but she got maudlin again as he helped her out of the car and got her to the front door of her flat, first making sure that the driver wasn't going to drive off and leave him. He was simultaneously holding her upright and scrabbling in her bag for her key.

'She was so young,' Hayley wailed, trying to hug him.

'You'll get over it,' counselled Daniel. 'Just try to think of happy things.' He opened the door with relief and gave her a gentle shove to get her inside. 'Bed time, I think.'

'Come with me,' she wailed. 'I don't want to be alone.'

'I think alone is best,' he said. 'You're going to prefer it when you wake up feeling crap tomorrow.'

'I won't. I want to be with yooooou . . .'

'You don't. I'm horrible, honestly,' he tried to shove her a bit further in, so he could close the door and escape. For a ghastly moment he wondered if he ought to go in and put her to bed, but then decided against it. She would be fine.

'It's not you, it's me,' he went on, flailing around desperately for things to say that would persuade her to let him leave.

This seemed to get through. 'Ah,' she said, nodding owlishly. 'You need more time.'

'I do,' he said, gratefully. 'I totally do, and then . . . well, who knows?'

She smiled. 'Night, night,' she said, suddenly seeming perfectly content, slamming the door in his face. He could see her through the window of the door, making her way along the corridor using the wall for support and guidance. Suddenly she disappeared. A door in the wall she was sliding along must have been open. Hopefully it was her bedroom.

7ᵗʰ December

The weather was so awful, Jack was so tired, and Kate was so monumentally hung over, she was immensely relieved the Christmas miracle task for the following day was just to stay in and make fudge to send to her parents and to Maureen.

'I love fudge! Can we eat some?'

'Probably.'

'We've got to save lots for Nana though.'

''Course.'

'Can we take it to her?'

Kate stopped stroking his hair. 'Do you want to? It's a really long way . . .' And expensive too, she thought.

'I want to see her,' he said, his chin wobbling. 'We haven't seen her for ages.'

'Okay, well, I'll see, but she might be too poorly,' said Kate. It had been a while. She called the nursing home every few weeks and the reports were consistent. Maureen was content. Or content enough. She was generally sunny and calm, amusingly dotty, and seemingly undistressed by her confusion. She had plenty to be distressed about, though; her eighteen-year-old daughter Daisy had left home after an argument, leaving behind her infant son Tom, and never returned. Maureen had dedicated herself to raising her grandson but had then seen him killed in Afghanistan just after he became a father to Jack.

Thankfully, Maureen usually had no memory of these sadnesses. When she asked where they were, on Kate's suggestion she was told Daisy was out shopping and Tom was at school and would be home for tea after football practice. She could then be distracted by some other activity, drifting off into a world where an entirely different logic applied.

'Don't touch,' squeaked Kate, seeing Jack reaching for a drip of molten fudge running down the outside of the pan.

'I just wanted a lick.'

'Boiling sugar!' she snapped. 'What have I told you?'

'I know, I know . . . really hot, sorry Mummy,' said Jack, crestfallen.

'No, I'm sorry, darling,' she said, ruffling his hair. She was tired. Dog tired. She had spent too many nights working on her jewellery, peering at it in the poor light, until her head pounded, and her eyes felt scratchy and dry. She must build up her stocks to make the most of Anastasia's party and all the while she was looking guiltily at the bags from the charity shop. Two camel costumes coming up, she thought. Great. Perhaps going to bed at two in the morning wasn't so bad when it was compensated for by a Sunday morning lie-in, she had told herself, but she hadn't factored in the entirely predictable fact that six-year-old boys don't do Sunday lie-ins. Jack was bouncing around in her bed at seven o'clock on the dot, wriggling, chatting and wanting her attention, so that was the end of sleep.

'How about we take this to Nana next weekend,' she said, pouring the fudge into the tin. 'She would love to see how much you've grown.'

'Will she think I'm Daddy?'

'Yeah, probably. Is that okay?'

'I don't mind. I think it makes her feel less sad.'

'I think it does too.'

'I'm pleased she feels less sad,' said Jack matter-of-factly. 'I wish I had something that made me less sad about not having a daddy.'

Kate swallowed, hot tears springing to her eyes. She turned away to put the pan in the sink, swiping her eyes quickly with the back of her hand.

'I know, darling,' she said, turning back with a watery smile. 'I wish you had something too.'

'I've got you, though,' he said putting his arms around her waist. 'I've got a mummy. Some little children don't have mummies *or* daddies. Like in wars and stuff.' His eyes widened as he looked up at her. 'What if you go too? Like Daddy did. Then I'll be like them. I'll have to look after myself and I don't think I know how to do everything on my own,' he said, staring into space, running through the complexities. 'You had better show me how to use the washing machine,' he said, practically. 'I will need to have clean clothes . . .'

'I'm not going anywhere,' said Kate, trying desperately to remember what the counsellor had told her about when he asked these sorts of questions.

'I'm not going to leave you,' she said, kneeling so she could hug him back. 'Daddy loved you very much and so do I.'

'But you're not a daddy,' said Jack quietly, into her shoulder, squeezing her tight. 'It would be nice to have a new daddy one day, too.'

'Would it?'

'One day,' he said. 'Maybe. I think I'll ask Father Christmas,' he said. 'In my letter.'

'Your letter?'

'Yes, I'm writing, but I haven't finished yet.'

'Can I see?'

'It's to Father Christmas,' he said, firmly. 'I have to post it soon or it won't get there in time.'

'Right,' said Kate. 'Well, maybe that's our Christmas thing for later this week. What do you reckon?'

After Jack had gone to bed, Kate laid out the coat on the floor, along with the other bits the kind lady had given them. Now the reality of making two camel heads from it all seemed ludicrous. She should probably ask Seema for help tomorrow. It was lucky tomorrow was the one day in the week they were both collecting their boys from school. Mind you, Seema, though a woman of many talents, had no sewing skills whatsoever.

By the time Kate had produced not one but two vaguely recognisable camel heads, both with long, fringed eyelashes made from the black felt the lady in the charity shop had miraculously found her, it was past midnight. For the second night running, she went to bed with tired eyes and an aching head. To top it all, when she finally lay there, staring into the darkness, she couldn't sleep. Thoughts about Tom's mother and whether it was seriously a good idea to take Jack to see her – quite apart from the expense – stopped her from relaxing enough to drop off.

At the moment Kate finally fell asleep, Daniel was in the tiny kitchen of the Crisisline office, stirring Coffeemate into two mugs. The claggy white powder floated initially and then dispersed, turning the murky extra-strength instant coffee into an unappealing orange-brown soup with an oil slick of fat globules on its surface. He added sugar to both mugs too – that always helped – and shook the biscuit tin experimentally. It was unpromisingly light and there was no rattle, just a faint swishing noise indicating the presence of biscuit wrappers. Empty ones.

He sighed. It was three in the morning. No corner shop or coffee shop was interested in staying open through the night in case he was in need of a sugar or caffeine rush to get him through his lonely shift. Not that it was completely lonely. Barbara was there in the booth beside his own. He could hear her soothing Bristolian tones, chatting matter-of-factly to the latest caller to phone the helpline that night. As he walked back towards her, he noticed how the two small desk lights in the darkened office created a glowing beacon in the darkness. That's what they were. The only other souls awake in the whole universe, or so it seemed to those who called them – drunk, angry, tearful, sometimes completely silent, unable to speak but hopefully able to take comfort from knowing that there was someone on the end of the line.

The silent ones got to him. They upset him, that heavy, oppressive miasma of misery coming down the line, sometimes a muffled sob, sometimes not even the sound of breathing, making him wonder if he was witnessing a death. A suicide. That had happened to him more than once. It happened to everyone working on the line if they volunteered for long enough. It changed you as a person, hearing someone die. It was a requirement of all volunteers that they undergo supervision sessions which gave them a chance to offload distressing stuff, preventing it from carving too deep a gouge into their own soul.

Another strategy they used to distance themselves from the pain of others was to use a different name for their phone selves. It wasn't compulsory, but Daniel had always done it. He was Jonathan when he answered the phone. It was also a double protection against ever picking up the phone to someone they knew in real life, although the chances of that were vanishing slim. Barbara was Daniel's supervisor. She was also the first person he met when he volunteered.

She smiled her thanks as he quietly put down her mug and sat beside her in the next booth, cradling his own mug as he idly listened to her call.

It sounded like yet another sex call. They got a lot of them. People – mainly men – phoned wanting to shock, talking inappropriately and often very obviously fiddling with themselves while they spoke. It was a policy of the charity to only end calls in exceptional circumstances, but they had recently adopted a rule which allowed volunteers to hang up if that happened. There were limits. In the Bristol office, their other option was to hand them on to Barbara, who was worldly and pragmatic enough not to mind.

This was clearly one of those calls.

'Gabriel,' she was saying, 'I don't think you *do* want to know what colour my knickers are, not really – they're those enormous Marks and Spencer flesh-coloured ones by the way, not attractive – but I do think you want to talk to me, don't you my love? I think you want to tell me what's upsetting you, don't you?'

Daniel raised his eyebrows and Barbara gave him a little nod in return.

'Gabriel?' she went on. 'I think you're playing with yourself while you're talking to me, and . . .'

She paused. Daniel strained his ears.

' . . . yes, I'm sure it *is* enormous . . . but Gabriel, I don't think you really want to talk about that . . .'

There was another indistinct rumble from the receiver. 'Or that. Gabriel, will you listen to me? Now, I am more than happy to sit and talk to you about the size of your private parts. I've got two grown-up boys of my own, I've seen it all and heard it all but, you know what? I'm just wondering why you drank a lot of alcohol tonight and decided to call the Crisisline, because you and me, Gabriel, we could be asleep in bed, couldn't we?' She paused again. 'No, different beds, Gabriel. Different beds, because I think I'm old enough to be your mum, and you need to take my word for it that sharing a bed with me – five foot nothing, north of twelve stone and long past my sell-by date – is going to do nothing to solve your problems . . . Gabriel?'

Barbara and Daniel strained their ears and waited. Sometimes there was a lot of waiting in silence. Not speaking was one of the most difficult things to learn.

She bowed her head, and put her hand to the headset, pushing the headphone a little closer to her ear.

'Gabriel,' she said, quietly, at last. 'I'm with you. I'm listening, my love . . . It's okay to have a little cry. You just carry on . . . If you want to talk, I'm here.'

Daniel drank his coffee, slowly. Barbara, next to him, was doing the same, her gaze resting intensely on a patch of wall in front of her, as she listened to her caller, not wanting to miss the slightest communication from him. Waiting.

'He hung up,' she said at last, taking off her headset and laying it on the desk.

'He'll call back,' said Daniel, resting a hand on her arm.

'I hope so,' she said, stretching her arms above her head and yawning. 'He worries me, that lad.'

She looked piercingly at Daniel.

'You worry me too.'

'Not for the same reasons, I hope. I don't want to sleep with you, honest. If I did, I'd say.'

'Thank goodness. But what's a nice boy like you doing volunteering on a Crisisline, stuck in here with a middle-aged deadbeat in the middle of the night, when you should be tucked up in bed with a loving partner.'

'Physician, heal thyself,' he volunteered, not meeting her eye.

His phone rang quietly, the red light on the dial flashing to indicate an incoming call.

'Saved by the bell,' he grinned, reaching for his headset. 'Crisisline,' he said. 'My name is Jonathan, and I'm listening.'

8th December

By the time he was heading down the street towards the office that morning he had fixed his sleep deprivation with the usual tactics: three hours' sleep, and as long and hot a shower as his boat bathroom could provide, with a cold burst at the end. It worked quite well. After a strong coffee and a bacon sandwich he would start to feel reasonably human. But it wasn't enough. It never was.

She was out there, alone, no customers to distract her from noticing him as he walked towards her. By the time he reached her, there was no ducking out. She was pale, with dark circles – almost purple – under her eyes, he noticed. She smiled up at him and ducked her head shyly as he reached her.

By the time he had stopped in front of her he had rehearsed and dismissed several potential comments. She looked up at him with a faintly quizzical but friendly smile. Did her eyes flicker up and down the street? Was she looking for rescue or welcome distraction from a customer or did he imagine it?

'You look knackered,' he blurted. Yikes, that wasn't good. Planning what to say hadn't gone well for him in the past but saying the first thing that came into his head wasn't playing too well either.

'I am a bit,' she admitted. 'You too?'

'Yeah . . .' he said. He shuffled from foot to foot, digging his hands into his pockets.

'So . . . get some rest, okay?'

She nodded, and continued looking at him expectantly, her crooked smile widening.

'Right . . . so . . .' said Daniel, rubbing his hands together briskly for no good reason. For want of anything else to do, he turned sharply on his heel and walked on, stiff-legged. He turned the corner and – again – beat his forehead with his hand, causing two women walking behind him to split apart, giving him a wide berth and each other raised eyebrow looks.

'I spoke to her,' he announced to Paul when he got to the office.

'Tree Girl?'

'Yeah.'

'Result! What did you say?'

'I told her she looked rubbish.'

'Nice one.'

They both stared into space, processing the significance of the encounter and contemplating how very, very much better it could have gone.

'First time you've spoken to her?' asked Paul, deciding to focus on the positive. 'First time this year, anyhow,' he corrected himself.

'Actually no,' admitted Daniel. 'I wished her a "Good Day" as I passed her last week, and I strong-armed this dodgy bloke in a bar that was bothering her. I stopped him chatting her up, which might actually have been what she wanted.'

'You did what? Genius, mate,' Paul shook his head in despair. 'To be honest I don't know how you haven't got them queuing round the block, all these women . . .'

'Yeah, me too,' admitted Daniel with a self-deprecating smile. 'She makes me nervous.'

'Just ask the poor girl for a coffee, for heaven's sake. Can you manage that? Repeat after me: "Would you like a coffee?"'

'Cheers,' said Daniel, irritatingly. 'If you're offering . . . milk and two sugars.'

Paul shook his head again. 'And I take it the Hayley situation isn't a thing?'

'You "take it" correctly. I'm not going to inflict myself on her. She's got enough problems as it is.'

'Yeah, sorry about that. Cara means well and all that.'

'I'm grateful, really, but I don't need you and Cara to help me mess up my love life. I'm perfectly capable of doing it on my own.'

'Clearly you are,' said Paul, admitting defeat. For now. 'Moving on to other matters . . .'

'Like coffee?'

'Like work.'

'Oh, that . . . go on then. Hit me.'

'Don't tempt me,' muttered Paul, riffling through papers on his desk. 'Here you go . . . we've just taken this on. Shop to let in Christmas Steps.'

'Nice,' said Daniel, reaching for the papers. 'Shouldn't take long to shift that.'

'You'd think, wouldn't you. However, it's a reject from Comptons, as it happens.'

'Rejected? By James "I'd rather sell my Grandma than leave a property unlet" Grady?'

'The same.'

'What's the catch . . .?' mused Daniel, his eyes skimming the details. 'No! This is a tragedy. You could have broken it to me gently. It's the "Oldie Sweetie Shoppie".'

'"The Oldie Sweetie . . ."' parroted Paul, exasperated. 'What are you? Five? Yeah, it's the Olde Sweet Shoppe. A bit of an institution, I gather. Clearly you frequented it.'

'I used to take Zoe there,' admitted Daniel. 'He had these gobstoppers the size of your fist. Even Zoe had to suck them down to size before she could get them in her mouth, and she had a gob on her – I used to tease her about it,' he recalled dreamily. 'We used to sit and watch old films with these ridiculous things. And liquorice allsorts. Proper ones. I swear they taste different out of one of those big jars . . .'

'Aaanyway,' said Paul, but his eyes softened sympathetically.

'Yeah, so . . .' said Daniel, returning to the property description. 'The rent's really very reasonable – yikes, the rates are sky high though.'

'The council decided to revalue it,' agreed Paul. 'They took the opportunity. To be fair Christmas Steps is long overdue for a rate rise. Half the city's due a review. We know that.'

'Why does our client not want to charge a rent in line with the rateable value? And why – especially as the rent is so low – hasn't he had his hand bitten off for the lease?'

'You can ask him that yourself. He's expecting you at three o'clock this afternoon.'

Kate was desperate for her morning break. Clapping her hands together wasn't helping with the cold any more. It just hurt, and her elf costume was too tight for her to stick her hands up the opposite sleeve like she did with her jumpers. Her face was so cold she was struggling to move her mouth and, talking to customers, she had started to sound like she had been to the dentist. She counted down the minutes, dreaming of curling her freezing hands around a hot cup of coffee. But it was not to be.

'Staff meeting,' said Wayne. 'Mr Wilkins has a cunning plan – and that's never good.'

'Oh, love,' said Pat, passing them on the way to the boardroom. 'You look frozen. I'm going to fill up my hot water bottle and bring it out to you when you do the next stint. You can tuck it under your top.'

Kate looked down at her chest doubtfully. She was sure Mr Wilkins would be delighted to see his Christmas elf with a bit more padding in the chest department, but she wasn't sure it would stay where it was put. Maybe she would have a bulgy tummy instead. A mildly pregnant elf, maybe . . . What the hell, as long as it was warmer.

'Now then,' said Mr Wilkins 'I know you're all wondering, how can Portman Brothers do even more to establish its good name in the community. As we all know, the firm is well known for its generosity to local charities and I am delighted to announce that the board has decided to launch a new and major fundraising project, to culminate at Christmas with a grand cheque presentation. Isn't that great?'

'Are they going to donate some of the Christmas profits?' Kate piped up innocently.

For a moment Mr Wilkins regarded her with blank incomprehension. 'Donate profits?' he said. 'Of course not . . .'

'Didn't think so,' whispered Pat, before immediately clapping her hand over her mouth, astonished and frightened by her boldness.

'No,' Mr Wilkins went on, 'much better than that, we want it to be fun,' he gave them all a sickly grin. 'Much better publicity to be fundraising actively . . . raffles, fun runs, that kind of thing . . .' he waved his hand, vaguely. 'Over to you all.'

A stony silence ensued. He stared them all down for an unconscionable time and then relented. 'Right,' he said, 'here is what we are going to do . . . We are going to need a committee. Kate, you are the chairman.'

'Did I volunteer?' she said, although – thinking about it – one of the tasks for her Christmas miracle was to do charity work. This might be useful.

'You did volunteer,' he said, looking at her beadily, 'because I know how keen you are to be a valuable employee and a contributing member of the team.' He paused, still glaring.

'Okay, fine,' she muttered, rubbing her cold hands together and blowing on them.

'I'll be your co-chair,' said Pat, and Kate smiled at her gratefully.

'So, the only other issue is a fundraising target,' said Mr Wilkins enthusiastically. 'I know you all like a challenge, so, as the last big fundraiser made eight hundred pounds, the board have agreed on a target of – wait for it . . .' he looked around the room expectantly, a foolish grin on his face, and said with a flourish, 'one thousand pounds!'

'Yay,' cheered the assembled group raggedly, with a conspicuous lack of enthusiasm.

'So, that's that . . . ooh, no, hang on . . . we, you, need to decide which local charity benefits,' said Mr Wilkins. 'The board declared you all should be allowed to choose, which I thought was extremely generous of them. Us.'

'Don't let it be the hedgehog rescue lot again,' muttered Kate. 'They were sweet, but I found fleas on me when I got home. Hedgehog fleas. They were seething, bless them.'

Pat shuddered.

'So,' Mr Wilkins went on, 'there were two the board put on the shortlist – now who was it again?' he fumbled with his notes. 'Ah yes, the Crisisline Bristol branch, apparently you call it if you're at your wit's end, and then . . . the Apple Café, run by mentally disabled kids and stuff, you know the kind of thing . . .' he looked up jovially. 'That's people who didn't have any wits in the first place.'

There was a quiet gasp, as people in the room assimilated what he had said.

'"Mentally disabled"?' mouthed Kate to Wayne quizzically. '"Witless"? Really?'

Wayne raised his eyes to heaven. 'Tosser,' he mouthed back, jerking a thumb in their boss's direction.

'I know the Apple Café,' said Kate aloud with a sigh of resignation. Some people you just couldn't even explain things to. 'I vote for that. It's just down the road from where I live.'

'Do you go in there?' asked Mr Wilkins incredulously.

'Sometimes,' said Kate. 'Me and Jack. They're open to anyone. It's not well known . . . but their raspberry white chocolate muffins are awesome.'

'Hands up for the Apple Café,' said Wayne. 'Seeing as Kate has to arrange stuff, I'm happy to go with her choice.'

All hands went up.

Kate checked her watch as the meeting dissolved into chatter. She had three minutes of her break left. Just time for a wee and then she was due back outside. Great.

'What will you do?' asked Pat. She had come out to the christmas tree stand with a hot wheat bag and – joy of joys – a thermos of hot coffee.

'Sorry, I know you don't have sugar usually, but it was already in.'

'It's amazing,' said Kate, sipping gratefully. 'And this wheat bag is incredible,' she added, wrapping it around her neck. The sudden warmth made her shiver.

'I'll get you one for Christmas,' said Pat, drily. 'Although I'd like to think you won't be out in the cold selling Christmas trees this time next year. We need better things for you and Jack. Better things than this . . .'

Kate shook her head, bleakly. Where would they both be this time next year?

'So, how on earth are we going to raise a thousand pounds?' asked Pat, breaking into her thoughts.

'Dunno. I could do without this, on top of everything else.'

'We've not been introduced properly,' said Daniel, when the little old man answered the door. 'Although I know you, and – I have to say – I am going to miss you and your shop hugely.'

'Thank you,' the man replied. 'My name is Noel Chandler but you can call me Noel. I remember you of course. You used to come in often with a young lady who has . . .' he paused, selecting his words.

'My sister Zoe,' intervened Daniel. 'She had a heart problem.'

'Had?' queried Noel with infinite gentleness.

'She died, coming up for a year ago,' said Daniel, his eyes thanking the old man for remembering, for being delicate in how he asked. People didn't know how to ask. Sometimes they markedly refused to, clearing their throats, looking at the sky, changing the subject to something – anything – more comfortable.

'Young man, I am so sorry to hear it. I very much enjoyed your sister's company.'

'And she yours.'

'But now, life has changed, as life tends to do – relentlessly,' Noel observed. 'It is the way of the world,' he smiled, clasping his hands. 'And I am glad I was there for your sister. I should not like to think I ever disappointed her by closing the shop whilst she still required it. Shall we?' he waved his arm at the front door of the shop.

Once inside, Daniel turned slowly in a circle, evaluating the space. 'So, it's small at just under three hundred square feet,' he observed. 'I am happy to re-assess the space, or – if you prefer – we can just adopt the Comptons evaluation and move on?'

'Comptons were fine. Let us take their evaluation as read,' said Noel.

'And yet you are looking to us to take on the job?' said Daniel. It was critical to understand why Comptons had not been successful. On the surface of it, finding a new tenant should have been swift and straightforward.

'Christmas Steps is a very special area,' explained Noel. 'I have lived and worked here all my life . . .'

'You live here?' asked Daniel, looking to the ceiling.

'I do. There is a little flat above. Two storeys. Tiny, actually, but perfectly adequate. I am alone,' said Noel without self-pity. 'It amuses me that people are always surprised. Where do you expect me to live? Actually, with children it is particularly amusing because they seem to think I am just – what? – sitting in the shop all day and night, every day of the week, waiting to spring to life when they come along . . .'

'I think I was a bit like that,' admitted Daniel. 'Do you know? I've been coming here with Zoe since we were tiny. Our Dad would bring us on a Saturday morning . . .' His eyes filled suddenly. They did that since Zoe died. He hated it. The feeling of not knowing when grief was going to roll over him, like a dark, powerful wave, sweeping his composure away in a moment as if it were a pile of match-stick flotsam. Sometimes he would even make a sound. A sob. Mainly he would manage to suppress it by holding his breath. He would turn away, surreptitiously wipe his eyes and turn back restored, as people pretended not to have noticed.

Noel didn't pretend not to notice.

'Our dear Queen said it perfectly,' he observed; '"Grief is the price we pay for love,"' he told Daniel, putting a hand on his arm just for a moment. 'And to quote Tennyson – as I believe it was – "Better to have loved and lost . . ."'

'That's so true,' said Daniel, taking a deep breath. He had to get a grip. He had never failed to be a professional before. Noel just seemed to hit a nerve. 'Sorry,' he said, turning back and straightening himself with a conscious effort.

'Don't,' he said sharply. 'Don't apologise. I won't have it.'

'No,' said Daniel. 'I won't. I won't apologise for being sad. You are quite right.'

'But there comes a time when you have to look forward, young man . . . and in a way, that is what I am asking you to help me with.'

'Right, yes, absolutely. So, you mention the flat upstairs but – just to check – you are only seeking a tenant for the shop, aren't you?'

'I am. It is all part of a bigger plan,' said Noel, gesturing for Daniel to sit on one of the two upright wooden chairs which were sitting at angles on the dusty floor, in an otherwise empty room. The light was dingy. Whatever sunlight filtered through into the narrow street was obscured by the whitewashed glass of the window. Daniel sat and, suddenly, felt more at peace than he had done for months. He looked expectantly at the shrunken old man beside him and settled in for the story he was about to hear.

'I have lived and worked here for more than seventy years now. Obviously, that makes me very old,' Noel said with a smile. 'And the demands of the business, the long opening hours, the need for a constant presence, means I have lived a fairly narrow life for that time. You might feel I regret that, but I do not. You might pity me, even. But you should not. I have been content. It has been the life I have chosen. My parents brought me here, as a young boy, from Germany, which was not a good place for my family to be at the time.'

'You escaped the Nazis?'

'We did. We were caught helping a Jewish family. In fact, we helped many, many families,' he said with pride. 'We got away with it for a long time, but eventually our card was marked, and we heard they were coming for us. We left in the dead of night, came here with nothing, and made a small life for ourselves. My family were confectioners in Germany too – marzipan mostly, some sugar work – and so it was natural to stick with what we knew. It has been years since we made the sweets ourselves – that part was not necessary here – but we built a reputation. When I was an adult I took over and when my parents died, it became something I did alone. I have now done it alone for as long as I feel I can.'

He paused.

'So,' interjected Daniel gently, 'how can I help you now? I'm interested to know why Comptons didn't succeed in finding you a tenant.'

'They failed – that man, James – he failed because he did not ask the right questions as you do. I am not looking for rent, it is not about money, it is about finding a person who can breathe life into the shop, who can cleave to our little community here in Christmas Steps and make it stronger. I have been presented only with a succession of ghastly people who want to open some "boutique",' he made a dismissive gesture with his hands, 'who want to take a short lease to make the most of some venal, commercial opportunity. I had a dodgy mobile phone sales person who wanted to take over the shop for six weeks only; it turned out he wanted to sell poor-quality phone cases, counterfeit handbags, cheap textiles – just in the run-up to Christmas – and then disappear again. That is the last thing this community needs. Every shop in Christmas Steps is like a different organ in a human body. We are more than the sum of our parts here . . .'

'Sorry, so . . .' Daniel asked, 'just to be clear, are you only interested in someone who wants to take over the confectionary business . . .?'

'No,' said Noel slowly. 'That would be delightful, but it is probably unrealistic. It is only because I own the property and pay no rent that I have been able to survive as long as I have. This ridiculous new, high business rate has put paid to the profitability of my business. It is gone now. I accept that.'

'That's so sad,' said Daniel. 'It's been a sweet shop as long as I remember.'

'We need to change or die. In my case, I am going to literally die soon anyway' – he said this without the slightest hint of self-pity – 'so it is important that this person has the energy, vision and goodness of heart to take on the battle.'

'And how will I find this person?' asked Daniel, smiling.

'You find them. When you have found them, you will know. I will know. You must bring them to me and I will tell you.'

'And the rent?'

'Irrelevant.'

As usual, Kate barely made it to the school gate in time.

'You needn't have rushed,' said Seema, looking cool and composed as usual. 'I could have taken the boys home and met you there.'

'I had a call. Apparently, Mrs Marshall wants "a word".'

'Uh-oh.'

'I know . . . not good.'

'Well, it might be good,' said Seema. 'It might be that Jack has done some amazing, astonishing, fabulous thing that Mrs Marshall is pining to tell you about.'

'Or not,' said Kate, flatly.

'Or not,' agreed Seema. 'I'll let you go and face the music then. See you back at ours?'

Mrs Marshall was waiting in the foyer, giving Kate the soothing, professional smile that she knew and dreaded.

'We are so glad you have come in . . . It's just a little chat, Mrs Thompson. We've been having a think about Jack and his needs,' she said, ushering Kate smoothly into the headteacher's office, where the others were already seated with cups of tea.

'It is our feeling,' said Mrs Marshall, slowly, 'that it would be helpful for Jack if we could take a closer look at his issues, with a view to seeing how we can best support him moving forward.'

'A closer look?'

'A professional insight.'

'At his issues?'

'Anger management, concentration and focus, executive function, cognitive ability . . .'

'What? Who?' Kate shook her head in confusion. 'Cognitive ability? Is Jack not normal? Is that what you're saying?'

'No, no, Mrs Thompson,' Mrs Marshall said earnestly. 'Of course, Jack is "normal". All children are "normal" but they are also unique, and we want to understand more about Jack's – uniqueness . . .'

Kate shuffled nervously. 'Okay, go on. Is there anything in particular?' she dreaded to ask. 'Anger, cognitive thingie . . .?'

'It's more of an emerging pattern of behaviours and learning styles,' said Mrs Marshall. 'I have asked our Special Needs Co-ordinator, Mrs England, to explain a little more.'

Kate turned expectantly. Mrs England was a quietly spoken, earnest, middle-aged woman whom Kate had been sent to speak to before. She had been reassuring then. Perhaps now it was a different story.

'Jack is a lovely boy,' she began, 'but . . .' she thought carefully, 'I feel he would benefit from an investigation by an education psychologist with a view to applying for an EHCP.'

'A wha . . .?'

'An EHCP – Education, health and care plan – is a binding document which compels the education authority to meet a child's needs as identified in their plan. It comes with a commitment. Funding. Resources.'

'So . . .' said Kate, floundering, 'you want to diagnose Jack. You want to say, "This is the thing that's wrong with him." Put a label on him.'

'We do not label children. This is not a diagnostic process. It is an opportunity to look in detail at the support Jack needs with all aspects of his access to education – and any other needs he may have – and then it helps to see more clearly which school is . . .'

'Which school?' interrupted Kate. 'This is his school. He goes here.'

Mrs Marshall nodded her head but would not meet Kate's eye. Kate stared at her imploringly.

Mrs Marshall cleared her throat delicately. 'Mrs Thompson, moving forward – and we really are simply trying to do the best for Jack – I suggest I apply for the EHCP process to start and see what the result suggests. As part of that, I have to ask, does Jack have a social worker at all?'

*

'They asked if he had a bloody social worker, for God's sake,' hissed Kate. They were both leaning up against the kitchen counter as Kate brought Seema up to date. As soon as Seema had seen her friend's face, she had dispatched the two boys to the sitting room, with CBBC turned up louder than usual and a packet of Monster Munch each.

'Wine,' said Seema, decisively.

'I know, I know, but it's just not my style,' admitted Kate. 'I do feel like it though. I feel like filing an official complaint.'

'I said "Wine", you idiot, not "whine",' said Seema, reaching into the cupboard for glasses.

'On a Monday?' said Kate, with mock horror.

'On a Monday,' she insisted, sloshing white wine into two glasses. 'This is a big one . . .'

'So I told them of *course* he hasn't got a social worker,' said Kate, returning to her point like a dog with a bone. 'I feel like I've been catapulted into a parallel universe. Suddenly he's – I dunno – different? Failing? Damaged in some way?'

Tears sprang to Kate's eyes and Seema tore off a bit of kitchen towel for her.

'It's fine,' she said. 'Don't panic. Jack's going to be fine.'

'But they don't want him at the school.'

'They didn't say that.'

'They sort of did. What if they do this psychology report thingie and then they say they can't help him. Do you think they'll expel him?' The thought lead to a fresh rush of tears.

'You need to calm down, girl. This isn't getting you anywhere.'

Kate's eyes widened at the no-nonsense tone. But then she nodded. 'You're right,' she said. 'I do.' She took a deep breath and let it out slowly. 'Do you think Jack is different to the other boys?' Her eyes were searching her friend's face for honesty.

Seema took her time. She took a slow gulp of wine and stared. 'I think,' she said at last, 'Jack *is* unusual.'

'How? I don't know what you mean.'

'You do know . . . in your heart, but maybe not your head yet. You're his mum so you see it. Describe it,' she suggested. 'Why don't you just – describe it – to me and to yourself. Right now, just say whatever pops into your head.'

'I've only ever been Jack's mum though,' said Kate. 'I can't compare with other children. How can I know? But . . .' She stared unseeing out of the kitchen window. 'It's like Jack is under siege the whole time. I look at his little face, and I can see he is desperately trying to – I don't know – make sense of everything. It's like he's being blasted by all this information. Like there are no filters, just a tidal wave of . . . stuff. And he takes it all in too. His questions . . . what, how, who, why . . . it's constant. It's like he's "always on" and then, suddenly, he gets totally overwhelmed and switches off. Glazes over. Gets angry sometimes then too. What is that?'

'I don't know,' said Seema, quietly. 'I don't think it needs to have a name, does it? It's just Jack. What matters is understanding what he needs. You're a good mum. You'll get him whatever he needs, I know you will. Just go with it. That's my advice.'

They both drank, silently, for a few minutes, lost in their own thoughts.

Suddenly, a huge crash destroyed their reverie.

'What the heck?' said Kate, jumping out of her skin. It had come from from the sitting room, followed by shouts of laughter from the two boys. There was another crash, and then another.

'I think they've finished their crisps,' said Seema calmly.

'Do we know what they're doing now?'

'My guess? Sounds like they're seeing whether they can jump from one sofa to the other, without touching the floor.'

'Nice,' said Kate. 'Do you mind?'

'Could be worse. Now show me these camel costume heads. I've been dying to see them all day.'

'Did Mrs Marshall say I was naughty?' asked Jack sleepily as Kate tucked him in.

'Absolutely not. She said you were amazing.'

'That's okay. I like my school.'

'There are lots of really cool schools though. Even better schools.'

'No,' said Jack, with certainty. 'I wouldn't want to go to another school. It wouldn't have Krish at it. That would be bad.' He added, 'I forgot my advent calendar!'

'Oh Jack,' said Kate. 'I reminded you twice. Now you've brushed your teeth . . .'

'I'll brush them again,' said Jack, hopping out of bed, all sleepiness forgotten.

'Send letter to Father Christmas,' he read on the scrap of paper Kate had hidden in the pocket. 'Oh yes, I've got to post it, haven't I, Mummy?' he said, around the chocolate which was now thoroughly coating his teeth.

'You have,' said Kate. 'Now off you go, you monkey,' she said, sending him back to bed with a pretend boot on the bottom. 'And brush your teeth again. Really well.'

9th December

The furry pants Kate had discussed in that uncomfortable conversation with Mr Wilkins were starting to sound more and more attractive. Even with two pairs of tights and three T-shirts under her elf tunic, she was freezing. Her face was numb, and her hands were aching with cold. Business was slow too, now that most people had their trees. With fewer customers to distract her, she tried to while away the time thinking up solutions to her newest pressing problems instead. The one about Jack and his school was too depressing for words, so she filed it in the back of her mind to return to later. The one about raising a thousand pounds for the Apple Café was more appealing; she was idly weighing up the pros and cons of carol singing versus getting the café staff to make and sell mince pies when – suddenly – the man was in front of her. She looked up into his kind, hazel eyes and smiled stiffly.

'You're really cold,' he said, not breaking her gaze.

Kate nodded, mutely.

'Okay,' he said. He stared for a moment longer, and then ran his eyes down from her face to her feet and back again. 'Right,' he barked, suddenly. 'Wait here. Don't go anywhere, okay?'

Kate shrugged. 'No chance of that.'

*

Twenty long minutes later, he arrived back in front of her, a little breathless. He had a Portman Brothers carrier bag in his hand.

'Look,' he told her, rummaging in the bag, 'what about this?' First, he produced a green woolly hat with an extravagant fluffy pompom. He held it out stretched, looking at her for permission.

She nodded, bemused, and he pulled it onto her head, gently tucking in a strand of her blonde hair that had fallen across her eyes, so she could see. His hand was warm as it brushed her cheek, and the hat was like a gentle hug. It was soft, thick and instantly warmer. 'Wow,' she said, 'that's brilliant. Do I look ridiculous?'

'No, cute,' he said, standing back to appraise his work. 'I thought green for an elf, I hope that's okay? Also . . .' He handed her a pair of dark green woollen gloves. 'They've got these flaps, see?' he demonstrated. They were fingerless but then there was a flap, buttoned to the back, which could be released and pulled over the fingers, turning them into mittens.

'Genius,' she breathed, pulling them on gratefully. 'I've been wanting some of these.'

'You can pull the flaps over, and then – when you've got customers – you can release your fingers to do the money thing,' he explained, unnecessarily.

She smiled. His simple enthusiasm reminded her of Jack. Actually, there was an intensity and focus on the problem solving that reminded her of someone else: of Tom. Her smile wobbled.

'Sorry,' he said, noticing, 'you must think I'm completely mad. Is this a bit random?'

'A little bit,' she admitted. 'But it's lovely. You're so kind.' Her smile wobbled again. 'What do I owe you?'

'Don't be silly,' he said, waving away her question without interest. 'And look, the *pièce de résistance*.' He rummaged in the bag again and produced a slim, orange plastic package. 'Ta da!'

'What . . .?'

'Aha!' he said, grinning, 'these are going to blow you away . . . you open the packet, then you put them in your shoes and they warm up your feet for up to sixteen hours. It's like . . . I dunno . . . but opening the packet sort of activates it and it gets hot. Good, eh?'

Kate giggled at his enthusiasm. 'Sixteen hours? Even Portman Brothers doesn't make me work for that long, thankfully. You are amazing. I feel so much warmer already. I'll do the foot thing when I have my break. I can't wait . . . But I can't let you do this . . . I don't even know your name.'

'You can,' he said. 'You need someone to look after you.' He looked at his watch. 'I've got to go.'

'And you still didn't tell me your name,' said Kate, too quietly for him to hear, as she watched him walk away.

'So,' said Paul, trying to get a grasp on what Daniel was telling him, 'you walked up to her and gave her a hat?'

'And gloves, yeah. Do you think it was weird?'

'Yes. Definitely. Eccentric-weird, possibly even creepy-weird but – mate – I have to admire your creativity. As chat-up lines go, I reckon bunging a bird a hat with a pompom on it has to be unique.'

'She was cold. She's warmer now,' said Daniel, to no-one in particular. 'So that's good.' And he had spoken to Tree Girl in a slightly more normal way than before. Slightly. That was good too.

'Plus, now we finally know her name?' persisted Paul.

'Ah,' he admitted. 'I forgot that bit.'

*

'Those are clever,' exclaimed Pat, when she saw Kate putting the foot warmers into her shoes.

'You're telling me,' said Kate, re-lacing her trainers. She needed to loosen them a bit to make room but – oh the relief – they were heating up already.

'So, a secret admirer, eh?'

'I dunno about that,' Kate flushed, and it wasn't the warmth of the staffroom. 'He's just this kind man,' she said. 'He's kind . . . And he's sad.'

'I can feel a rescue coming on,' chided Pat. 'And I do wonder whether you've already got enough on yourself, without turning yourself inside out for another sad story. What about this ridiculous fundraising thing? Why is Mr Wilkins loading everything onto you? I could cheerfully murder him.'

'He knows I'll do it, because I need my job,' said Kate wearily rubbing her face.

'Talking of which,' said Pat, 'this'll cheer you up. See what I brought in this morning?' she was pointing at a cardboard box on the worktop.

Kate went over, her curiosity piqued. 'What's all this?' she said, rummaging. 'Chocolates, bath stuff, oh – bottle of Scotch – great. Cloakroom tickets? What's it all for?'

'Staff raffle. My friends at the Women's Institute. At the meeting last night I told them I was co-chair of the fundraising committee here, to raise a thousand pounds and – bless them – they gathered up the raffle prizes we go round and round with and told me to bring them here. The cloakroom tickets too . . .'

'What do you mean they "go round and round"?'

'We have a raffle every couple of months and – to be honest – there's a bit of re-gifting, shall we call it? The girls were more than happy to donate all this. We can ask staff to buy tickets. I thought a pound a strip? It won't raise a thousand but it all helps doesn't it?'

'You're an angel,' said Kate. 'Really! It's brilliant . . . we'll just set them all up here . . . make it all look a bit enticing.' Now she knew more, she peered into the box again doubtfully, wondering about use-by dates.

'What else shall we do though?' Pat fretted. 'I don't want us to let them down. Shall we go there, and have a chat with people? Kick some ideas around?'

'I was thinking of doing just that,' said Kate, with relief. 'It's a brilliant place, you'll love it. When are you free?'

'Soon, my love. Tomorrow? But never mind that . . . what else is it? Has that Mr Wilkins upset you again?'

Kate sighed, hugging her cup and bowing her head over the table that separated them. 'How did you guess? No, it's not Mr Wilkins, although obviously he is an arse and it does upset me that he wants me out of here . . . No, I had a meeting with the school about Jack yesterday.'

'That lovely boy of yours. He's not in trouble, is he?'

'Sort of, yes. They want him out.'

'Ridiculous! What's he done? I can't believe he would have done anything. He's just not . . .'

'No, to be fair, it's not that . . .' Kate searched for an explanation. 'They're starting to say his needs would be best met elsewhere.'

'What needs exactly?'

'That's the thing,' sighed Kate, going on to explain what she had said to Seema, his tendency to zone out, the feeling she had that he was overwhelmed sometimes. She told Pat about the huge tantrums he had had at two and three years old. Normal two-year-old stuff, everyone had said at the time. And, of course, Tom had been killed around that time. The tantrums had been massive. Epic. Once seen never forgotten, and yet they had passed. Jack had got somewhat better at managing his own emotions, but not enough to fit in, it seemed. Kate had sometimes allowed a tiny voice in her head to whisper that Jack might be autistic, but he couldn't be, could he? His unusual behaviour didn't fit with the autism Kate knew of from what she had read in the papers. That wasn't Jack. And yet . . .

Pat listened as Kate talked. She was knitting, as usual, her needles clicking rhythmically, comfortingly, as she sat, nodding occasionally, making encouraging noises.

'So,' said Kate at last. 'Here we are. They want to examine him. Report on him. They've already warned me they think he might need to go to a different school, but they haven't said properly why yet. Or where.'

'The "where" I might be able to help you with,' she said obliquely. But Kate was beyond hearing subtlety and inference.

'I don't want Jack to change schools,' Kate wailed, tears springing frustratingly to her eyes again.

'Also,' said Pat, persevering kindly but firmly, 'you need to know that Jack is in the right place to meet his needs. He's a gorgeous boy. Don't worry. But if he's not thriving where he is, then you have a duty to find somewhere he's better suited.'

'Of course, I do. You're right. I need to get a grip.'

'You've been through more than a lot of people go through in their lifetime,' said Pat. 'Don't be hard on yourself. Now,' she went on, 'On the subject of schools, there's someone I think you should meet . . .'

'Who?'

'My sister Ursula.'

'Why?'

'Because I think she would be interested in Jack. She's the principal at Greystone Manor Prep, do you know it?'

'Vaguely, but it's a posh private school isn't it? Navy uniform, boys in shorts and long socks, boaters? You see them all swarming around the Cathedral in the summer.'

'Those are the ones.'

'Private school is completely out of the question, Pat.' She was aghast that Pat had even suggested it. 'Anyway, no one is suggesting Jack needs a posh school with Latin grammar, the cane and rugger practice . . .'

Pat held up a hand. 'It has elements of that – no bad thing for many boys – not the cane, obviously, there's none of that nowadays – but Greystone Manor is no ordinary private school. Go and talk to Ursula,' she implored. 'I'm going to give her a call.'

'You've got to do your letter to Father Christmas,' Kate reminded Jack when they got home.

'More writing,' he complained. 'I've been doing that at school all day.'

They were both cold and tired. The dark flat was always chilly and uninviting when they first returned at this time of year. She longed for the days when it was still light when they got home. It was getting towards the shortest day and that, she reminded herself – at least that – was a turning point.

'It's exciting writing to Father Christmas, though,' she said. 'Have some milk and a biscuit. Then we can sit down and do it together.'

Kate bustled about the flat, checking the meter, switching on the electric heater at least for a little while, turning on the lights and drawing the thin curtains. 'We'll soon get it cosy,' she said. 'Get out your paper and pencil, monkey boy. We can post it tomorrow on the way to the bus.'

She left him alone at first, starting on dinner while he wrote laboriously, tongue poking out of the corner of his mouth.

For all his talk, he had made little progress previously. He found getting his thoughts down on paper frustratingly difficult and had to be hectored to get it done. When she could see he had covered half a page, in his huge, scrawly writing, each line drifting off at a steep angle downwards, she looked over his shoulder.

'Good job,' she said. 'Can I read it?'

Jack sighed. 'Suppose so. It won't happen anyway. What's the point?'

'You're far too world-weary for a six-year-old,' she teased, but her heart gave a twist in her chest.

Dear Father Crismas, it said. *I don't want lots of toys becos we dont have much room, becos we dont have much munny. We need a new daddy me and mummy do becos we are sad and a daddy will have munny and mummy wont have to work so hard and be tired. Thank you. Love Jack.*

'Do I do a kiss at the end?' asked Jack.

'If you want to,' said Kate. It came out squeaky because she was trying not to laugh. Or trying not to cry – one of the two, she wasn't quite sure which.

'I don't want to,' he admitted. 'I don't know him, and I wouldn't want to kiss him in real life 'cos he's got a big beard.'

'No, okay.'

'And you shouldn't have to kiss people if you don't want to,' Jack went on seriously. 'We did it in school. It's all about sent.'

'Consent,' corrected Kate, automatically. 'No, okay, no kisses for Father Christmas, that's fine.' She put her arm around his little, bony shoulder and gave him a squeeze. 'Well done sweetie. Put it in the envelope. We'll check the address we need after dinner, shall we? Come and wash your hands now. It's macaroni cheese. You like that, don't you?'

'Is that going to work?' said Jack, doubtfully, once they had returned to it, after tea.

Google had informed them, with considerable authority, that the correct address was 'Father Christmas, Lapland', which didn't seem enough.

'It is a bit odd that there's no postcode,' agreed Kate. 'But I'm sure it'll be fine. There. Put the stamp on for me. It's first class, so that's good.'

'Will he reply?' asked Jack, later, as he got ready for bed.

Kate thought hard. 'I think he will, eventually, but we have to let him sort things out his way,' she said, diplomatically. 'He'll do what's right for us. Sometimes that's not exactly the same as doing the thing we've asked him to do.'

'Like God,' said Jack, putting his toothbrush back in the mug thoughtfully.

'I suppose so.'

'I don't like God taking Daddy away,' said Jack. 'I don't know what he was thinking. That was a rubbish thing to do.'

Kate hugged him. 'I know, darling. We just have to keep going. It's nearly Christmas! That's a good thing, right there, isn't it?'

'And we're stirring the Christmas pudding tomorrow,' said Jack, remembering the slip of paper in the advent calendar. 'I can make a wish. I know what I'm going to wish for already. It might seem a waste to do the same thing,' he paused, 'but I think it'll be good. We don't want God to think we're asking for too many different things . . .'

'Very sensible,' said Kate, kissing the top of his head. He smelt like 'boy', a mix of warmth, grubbiness and shampoo. 'It's cold tonight, darling,' she said. 'Want to sleep in with me?'

'It's all right, Mummy,' said Jack. 'I'll be fine.'

She felt quietly bereft. Had the day already come that she had spent her last fractured night next to this squirming, kicking child, all limbs and energy. Had she woken beside him for the final time and not even realised? As a family they would all pile into the bed to watch cartoons on a Saturday morning before Tom went for a run. With Jack waking them at five in the morning most days, it allowed the two of them to grab a sneaky doze, knowing he was safely stationed between them. Then she did it a lot when Tom was killed. When Jack was having night terrors – when she was too – they both gained comfort from waking next to another living, breathing human being. She would put him in her bed whenever he was ill, too, so she could check on him more easily, feeling his forehead, dosing him with Calpol and giving him sips of water throughout the night, gazing at him anxiously for early signs of the sickness parents dread – meningitis, sepsis. She felt constantly as if she was warding off terrible disasters, protecting his frail body with her own. Because appalling things did happen. She knew that. There was no innate sense of fundamental safety and rightness in life anymore – not for her. For Jack, her sole intention in life was to create safety; and yet here she was, bringing him up in a dodgy neighbourhood inside a dingy flat with no garden for a little boy to run around, no space for a Christmas tree, a school that didn't understand him and didn't want him, no male role model . . .

She sighed sadly and pulled Jack's door just ajar, so he could see the light in the corridor if he woke. She had things to do. If Christmas pudding stirring was going to happen she needed to find money for the ingredients. With luck, her coat pockets and the space behind the sofa cushions would cough up a quid or two.

10th December

The Apple Café was only about a quarter of a mile from the flat. She and Jack sometimes went there on a Saturday morning, walking through streets made ugly with graffitied swearwords, boarded-up buildings and betting shops, although optimistic little artisan food and coffee shops were beginning to pop up here and there. The two of them usually took the route through the back streets, swapping the high street for lines of Victorian terraces. Occasionally there would be a stained old mattress dumped on the pavement but here the decay was fighting with signs of defiant gentrification – smart grey shutters on windows and pairs of bay trees either side of front doors. For all that, it was a far cry from the bright, shiny streets of Portman Brothers with its wide pavements, its huge shop windows and its enticing, unaffordable lifestyle, which came so naturally to many and seemed so completely unreachable for Kate.

At least Mr Wilkins had agreed she could go into work late, so she was visiting the Apple Café on company time. Pat had agreed to meet her there and, when she arrived, the older woman was already inside. Kate could see her, beaming, as she chatted with the girl behind the counter. She was clearly admiring the wide variety of cakes set out on the counter under a series of glass domes.

Tucked in between a charity shop and a newsagent, the café had a tiny outside space where the staff would place two pairs of chairs and tables for patrons to sit outside. There was no furniture there today. Who would want to take their coffee outside with its lead-grey skies and intermittent frozen rain?

Kate shivered as she opened the shop door and stepped into the brightly lit café. The little room was crammed with aluminium furniture, made cosier that day with wipeable green gingham cloths, each table adorned with a small zinc pail and a pot of thyme.

'Kate!' said Pat. 'Will you look at these incredible meringues? Beth here tells me she made them herself.'

The girl behind the counter bobbed her head and smiled shyly.

'I can't believe the talent,' Pat went on. 'I tell you I wish I could produce something like that.'

'You have to heat the sugar,' the girl said, quietly. Her voice was low and charmingly gruff. 'That's what Brian showed me. He taught me that.'

'Well,' said Pat, 'I want to meet this Brian. He's obviously a genius.'

'No sooner said,' came a voice from the doorway behind the counter. A tall, well-upholstered man with a shaved head and well-trimmed grey beard was ducking slightly to come through the doorway.

'I am Brian,' he said, holding out a meaty hand to Pat, and then to Kate. 'And Beth's right. You have to heat the sugar.'

'I never knew,' said Pat, clearly impressed.

'Beth knows her stuff,' said Brian, gesturing for Kate and Pat to sit down at one of the larger tables. 'Tea for you ladies?'

'I'd kill for coffee,' said Kate. It was nearly ten o'clock and she hadn't had time for her usual caffeine fix that morning.

Getting a worn-out and grumpy Jack off to school had been even harder than usual that day.

'Latte? Cappuccino? Flat white?' offered Brian, laughing at Pat's amazed response.

'Oh yeah . . . we take our coffee pretty seriously here at the Apple . . . we got a grant for that giant of a coffee machine and three of our staff have just come back from a barista course. Hey, Will!' he suddenly shouted, making the women jump.

'Sorry . . . these ladies would like you to stand by for a coffee order, mate,' he said to a young man who emerged shyly from the dark room at the back. He was wearing a striped blue and white apron and smiled at them both before ducking his head. He had a charming smile, made all the more endearing by his unusual appearance. He was thickset with stubbly red hair, a wide face and a clumsy manner. Kate could just imagine him being crucified at school.

'S-s-s-standing by,' he said, twisting Kate's heartstrings further as she realised the young man had a learning disability and a stammer too.

'Latte would be amazing,' she told him. 'You're a lifesaver.' He looked thrilled.

'Same here too please, my lovely,' added Pat, who – Kate knew – usually drank tea, but clearly wanted to make it easier for him.

'So,' said Brian, addressing Kate, 'I recognise you as one of our few genuine public customers.'

'I don't come in much,' admitted Kate, 'but me and Jack – that's my son – we come in sometimes at the weekends, when . . .' She nearly said *when we can afford to*, but didn't want to indicate to Brian the café's prices were too high for her. Instead she settled for a half truth. 'We come in when we're in the area. We go to the park sometimes.'

'Yes, at least we've got the park nearby,' Brian conceded, 'but we're not exactly in a "destination" location, we know that all too well. Not that we're not lucky to have a venue,' he added quickly. 'How much do you know about the Apple Café?'

Both women shook their heads.

'Okay, so, we're a charity obviously. There was a founding benefactor from as long ago as anyone can remember; a parent, I believe, with a child who had Down's syndrome . . . they wanted their child to have somewhere to go in the daytime – the type of experience someone just going to an ordinary job might have.'

'Of course,' said Pat. 'People want to work. It's a normal thing.'

'Exactly,' said Brian, beaming. 'You get it. Structure to life, purpose, pride, income . . . Unfortunately, work opportunities for adults with learning disabilities are few and far between. Employers don't want to know or aren't supportive enough, so we've had to create the opportunities ourselves. This used to be just a social club. When I first started working here it was like a day care centre to get people like Beth and Will out of the house. Respite care, you could even call it. Pretty boring stuff. A pool table, a telly, some craft activities that no-one was really into. I was brought in because I knew about the cooking and baking side, but now I'm the manager, basically.'

'Is that what you are?' said Kate, surprised. 'I wouldn't have thought . . .'

'No, well, I wasn't massively employable at one point,' admitted Brian. 'I had mental health problems and bailed out of my job. I was a head patissier in a top five-star hotel chain,' he said with obvious pride. 'It nearly killed me. I came here because I needed to do something with less pressure and – to be honest – I can't imagine a more rewarding workplace. I don't want to work anywhere else now.'

'That's amazing,' said Kate. 'No wonder the cakes here are so good.'

'It's the staff,' insisted Brian. 'I'm not nearly as hands-on as you might think. Nowadays I'm training, mainly. We do real qualifications too. Everyone starts with their Food Hygiene exam. Some take longer than others . . . everyone gets there in the end. That's a proper, externally recognised qualification, by the way. Then we get onto learning about recipes and stuff. Everyone's got their own interest. Will was really keen on learning about the drinks and he totally knows his way around that coffee machine now.'

Kate and Pat looked over as Will came proudly and slowly towards them, a latte in each hand, his tongue poking out of the corner of his mouth in concentration.

'I'm really impressed,' Kate told him, as he put them down, slopping them onto the table only slightly. She grabbed a napkin and whisked away the spill almost before it happened. 'I'd be terrified of that thing,' she said, waving at the countertop-sized giant of polished chrome.

'We c-c-c-call it the dragon,' he told her, 'because steam comes out of its mouth.'

'Good name.' She took a sip of her coffee. 'Perfect,' she pronounced.

'So, the other thing I do, is trying to keep us financially afloat,' said Brian, leading them neatly around to the reason for their visit, 'and that's a real brain ache, I can tell you.'

'Yes, so – absolutely,' said Kate. 'We at Portman Brothers are aiming for a grand over the next couple of weeks – which isn't a fortune, I appreciate.' Kate looked around. It was a humble little place, but she was pretty certain the overheads were considerable, even so.

'It isn't a fortune,' agreed Brian, bluntly, and then he laughed. 'Sorry. Tact isn't my greatest skill, as the trustees frequently tell me. Apparently, I should be fawning over you, telling you what a huge benefit a thousand pounds will be and how extremely grateful we all truly are for your massive generosity.' He tried out a sickly, grateful, sycophantic smile, which looked entertainingly grotesque on his handsome-ugly face with his stubble and his boxer's nose.

The women laughed, and he joined in. 'Seriously though,' he went on, 'a grand is not to be sneezed at, and there is something else we need from you, which really will make a difference.'

'Go on,' said Pat.

'Hardly anyone knows we're here. Mainly our customers are limited to the family and friends of our staff. Those who do know we exist tend, present company excepted,' he nodded at Kate, 'to assume we don't serve members of the general public.'

Kate and Pat nodded.

'And then,' he went on, lowering his voice and glancing at Will and Beth, who were assiduously wiping down the counter and tables, 'the other issue we face is that an awful lot of people don't quite know how to behave when they meet someone with a learning disability.'

Pat started to look affronted on Will and Beth's behalf, but Brian continued, 'Listen, we don't think badly of people for ignorance. Not so long ago, people with learning disabilities spent their lives in residential homes. That was the norm. The shocking and damaging effect of that is that people just didn't see people with Down's syndrome – and people like Will who has Fetal Alcohol Syndrome – walking down the street, working, serving them in shops and so on . . . it's natural. In the majority of folks, the antipathy isn't rejection, it's fear . . .'

'How could someone fear a person like Will,' said Kate in a low voice, matching Brian's reduction in volume, but Brian would brook no criticism of Joe Public.

'I've always seen it as more of a worry about saying or doing the wrong thing,' he said, charitably. 'Will's a lovely bloke, but it's not always easy to understand what he's saying, and he looks different in a way that people don't even recognise, which makes it harder in some ways. At least people generally understand that Beth has Down's. They then tend to make unhelpful assumptions about her, but at least they understand – or think they understand – what her issues might be . . .'

'I agree with you Brian, I'm not sure a thousand pounds is going to make a lot of difference,' said Kate, deflated at the scale of the task.

'So, what I want from you is more.'

'They won't be up for more than a grand,' said Kate, apologetically. 'And it's up to us to raise that. It's not even a donation . . .'

'I don't mean money. What you've got is presence. A bloody great big frontage at Cabot Circus. Tens of thousands of people through your door, especially at Christmas. What we want is a piece of that.'

'O-kay,' said Pat. 'What have you got in mind?'

Kate looked at her older friend. She had a fierce laser-focus and determination that Kate had never seen before.

Brian pushed up his sleeves and leaned towards Pat in recognition of her commitment.

'Right,' he said. 'I don't completely know . . . but I want Portman Brothers to help us reach out; to show what we're made of. I tell you what – the world doesn't know what it's missing! Never mind Ruth's meringues – they're impressive – but Craig's salted caramel brownies are epic, once tasted never forgotten, and baking and Christmas were made for each other. We're getting sixty Christmas puddings out of the door in the next fortnight. That takes some doing . . .'

Kate slapped her forehead and made a noise which – whilst containing no actual words – expressed real anguish.

Brian and Pat looked at her with concern.

'I need Christmas pudding,' she said, by way of embarrassed explanation for the cry.

'Don't worry,' said Brian, gently, 'if that's all it takes to turn your world the right way up again we can sort you out, no problem.'

'It's worse than that,' explained Kate. 'I'm sure your Christmas puddings are amazing, but I've got to produce Christmas pudding mixture for my little boy to stir, tonight. I'd just forgotten. It's when you said . . . I'm glad you reminded me. I've just got to . . .' Kate's face twisted in worry, 'got to buy the ingredients,' she looked at Pat, blushing. The awful truth was, she was so broke, she was probably going to have to just full-on come out and ask her lovely friend for some cash, which was going to be both humiliating for her and unfair on Pat, who wasn't getting paid any more at Portman Brothers than she was, probably.

'As it happens, we've got six kilos of Christmas pudding batter sitting in the mixer out the back. I'm just waiting for staff to come and put it into the basins. I can bung a bit into a tub for you to take away, no problem at all.'

'Really?' said Kate, her shoulders lowering slightly at the thought of one less battle to fight that day. 'I'm a bit surprised . . . to be honest I was expecting you to tell me you made them all months ago. I've never made one before. I had this idea they have to mature for months.'

'They do,' said Brian and Pat in unison before meeting each other's eye and laughing. Pat gestured to Brian. 'You tell her, you're the expert.'

He demurred with a nod of his head, but turned to Kate. 'You're not wrong,' he said. 'These are next year's puddings. We give them twelve to fourteen months ideally.'

'Ah,' said Kate, her ideas of nailing a problem adjusting slightly and disappointingly. 'So, I can't get away with having Jack stir a bit of your mixture and then cook it up for Christmas Day then.'

'Not really,' he laughed. 'Tell you what, boil it and stash it away, and I'll slip you one of our mature ones too. That way you can pretend . . . plus next year will be sorted too.'

'That's one problem solved,' said Pat. 'And I've just had the most fantastic idea . . . how about we have a bake-off?'

'Go on,' said Brian, beaming encouragingly.

'Well, I don't know . . .' said Pat, waving her hands, 'but some sort of competition – maybe Portman Brothers staff versus Apple Café staff . . .'

'We'll win,' interjected Brian.

'Good! That'll banish some misconceptions, and the local media will love it.'

'True. And the board directors will love it too,' interrupted Kate. 'They can do the judging . . . give the prizes . . .'

'Our Mr Wilkins'll be thrilled with that,' said Pat, knowingly. 'If it were a prize for the biggest ego . . .'

'But how is this going to earn money?' said Kate. 'I know you said the dosh wasn't important but – if nothing else – I'll get it in the neck if we don't raise at least a thousand.'

'Really? Nice people you work for,' he observed, his brow lowering momentarily. 'Anyhow, I wasn't suggesting I didn't want your money, but raising dosh isn't a problem with this idea. If the competitors don't mind – and I don't see why they should – we can sell the cakes they make. It can be seasonal, the best mince pie, best Yule log, et cetera . . .'

'That could definitely work,' said Kate. 'We could sell the cakes out of the Cabot Circus store where we've got the footfall and, at the same time, promote the location of the café to encourage people to visit in the new year. The staff here could do the selling alongside Portman Brothers' staff.'

'Our lot will love getting out and about. This idea has got legs, girls, but we don't have much time. It'll be Christmas in a couple of weeks. Your top bods and mine will be wanting to do some sort of photocall before Christmas to announce how successful it's been. That's not long away . . .'

'Doesn't take long to rustle up a batch of mince pies,' said Pat, with a competitive glint in her eye. 'That Beth's more than a worthy competitor. I'll be pulling out all the stops, and she needn't think I won't,' she muttered.

'That's the spirit,' said Brian with frank admiration. 'Now, we'd better get down to some planning . . .'

Brian was as good as his word. Kate and Pat left buzzing with caffeine and with tummies definitely more expanded than before, after being persuaded to try not only the mince pies, but the stollen too, and a piece each of the Apple Café's special spiced apple Christmas cake, which they both pronounced delicious. He had insisted that Kate take away a tub of Christmas pudding mixture to stir with Jack, as well as a near-black canonball-shaped Christmas pudding for them to eat on Christmas Day.

'What a kind and lovely man,' declared Pat, as they made their way to the bus stop and on to work.

Kate was amused to see her friend was glowing and quite pink in the face. 'You've got the hots for our Brian,' she teased.

Pat flushed even deeper. 'He and I are both far too old for all that nonsense,' she said, stoutly.

'Mmm,' said Kate. 'I don't buy that, Pat Walker. You're not too old for anything. Not even romance. Actually, especially not romance. Why the heck not?'

'We've never made our own Christmas pudding before have we, Mummy?' said Jack, poking a wooden spoon at the Christmas pudding mix Brian had given them. 'Do I like it?'

'You'll like this,' said Kate. 'Actually, I think you do like it, but I don't think we've had it for a couple of years,' she admitted guiltily. 'Do you remember Christmas at Nana's house? You ate it then. It was when . . .' She was going to say, *when Tom was still alive.*

'I don't remember,' said Jack. 'It must have been when I was really little.'

'You were, my darling. But we're going to eat Christmas pudding this year. You and me. We're going to cook it ourselves, how about that?'

'I hope it's nice,' said Jack. 'It doesn't look very nice at the moment.'

She had to agree. It was beige, gloopy and filled with unidentifiable lumps. 'It smells amazing though,' she said, sticking her nose into the bowl and sniffing hard, then deliberately putting her face right in.

'You've got it on your nose,' shrieked Jack.

'No I haven't,' said Kate, 'whatever do you mean?' She looked around wildly, the glob of mixture threatening to plop onto the floor. 'How rude of you . . . my nose is absolutely fine . . .'

Jack was in fits of laughter and Kate couldn't remember the last time they had just messed around like this. Playing the fool had been Tom's job. Kate was the sensible one, treating them both as kids more often than not, and telling Tom off when things got too silly. Her own silly streak had got lost over the years, buried deep under the weight of responsibility and grief.

Eventually, with her nose wiped clean, they got down to the serious business of stirring the pudding.

'I used to do this with my mummy,' Kate said, leading the way. 'It has to be anticlockwise, like this, see . . .? And then you make a wish.'

'I know what anticlockwise means,' said Jack. 'It means like a clock hand goes but the other way.'

'Clever you! Now make a wish . . .'

'I wish my Daddy wasn't dead.'

She put her arms around his bony little shoulders. 'I wish that too, darling,' she murmured in his ear. 'But let's make a wish together for something nice to happen in the next year because the past can't change, can it?'

Jack stiffened. 'Sorry, Mummy.'

'Never be sorry, darling. Daddy wouldn't want that.'

'But I'm sorry 'cos I don't want to make you sad.'

'You can't. You make me really, really happy. You're my best thing in the whole world.'

'You're my best thing in the whole world too,' said Jack, leaning back into Kate's arms.

'I'm going to wish for a new daddy to come one day and it has to be someone we both like,' he declared, giving the pudding a decisive anticlockwise stir. 'There. Done it.'

'You are too amazing for words,' said Kate, giving him a tight squeeze. 'I love you, monkey boy.'

It was six o'clock in the evening, but Daniel was working late – something he was able to do now he no longer had Zoe to rush back to.

Working late was not only 'possible' now, it was also frequently necessary. Work was taking longer than it should. He spent far too much time staring out of the window, over Broad Street, idly watching the crowds below, thinking about Zoe, about his parents, and longing for life when it was simpler, when he was at home with his family, in their rambling old house in Clifton. It had been a typical townhouse, with endless stairs to endless floors but with a gem of a garden, larger than any allowed in new houses, stretching back and back behind the house, an oasis of green in the middle of the city. His and Zoe's bedrooms used to be in the loft space but – as Zoe became more ill – she was moved to the back room on the floor where the family spent the most time, giving her fewer stairs to climb, sparing her failing energy and keeping her at the heart of family life . . .

Despite all the difficulty, life had been fun. His grief at its ending was still a physical ache in his chest. When the longing for the past became too great, he steered his daydreams to other matters. Increasingly, he filled his thoughts with the Christmas Tree Girl, remembering word for word their encounters and wondering if her days were now a tiny bit less arduous for being a little less cold.

But the thoughts preoccupying him that evening were work-related. His meeting with Noel had taken him aback. The gentle little man had clearly placed such faith in him, Daniel, to do this thing right; to find a tenant for the shop who could take on this mantle, this responsibility.

'Literally no rent,' Paul had exclaimed disbelievingly, when he filled him in.

'I didn't say "no rent". I think he just meant that there was a greater need for the right person than for rental income, although he doesn't look affluent at all. I am sure he could do with the money.'

'How are you going to find the right person, though?'

'That's another question. I think I'll know them when I see them. I just hope Noel agrees. He's an odd man. I like him.'

'You won't lack candidates. It's a prime spot. That Christmas Steps area is becoming very sought after. I can see it going to a retailer flogging some pretty high-end stuff – a designer boutique? The London designers are starting to want representation in Bristol. Their own store. People like Versace, maybe? Emporio Armani?'

'He definitely won't go for that,' said Daniel, with certainty. 'Anyway, it's too small.'

'Right, well, how are you going to do it? Some kind of auditiony search-for-a-star thing? Bush tucker trials? Sob stories about people's lifelong ambitions and poorly grannies?'

'Nope.'

'What then?'

'Dunno,' admitted Daniel.

And then he had an idea.

11th *December*

'The other pressing issue,' said Pat, seeing Kate frantically scribbling plans for the bake-off in her notebook at break, 'is what we are going to do about Jack.'

'It's the meeting at the school today,' said Kate, looking stricken. She had been trying to forget. 'They're assessing him this morning, all the execution squad – sorry, I mean expert educationalists – and then I'm going in to be patronised and instructed on what's going to happen next this afternoon.'

'You mustn't worry,' said Pat, her head on one side. 'I know you will . . . but the good news is I spoke to my sister, and she wants you to go and meet her on Friday. You knock off at two o'clock, don't you?'

Kate nodded.

'Thought so. She said to be there at three and she'll give you a tour and have a chat.'

'I'll have to get Helen to look after Jack. She doesn't usually do Fridays.'

'Take him.'

'I don't want him to see . . . not yet. I don't want him to want something he probably can't have; and he's not keen to change. If I need to persuade him then I need to do it my own way.'

'See what happens,' said Pat.

'You're so kind,' said Kate, hurriedly and belatedly. 'I can't thank you enough. And your sister.' She took a gulp of her now cold coffee. It was nearly time to go back outside. She shivered at the thought. 'You've not mentioned her before.'

'No. Well . . .' Pat hesitated. 'We haven't always got on. No real reason. She's very bossy, as you'll see. She's older. She took herself off to university – first in my family to go. She always wanted to be a teacher and now she is one,' said Pat, 'so that's good.'

Kate heard a hint of resentment in the last phrase, which was a shock – Pat was always so positive about everyone.

'Does she have a partner and children?'

'Nope. A career was all she wanted. I think she's probably gay,' Pat confided, 'and in my generation it isn't so well accepted.'

'In your generation . . .' Kate teased. 'You're not a hundred years old, and nor is your sister, I imagine.'

'It wasn't long ago! You youngsters forget too easily . . . She could have found a partner, of course she could, but it would have been hard for her in ways it's difficult for people your age to imagine, and she didn't. More than anything, it was that she was too busy doing all these amazing things . . . building up schools. She's moved around a lot as one of those super-heads, you know, turning around failing schools. Greystone Manor is her first private school and it's not the norm. As you'll see.'

'And you've never been married?' Kate was ashamed of herself for never having asked the question. She had never got the impression from Pat that there was a partner, or even that there had been, but she had to admit, she had never properly enquired.

'Never married. Never engaged. Can't say I've never been kissed but I can say I've never been swept off my feet. If anyone tried it now, they'd be in danger of doing their back in,' joked Pat, complacently. 'It's fine,' she added, seeing

Kate's look of uncertainty. 'Our mother wasn't impressed with us for not producing grandchildren, but me and Ursula are a pair of old spinsters for one reason or another, and that's just how it is. The difference is, Ursula built an impressive career and I've stuck by my mum because one of us was always going to.'

'It's never too late though. Brian could sweep you off your feet,' teased Kate. 'He looks pretty burly.'

'Now, now,' admonished Pat, but she was smiling. 'I'll be doing you no more favours if you start stirring my perfectly nice life up for me, thank you very much.'

'It's an interesting idea,' said Brian, as Daniel wriggled the key in the lock of the Olde Sweet Shoppe, 'and it's definitely nice to see you after all this time,' he added as Daniel finally succeeded in opening the door and waving him inside. 'We've all been wondering where you'd got to.'

'I know, I'm sorry,' said Daniel, placing his hand on Brian's meaty arm. 'I've kept meaning to come.'

'It must be hard.'

'Yeah, memories,' Daniel agreed. 'Zoe loved spending time at the Apple. I just can't quite imagine – face – being with you guys and her not being there . . .'

'Beth misses her.'

'Yeah. Well, you knew they've been friends since they were tiny, didn't you? Did they ever tell you? They were at this special needs playgroup together when they were two years old. Beth's mum and our mum became friends, so they spent a lot of time together, growing up . . .'

'It's hard for a young woman Beth's age to lose a friend like that.'

'Hard for everyone,' Daniel agreed. 'Will you say hi to her for me?'

'Come and say hi yourself,' Brian told him, not letting him off the hook. It would do Daniel good to come to the café.

The two men toured the little shop. It didn't take long. Daniel briefly explained the need to find a tenant his client Noel could approve of, and his reason for thinking of the Apple Café.

Brian heard him out, nodding thoughtfully as he outlined the situation with the high rates but massive flexibility over rent, if the 'right' tenant could be found.

'Yeah, the rates thing isn't going to be an issue with charities,' said Brian. 'As you know, we get a major discount on business rates.'

'You do, of course,' said Daniel.

'It's just too small, though,' said Brian, regretfully. 'It's great of you to think of us. I love that you did . . . but I can't teach our staff in that tiny space out the back and – realistically – this shop unit's too small to be a financially viable café. There's not enough room to fit in the punters. We couldn't achieve the turnover. Although I could see it as a sandwich takeaway place, maybe . . . Coffees to take away, soup, possibly even a lunchtime sandwich delivery service . . .' he mused. 'But it's not for us,' he added briskly. 'Plus, the café two doors up wouldn't thank us for it. It would be a fight to the death between the two.'

'Of course,' said Daniel, hitting his forehead. 'I wasn't thinking. My client did say it was important to think about the balance of local businesses, all part of one organism, et cetera. I was just so hung up on my idea about giving the Apple Cafe a more central venue.'

'You're not wrong, my friend, we do badly need a location with a bit more visibility,' admitted Brian. 'Which reminds me, I was having just such a conversation yesterday with two lovely ladies from Portman Brothers . . . Now this might be our big break. Let me tell you all about it, because we might need to get you involved.'

'I can't imagine any worthwhile project where you might urgently need the skills of a chartered surveyor.'

'No, nor can I,' agreed Brian, 'but if I think hard enough I am sure I can come up with *something* useful you can do . . .'

It was odd walking to the school gate without crowds of other mums around. It was still an hour until home time. An hour was a long time to be sitting listening to smug-faced professionals with letters after their names, telling her things she didn't want to hear about her boy. Even the thought of it brought on a wave of outrage. It flooded through her as she pushed open the door into the school lobby, so she arrived at the reception desk, infuriatingly, with a brick-red face and hot tears suddenly flooding her eyes. She dabbed them away surreptitiously.

'I'm expected,' she said to the cod-faced woman – Kate couldn't remember her name – who sat in the little cubicle with the hatch. This piece of architecture gave the impression that parents and other adults were dangerous creatures who must be cordoned off from school life behind a glass screen, allowed into the inner sanctum itself only once they had completed a series of challenges, such as the signing-in form.

Kate knew the drill. She took the clipboard with the signing-in register – tied to the counter for fear it might be stolen by a ruthless clipboard thief – and angled it expertly so it was within reach of the solitary biro. Inexplicably, the biro was attached, via an unattractive wodge of Sellotape, to a piece of string that was slightly too short.

The old fish-faced woman appeared satisfied, albeit reluctantly – even though Kate had signed herself as 'Wonder Woman' in a moment of childish irritation. The woman knew exactly who she was. There was no need. She gave Kate a sideways look and pressed the buzzer to open the door.

The reaction from the headteacher was slightly more cordial.

'Mrs Thompson,' she said. 'Thank you so much for taking the trouble to come in. Here we all are.'

The seat intended for her was obvious. A small, plastic chair, lower than the others, facing a rank of four women, each with notebooks, pens, and professional smiles.

'Allow me,' said Jack's teacher, Mrs Chandler, who looked like Theresa May and flushed with delight when people pointed it out. She had taken to wearing two-piece suits in bright colours with draped bits on them to encourage further positive comparisons. Kate quite liked her. She also liked the head despite it all, because when she and Jack arrived – grey and bedraggled from the traumatic few months following Tom's death and knowing nothing and nobody in the area – Mrs Marshall had defied the local education authority to put Jack into the school even though there wasn't a place. And now she wanted him out.

'Mrs Thompson,' she said, smiling warmly, once she had peremptorily introduced the team, announcing names Kate tried hard to remember, but they were mainly a blur of noise. They sat in a crescent around her low chair like hyenas crowding around their prey. 'I want to say how much we have all enjoyed working with Jack today, and how cooperative he has been too. You should be proud of him.'

'I am,' said Kate, raising her chin and trying hard to contain the slight wobble Mrs Marshall's kind words elicited. 'I am very proud of Jack.'

'And we all want the best for him, of course,' Mrs Chandler went on.

'Of course.'

'So, I thought it would be helpful to ask you your own impressions of Jack and his learning over the last two years, also perhaps his interactions with his peers and the teaching staff.'

'He's had his moments,' admitted Kate, meeting Mrs Chandler's eye as they both silently recalled a couple of the more exciting ones. There was the occasion where he climbed onto the roof of the canteen and sat, feet dangling over the edge, refusing to come down because he could see a hot-air balloon in the distance and wanted to see where it landed. Kate had pointed out he would never have been able to do it if the school caretaker hadn't left the ladder there after clearing out the gutters, but it was a memorable occasion for the wrong reasons . . . And then there was the time when – as Kate frequently reminded people – Jack had *not* thrown a chair at a teacher. He absolutely hadn't. Although he had threatened to do it – she didn't deny that – it was because he was furious that the teacher had wrongly accused him of another child's crime in dropping a cheese sandwich into the class fish tank. It was difficult to determine whether his huge rage was triggered more by the injustice of the false accusation or the distress that anyone would think him capable of harming the fish, of whom he had grown inordinately fond.

'So . . .' Kate ventured, 'yeah . . . he's had his moments . . .'

The assembled company bowed their heads briefly in acknowledgement.

'And then there is Jack's learning,' said Mrs Marshall, briskly. 'What is your impression of that Mrs Thompson?'

'I–' Kate was flummoxed, she was not the one to judge, surely. 'He seems to make *some* progress. It's tough, and I don't have other children to compare with, so . . . He's not that keen on reading and writing. We do stuff at home . . .'

Mrs Chandler intervened. 'We have been carrying out some observations today, Mrs Thompson, and – as I am sure you have gathered yourself – we all think Jack is a lovely boy and bright in many ways. He does seem to lack' – she paused momentarily – 'to lack "application", shall I call it?' She looked for ratification to the stern woman who had been introduced as an educational psychologist. 'And so it has been exceedingly helpful to have the input of our experts today, to try to understand more about Jack's special needs.'

'Special needs?' echoed Kate, blankly. 'Jack has "special needs"?'

'That's right,' said the woman. Kate now remembered she had been introduced as Maura, or it could have been Flora . . . although she looked pretty fierce, not much like a Flora. Kate belatedly realised she was watching the woman's violently red-lipsticked mouth but not processing any of the words that were coming out of it. Instead the words 'special needs' were echoing in her head like a football chant. It was hypnotic. With effort, she tuned in to what the woman was saying.

'. . . So Jack's scores were coming out at the very top end for verbal intelligence but much lower in other areas such as semantics and written comprehension . . . His scores for concentration and focus were . . .' she rifled through her paperwork, 'ah yes, well, they were first centile.'

'First centile?'

'Concerning,' said Maura, baldly. 'It essentially means that, if there were one hundred children of Jack's age in the room, taking the test with him then, on average, his score would be – well – the lowest.'

'Crikey,' muttered Kate.

'But then there are these much higher scores,' Maura waved her hand at the page. 'I'll send you and everyone involved a proper, written report, but Jack has got what we colloquially refer to as a spiky learning profile. It means his low scores in some areas are down to specific difficulty rather than to an overall low attainment potential.'

'In other words, he's not thick.'

'That's not an expression we use.'

Kate's heart sank further. 'He can't really read yet. Not yet,' she said through frozen lips. 'He will read though. Won't he?'

'Yes, Mrs Thompson,' intervened the headteacher again. 'Jack will certainly read. And he will write. He should do well. But is it not useful to pick up on these issues now and ensure he gets the help he needs?' She put her head on one side, like a budgie.

Kate's stomach roiled. She got a whiff of her own nervous sweat. She must stink. She wanted to go back to the flat and curl up in a ball.

'Mrs Thompson,' Mrs Marshall said, in a low, calm voice, the sort of tone you might take with a dangerous lunatic who was threatening to do something horrendous, 'when Jack first joined the school he was a very disturbed and distressed little boy . . .'

'I know,' sobbed Kate. Tears sprang hotly and she pressed her fingers to her eyes to push them back in. 'He lost his father. It was awful. I know –' She looked unseeing at the display board behind the women's heads. 'I know he was angry, wild, unpredictable . . . and naughty,' she admitted, meeting Mrs Marshall's eye again. 'He was naughty, but he's better than that now, isn't he?'

'He is, he is,' she said, making a downward patting movement with her hands that was clearly meant to soothe but just looked like she was trying to get someone to turn down the volume. 'We knew we needed to let Jack find his feet, and of course we know how difficult it has been for you both, what with the terrible loss you both faced, but – whilst we are rightly reluctant to label children when they first join the school in Reception, it is really important that we pick up on the children who are struggling for one reason or another by the time they get to Year Two. And Jack is in Year Two now,' she held out her hands in justification, 'so . . .'

Kate jumped in. 'So . . . what? It was wrong to label him when he came here but now it's right?'

'In the real world,' counselled Mrs Marshall, 'whilst we absolutely see each child as an individual, a "label" – as you call it – can be a means to an end, providing resources, attention, access to funding . . .'

'Actually, you said "label" first,' said Kate, sulkily, before realising how childish she sounded. 'Okay, fine,' she went on. 'You want Jack to leave the school. You want him to get help. I get that. Where, exactly do you want him to go? Where is this amazing additional resource that he needs? It had better be close by, because I've got a flat I can just about afford and it's only down the road. If he's going to have to go miles away then that's going to be a problem because I have to go to work too, you know . . .'

'As it happens, there is an excellent facility just ten minutes from here,' beamed Mrs Marshall. 'One of just two PRUs for the entire LEA is just around the corner.' She seemed thrilled with herself for announcing this, which made Kate's spirits rise a millimetre.

'LEAs? PRUs?'

'Local Education Authority,' clarified Mrs Marshall. 'And PRU is,' she cleared her throat and looked out of the window, 'PRU stands for Pupil Referral Unit.'

'What?' snapped Kate. 'A Pupil Referral Unit? Isn't that where expelled children get sent?'

'Actually,' piped up the long-faced woman in the corner who had not yet spoken, 'children don't automatically get sent to the PRU if they get expelled. Usually it's when children have been expelled from at least three other schools,' she explained earnestly.

The other women turned, as one, and glared at her.

'Oh, that makes it much better,' said Kate sarcastically. 'Why does he have to go there? You said yourself he's not a bad boy. You're not even expelling him. Are you?' Mrs Marshall looked down at her hands.

'Are you?' Kate demanded.

'Mrs Thompson,' said the educational psychologist woman with heavy patience, 'we absolutely do not see Jack as being a – well, a *very* – disruptive child; not the usual PRU child in many ways. However, we simply think it is worth considering because our PRUs are extremely well resourced. Naturally enough many of the children – almost invariably boys at primary-school level, by the way – also require the kind of expert special guidance and intervention that we believe Jack would benefit from enormously. If the PRU is the place to get it, then . . .' She too held her hands out in a shrug.

'But where do other children like Jack go? The ones who need extra help but who aren't properly naughty? Why does he have to be surrounded by children who have real behaviour problems? That won't be good for him, surely?'

The other women stayed silent. No one would meet her eye.

'What about Greystone Manor?' she said.

At this the women smiled and shook their heads. 'Well, of course Greystone Manor would be lovely,' said the long-faced woman with a world-weary smile. 'If budgets were endless all our children would go to schools like Greystones. However, in the real world . . .' she trailed off.

'I heard the LAE – I mean the LEA – did sometimes fund children in the public sector to go to Greystones, if they needed the kind of help it offers.'

Longface blushed. 'You may well have heard that, but I can assure you, securing the funding is a very different matter. I'm not saying it never happens' – her face communicated that it pretty much never did happen – 'but if that's your plan, I wish you luck. You'll need it.'

'Fine,' said Kate, springing to her feet. 'Because Greystone Manor is where Jack is going to be going. Thank you so much for your time, your advice and your encouragement,' she said, sweeping her gaze from one end of the line of women to the other, nearly spitting out the final few words, as she gathered up her jacket and bag, rattling the door handle slightly in her keenness to get out and trying forcibly to resist the impulse to slam the door. She succeeded and allowed herself a moment of pride at her restraint. To be fair, the women were doing their best for Jack, but it was hard hearing that others didn't think of your son in the same glowing light that you did. It was very hard. She wished she had Tom to share her delight in him and tell her he was perfect, despite what anyone said.

The other parents turned to watch with interest as Kate flew out of the building as if propelled by some invisible force. She gathered herself, pulling her jacket around her and smoothing her hair, before walking slowly to join the crowd at the school gate. A couple of the mothers snickered and turned away. Kate looked for Seema but then remembered she didn't pick up on a Thursday. She had no allies.

She was not left alone for long. There was a parting of the waves in the crowd which quickly manifested itself as

Anastasia arriving. She was impeccably poised as usual, her hair and make-up immaculate as if she had done nothing all day since dropping her son off that morning other than polish herself to perfection. She had a tendency to announce that Thursday was her "me day" although Kate had wondered before what it was that stopped all the other days of the week from being Anastasia's "me days" too.

Kate dropped her head and tried to disappear. The last thing she wanted was an ego-bruising interaction with Anastasia.

'Kate!' Anastasia cried.

Damn.

'Anastasia,' she replied, summoning up a ghastly smile.

'I'm glad I've caught you,' said Anastasia, her eyes raking appraisingly over Kate from head to toe, and – from the downward quirk of the corner of her mouth – finding Kate wanting, as usual. 'The jewellery evening . . . I've been thinking.'

'Oh good,' said Kate, her heart sinking. What now? Canapés? Jugglers? A fun fair?

'Yes, I'm just concerned,' Anastasia put on her concerned face. Kate was expecting a furrowed brow but there was no sign of that. For Anastasia brow-furrowing was – well – frowned upon – and, in any case, probably physically impossible as a result of all the botox.

'I'm concerned,' Anastasia went on, 'that it might be too much focused on the selling. I don't want my friends to feel they've been taken advantage of. That they've been brought to my house just for me – you – to sell them stuff.' Anastasia made it sound as if the selling was a purely exploitative process, bearing no benefit for the buyers at all.

'I am focusing very much on things which would make good Christmas presents,' Kate reminded her.

'Yeah, sure, I'm certain you'll sell lots,' said Anastasia. 'My friends are generous like that, as I am sure you know.'

Kate wasn't sure she did know that Anastasia's friends were nice girls. If Anastasia was anyone to go by, they weren't nice at all.

'So, I just thought it would be great if they had a chance to have a go themselves!' she announced, thoroughly pleased with herself for her sterling idea.

'What? At making jewellery?'

'Well, obviously making jewellery, what else did you think I meant,' said Anastasia, suddenly terse.

'There's not a lot I could teach in such a short time.'

'Teach? It's not rocket science, is it? Surely, they can be allowed to thread some beads onto a bit of wire or something . . .' said Anastasia meanly, adding, 'I do think people tend to want to complicate things, just to – I don't know – make themselves look clever perhaps?'

Ouch. That was an Anastasia special. Kate took a deep breath. The temptation was to tell her where to stick it, but luckily for Anastasia the adrenaline coursing through Kate's veins after her encounter with the special needs team had ebbed away.

'Fine,' she said. 'I'll see what I can do.'

'Lovely,' said Anastasia, tightly, turning away. Within moments she was huddled with her little group of friends, and Kate could tell she was getting a slagging off. Every now and then one or other of them would glance in her direction and then lean in to share another observation with the rest of the group.

As soon as Kate got home and had Jack ensconced in front of the telly with milk and a marmite sandwich, she called Helen.

'I know you don't usually do Fridays for me, but I just need you to take Jack while I go and speak to this woman at Greystone Manor,' she asked tentatively, once she had briefly filled Helen in on the situation with school.

'Why don't you take him with you?'

'Because, despite my declarations to those snotty women who told me he wouldn't get in, I am pretty confident he won't. And it's probably really nice, and there's no point upsetting him because you know what he's like about change. Although I actually have no clue what I'm going to do if I can't make it work. I hope it's horrible. That would solve a problem in a way . . .'

'You should go and look at the PRU, you know,' said Helen, tentatively. 'You never know . . . it might be okay.'

'Not you as well,' said Kate, feeling betrayed. 'He's not going there. So, will you – can you – do it tomorrow?'

'Of course. I'll do anything to help you and Jack. You know that.'

12ᵗʰ December

'Kate?'

The voice on the phone was gravelly and faint. Kate sat up in bed and held the phone closer to her ear.

'Blimey, Helen, you sound terrible!'

'I'm not great. I've been throwing up all night and I feel like I've been hit by a bus. It looks like this gastric 'flu thing. I can't even get out of bed without keeling over. Jason's having to take a day off work to look after me.'

'You poor thing,' Kate exclaimed, already rapidly recalibrating her day in her head. Damn. The timing was terrible.

'I'm so sorry, I just don't think . . .'

'Of course not,' Kate interrupted. 'You can't look after Jack today, that would be ridiculous.'

'I wouldn't want to give this thing to him . . . or you, but it's a problem.'

'Never mind that; you just look after yourself. Get Jason to take care of you and tell him he'll have me to answer to if he doesn't,' she joked.

'Come on you, what've you got this afternoon?' she said to Jack when she got off the phone.

'Maths and carpet time on Friday after lunch,' said Jack, pulling a face.

'Not today you haven't,' she said, ruffling his hair. 'The weekend starts early. I've got some finding out to do, and you're coming with me.'

The school was less keen on the change in plan.

'Mrs Marshall does not encourage school absences for any reason,' said the receptionist oppressively. She pursed her lips.

'Mrs Marshall is encouraging Jack to be permanently absent from this school, as it happens,' Kate said bitterly, 'and I have to collect Jack at lunchtime because I will be unable to get back here in time to collect him at the end of the school day. Please therefore ensure he is ready for me at one o'clock.'

Daniel was not having a good day. His morning had been taken up with a lucrative, long-term client who owned a significant chunk of Bristol and was constantly on the prowl to see how he could extract more money from it. Daniel's job was to review Sam Bird's portfolio and advise on steps involving rents, acquisitions and sales. This morning he had been escorting him around several commercial properties, but something prevented him from including Noel's shop. Mr Bird was looking to buy and not rent, in any case, but he was not one to accept no for an answer. That was another reason why Daniel had not mentioned it. There was something extremely distasteful about the thought of allowing Noel to be pushed around by someone with a different agenda.

Now, he had to admit, he had a problem. What with Brian from the Apple Café turning it down, he had made no progress with Noel's request for him to find a suitable tenant.

'I'm going out,' he called to Paul as he shrugged on his coat. It was nearly three o'clock on Friday afternoon and the light, on this already dull day, was fading already.

'You coming back?'

'Probably not,' admitted Daniel. 'It's Friday.'

'Part-timer,' Paul accused him without heat.

But Daniel wasn't on a skive. He pulled his coat collar around his ears – the wind was vicious – and headed off to Christmas Steps.

Not being a talented shopper, he had never paid attention to the other shops on Christmas Steps. Now, he stood at the foot of the steps looking up, disconsolate and demotivated, sad to see the Olde Sweet Shoppe so altered but checking out its neighbours with a more professional eye. There was a wedding dress shop, a florist, a café and a strange little shop selling old-fashioned menswear – cravats, silk handkerchiefs and ties, braces. Did people ever wear such things? How did it survive?

Taking a deep breath, Daniel shook himself and decided to open a conversation with someone. Talking was the key. Looking around him, he headed for the shop most brightly lit. It was the wedding dress shop.

The doorbell clanged as he entered, and a young woman appeared from an inconspicuous doorway beside a rack of wedding dresses. She was striking, and she knew it – a shock of short, pink hair was the initial impression, and the rest dropped into place as a tall, willowy figure, with chiselled cheekbones and extensively ripped jeans. On closer inspection she also had a constellation of tiny diamond studs, a scattering in her ear, including the lobe and cartilage, and another on the side of her nose.

'Hello?' she smiled.

'Hi!' he looked around. 'Er . . . so, wedding dresses, eh? I assume I'm not your usual customer.'

'We serve all sorts,' said the woman solemnly, suppressing a smile. 'Is it for yourself?'

'Um, no.' Daniel was flummoxed. 'Do you get that?'

'Absolutely. We do a wide range of larger sizes, especially for the shoes,' she said, waving at a stand of elaborate shoes, all either white or shades of cream. 'We are very discreet.'

'Mmm, thanks, but no thanks . . . I don't think white lace is really me.'

'Ecru or taupe can be very flattering on some skin tones,' she teased gently.

'Huh?' said Daniel. 'What the heck is an ecru?' He scratched his head. 'You know about paying rent, right?' he dived in, without preamble.

'I do,' she inclined her head.

'I mean, is this your business?'

'Yeah,' and then when Daniel looked surprised she squared her shoulders. 'You think I'm too young, don't you? I know my stuff . . . but actually it's me and my girlfriend. Partner. We co-own.'

'Sorry, no, absolutely,' he said striking his forehead with his hand. 'I don't really know what I'm asking . . . I'm a chartered surveyor, just trying to get a handle on how to market the empty unit up the street.'

'Noel's place?'

Daniel nodded.

'I'm Grace,' said the young woman, holding out her hand to shake. 'Cup of tea?'

'Go on then. I'm not stopping you working?'

She shook her head. 'It's a quiet time for us, this close to Christmas. People get engaged to each other over Christmas and the New Year, so January is always mental. We have Christmas weddings too, but we're pretty much there with all that. I delivered a dress yesterday, just one more to go, final alterations to do. The bride keeps losing weight. They do that. It's the stress . . .' she chatted, as she pottered efficiently around the little kitchenette in the back of the shop, while he leaned against the door frame, watching.

'So, how are you helping Noel, exactly,' she said handing him a steaming mug.

'I'm not at liberty . . .'

'Oh, don't be ridiculous, he's practically my dad . . . okay, my grandad. He's wanting to give up the shop. We all know that. We're worried about him. You know he's in his nineties, right?'

'I sort of do,' admitted Daniel, 'but he's amazing. More like someone in their seventies, if that. He looks ageless.'

'He's the father of Christmas Steps,' said Grace. 'Especially with a name like Noel.'

'Oh yeah, I hadn't thought . . .'

'Christmas Day is his birthday. His parents had a sense of humour. It could have been worse. Noel is a nice name.'

'It is.'

'And he's a really, really nice man,' said Grace, giving Daniel a fierce look.

'I know.'

She looked at him appraisingly over the rim of her mug for a long few seconds. 'Sorry. Let's start again, I'm just nervous about the whole thing with Noel. We're all worried about him. And then there's all this other stuff that's going on with the rates. We're fighting for our lives here. At least that's what some of us feel.'

'Tell me.'

'The City Council is reviewing all our rateable values. And they ain't going down.'

'I saw that. Clearly the rateable value of the Olde Sweet Shoppe went up recently. Mind you, if you own your unit that's a good thing. It means the market value must have risen.'

'That means nothing to us. Most of us along here don't own our shops. Noel is the exception.'

'Okay, and you're worried your rents might rise.'

'It's a real possibility . . . If rates are supposed to be – what? – forty per cent of the rent and they're currently higher, then landlords are going to come into line aren't they? Mind you, if the rates dropped I don't suppose rents would drop would they?'

'Have you contacted your landlord?'

'It's an offshore company. We don't get any correspondence from them except rent demands. They basically ignore us if we contact them about repairs. Me and my partner have had to do loads to this place. The guttering, the drain outside . . . The guy who rents the flat upstairs is really decent and he shares costs with us.'

Daniel's heart went out to her, she looked so despondent.

'And you're all in the same boat?'

'This place, the café, the cake shop and the gentleman's outfitters are all owned by the same guys. The florist, Jenny, she's in a better position because she owns her building and lives in the flat above. Her rateable value went up at the same time as Noel's and by a similar amount, so it's definitely a blanket thing. Obviously, she and Noel haven't got the rent worries though.'

'Why don't you move out of here and rent the other shop off Noel? At least then you'll have a decent bloke for a landlord.'

'Nice idea,' said Grace regretfully, 'but Noel's shop's half the size of this one. I couldn't make it work.'

'Shame,' said Daniel, seeing her point. 'The landlords would be idiots to put all your rents up to a level you can't afford,' he reassured her. 'You'd all move out, close down, they wouldn't get anything then.' But even as he was saying it, he knew the truth. Any commercial landlord – like his client this morning – would welcome the chance to put a unit back out on the market at a higher rent if they could. Christmas Steps would just evolve. It would attract tenants who could afford to pay more. Like a herd, they would all come together – those high-price boutique shops – and the current atmosphere of Dickensian charm would be gone for ever. That was the way of the world.

Suddenly a thought struck him. 'What did you say your landlord's name was?'

'I didn't. I said it was an offshore company. 'Eagle Ltd' or something. Actually, not Eagle, but I think it's a bird, I've got the paperwork somewhere.'

What were the chances? Daniel thought to himself. Of course, he should have known . . . His client Sam Bird had not only created a series of offshore companies in which he hid his money but – as he was a narcissist – they were all named after birds. It was too much of a coincidence. He would check when he got back to the office. Normally he prided himself on having a better memory of his clients' property portfolios, but his impression of this client was more about the man himself; a tough-talking no-nonsense Northerner who had made a ton of money and liked people to know it. He was ruthless and mercenary and Daniel suspected would have little sympathy for these tenants, if they were in fact his.

'Would you speak to them for us?' she pleaded, breaking into his thoughts.

'What?' Daniel jumped guiltily. 'Speak to who?'

'The council, of course. About the rateable value review?'

'Yeah, sure. I've got a contact, but I don't think . . .' he took another gulp of tea. 'Honestly – I feel for you all. You're getting it from both angles here, rent and rate hikes, you're all going to have to make a plan. To raise your game. Find a way to make your businesses produce more money.'

'Oh yeah!' she mocked. 'Doh, why didn't I think of that?'

'Sorry.'

Then she forced a smile. 'No, *I'm* sorry. You're right.'

'Will you do something for me?'

'If I can,' she was guarded.

'I just want you to have a think – and this could help you all too – what sort of business could go into the Olde Sweet Shoppe that would complement what is already here.'

'Okay,' she said doubtfully. 'I can think about it, and I'll get the others to think too.' She gave him a considering look. 'Why don't you come to our meeting next week?'

'Who, what, when, why?'

She smiled. 'In the café, next Tuesday at six o'clock, a few of us from around here, to talk about rate rises, rents, viability, all that jazz . . . yeah?'

'Sure. That could be good.' Why not, he thought to himself. He had no other clue how on earth he was going to find what Noel was looking for. The normal rules didn't apply. Plus, he needed to find out whether Sam Bird was indeed the landlord here and come clean with them all that he had this other agenda to meet.

When Kate and Jack arrived at Greystone Manor her anxiety did not improve. She had passed it many times; it was on her bus route to work. Logistically, it would work well, but seeing the lovely old building – with a small boy in uniform trotting in with his leather satchel and holding the hand of a mum who reminded Kate of Anastasia – made her even less confident that it was an option. There was a grand circular in-and-out gravel drive, with two pairs of wrought-iron gates. She and Jack trudged in through the one marked *Entrance* and crunched up to the front door, a double, high, oak affair with a magnificent knocker.

'Can I do the knocker, Mummy?' asked Jack.

'I'll have to pick you up,' said Kate, reaching down. But as she did so, the door opened, and a thinner, more polished version of Pat appeared before them in a cobalt blue two-piece skirt suit, a blouse with a pussy-cat bow, and neat, sensible court shoes.

'Mrs Thompson,' she said. 'And Jack too! What a lovely surprise,' she added, bending down to be on eye level with him. 'I didn't think you would be able to come but I'm very glad you've made it too.'

Kate blinked. 'I'm so sorry, childcare,' she muttered, trying not to stare, but failing.

'Of course, it's no trouble at all,' said "Pat", smiling.

'You're . . .'

'I know. It's disconcerting, isn't it?'

'Pat told me you were sisters, but she said you were older.'

'Twelve minutes older, and don't you forget it,' joked the woman. 'I'm Ursula Moore,' she said, holding out her hand. 'Pat's twin.'

'Cool,' said Jack. 'I know about twins. You were the same egg.'

'That's right,' said Ursula, unabashed, giving Jack her full attention. 'We are identical twins, with exactly the same DNA. But,' she held up her hand, 'do you know whether identical twins have the same fingerprints?'

'No,' said Jack, intrigued.

'What do you think then?'

'Erm . . . I think you do.'

'Actually, we don't,' said Ursula, raising her eyebrows. 'Isn't that interesting?'

'Yeah, that's really amazing,' said Jack, fascinated. 'What about other stuff . . . like . . . do you have moles in the same places too?'

'Sorry,' said Kate, pulling an apologetic face.

'Never apologise. Curiosity. That's what I'm looking for. I don't know enough about my sister to know exactly where her moles are, but my guess is we do not. Now,' she said, looking at her watch, 'the other boys are just about to go into their second lesson of the afternoon, which is biology, as it happens . . . would you like to go and see what they're up to?'

To Kate's amazement, Jack willingly trotted off with one of the other teachers, leaving Ursula and herself in the office alone.

'So, fill me in,' said Ursula, once Kate had been given a cup of tea by the lovely secretary, who was a delightful contrast to the receptionist at the school they had just left.

Kate did so, her voice shaking with outrage when she recalled the way the woman from the Local Education Authority had wanted to send Jack to the PRU.

'It saves them money,' explained Ursula, nodding sagely. 'That's why they are pushing you to accept it. Funding children to come to a facility like this is painful for them. They say they have a commitment to providing all children with the support they need – it's a legal requirement, actually – but they cut costs and corners if they can.'

'But how can I get them to do it?'

'First things first, let's work out whether this is the school for Jack. If it is, then – yes, it's a challenge – but we'll see what we can do about the funding problem. I've had the reports from the LEA on Jack's learning style . . .'

'You have? That was quick.'

'We know people,' acknowledged Ursula with a modest smile. 'On the surface of it, I am confident we can meet his education needs, but I'd like to spend some time with him myself. I'm glad you've ended up bringing him, but first, let me tell you about Greystones . . .'

'So, it's mainly a private school,' said Kate, checking her understanding, when Ursula reached the end. 'Don't they tend to have really high entry requirements?'

'You're right, that's usually the case. Parents who want to put their children into private schools tend to find the ones with additional or unusual learning requirements struggle with the entrance exams. Those are the schools who show off about their academic results which are – dare I say it – the inevitable outcome of cherry picking. What we do here is cater for boys who need to learn a different way and whose achievement is often, but not always, measured by different criteria. We don't lower our expectations, though. Not one bit. If Jack is capable of passing a string of conventional exams, then he will do that here. But let me show you . . .'

The grand old manor house was only half of the school. A modern single-storey building behind it housed most of the classrooms. The old building smelt of beeswax and disinfectant. Kate was shown the high-ceilinged, wood-panelled library and the dining room with its benches and long tables – the round, jolly cook greeting her warmly as she wiped the food remains from lunch off the tables in preparation for tea. The chocolate cake they were having was already cooling on the sideboard in two, enormous oblong trays.

'They're growing fast, these boys,' she explained, seeing Kate looking at the cake. 'They need calories and plenty of them. I make sure they get their five a day too, of course.'

In every room they went or peered into, there were small groups of boys, in their grey shorts and navy blazers, shirts tucked in and ties neatly knotted. Each group had at least one adult present, leading the boys in some endeavour that they clearly all found completely absorbing, such was the quiet air of rapt attention.

'We aim for calm,' explained Ursula. 'A lot of these boys shut down when they are surrounded by chaos and noise. It overwhelms them and, of course, they are in no state to learn like that. We teach in short bursts, too, with lots of hands-on activities and repetition. We ignite curiosity and then let the boys explore.'

Kate's heart swelled. This was the place for Jack.

Continuing their tour in the new part of the building, they came across him, in a group of six other boys his age, carefully examining a tank of what looked like brackish water and pond weed, with some rocks creating a sort of promontory at one end. They barely looked up as Kate and Ursula came in, but Jack saw them instantly and came towards them.

'Mummy,' he said. 'Look. We're learning about –' he paused and went on slowly and carefully, 'meta-morph-osis. It's when something turns into something different, like what frogs do, look!'

'Metamorphosis, Jack, good, well done,' said the teacher, a fresh-faced young man in a tweed jacket and sharply pressed flannel trousers.

'Are you having a good time, darling?' asked Kate, pulling Jack against her for a sideways hug.

'Yeah, this is really amazing Mummy. Can we stay a bit longer? We're going to have break next and there's chocolate cake on Fridays.'

'So I gather,' smiled Kate. 'I think we're not quite finished, are we?' she asked Ursula.

'Jack, will you come and have a chat with me, while Mummy carries on her tour? I'll make sure we're done in time for break.'

'Okay,' he said, happily. 'See you, Mummy.'

Another cup of tea, this time with a slice of warm chocolate cake, was brought to her as she waited in the reception area. She was sitting with the sweet lady who seemed to be doing everything from making the tea, to answering the phone, to welcoming anyone who walked through the door – deliveries, parents, *et al.* She managed all of this with a smile and an air of unflappable calm.

Ursula was matter-of-fact. 'Jack is a delightful boy,' she said. 'I would very much like to offer him a place. However, I am bound to tell you the majority of applications for state funding are unsuccessful. It would be unkind of me to give false hope.'

'I'm desperate for you to offer a place to Jack. What would the fees be if I just paid for him myself?'

Ursula mentioned a five-figure sum that exceeded Kate's entire annual salary – and that was for a job that she was probably just about to lose anyway.

She hung her head. It was impossible.

'Chin up, girl,' Ursula said, suddenly sounding exactly like Pat. 'I don't agree with my sister over much,' she went on, 'but I'm glad she sent you. It's up to you now. I can only help so much. Jack has a huge advantage over all the other state-educated children who need us. He has you.'

Kate shook her head, tears filling her eyes, but Ursula was having none of it.

'You are going to have to fight. I'm sorry . . . but you will. Get onto the LEA. Know their jobs better than they do. Know Jack's rights. Kick their arses.'

Kate blinked at the surprisingly robust language.

'Yes,' Ursula went on, unapologetically. 'You need to kick their arses. You contact your MP. You contact your local paper. You embarrass them into complying with their legal obligation to provide your child with the education he needs. I will concur, I will write the letters, provide the forms, but I can't do this for you.'

As she escorted them both to the door, she rested her hand on Kate's arm. 'I'm so sorry you have all this on your shoulders,' she said quietly. 'Pat told me. It's almost too much to bear, but you're strong. A mother's strength is a joy to behold. Keep going.'

Kate was not at all sure Ursula's faith in her was justified. As she and Jack went home, she was barely listening but merely making the appropriate noises as he chattered on about his exciting afternoon, the boys he had met and the stuff he had learned. She couldn't remember him ever doing that on the way home from his current school. Not ever.

'What Christmas thing are we doing tomorrow?' asked Jack sleepily as Kate sat with him on his bed, stroking his hair.

'Well, it's the weekend, so we're having Christmas pancakes for breakfast . . .'

'Yay!'

'And then we're doing Christmas cleaning . . .'

'Boo.'

'And then we need to do Christmas homework,' she teased.

'Muuummmy . . .'

Kate smiled. 'And then . . . we're going to the St Nicholas Christmas Fair. Is that Christmassy enough for you?'

'What's at the Sir Nicholas Christmas thing . . .?'

'*Saint* Nicholas,' corrected Kate, gently. 'Saint Nicholas is sort of the German version of Father Christmas, so the

Christmas Fair is all about German Christmas celebrations, which is great, because Queen Victoria's husband Albert – he was German – pretty much invented Christmas in this country: Christmas trees, candy canes, gingerbread . . . er . . . Christmas cards, all that . . .' she added, having pretty much exhausted her knowledge of German-inspired Christmas traditions.

'Brilliant,' said Jack. 'And you're not selling trees?'

'Not tomorrow, monkey boy. I'm all yours.'

'We need to get our own tree,' he murmured sleepily as his eyes drifted closed. Kate watched him, smiling, but didn't reply.

13th December

Daniel finally fell asleep only to wake again with the dawn. It was probably the gentle rocking as the big pleasure boat went by on its way to the pier to prepare for the first of its tourist trips of the day, its bow wave lifting the narrowboat in a barely-there shift and yaw. There was the soft lap of waves on the bow, the familiar condensation running down the insides of the windows . . . His bed was faintly damp, and he was too cold to sleep any more.

In the summer his friends envied his home and felt he wasted the pulling potential his unusual accommodation offered. In the winter, no one disputed that a boat, even one moored on the Bristol canal basin right in the heart of the city, wasn't a home for the faint-hearted. It was hard work living in a place without the convenience of power, warmth, unlimited fresh water from the tap, and the easy removal of wastewater. On the river, all these essentials of a civilised life were hard won in a series of chores which Daniel never resented. Instead he found the constant need to collect fresh water, empty waste, plug into the power, recharge the batteries and replace the gas cylinders presented a comforting physical routine.

With Zoe there, the importance of keeping the boat warm, dry and well-resourced was paramount. It had given Daniel a sense of purpose when all hope was lost. She had died whilst rocked gently in her cabin, held in Daniel's arms as they both idly watched their waterborne community, the people, boats, birds and the river itself, flow past the porthole. It was an implacable continuity that was a profound comfort. He had dozed and then, on waking, he had found that quietly, imperceptibly, they had gone from two to one – and he was alone.

He was bad at being home alone. He cleaned and tidied the living space, which was small and didn't take long; he had made a trip to the nearby convenience store to restock the fridge; and then he was ready to get out. To go anywhere.

Wandering from the docks into the centre of town, he found himself at the Christmas Market in the St Nicholas shopping centre, a covered Georgian arcade filled with Christmas sights and smells. Especially smells. As if sleepwalking, and invisible to the throngs of families brushing against him, he haunted the aisles.

Why was it that smell was so evocative? He had brought Zoe here in her wheelchair exactly a year ago. They had known time was short, of course. The expedition had been carried out with military precision: warm clothes, medications, timings perfect. Scant strength gathered up following a late-morning nap, he and Zoe had sallied forth from the houseboat on a mission to buy candy canes and a gingerbread house and then – strength allowing – they would take the car to Cabot Circus to choose the perfect tree. Of course, getting the tree onto the houseboat would be ridiculous, but the plan was to have it on the deck outside, still lit and decorated but, as Zoe had pointed out, happier in the chill than in the average suburban, centrally-heated house.

The replay of the video in his mind of that afternoon when they chose the tree was so vivid – his excuse for interaction with Christmas Tree Girl leapt upon and savoured

– it was more real than his surroundings. His head filled with a memory of how her blonde plait had a lock of hair escaping from it that she needed to tuck behind her ear as she chatted with Zoe. He was brought up short by a thud – a solid obstacle in his path. Dragging his mind back to the present, he looked down and was astonished to see the same blonde plait.

'God, I'm so sorry,' he said, his hands shooting out to steady her as she rocked on her feet. 'I totally wasn't looking where I was going . . . I was thinking about you.' He blurted it out, his hands still holding firm to her upper arms.

She smiled up at him. 'I've been thinking about you too,' she said, before putting her hand up to her mouth to stop the words. 'Not in a weird way,' she added. 'Obviously.'

'God no,' he agreed. 'Me neither.'

'I was actually wondering when you were going to come and get your tree,' she said, in a rush. 'You and . . .'

'Zoe,' he said. They were still standing chest to chest, just inches between them, neither drawing away.

'I never asked her name,' said Kate. 'Zoe. That's lovely.'

A long moment passed.

'She's gone, isn't she?' said Kate, so quietly that if Daniel hadn't still been so close, nearly touching, he wouldn't have heard.

He nodded, his eyes holding her gaze, watching them fill with tears. Or was it his own. He couldn't tell any longer.

And then, because it was the most natural thing in the world, he felt her arms slip around him and his went around her in response. She pressed her head against his chest, and one of her hands moved up and held him gently on the back of his head. They stood joined, the other shoppers parting and flowing around them like they were rocks in a river. Despite being nearly a foot shorter than him, she rocked him in her arms, as she would do with Jack when he had suffered the greatest hurt in the world.

Daniel closed his eyes and, as they swayed together, he breathed, taking in the faint jasmine scent of her bright, blonde hair. A peace he had not known for nearly a year poured into his body, filling him up and buoying him as if he was floating in a warm sea.

Eventually, he sighed, and, as one, they both drew back a little, so they could look at each other again.

'And I'm Daniel,' he said, as if there had been no gap in their conversation at all. As if the world had not just changed, totally, and for the better.

'Kate.' She smiled. 'And this is my little monkey boy Jack. Or not . . .' she added as she glanced down to see he was no longer standing beside her. She spoke without alarm, but turned away, scanning the vicinity, peering into the crowds of people who had been milling around them as they embraced.

'He knows not to wander off. Where's he *gone*?' she said, and the last word in the sentence was flooded with a sudden tension.

'He can't be far,' said Daniel, suddenly alert, his hand on her upper arm. 'Don't panic. Look, you stay here. It's important you don't move away from the last place you saw him. Chances are he's just wandered off and he'll make his way back.' He too was scanning the crowds. 'What's he wearing?'

'Jeans, a hoodie. It's red.'

'Don't move,' he told her again. 'I'll be back really soon.'

In moments he was out of sight. Kate put her hand to her chest, feeling her thudding heart through her coat and scarf. It was beating so hard her whole body was rocking with the force. The urge to run was overwhelming, the instinct was to get herself to the corner of the row, each corner, each row, looking for even a glimpse of him. But Daniel was right. She had to wait.

In what felt like hours Daniel was back, jogging towards her, not panting much but enough to constrain his speech a little.

'I've told everyone at the exits to stop anyone trying to leave with a small boy in a red hoodie. They're all on the alert.'

'Would someone have actually taken him?' This was a fresh horror. Kate's pounding heart shook her entire body and she felt a prickle of cold sweat form on her upper lip. Her mind flooded with terrible stories of planned child abduction in public places, the perpetrators changing clothes, dyeing hair, drugging the children to prevent their escape . . .

'It's not that,' he said grasping her shoulders to calm her. 'Why would it be? Don't imagine the worst. I was taking precautions, that's all.'

'It happens, though,' said Kate desperately.

'Okay, look. I'll stay here now, in case he comes back – *when* he comes back. You go and look now, but stay in the market, he will be somewhere here.'

She didn't need a second invitation. Unlike Daniel she was too small to see over people's heads, but then Jack was so small she could miss him by looking up high anyway. Instead, she ran across the top of the rows of stalls, ducking down to peer between the legs of the crowd along each of the aisles, torn between looking thoroughly and feeling she should rush on to the next row. She was too breathless to shout his name. It felt like one of those nightmares where you want to run and scream and your body feels drained of strength. People were moving around. Jack could be moving around. She could be just yards away from him, but missing him, going around in circles. She was sweating, panicking, more afraid than she had ever been in her life. To have something happen to Jack was unthinkable. But bad things happened to good people. Losing Tom had taught her that. People were looking at her oddly, but no one approached.

Then a hand fell heavily onto her shoulder, making her jump. 'You look like you've lost someone.'

She turned and found herself facing an older man with heavy dark eyebrows. He looked familiar.

'I have,' she panted, 'I have. I've lost my little boy.' Her mouth turned down and she put her fist against it to hold in the howl that was suddenly trying to get out.

'What's his name? What's he wearing?' said the man, abruptly.

'Jack. He's called Jack,' she said, openly crying now. 'He's got a red hoodie on.'

'Indeed, he has. Sorry, had to check, needed to make sure you were the real deal.'

'What? Not a child abductor, you mean?'

'Something like that. And I'm not one either, by the way. Don't worry, he's fine. Come on. He's currently entertaining my wife and doing a grand job of it too.'

The man, who still had his hand on her shoulder, steered her to the entrance of the market at the back. There, next to a woman who was crouched down chatting to him, was Jack.

The woman, with kind, dark eyes, looked on sympathetically as Kate swept an uncomprehending Jack into her arms and sobbed briefly into his neck.

'Children will be the death of us,' she said, handing Kate a tissue.

'Ours are grown up,' agreed the man, 'and they still frighten the life out of me. We managed to keep them alive, just about, when they were little, and we were always mislaying them, weren't we darling?'

The woman smiled at him. '*You* were.'

'I'm glad they give you the odd day off from selling Christmas trees,' he went on.

'I thought I recognised you,' said Kate, shyly. 'You bought two, to save arguments.'

'Is that what he said? That's just an excuse,' said the woman. 'He insists. He's just like a little boy at Christmas. Loves all the preparation, adores impressing the grandchildren, wants everything to be huge, sparkly, larger than life . . .'

The grumpy-looking man grinned, his face transforming. 'Maybe I do,' he admitted. 'Perhaps I'm not quite the Christmas Grinch I pretend to be.'

It must only have been minutes, Kate thought as she and Jack went back to where he disappeared. It felt like hours. She hoped Daniel would still be there. And he was.

They were too far away to speak when he saw her. He communicated his relief with an exaggerated knee-sag and brow wipe. He was holding two steaming paper cups from the stall beside the spot where he had been anxiously waiting and he handed one to Kate as she arrived.

'Mmm,' she said, sniffing it. 'Pure Christmas in a cup.'

'It's glogg.'

'Not mulled wine?'

'Yes, mulled wine, Swedish-style. It's got nuts and raisins in.'

'Glad you warned me,' said Kate, who had just taken a sip and had a disturbing sense of something solid bobbing around and nudging her lip.

'Should we be drinking alcohol in the daytime?'

'Definitely, after that.'

'Where did you get to, Jack?' said Kate, making a conscious effort to keep her voice light. Daniel met her eye, sympathetically.

'All I did was went around the corner,' he explained. 'To look at the toy soldiers. They were like Daddy's ones. I just wanted to see. I was right there. You were really close . . . And then, when you didn't come,' he admitted, 'I got bored so I went up the end to see Father Christmas, to make sure he got my letter all right.'

Daniel smiled, his eyes softening. 'I can see how it happened, mate,' he said, ruffling Jack's hair.

'Yeah, so . . .' Jack was on a mission to tell his story now. 'I went to see Father Christmas but – do you know what?' He looked at them both, wide-eyed, 'I don't think he was the real, proper one, because he didn't know about Daddy. He tried to pretend he did, but I had to tell him, and then he looked sad. But if he was real he would have known . . . and I did say in my letter too, didn't I, Mummy?'

'You did, darling . . . I'm sorry. He should have known.'

'Yeah, so that's how I know he wasn't the real one. And also,' he leaned towards them both and lowered his voice, 'I saw this weird stuff on his face and – do you know what?'

Daniel and Kate responded appropriately, stifling grins. 'What?' they said in unison.

'I actually don't think it was a real beard. I think –' He paused for effect. 'I think it was stuck on.' At that Jack leaned back again, looking to see what effect his revelation might have had on them both.

'Mate,' said Daniel. 'That's a pretty strong statement you're making there . . . but you could be right.'

'We should tell someone.'

Daniel pretended to consider. 'Mmm,' he said. 'Maybe not this time, eh? We'll let him have this one, shall we? He's not the proper Father Christmas and I'm afraid, mate, there's a lot of it about. But he's probably just being helpful, don't you think?'

Jack looked serious. 'Good point,' he said. 'We'll let him get away with it. Just this once, mind.'

Once Daniel, with Kate's permission, had distracted Jack from his Santa conspiracy revelations with a stick of candy-floss the size of his head, Kate had drained her drink and eaten the nuts and fruit. With a sigh of regret, she tipped her head right back to get the last drops, but she was calm again and warmed from within.

'Wow, that was good,' she said.

'Same again?'

'God, no. I'm sure it's massively alcoholic. I'm glad I'm not driving.'

'I think the traditional recipe includes vodka,' admitted Daniel, finishing the last of his and holding out his hand for her empty cup so he could put them in the bin.

'I'd like to hear more about Zoe,' said Kate gently when he returned.

'I'd like to tell you more about her. Not today, though. I think you've had enough drama for now.'

Their eyes met and too much time passed before they broke the gaze, leaving them both awkwardly fidgeting and looking anywhere except at each other.

Kate handed him her phone. 'I'd love to say tomorrow but I can't, unfortunately. We're going to see my husband's mother. But soon. Put your number in? We'll meet, and you can tell me. I want to know.'

So, where there was a husband's mother, there must be a husband, thought Daniel as he walked slowly and thought-fully back to the boat. Poking his feelings delicately he was dismayed to discover this depressed him very much. Could fate be so cruel? It was time to admit to himself, he hadn't felt that strongly about any of the women in his past – before Zoe came to live with him. Correction: he had never felt that strongly about anyone, full stop. Especially someone he didn't even know. The whole thing was a nonsense, and yet the connection, was there – the shared sense of loss. For some stupid reason – he imagined that meant she was alone. Wishful thinking.

14th December

Bracing herself, Kate hopped out of bed, teeth chattering, and piled on a jumper, dressing gown, thick socks and tracksuit bottoms over her pyjamas, tiptoeing quietly so she could get the heating on and the flat warmer before Jack woke up. She would have poked her nose in through his door to make sure he wasn't sound asleep and blue with cold with his duvet on the floor – he was a restless sleeper – but she didn't want to risk waking him. She would get some breakfast on the go first.

They were due to be on the coach to Frome at eight o'clock. From there they could catch a bus to Maureen's care home. There were not many buses on a Sunday so the whole journey had to be planned like a military operation. A missed connection would be a disaster. For the millionth time she regretted having to sell the car after Tom died. It was nothing special and she got very little for it, but the cost of taxing and insuring it, together with the impracticality of keeping it parked and not collecting parking tickets in Bristol, made it an unnecessary luxury and complication. Plus, living where they did, even a clapped-out Ford would probably have been stolen by now. Either that or she would have come out one morning to discover it propped up on bricks with its wheels gone.

She whacked on the electric heater in the sitting room cum kitchenette, trying not to think about the cost, and got some porridge on the go. As she stirred the pan, she looked out of the window. The sky was grey, heavy and low with cloud.

'Is it porridge?' said Jack, trailing in looking sleepy, his hair on end in the most enchanting way.

'Good hair,' said Kate. 'Yes, it is.'

'Aw . . . I don't really like it.'

'What? Porridge? Porridge is amazing. Body builders have porridge for breakfast.'

'Is there golden syrup?'

'Yes, as it happens.'

'Can I put it on myself?'

'Er, no thanks,' said Kate, wise to that. 'We're having syrup with our porridge, not porridge with our syrup.'

'More than that, Mummy,' he said, watching intently as she squeezed the syrup bottle. There wasn't much left. That was another item for her growing shopping list and shrinking purse.

'There, that's loads,' she said. 'Now, why don't you go and get your duvet? You can eat it snuggled on the sofa with the telly on, just this once.'

Within minutes the coach was fuggy and warm, like a tropical hot house, and it was packed, too. Thanks to a kind lady offering to move, she and Jack had managed to grab a set of three seats for the two of them.

'It's really hot, Mummy,' Jack complained, pulling distractedly at his coat.

Kate helped him take it off and folded it into her lap.

'Lie down, darling,' she told him. 'Put your head on my knee and I'll tell you a story.'

Jack was soon dozing as Kate had hoped, which gave her a chance to think, looking out of the window at the leaden skies and dreary rain-sodden landscape. It must only be one or two degrees too warm for the rain to turn to snow, she thought. Bad weather was going to make next week tricky. She had lots to do, with work, the Apple Café project and fighting for Jack's education. And then there was Daniel, she remembered, pleased at the thought she would see him again, perhaps help by listening to his memories of Zoe. God knows, she was grateful for her friends listening to her when she railed and sobbed about having lost Tom. She carefully slid her phone out of her pocket without disturbing Jack and found his contact details. She tapped out a quick text, offering to meet him the following afternoon. She always had a couple of hours to spare on Monday afternoon before she had to get Jack. If she needed longer, she knew she could ask Seema to help. That done, she leaned her head on the window and daydreamed, about Tom, about their life when they first married.

Maureen had been lovely, not the traditional difficult mother-in-law at all – grandmother-in-law technically, of course. She had welcomed Kate warmly, feeding them both far too much whenever they came to see her, and absolutely – unequivocally – adoring Jack from the moment he was born. His birth had triggered happy memories for Maureen, bittersweet memories of raising Tom. She stayed for a week after he was born, and she would sit with Kate and baby Jack, dreamily recalling her own daughter Daisy. It had been so sad listening to her tell how Daisy had disappeared at just eighteen years old, weeks after giving birth to Tom. Her departure had launched Maureen into a second burst of motherhood as she immediately stepped in to raise Tom herself. She had clearly been a great surrogate mum, as Kate often said. She had been just as keen to be a brilliant (great) grandmother and Kate had had to beg her to stop buying clothes and toys. There was barely room for it all in their cramped army married quarters.

'How much further?' Jack complained.

'Not much,' encouraged Kate. 'Anyhow, you know the way. It's just around the corner, isn't it?'

'It's too far,' he said. 'And we've got to get back.'

The owner – whom no-one ever saw – might be venal, but the staff of the home were motivated and kind. Someone had put pots of bulbs either side of the front door, the green beaks of whatever would later flower showing themselves already, despite the cold. The windows gave a view into warm, brightly lit interiors, and Kate was so desperate she was even thinkingly longingly of the weak, grey tea she was generally served there.

'Mrs Thompson,' said the manager, Carol, popping out from her little, paper-filled office behind the reception desk. 'How lovely to see you, and Jack too! Maureen will so enjoy your visit.'

'Is she well?' asked Kate.

'Well enough, dear. You'll judge for yourself. I think you will see changes, but that's to be expected.' She raised her eyebrows meaningfully. 'She has better days, bless her, but it's fair to say we're using a wheelchair most of the time now.'

'She can't walk?'

'Mobility, speech and – er – continence, do gradually disappear in the final stages,' she said, dropping her voice tactfully. 'I'll let you find your own way.'

'So, Jack,' said Kate, kneeling in front of him to straighten his jumper and smooth down his hair, which had sprung up again at the back, 'You know how Nana is?'

Jack nodded.

'She probably won't remember you, but she'll be glad you're there, okay?'

'We're going to give her the fudge, aren't we? Can I give it to her?'

''Course you can,' said Kate, handing him the tin from her rucksack.

Maureen had been stationed in front of the window in the large day room and they could see her right from the end of the corridor as they walked towards her. She didn't move. There was a side table bearing a mug and a small plate of biscuits, untouched. The wheelchair was angled so its occupant could see both the view outside and the interior of the room, but the little figure in the chair was hunched, head on her chest, eyes closed.

'Maureen?' said Kate, kneeling beside her and taking the frail, bony, bird-like hand in her own.

The old lady opened her eyes and turned her head. As soon as she saw Kate she broke into a huge smile, her blue eyes twinkling and her face lighting up in recognition.

'Hello darling,' she said, brightly. 'How lovely to see you again. Have I ever told you how much you look like my daughter-in-law? Well my grand-daughter-in-law actually. She was such a lovely girl . . . now what was her name?' she gazed out of the window, rummaging through her failing brain.

'Kate?' suggested Kate, but Maureen was oblivious.

'Daisy!' she declared at last. 'Yes, that's it. Daisy.' She turned back to Kate delightedly. 'I knew I'd remember. I'm good at names.'

'You are,' said Kate, smiling back at her. 'And here is Jack,' she said, getting his hand in her own and pulling him closer. 'Say hello, Jack,' she whispered.

'Hello Nana,' he said, cheerfully. Kate's heart swelled with pride.

'Tom!' she said, beaming. 'You gorgeous boy. I knew you'd come back.'

'I'm Jack,' he said. 'But that's okay, you can call me Tom.'

She nodded. 'My lovely Tom,' and then her face clouded. 'He died, you know,' she said, turning to Kate. 'My Tom was killed, it was so sad, and this little boy looks so much like him.' A tear welled up and tracked down the wrinkled cheek.

'I know, Maureen. I know,' said Kate helplessly, patting the old lady's hand.

Why did they come? What difference could it possibly make, other than upsetting this poor lady, whose mind was in such tatters that thoughts just drifted through it like gossamer on the wind?

'He does look like Tom, doesn't he?' she went on, matter-of-factly. 'He's just like his Dad. And he has really been looking forward to seeing you, Maureen.'

'And we brought you a Christmas present,' said Jack, producing the tin of fudge with a flourish. 'Look, Christmas fudge, would you like some?'

'How yummy,' she said. 'You know, my little boy used to like fudge,' she said, conversationally, after Jack had managed to persuade her to take a piece.

Kate was glad to see her eat something. The main external difference in the old lady was a dramatic weight loss. The differences in her brain function were also quickly becoming tragically apparent. But she was clearly delighted to have them there.

'Mrs Thompson, could we perhaps have a brief chat?' said Carol. She had brought Kate a cup of tea and Jack a glass of squash, which he was thrilled with as it was strictly rationed at home.

'Jack?' queried Kate, as she got up.

'I'm fine Mummy,' he said. 'Me and Nana are going to eat the fudge and look out of the window.'

'He remembers her as she was,' remarked Carol. 'The children tend to be better than we imagine at dealing with dementia. They relate on a simpler level, which can be quite appropriate and helpful.'

'She was such a lovely Nana to him,' said Kate, welling up for the first time since she arrived.

'Look at it from her side, not yours,' counselled Carol wisely. 'She is unware of what is happening to her now. She doesn't question the changes you see. She is living in the moment.'

'When she's not living in the past.'

'Absolutely. If she thinks Jack is your husband as a boy . . . so what? He's a lovely-looking child, by the way.'

'Thanks, I know,' said Kate. What would be the point in denying it? 'Tom was handsome,' she remembered. 'I thought he might be a bit big-headed because he was so good looking . . . But he wasn't.'

'I'm sorry I didn't meet him.'

Kate shook her head, summoning a smile, with difficulty. 'That's life.'

By this time, Carol had walked her down the corridor to a little meeting room.

'Is it the fees?' Kate asked when they sat down.

'Those and something else . . .' She looked awkwardly at Kate. 'Let's do the money bit first,' she said briskly, snapping open the file she had been carrying.

'So, as you know, your mother-in-law is funded by substantial social services support along with a top-up fee from the proceeds of her house sale and a small monthly pension, but I believe you are aware that now she has spent nearly four years with us, the money is shortly to run out.'

'I did know that,' said Kate, picking at a fingernail anxiously. It had been in the background of her thoughts like the ominous mood music in a bad horror film, letting the audience know more doom and gloom was shortly to arrive. She had had little involvement with the matter; there was a bank account with the money in it. Each month an unfeasibly large sum was transferred to the home. Each month, the sand ran out of the hourglass just a little more. There was a grotesque race going on, with all bets off on whether Maureen would get to the finish line before the money did.

'When does it run out?' asked Kate.

'Well, you're in charge of the money, but – according to the conversation we had when Maureen arrived – it won't last much more than another few months.'

'Then what? You chuck her out?' The concern and distress seeped out in between her words, making them land more forcefully than she intended.

'We wouldn't do that. Not exactly . . . but . . .'

'What?'

'The other pressing and potentially troublesome issue is that we have been asked to reapply for the funding, which I have done. The parameters on what constitutes social care and what is medical are constantly shifting and open to interpretation. It is a concern that this re-evaluation is taking place.'

'But she's worse now than she was when the funding was first allocated,' protested Kate.

'I know. It's a nonsense,' agreed Carol. 'And let us be frank, it is a money-saving exercise, pure and simple. I have to warn you, I have known residents in a poorer state than Maureen being judged as ineligible for ongoing funding. It is something that has become increasingly common in the last couple of years. It's very distressing for everyone.'

'I absolutely will not allow Maureen to be upset over this. I absolutely will not. Over my dead body. You won't say anything, will you?'

'Of course not,' said Carol, patting her hand sympathetically, 'what on earth would be the point?'

'So, what do we do?'

Carol looked relieved, and – with business-like efficiency – she produced a sheaf of paperwork from her folder.

'There are a number of other benefits that can be applied for, which will all help. I have filled in the forms as far as I can. You are Maureen's attorney, of course, so I just need you to sign here and here . . .' She pointed, and Kate duly signed.

'I will put in the forms and keep you posted.'

'What will happen when it runs out?'

Carol wouldn't meet her eye. 'Let's just . . . do this,' she said eventually and then paused, clearly psyching herself up. 'Also, Kate . . .'

Kate looked up at her enquiringly.

'Maureen is deteriorating, as you can see – I mean she's pretty good today, actually – I'm glad you've seen her like this – but increasingly now she's not really with us. Her physical health is failing quite quickly now too. We need to have some difficult discussions . . . Kate, I have to ask you what you think Maureen would want us to do if she became more unwell, this winter. There's flu going around, for instance, and you appreciate our clients are vulnerable. We take precautions of course. Naturally. But . . .'

'Could something like the flu kill her?'

'It could, and,' she cleared her throat, 'it especially could if we were not, perhaps, automatically treating her with heroic measures . . .'

'What do you mean "heroic measures"? I want you to keep looking after her if she gets ill.'

'Yes of course, of course . . . but if she were to become very unwell then the question as to whether she would want us to take really drastic steps to maintain her life at all costs would have to be asked . . .'

'What does she say?'

'Kate, it's difficult to have that kind of conversation with Maureen now, hence our asking you – as her registered attorney – to help us make sure her long-term wishes are enacted.'

Kate shook her head. It had been Tom's idea that everyone should have power of attorney, him for her, her for him and both of them for his grandmother – just in case something happened to him. Which it had. Now, the responsibility, tackled on her own, appalled and crushed her.

'Let me see her,' she said, standing up suddenly. 'I need to hear what she says for myself.'

She arrived back in the lounge, propelled by a drive that dissipated as she stood in the doorway watching Maureen and Jack together.

'Jack,' said Carol. 'Let me show you our chickens. Your Nana loves to come and feed them sometimes but today I think I'd like you to help me, so she and your mum can have a chat. How about it?' She held out her hand and cocked her head invitingly. Kate threw her a grateful look and sat down in the chair Jack had vacated.

She took Maureen's hand and smiled at her.

'He's such a lovely boy, that Tom,' said Maureen, staring after Jack fondly. 'I always brought him up to mind his Ps and Qs. "Manners maketh the man," I told him. It costs nothing to be polite.'

'You did a grand job,' said Kate.

'I did, didn't I? He's wonderful, if I say so myself,' she said, looking fondly at Jack out of the window. 'You look ever so much like my granddaughter-in-law, you know.'

'I get that a lot,' she agreed. 'I'm sorry about Tom. You must miss him.'

'Oh, I do . . . I do. But you mustn't worry about me. I'll be seeing him very soon. And my Derek.'

Kate sighed. It was pointless telling her that Derek, her husband, had been gone for even longer than Tom. He had barely remembered his grandfather.

She stroked the old woman's hand absentmindedly while she wondered how to have the conversation required, but then Maureen took the matter into her own hands.

'They're dead, you know,' she said suddenly.

'Who's dead?'

'My family. My husband, probably my daughter for all I know, and then even my grandson, Tom. You would have liked him. It's not right you know . . . to have your children go before you.'

'I'm sorry.'

'Don't be. I'm nearly there,' she went on, smiling happily out of the window at Jack, who was holding a pan of chicken food as Carol fiddled with the latch of the coop.

'Nearly there?'

'Nearly there,' repeated Maureen. 'I want to be with them now,' she said, her chin wobbling like a child about to cry. Kate's eyes filled in sympathy.

'Do you want to die?' she asked.

'Of course I do, dear,' she said, her smile returning.

Kate stood and kissed Maureen tenderly on the forehead, making her smile even wider, her arms reaching up to cradle Kate's face in her hands.

'Be happy,' she said, looking into Kate's eyes searchingly. For a moment, she could see the younger woman there, the energetic, kind and wise woman who had welcomed Kate into her tiny family. 'You need to find yourself a man,' she went on. 'A nice man. Like my Tom. He would suit you down to the ground.'

'I could never replace Tom,' Kate told her sadly, but the moment of clarity was over. Maureen's eyes clouded, her mind drifting to some place Kate couldn't reach. As Kate straightened up, she looked back up at her.

'You look ever so much like my granddaughter-in-law,' she said.

Late that night, once Kate had got a cold and exhausted Jack home after their long journey, she dug out the sign-in details for the savings account where Maureen's money was. Carol was right. There were the monthly payments to the home – she hadn't looked at it since the last fee rise had forced her to go in and change the standing order amount. Other than that, there had been no activity, just a pathetically low interest payment on the balance. They had lowered it again, surreptitiously. She didn't remember getting notification. The money was disappearing, and at a rate which – according to her quick calculations – meant the standing order would bounce in less than six months' time. If the social care package was removed or reduced, then funding would hit the wall within just a few weeks.

She filed the login details back in the folder she used for stuff relating to Maureen and added the copy of the *Do Not Resuscitate* order to the fat wodge of paperwork that was Maureen's Lasting Power of Attorney. In with it was Tom's copy of his own. She had kept both of them together, never thinking she would need them. Struggling to push it all back into the file, she extracted Tom's and put it in the recycling bin instead. It was about time.

15ᵗʰ December

'You gave him your mobile number? Seriously? You don't know anything about this Daniel bloke,' complained Wayne when they got to their first coffee break on Monday – the traditional weekend report and download session for them all. 'He could be a nut job. Why can't you just pick up randoms online like normal birds do.'

'Normal birds who pick you?' teased Kate.

'Yeah,' he shrugged defensively.

'Not that normal then,' she joked, 'and anyway it's totally not a dating thing. He's sad. I'm sad. I sort of know him. Well, I feel like I do . . .' she trailed off.

'Talking of "things to discuss",' Pat reminded her, 'we must catch up about the Apple Café thing. I've been preparing for this mince pie bake. My idea is that the workers at the café could make mince pies, bring them to the store and then, I am sure, Mr Wilkins will allow us to help them give them away and ask for donations.'

'Can't they just sell them?' asked Kate.

'I'm not sure they can, dear,' explained Pat. 'I think that's complicated. Better if they give them away.'

'Actually, I agree,' said Kate, thinking. 'I can see that working really well in fact. It's not just about the fundraising. It would be great for the café workers to just chat to people . . . form relationships . . . let them know the café is there and open to visitors . . .'

'They need to be handing out some information about the café with the mince pies,' said Pat excitedly, warming to the theme. 'Who will do that?'

'I think you should go and speak to Brian about it,' suggested Kate, spotting a matchmaking opportunity.

Pat flushed. 'He's not got time. I wouldn't know what to say . . .'

'Or I could go?'

'No, no dear,' said Pat hastily. 'You're busy too. I'll go, perhaps after work today.' Unconsciously she patted her hair. 'I look a right state,' she muttered to herself, 'I should have made that hair appointment . . .'

'You look lovely,' Kate reassured her. 'And you look remarkably like your sister, by the way.'

'Ah yes! How was she?' Pat suddenly looked tight-lipped.

'Fine. Spoke highly of you.'

'Did she?' She sounded mollified. Kate and Wayne glanced at each other in surprise. 'Ursula's fine, but we don't get on particularly well. It's just a sister thing. She knows her job, though. I hope she can help.'

'So do I,' said Kate, with feeling. 'And my other big thing – going back to the Apple Café project – is to organise this bake-off competition.'

'Baking competition?' said Wayne, his eyes lighting up.

'Yeerrs?' said Kate, surprised at his enthusiasm.

'Count me in!'

'Do you bake?'

'Do I bake . . .?' Wayne gave a disparaging laugh at her ignorance. 'I'm a ninja baker. How do you think I pull all those birds?'

'I thought there had to be something.'

'Seriously darlin', I do bread, pies, pastries, big, massive cakes an' that.'

'How about fairy cakes – pink icing, silver balls, swirls of buttercream, I love a fairy cake,' teased Kate.

'Nah, I'm not doing nothing girlie, I'm not a pouf, innit. I do hard man stuff. Endurance cake baker, that's me.'

'I hope you'll enter the Christmas cake competition then,' said Pat. 'It's going to be a fight to the death, mind, I should have thought it would suit you down to the ground.'

'Yeah,' said Wayne, allowing an endearing smile to break through the machismo. 'I'll do that. Seein' as it's for charity an' all. I'm gonna win, mind.'

'I am sure you will,' said Pat in the voice she usually reserved for her grandchildren, 'but you will have to work. From what I've seen those young people at the café are going to be hard to beat.'

Daniel was nervous. He now wished he had asked Kate to meet him in a café or something. Somewhere neutral. That would have been better. It probably looked a bit dodgy asking a lone woman back to his lair, and according to Paul he had already been inadvertently acting like a stalker already. He wouldn't be surprised if she didn't show. He astonished himself at the wave of sorrow he felt at the thought she would blow him out. Somehow, though, he wanted – needed – her to see the real him. A real, live Daniel in its natural environment, he joked to himself, as he did a visual check around the narrowboat's tiny lounge area. Since Zoe had died, he had taken over the 'big' bedroom to the front of the boat, with the shaped mattress which fitted into the whole of the pointed bow to make the most of the space. That meant he no longer had to convert the sofa to a bed every night, and not having to store away the bedclothes had created a bit more space too. The cushions on the narrow, padded bench – you could barely call it a sofa really – were thoroughly plumped and carefully positioned. He had managed to find a poinsettia in the market. Zoe had always asked him to buy one at Christmas, when there was so little else available: it was a welcome splash of colour. The tiny galley kitchen, within arms-reach of the sofa, was scrubbed clean; the kettle, teapot and a pair of matching mugs – bought specially for the occasion – were standing by. He really wasn't sure what Kate would want. She looked like a yoga bunny, the kind of girl who drank some sort of decaff, skinny, soya chai, whatever that was, with hazelnut syrup and a sprinkling of mung beans or something . . . He was more of an espresso man himself – hot, black and a big spoon of brown sugar – so he needed nothing more than his trusty stovetop espresso maker, which he also had standing by now. He had gone out to buy biscuits from the fancy delicatessen on the harbour. The cute girl behind the counter, who fluttered her eyelashes at him suggestively, had managed to get him to spring for some astonishingly expensive and complicated looking green tea, matcha powder stuff, which she told him was full of antioxidants and consequently all the rage. Just in case Kate did insist on non-dairy – so many girls regarded cow's milk as akin to cyanide – he chucked in a litre carton of dodgy looking soya milk too.

And now here he was, scanning the tiny space anxiously, waiting . . .

'Helloo?' Kate called, as she stood uncertainly on the jetty. This had to be the one. A blue painted narrow boat, Daniel had described it as, with a green roof and the name *Wonderland* painted on the side. There were cobalt-glazed pots on the small deck, nothing growing in them as far as she could see. In fact, they looked neglected and forlorn, with the remains of flowers now just grey-brown twiggy growth.

Whoever the keen gardener was hadn't been there recently. And then she remembered. It had probably been Zoe.

'Well done. You found it,' said Daniel, climbing up out of the cabin and holding out his hand to help her onto the boat.

'It's fine,' he said, 'you won't fall. I'm liking your hat, by the way.'

'Great, isn't it? Designer, you know,' she joked, patting the green woolly pompom hat he had given her. She pretty much wore it all the time. 'How did you and Zoe manage? With the wheelchair and everything?'

'Oh, she didn't need it all the time. It was just for when she might have to stand up for a long time or walk a long way. She couldn't do that. Not in the end. I just kept the wheelchair in the car and then carried her down here.'

He showed Kate down the steep wooden steps into the cabin, hovering anxiously behind.

'You'll need to duck your head,' he warned.

'Wow, it's amazing,' she said, taking it all in. 'You'd have to be awfully tidy to live in such a small space. I couldn't do it,' she admitted.

'It's a discipline. You get used to it.'

'Go on then, let's give the matcha thingie a go,' she said gamely, when he had run her through the extensive beverage choices.

'I thought you'd be into that sort of stuff,' he admitted, attempting to read the label on the packet but then just chucking a good few teaspoons of the frankly vile-looking green stuff into the two cups and pouring water on.

'It's interesting,' she said, looking into her cup when they had sat themselves down on the narrow sofa, thighs nearly touching. She stirred her mug cautiously, but the effect was just to make the large clumps of green into smaller clumps of green. 'Is it supposed to be like this?' she asked with a grin.

'Oh God, I've no idea,' admitted Daniel, poking one of the lumps with his spoon. 'Here goes though . . .' he took a large gulp and his face convulsed in disgust, making Kate burst into peals of laughter.

'You're not selling it to me,' she said, taking a sip of her own and immediately having to try not to gag.

'Yikes, that's bad,' she admitted, putting the mug carefully down on the little table and regarding it as if it might bite. 'I'm sure it's amazingly good for you – or something . . .'

'Sorry,' he said, picking up both mugs and pouring them down the plughole. The lumps resisted, forming a claggy layer in the bottom of the sink, and floating on the water Daniel ran in an attempt to wash them away. To top it all, the water slowed to a trickle and then stopped.

'Damn. Water tank's empty,' he said. It was a morning job and he had been so distracted by Kate's visit he had clean forgotten.

'I'm beginning to see it's not as cool living on a boat as most people think.'

'Sorry,' he said. 'Builders' tea?' He was lucky there was still recently boiled water in the kettle.

'Yes, please,' said Kate, with relief.

'So, when did you lose Zoe?' she asked, when they were settled again, this time with chipped, mismatched mugs. They were filled with reassuringly familiar orangey brown tea, strong, milky and – in Daniel's case – sweet.

'It was January she died, so not long into the new year. You saw her just before Christmas, of course. She was incredibly unwell by then. We were just hanging on, really . . . There was no hope.'

'What was it? Cancer?'

'Heart,' said Daniel, succinctly. 'She had a congenital heart defect. It led to unsurvivable complications. She had everything – pulmonary hypertension, heart failure, she was on oxygen, the tiniest thing exhausted her . . .'

Kate put her hand on Daniels, which was resting on the table.

'I'm so sorry. She was young. And she was lovely.'

'She was,' he smiled.

'Could they not operate?'

'They wouldn't,' he said, his face becoming grim. 'Not when she was younger. And then, they couldn't. It was too late.' He stared intensely at the little table between them. 'She had an AVSD,' he went on. 'That's an atrio-ventricular septum defect. A hole in the heart, basically.'

Kate nodded, giving his hand a squeeze.

'Why wouldn't they? Operate, I mean . . .'

Daniel looked at her. 'Because she had Down's.'

'No! Surely not . . . that's . . . it can't be right?' She looked appalled, tears springing to her eyes.

He sighed. 'Yep, I know, it's not what's supposed to happen. You won't get anyone admitting to it out loud. We didn't understand at the time. If we . . . well, if my parents had known, there was a window, when she was a baby, when they could have tried a surgical repair. My parents were talked out of it, but it seems pretty clear now, she would have been offered the surgery if she hadn't had Downs. By the time we realised she had been discriminated against, it was a case of accepting she would die young. She had a longer life than any of us expected.' He stared out of the window at the brown river, the grey sky, hinting at snow. 'She had an amazing life, really.'

'She was lucky to have you.'

'I was lucky to have her.'

'The first Christmas is hard.' It was a statement not a question.

'It will be. God, December . . . It's so depressing anyhow, no wonder the pagans decided to have a bit of a party to keep their spirits up in midwinter. I just don't want to have anything to do with Christmas this year.'

'I've got Jack,' she said. 'I've got to "do" Christmas. For his sake.'

'And your husband?'

Kate looked at him in surprise. 'My husband?' she echoed, stupidly.

'Uh-oh, he died, didn't he?' said Daniel, suddenly realising and feeling a fool. He smacked his forehead. 'I'm such an insensitive idiot. First, I somehow assumed you had lost him because – well – you just look like you've lost someone. Then I realised I didn't actually know and I was jumping to conclusions. Then, when you said you were visiting your mother-in-law, I thought I must have been mistaken. And then I thought well, maybe you're just divorced or something. I mean that can be awful enough, apparently . . .'

Kate straightened her shoulders and took a deep breath. 'You should trust your instincts,' she told him. 'My husband Tom has been gone for four years now. Dead, not just divorced. I'd like to tell you it gets easier, but in truth . . .' She spread her palms and tilted her head sympathetically.

'How?'

'He was a soldier – killed in Afghanistan. The usual crap – dodgy equipment, inadequate leadership, exhaustion . . . He was blown up by an IED. I don't even know why they sent a person-shaped coffin. A box would have done. A small one at that . . .' Kate's face was hard. She had learned to be angry. To say unspeakable things that upset people, to express her rage at the horrible, senseless, violent loss.

He nodded calmly. He didn't try to touch her. Not now. He knew from his work with the Crisisline, from his own grief, that she just wanted – in that moment – to be angry. He was quietly touched that she allowed him to see it.

They both sat, beside each other, looking out at the heavy sky, the river, whipped into small frothy crests by the bitter wind.

'How old was Jack when it happened?' he said quietly at last. 'He would only have been – what? – two?'

'Yes, just two. He has memories of his Dad. Sort of. We go over them quite often to – I dunno – reinforce them. I want him to have that.'

'So now he's six?'

Kate nodded.

'Four years is a long time to be alone.'

'I'm not alone,' said Kate, stoutly. 'I have Jack. You're alone,' she added, with unintended bluntness.

'Zoe was always trying to fix me up with people. She didn't want me to not have anyone when she . . .' He paused and then gave a snort of laughter at a memory recalled. 'Yeah, she was quite the matchmaker . . .'

'So, have you ever had anyone? Sorry, not "had", although, yes, I do mean that actually. Have you ever had a relationship with a woman? Or a man, of course,' she added.

He laughed again, longer this time. 'What do you think?' he teased gently. 'I'm thirty-two and I'm not a monk. I'm afraid I was a bit of a tart before Mum and Dad died – I prefer women by the way – but they went suddenly, just six months apart, and then obviously it was just me and Zoe . . . Yeah,' he went on at last. 'I grew up then, all right, and no, I haven't "had" anyone since.'

'We're a right pair, aren't we? Staring down Christmas like we're looking down the barrel of a gun,' admitted Kate. 'What are you going to do for it? Do you have any family left at all? There must be someone . . .'

'Not really. Elderly aunts who live miles away. I've got a volunteer job I do. I'll probably be tied up doing that. Lots of the others do have families, so they won't want to work over the holidays. I'm happy to fill in.'

'Talking about work, what do you do, and why aren't you doing it as we speak?'

'In my proper work I'm a chartered surveyor specialising in commercial property, which is exactly as dull as it sounds. And I'm not doing it today because I am on enforced holiday. I haven't . . . well, I haven't wanted to . . . take my annual leave this year and I'm supposed to use it before the end of December so . . . now I have a week off. They made me.' He held out his hands and let them drop.

'What are you going to do?'

'Put my record collection in alphabetical order.'

'You haven't got one,' said Kate, looking around the tiny space.

'Haven't I? Damn, can't do that then.' He put his finger on his mouth, pretending to think, but came up with nothing.

'Me and Jack, we're doing Christmas things every day,' ventured Kate. 'We've got this advent calendar . . . I decided we would do it. Celebrate the run-up to Christmas properly; change the way we've been living for the last four years. It's hard to explain . . . I made a decision I would find my way back this year, make Christmas special again and use it as a springboard for the rest of our lives. Get happy. That's the plan, anyhow,' she said uncertainly, remembering Seema's list of things she had to do – a list she had made little impact on so far. 'Does that sound ridiculous? It *is* ridiculous, I know.'

'No, it sounds very sensible. Well, maybe not sensible, but definitely a good idea. What's the plan for tomorrow then?'

'I haven't decided yet,' she admitted. 'I've got this list of things we have to do but none appeal for tomorrow, to be honest. I was hoping it would snow.'

'You don't want much, do you? I can't remember the last time we had proper snow in Bristol. Well, I can, but crikey, I was a teenager,' he said, thinking back. Zoe had been really small then. It was her first experience of snow and she had been utterly transfixed. Funny how so many of his life experiences were all the more intense and fantastic because he had seen them through his sister's eyes . . .

'It might snow,' said Kate, peering out at the leaden sky hopefully. 'It's definitely chilly enough.' She gave a shudder.

'Are you cold?' he said, jumping up. 'I'll put another log on.' He reached for the little basket by the stove and selected another chunk of wood to put into the little wood-burning stove that glowed cosily in the corner.

'I wish we had one of those,' she said, longingly.

'Where do you live?'

'We're in a flat off St Peter's Road. It's warmer than it might be because it's above a launderette, but it still gets cold. Poorly maintained sixties architecture isn't known for its insulation.'

'You sound like a chartered surveyor,' he joked. 'You know, there's grants for improving substandard properties, to help landlords improve the quality of their buildings. I should take a look for you.'

'We're not going to be there for ever. I want us to get something better. I want Jack to have a garden. Or something like this. Jack would love it!'

'You should bring him.'

'Yeah, maybe . . .' Kate's smile didn't slip but she shifted a millimetre away.

He noticed. She was wary and that was fine. He was too.

When she had gone, the boat suddenly felt oppressive and claustrophobic rather than cosy. Kate had left her hat behind and she would be missing it now. The cruel wind was swirling tiny flakes of sleet across the water. Not snow, but close to it. Kate might get her white Christmas after all, he thought. The yawning loneliness of the week he had on holiday stretched before him. 'Me time' wasn't good. He was lousy company.

'You don't have to do all the shifts, you know,' said Barbara.

'I might as well. No one else wants them and I've got nothing else to do this week. I've been practically laid off work, as in they won't let me go in. And I've got plenty I could be getting on with too,' he said, remembering the Olde Sweet Shoppe, which he had made no progress with. At least he had the local retailer meeting to go to tomorrow evening. Something in the otherwise empty diary.

'Christmas shopping?' said Barbara. 'Who for?'

'Fair enough; I don't have a very long list,' said Daniel. Then he added, 'Listen, my experience is relevant to helpline users. I'm alone at Christmas. Half our callers are now telling us they feel more crap because of Christmas – loneliness, alienation, poverty . . . it's a "thing".'

'Fine. It's a "thing"', admitted Barbara. 'But it's not your thing. Not as in solving the problems of the world on your own, lovie. I gather you had another bad ending on your shift last night.'

Daniel nodded his admission. 'Thirty-year-old man, girl-friend problems, fallen out with his family, no job, no prospects, no hope. Same old.'

'Could you not intervene?'

He shook his head. 'I couldn't get him to tell me where he was before he lost consciousness. He knew the drill. He wouldn't say, and he knew what that meant. He just didn't want to die alone.' And he hadn't. Daniel had stayed with him, on the phone, long after the last signs and sounds of life. It had been an overdose. About thirty codeine and paracetamol capsules, prescribed for the man's back pain. Thirty tablets were all it took to be convincingly over the lethal dose. Daniel had only hoped the codeine would be enough to kill him. There were too many incidents of the opiate wearing off and the poor souls waking up, but then the paracetamol getting them anyway after several days of liver failure. Then it was a hospital death, long drawn out and painful. The worst thing of all was when second thoughts had kicked in and the person wanted to live but it was too late for the extended suicide process to be stopped. Yep, Daniel hoped the codeine had done its work.

'Such a waste,' sighed Barbara. It was a credit to her humanity that – with all her experience – her sense of outrage at lives lost to suicide was undimmed.

'It's the business we're in. Young men in particular. You know that. Some you win, some you lose,' said Daniel, wearily, rubbing his face with his hands. He would never subject his family to the shock of suicide. It was an act of violence, not just against yourself, but against everyone who knows you. People left behind described it as being like a bomb going off. He spent time talking to those people too.

'Do you ever ask yourself why we do this?' he said, turning to Barbara with a frank look of despair.

'I certainly ask myself why *you* do this? A young, handsome man, who should be out living his life, not picking up the pieces of other people's mess.'

'Ah, but I do it so well.'

'You do, unfortunately. And how are you?'

'Bored this week, hence the shift volunteering.'

'Hmm,' said Barbara, looking out of the window. 'What you need to do is take some time to yourself,' she said. 'And if it snows like they are saying it will, none of us will be going anywhere, so I suspect you'll get it whether you like it or not.'

16th December

The following morning, Jack came excitedly into Kate's bedroom, jumping right into the centre of the bed, which was – unfortunately – where Kate's legs were.

'Ouch,' she said, blearily rubbing her eyes. 'Watch out, monkey boy! Where's the fire?'

'Not fire, Mummy, snow . . . look! It's really snowing. See?'

Kate sat up. She didn't even need to get up. From the bed she could see the air was a thick flurry of large snowflakes, dark against the heavily clouded sky but pure white as they drifted across the buildings of the street opposite, blurring the ugly shop signs and dressing the grey pavements with a thick coating of pure, fondant icing. She joined Jack at the window, wrapping around his slight shoulders the shawl she kept at the end of the bed. 'It's settling,' she said. 'I'll have to see whether school's open.'

'Might it be shut?' said Jack, delighted.

Kate's heart sank at the thought it might. When it came to snow she was as excited as the next grown-up – in other words, not very. Snow wasn't nearly as fun as it had been when she was a child. She doubted Portman Brothers gave a stuff about schools closing and the resulting childcare problems.

She grabbed her laptop and quickly navigated to the school website. They may not have closed. If she could just get Jack there, if the buses were running, she'd be all right.

But no. On the homepage there was a stilted little note from the headteacher citing extraordinary circumstances, well-being of students and staff, health and safety, yada, yada . . . Absolutely fine for all the middle-class mums like Anastasia who didn't have proper jobs anyway and would be doing snow-related, cool, educational stuff with their kids that lent itself to cute, Instagrammable photos. Just to punish herself, Kate checked out Anastasia's Instagram account. Yup, there it was, cute kids in pyjamas collecting carrots and bobble hats for the snowman they were going to build in the garden after homemade waffles for breakfast. People like Anastasia didn't have bosses who were looking for an excuse to terminate a contract.

She picked up her phone and wondered whether to text Helen or call. She called.

'I'm so sorry, darling, I know exactly what you're going to ask,' she said, before Kate had even spoken.

'And . . .?'

'We're all in the same boat. I've had calls from pretty much all my other parents. It's first come, first served, unless I normally do Tuesdays for you.'

'Which you don't.'

'Which I don't,' Helen agreed with regret. 'And you know I've got my quota. Ofsted will have my guts for garters if I go over.'

'I know, I know. That's fine, don't worry. I'll work something out.'

With a sinking heart, she called work next. Using the direct line for the Human Resources department, she was surprised not to get the absence answerphone but a human – more specifically, the human who had been so crushing and discouraging when she had talked about her contract the other day.

'Kate,' Sarah said, not unkindly. 'Can I guess?'

'I've tried really hard,' said Kate. 'There's just no way I can get childcare, everyone's completely booked . . .'

'So, what you're saying,' she replied, 'is that you're too ill to come in today.'

'It's looking after Jack that's the problem. I'm fine.'

'No, you're not,' Sarah said, heavily. 'You're vomiting. You probably ate a dodgy prawn. Better still, it's viral and to avoid spreading it you should probably take a couple of days off. At least.'

'I should?'

'You should. However, you are predicting a miraculous recovery just in time for the end of the period you can self-certify, by which I mean the period where you can tell us you're ill without proof from your doctor.'

'I am?'

'You are.'

'And what is the timing of my miraculous recovery exactly.'

'Well, it has to be within five working days, so don't take the piss or anything,' Sarah muttered. 'I'll see you later this week. Enjoy.'

On putting down the phone, Kate's spirits lifted.

'So, turns out it *is* a day off, for both of us,' she said to Jack, 'and let's start with a nice, warming breakfast, eh?'

'Porridge?' he said, doubtfully.

'Porridge.'

His face fell. 'Not pancakes?'

'What? Pancakes on a Tuesday?' exclaimed Kate, with a fake shocked expression.

Jack wasn't fooled. 'Yeah!'

'Oh, go on then. Brush teeth first please.'

While he ate, Kate considered her options. Which were sadly limited. There was very little traffic outside and the cars were having a terrible time, creeping along cautiously. They were definitely slipping and sliding on the corners and this made her nervous about taking Jack out walking anywhere. The buses didn't look as if they were running. They were quite a way from any really good parks. The one just up the road was tiny and generally full of dog poo, which was even harder to avoid with snow to camouflage it until it was too late. To top it all, she had left her woolly hat at Daniel's boat yesterday and didn't have another one. It was going to be cold. She pondered, sipping her tea slowly.

'Kate? Kate?' came the cry up the stairs. She recognised the voice. It was her landlady, the launderette owner, Mrs Akintola.

'I'm in my pyjamas,' she shouted back.

'Better and better, darlin'' the voice shouted back. Kate opened the door.

'Ah, there you are dear. I have a handsome young man here, asking for you.'

'Mrs Akintola, you shouldn't have,' she joked. 'It's not even my birthday.' She assumed the older woman was going to produce one of her apparently innumerable handsome sons, probably to go up and fix the dripping shower head Kate had mentioned the week before. It might not be a brilliant flat, but Mrs Akintola was pretty good on the ongoing repairs.

'I'm sending him up,' she said, standing to one side, but instead of the smiling face of Dwayne, Daryl, or the other son whose name Kate could never remember – Dorian? – to her immense surprise the man who appeared was Daniel.

'Well, I knew it was someone beginning with D,' she reflected. 'What a surprise!' she said aloud, standing aside as Daniel arrived at the top of the narrow stairs and awkwardly raking her fingers through her thick blonde hair. She was sure she looked a sight.

'I thought you'd need your hat,' he said producing it out of his pocket with a flourish. 'You've been trying to get rid of it, haven't you? Be honest . . .'

'Certainly not, I am extremely attached to my hat,' she protested. 'I was just thinking how sad I was that I left it behind, but I wasn't expecting this marvellous delivery service. How did you even find me?'

'Sorry, I hope it's not too weird of me,' he said, waving to Jack, who sat at the tiny table with a forkful of pancake on the way to his mouth. 'You said you lived above a launderette in St Peter's Road and I checked on Google. There's only one launderette in the area so my chances were pretty good.'

'And you talked your way around Mrs Akintola.'

'That wasn't hard. I think she liked me. I think she thinks there might be something going on between us,' he added cheekily.

'Yeah, well, there isn't,' said Kate firmly, but with a hint of a smile. 'Tea?'

'Builders'?'

'Definitely.'

'Thank God for that. Yes please.' He went over to Jack. 'Nice to see you again, mate,' he said holding out his hand just as if he were meeting another bloke down the pub.

'Nice to see you too,' said Jack in reciprocation, holding out his hand for a firm, decisive handshake.

'I brought your mum's hat,' he said, in a factual, no-nonsense exchange of information.

'We're going out in the snow,' responded Jack in a similar vein.

'Good idea. Have you decided where?'

'That's slightly the point,' admitted Kate. 'There are no buses, I suspect, and there's not much green space around here.'

'Dare I suggest a cunning plan?' said Daniel, he looked enquiringly at Kate, hyper-sensitive to the slightest hesitation from her.

'Feel free.'

'I have a car.'

'In this weather? I'm not sure . . .' she said, remembering seeing the cars outside sliding around.

'I have snow chains.'

'In Bristol?'

'Yep.'

'Where – to quote you just yesterday – "it never snows"?'

'I did say that, didn't I?' he grinned. 'Me and Zoe used to go to this amazing place in North Wales and I bought a set of snow chains there once because we got caught out by snow in April, which we definitely weren't expecting. Now I'm glad I did.'

'Okay, well, that's good . . .' said Kate, still unsure.

'We can go to Brandon Hill, can't we Mummy?'

'That was exactly what I was going to suggest, dude,' said Daniel. 'Gimme five.'

Jack wacked Daniel's hand with enthusiasm.

'Hang on, hang on . . . I'm sure Daniel's got better things to do with his time.'

'Better things than going to Brandon Park in the snow?' he said. 'What do you mean? It doesn't get better than that.'

'Yeah, Mum,' said Jack, triumphantly, going to stand next to Daniel in solidarity.

So, this is what it's like to have two parents to play off against each other, thought Kate, amused. He had been a bit too young or guileless to learn that trick when Tom was still alive. 'In your pyjamas?' she enquired, as close to admitting defeat as she was prepared to go.

'Tea,' she said to Daniel, handing over the mug as Jack scampered off to dress. His challenge was to find – on Kate's instruction – a vest, shirt, jumper, fleece and two pairs of socks. She hoped his waterproof trousers would still fit. Being short of money meant she dreaded waking up one morning and discovering too many things had been grown out of in one go. School shoes were bad enough, but it was having to replace gym shoes, wellies and trainers all at the same time that kept her awake at night. Trousers were habitually a bit too short. Long socks were a godsend for filling in the gaps; she never bought short ones.

'He's great,' said Daniel, sitting on the sofa and watching, relaxed, as she moved around the kitchenette tidying away breakfast.

'Have you really got nothing better to do?' she said, sounding ruder than she meant. She genuinely didn't want him to feel he had to.

'It's not just your hat and the snow chains,' he admitted. 'I've got the full snow kit in the car. Shovel, blankets, thermos flask . . .'

'We're not in the Norwegian fjords,' said Kate with a smile.

'And a sledge,' he finished, in triumph.

'A sledge?' said Jack, coming back into the room, already looking hot in all his layers. 'Coooool!'

'So, here we have a man who lives on a boat, in the middle of the city, and has snow chains. And a sledge. Where do you put it all?'

'I have a lock-up garage,' he admitted. 'You should see the decluttering I had to do when we sold my parents' house a few years ago. I travel light now: nothing but the essentials.'

'Snow chains, thermos flask and shovel-type "essentials",' smiled Kate. 'Who are you? Bear Grylls?'

'I've never been on a sledge,' said Jack, staring, wide-eyed at the amazement of how well his day was now going with the introduction of this man, who had started turning up miraculously in his life with hugely covetable items like candyfloss and sledges.

Kate turned away, stacking the breakfast things busily, plates and spoons clattering.

Daniel touched her arm.

'Okay?' he said quietly.

She turned to him, bowing her head so he wouldn't see her distress. Except he already had.

'I'm fine,' she said brightly, for Jack's benefit, and then, *sotto voce*, 'It's just . . .'

Daniel waited, his hand on her forearm, a comforting weight.

'It's just that Tom went sledging with him once. Only once when he was – what? – eighteen months old, perhaps. I'm sad he doesn't remember, that's all.'

He gave her a comforting squeeze.

'Anyway,' she said, briskly pushing her hair back from her face, 'let's be off before it melts, I'll just get some snacks together.'

Even with the snow chains, Daniels' car felt unstable on the side roads where the snow was still fresh. Kate sat, with her fists clenched, concerned that he would slide into one of the parked cars that lined the streets. The majority were still blanketed in snow. Clearly most of the population of

Bristol was staying put today. Daniel did his best to stick to the main roads where the snow had already been turned to mush by the traffic. It took twice as long as it might have done to get to Brandon Park. When they got there, he manoeuvred expertly into a space just vacated by another sledging family, yards from the park entrance.

'Look Mummy,' said Jack excitedly, pointing.

The park had been invaded by families with sledges. Some children were sliding down the hills, just on black bin liners. Some had skiing outfits on, complete with sunglasses and salopettes, clearly from posh skiing holidays. That was a hundred pounds worth of clothes, put onto growing children, thought Kate. What must it be like to do that – not worrying about the clothes barely, or never, being worn? What must it be like to not worry about waste, about not being able to afford shoes for them, or how to pay for school outings? Actually, they probably bought the kit every year to go skiing. In France perhaps. Or even Canada, probably.

'Wake up, we're here,' teased Daniel. 'You were a million miles away. And not in a happy place either, by the looks of it.'

'Sorry,' said Kate, summoning a smile. 'Thanks again for this.'

'No worries. Now, what do you reckon, Jack? Over there?' He pointed at one of the gentler slopes, where there was a well-established run of compacted snow and a stream of small children mainly with parents in tow, sliding down and trailing up the hill again to queue at the top.

'Or there,' said Jack, pointing in the other direction where teenage snowboarders were throwing themselves down a steeper slope. Probably one in three were crashing dramatically, to derogatory shouts from the others.

'Let's maybe work up to that one, dude,' said Daniel.

Kate gave him a grateful look.

'I hope you're going to have a go?' he said.

'I'll just watch, if you don't mind.'

Kate tagged onto the outside of the group of mums, who were weighed down with discarded possessions, draped about with coats, scarves, snacks and drinks. She knew from summer day trips that there was a cool little café in the park too – a wooden building with sofas and six different types of coffee. She rummaged through her purse anxiously. She could just about do a few hot drinks and maybe a flapjack or something for Jack. It was the least she could do for Daniel, buy him a coffee.

'Did you see, Mummy?' shouted Jack, waving at her as he and Daniel arrived at the bottom of the hill.

Kate put two thumbs up and grinned back.

By the time he and Daniel had trailed up and slid down three times, Kate could no longer feel her feet, which was almost a relief. She knew they were wet through because her shoes were in no way waterproof. She hadn't owned a pair of wellingtons for a few years now, since the old ones fell apart. She didn't mind. She couldn't bear Jack not being warm and dry, though.

'Do you want a go?' he called, as they joined her.

'Yes, go on, Mummy,' said Jack, 'I really want us to all go down together.'

'Will we fit?'

'Of course,' said Daniel. 'Me and Zoe have been on this sledge. It was fine.'

Kate obediently walked up the hill and queued.

'Come on,' said Daniel, sitting on the very back, legs apart. 'You here, and then Jack on your lap.'

Kate positioned herself, between his legs, as far to the front as she could. There wasn't going to be room for Jack.

'You're going to have to get a bit closer than that, I'm afraid.' He put his arm around her waist and slid her back towards himself. 'Sorry,' he apologised, awkward at the over-familiarity. She could feel a blast of welcome warmth from his body heat, even through her coat and jumper. She allowed herself to relax back just a little.

'That's better,' he murmured, his mouth right by her ear. 'Now you, Jack.'

'Yay!' Jack jumped on and pulled his knees right up to his chest, and Kate wrapped her arms around him protectively.

'We aren't going to hit anything, are we?' she asked, acutely aware that Jack would take all the impact if there was a front-on collision.

'No. I promise,' said Daniel. 'Relax. Actually, cancel that. Don't relax. Brace yourself!' And with that, he pushed off.

Kate screeched but, after a couple of seconds, her screech turned into helpless laughter as they bumped precipitously down the hill. They were so low down, the ground felt as if it was absolutely racing past them. She hung onto Jack tightly as he giggled and shouted.

It seemed to go on for ever but then, finally, they slowed a little as the hill flattened out. Daniel put out a leg to slow them and they slid around to a halt.

'Wow,' she said. 'That was, unexpectedly, really fun!'

'I know. You should do more stuff like that.'

'So should you.'

'I need a child to justify behaving like one.'

'You can borrow mine, any time. He's loving it.'

'Thanks, I'll take you up on that,' said Daniel, suddenly serious. He looked at her as if he had just thought of something, looked away and then back again. 'But all the better if you're there too,' he added, watching her face with a flicker of anxiety.

'Sure,' said Kate, a twitch of a smile curling one side of her mouth. She looked down at Jack. He was still game for another go, judging by his beseeching looks at Daniel, but she noticed his hands were mottled red and white and his rosy cheeks were set off attractively by slightly blue lips.

'You cold, darling?'

'No,' he said, sensing an outbreak of sensibleness which should be resisted at all costs.

Daniel sized them both up. 'I'm, freezing mate,' he told Jack. 'I could do with a hot chocolate, couldn't you?'

'Awww . . .' Jack started, but Kate stayed him with a look. 'Poor Daniel,' she said. 'You've been working him pretty hard, you know, and I wouldn't mind a cup of tea myself. Let's go to the café to warm up.'

Seeing he was outnumbered, Jack capitulated. They joined a ragged trail of people heading to the café in the middle of the park. The windows were running with condensation and the outside seating area was deserted, the plastic chairs and tables capped with white snow, most of it marked by the sweeps of little hands collecting it up for snowballs. There were a couple of desultory attempts at snowmen, but mainly the focus was on getting inside and getting warm.

In the long queue, Kate noticed Jack hopping from foot to foot.

'Is that the wee-wee dance?' she whispered.

'Nooo,' insisted Jack, rooting his feet to the ground, but she noticed he started hopping again as soon as she turned away.

'Are you sure?'

'Yesss,' he said, furious. 'I don't need a wee.'

Kate insisted on paying for a double espresso, a cup of tea and a huge hot chocolate with an unfeasibly high swirl of whipped cream, marshmallows and chocolate shavings. Daniel swiftly and surely sliced through the dithering families with the tray in his hands. Like a snake-hipped Italian waiter he wove his way amongst them, miraculously arriving at one of the sought-after tables with padded banquettes just as a family was getting up to leave. He put down the tray by way of marking his territory, encouraging Kate to sit down. After he had helped the departing family clear away their mess, he returned and slid in beside Kate, with Jack beyond her in the corner.

Just as she was gratefully lifting her steaming mug to her lips, Jack announced, 'I need a wee, Mummy.'

'You are kidding,' she said, without rancour. 'Do you want to go on your own?'

A flash of mild panic crossed Jack's face.

'If I take you, we'll have to go in the ladies' loo,' she told him.

'I'm not going in the girls' toilets,' he said, horrified.

Daniel got to his feet but then froze, looking at Kate for approval. 'I could take him if that's okay? You drink your tea while it's hot. Plus, there'll be a massive queue in the ladies. Zoe was always telling me that. She'd make me take her into the blokes' loos. She didn't care.'

Kate laughed. 'Thank you,' she said. 'That would be great.'

Daniel looked relieved. 'Right, come on you,' he said, his hand resting on Jack's shoulder, gently steering him.

Jack had got to an age, already, where he was very reluctant to let Kate touch him in public. If that had been her he would have wriggled away, she thought, watching the two of them walking away: Daniel with his broad shoulders and brown hair curling onto his collar, Jack heartbreakingly small, his bobble hat bobbing up and down as he practically skipped with joy at how his day was panning out.

As they disappeared Kate's phone quacked. It was a text from Seema: *Me and Krish are at Brandon Park, fancy joining?*

Clearly Seema had managed to wangle a day off too, thought Kate, with delighted surprise. Maybe she had eaten a legendary dodgy prawn as well. There was a lot of it about, clearly.

There was a line of three men at the urinals.

'Want to go in the cubicle?' whispered Daniel. He had always found standing at the urinals as a boy a daunting prospect.

Jack nodded and took himself off obediently.

Daniel leaned his shoulder onto the wall and folded his arms. Luckily the cold weather had neutralised the usual smell.

'You waitin' for somethin'?' A belligerent voice sounded close to his ear.

He turned, to see a scowling, bald-headed man in a football scarf. He looked remarkably like a gorilla. He appeared to have no neck and underneath the leather jacket there was a general impression of bulkiness that hinted at some overly macho gym work along with too many pints and pies.

A spirit of mischief filled him. 'I'm waiting for a little boy,' he said, meeting the man's eye and cocking his eyebrow.

The man's scowl deepened. 'I know your type,' he growled, but just then, the lock snicked and Jack emerged from the cubicle.

'Ah, found one,' continued Daniel. 'He'll do.' To Jack, he said, 'Don't forget to wash your hands.'

Gorilla Man turned to Jack. 'Is this your Dad?'

'No,' he replied happily, squirting too much soap onto his hands. 'I just met him.' Jack looked around conspiratorially and lowered his voice, leaning towards the man. 'He told me Father Christmas wasn't real . . .'

Gorilla Man threw Daniel an outraged look. 'Did he?' he said, squaring his shoulders, but after giving it a couple of seconds of consideration, he clearly couldn't decide what to do next. 'I'm watching you,' he told Daniel as he brushed past him, deliberately knocking him off balance.

'Is that man your friend?' said Jack, slipping his hand into Daniel's.

'I don't think so, no.'

'Look who I found?' said Kate as they re-joined her at the table.

'Krish!' said Jack delightedly. 'You've got hot chocolate too? Cool . . .'

Kate introduced Seema to Daniel, kicking Seema under the table as she cooed, 'Well, hello handsome, which Christmas tree did Kate find *you* under?' She held out her arm, hand limp at the wrist.

'Hi,' said Daniel, in return, shaking it firmly.

Kate admired him for not kissing it, although Seema clearly wouldn't have minded.

'Krish and Jack are at school together,' explained Kate.

'Kids are a great way to meet people,' agreed Daniel. 'Kids and dogs, apparently.'

'And how about you?' Seema went straight in, without shame or embarrassment. 'Do you have kids? Dogs? A "friend" you are – how shall we say? – particularly close to? Like Kate, for example?'

'Seema!' gasped Kate, kicking her again, but she just laughed and moved her legs away.

Daniel laughed too, a proper laugh that creased the skin around his eyes. 'No, on all charges, although my sister was with you on the dog thing. She was always pestering me to get one because she said I could use it to pick up random women.'

'Did she want you to pick up random women?' asked Kate, intrigued.

'She didn't want me to be lonely when she . . .' he stopped.

'I'd love a dog,' interrupted Jack, overhearing. 'Mum says we can't, though. Because we live in a little flat with no garden and she's out at work all day.'

'One day we might, darling,' she replied, ruffling his hair, which was spiked wildly now he had taken off his woolly hat. 'One day . . .'

Jack had finished his hot chocolate now, scooping out the last bits of foam with his spoon and then wiping his mouth on his coat sleeve.

'Can we go up the Tower,' he clamoured. 'Me and Krish?'

The Cabot Tower, a brick Victorian folly, stood at the highest point of the park, with a steep, spiral staircase to the top. Kate resorted to it when Jack really needed to burn off energy. The views were amazing when you got to the top. But today the two women groaned in unison.

'You'll kill me,' said Seema to Krishna, his dark brown eyes alight with excitement at the thought. 'I've already done my work-out this week.'

'We can go on our own,' said Jack.

'I don't think so, darling. Surely you haven't got the energy after all that sledging?'

'I have, I have,' his lip wobbled slightly, his emotional state made fragile by too much excitement and too much sugar.

'I'll go,' said Daniel, smiling.

'You can't! It's really a tough climb, believe me. You don't know what you're saying.'

'Listen, I'm a Bristolian,' he said with a laugh. 'I know about the Tower. I've been up those steps man and boy. And I need to get some exercise.'

'Well?' insisted Seema loudly, before Daniel was even out of earshot. 'Where *did* you find him?'

'Have I ever told you how subtle you are?' said Kate. 'That's what I've always liked about you. Your diplomacy. Your tact . . .'

'Yeah, yeah,' Seema dismissed Kate's sarcasm with a wave of the hand. 'Tell me absolutely everything about you and this *über*-fit man. Starting from the beginning.'

Children were fun but God they were knackering, thought Daniel as he and the boys traipsed, seemingly endlessly, up the narrow tower. The climb was always a pain in the arse, the winding stone steps, the squeezing against the wall to let people who were coming the other way get past. Doing all that whilst herding two excited boys had added an extra challenge. At the top, the iron railings seemed inadequate to keep them safe. The usual almost enjoyable rollercoaster lurch in the pit of the stomach at looking down over the edge seemed magnified today, as if he was experiencing it on behalf of his young charges too. He made himself feel better by holding both of them firmly by the scruff as they stood, looking out over the city to the snowy hills in the distance. He hadn't been up here for years. It was worth it. He inhaled deeply, filling his lungs with the cold, crisp, enlivening and cleansing air. Amazing.

'I need a wee,' announced Krishna.

'You go back to your mum and tell her we'll be with you in a minute,' he told Jack as he steered Krishna towards the toilet block.

'So! Now you've got another little boy,' sneered a voice as Krishna disappeared inside.

Daniel turned, and there – again – was Gorilla Man with a triumphant leer on his face. 'I suppose you're going to tell me this one's your son, an' all.'

There was the small matter that Daniel had not, in fact, told him Jack was his son, but he decided to let that one go.

'What's your point?' he said, dangerously quietly.

'My point,' said the man, putting out a finger as if he was going to prod Daniel in the chest but then thinking better of it, 'my point is that here you are, hangin' around a public toilet, again. And this time you can't even tell me this boy's yours – because he can't be, can he?'

The man clearly felt his logic was unimpeachable.

Daniel put his head on one side, pretending to think. 'Sorry,' he said, 'am I misunderstanding, or are you saying – and correct me if I'm wrong – this boy can't possibly be my son because – what? – because he's darker than I am . . .?'

'Yeah,' the man sneered, his head back, lip raised in a snarl. 'That's what I'm sayin'.'

Daniel took a moment. His instinctive response was tempered by the knowledge that Krishna was just about to come out and expected him to be a safe, reliable adult. Instead of punching Gorilla Man on the nose – which would have been extremely satisfying – he leaned in close. 'Right, so I've had enough of you now,' he announced with chilling calm. 'I don't care if you fancy yourself as some one-man anti-paedophile vigilante superhero or what your bloody problem is, but if I hear any more of your vile, nasty, evil-minded and also frankly racist poison I will lose my temper. And this is a family show so – believe me – you don't want that. Got it?'

Gorilla Man paled. For a moment his lips tightened and his jaw jutted, but then he met Daniel's eyes and he recoiled physically.

'Yeah. All right mate,' he said, stepping back, holding his hands up in submission. 'No offence.'

'Mum says Daniel lives on a boat,' announced Jack to Krishna when they got back to the table. It was clear the women had been talking about Daniel, because they hastily shut up when they saw him coming. Kate was blushing.

'Can we go and see your boat?' pleaded Jack. 'It sounds really cool. Mummy's seen it, haven't you Mummy . . .'

'Have you?' said Seema, doing a double take, eyes wide, like a pantomime character.

Kate didn't kick her this time. There was no point; it didn't stop her misbehaving.

'I had a cup of tea with Daniel in his boat,' she said primly. 'It was very nice. I'm not sure I'd like to be there in this weather, though. Aren't you cold?'

'Not with the woodburner,' said Daniel. 'And I'd love you all to come, but it can't be today I'm afraid. Even though the office is closed, I have to do some work this afternoon and then I've got a meeting this evening, so . . . we'll have to arrange another time, all right boys?'

'Absolutely,' said Seema, satisfied. 'I think a trip to the boat is a really good idea, Daniel. I am delighted you are getting to know Kate better. And Jack,' she added.

'Likewise,' said Daniel, winking at Kate.

'See? Dead subtle,' muttered Kate, sarcastically, missing his wink because she was too busy grimacing at Seema.

'Now, I'm sorry guys,' Daniel went on, this time to Jack, 'but I had better get you and your mum home.'

*

He dropped by Paul's house on the off chance that Paul would be home and, ideally, Cara wouldn't. He was in luck.

'I nearly decked the bloke,' Daniel admitted to his friend, troubled at his reaction in the public toilets.

'Not like you, mate,' agreed Paul. 'You're always the one who's all calm and lovely and sweet. At least that's what all the girls who've ever dumped you have said. They all secretly want a bad boy – and that's the truth.'

'I'm just not a "ten pints looking for a punch-up" kind of guy. That's you, if anything. At least it was you before Cara got hold of you and civilised you.'

'A bit harsh, mate.'

'True though, I was always having to get you to let it go 'cos you're tanked up and some bloke looked at you in a funny way, or something.'

'I don't remember that.'

'No, well you wouldn't.'

'So, you felt rage then,' said Paul, returning to the point and away from his own shortcomings. 'Like the Incredible Hulk, all green and bursting out of your shirt, yeah?'

'Yeah, kind of,' admitted Daniel, remembering his altercation with Gorilla Man. Normally he would brush off that kind of episode without it even raising his pulse.

'You know what it is, don't you?'

'Obviously no, or I wouldn't be asking you,' said Daniel with conspicuous patience.

'You're defending them. Defending this Kate girl, her son, her son's friends . . . they're your "tribe".'

'My "tribe"?'

'It's a primal instinct. You may not be admitting to yourself that you feel this connection, but your instincts are telling you to protect her, them, the whole lot . . . They're your people. Your "tribe".'

'Who knew?' said Daniel, wonderingly. 'And the most remarkable thing is,' he admitted to Paul, 'I think you might actually be right about something at last.'

Leaving Paul's house in the snow, Daniel wondered if the meeting between the shop owners at Christmas Steps would still be on, but with their own businesses to run they evidently had to be made of sterner stuff. He reported to the café ten minutes early but his friend from the wedding dress shop was already there.

'Daniel,' she said. 'You came.'

'Grace,' he said. 'I did.'

'This is Daniel,' she explained to the four others who had arranged themselves around the largest table in the café. 'He doesn't really know why he's here, but I thought he should come. He's helping Noel find a new tenant, plus he's got all this inside info about rates and stuff. It's literally his job.'

'Yes, I really am that boring,' agreed Daniel. 'Thanks for having me. I understand things are a bit tricky here at the moment.'

'I'm Adrian,' said a thin, elegant man in his fifties who was wearing an impeccably knotted yellow tie and matching silk handkerchief in his breast pocket. 'You're right. We're glad you're here.'

'You run the gentleman's outfitters?'

'That's correct. It was my father's shop and his father's before him. We've got history. I'm hoping I'm not the one who oversees the end.'

'Me too,' agreed Daniel. 'Have your rates gone up too?'

'They have. All of us have now had letters. It's been a dramatic rise.'

The rest of them nodded in agreement.

'I'm Jenny,' said the woman nearest him, grey-haired but with a youthful yoga-toned figure. 'I'm the florist. The Lavender House.'

'I know the one. I don't know much about flowers though,' admitted Daniel. 'Grace mentioned you own your shop?'

'And I live in the flat above. So, I'm like Noel,' she explained. 'Obviously we aren't worried about rent. We're lucky, but – even so – the higher rates are a blow. I'm already working on narrow margins.' Stifling a yawn, she laughed apologetically. 'Sorry. We florists have early mornings, collecting our stock from the markets. This is a late night for me.'

'I'm Graham,' said a bearded man, coming out from behind the counter and sitting down with the rest of them. 'This is my gaffe. I've seen you before.'

'Yeah, I've been in here a few times. You've got a good memory though. You must see thousands of people.'

'I don't know about thousands, but the footfall's not bad,' he said. 'We have a good reputation locally – it's fine – but if the rents are following the rates, which I'm guessing they will, it's a case of "Houston, we have a problem." I'm not going to be able to sell enough Portuguese custard tarts to cover that.'

'Those custard tarts are good, though,' said Daniel, remembering the ones he and Zoe had always enjoyed with their coffee there. If Graham remembered her, he wasn't saying, and Daniel was grateful for it.

Instead, Graham went on: 'I'd like to do more outside catering for events, small events, maybe up to fifty people – private parties, funerals and stuff . . . I'm not sure we're doing enough to let people know we're up for it, though.'

'I didn't know,' admitted Daniel, 'but don't judge it on me. Like I said, I don't know much.'

'Tell us about rates,' prompted Grace.

'I will,' said Daniel, wrapping his hands around the mug of tea she handed him. 'But first . . .' he looked enquiringly around the table.

'Louise,' said the remaining woman who was sitting next to Jenny. She had striking red hair, green eyes, and a plump, curvaceous figure which her fifties dress showed off to perfection. 'Cakes,' she said, economically, giving him a little wave.

'Ah, yes,' said Daniel. 'Posh cakes. Wedding cakes.'

She nodded with a smile.

'You're an eclectic bunch, then.'

'With one common goal,' said Adrian, 'finding a way to steer ourselves out of this catastrophe waiting to happen. Our landlords don't seem to appreciate that we are trading on a knife-edge here. Christmas Steps is really special. We're a little bit of a tourist draw, but also, these small shops this close to the centre of town are a precious resource for independent traders. There are plenty of big expensive units in Broadmead and at Cabot Circus for the chains and the big boys. Let us keep our diversity here.' Adrian had gone quite red in the face, and when he finished he bowed his head, seemingly needing to collect himself. Daniel guessed he didn't normally allow much to ruffle his demeanour. Louise patted his hand and he turned his head to smile at her gratefully.

'This place is magical,' said Jenny, taking up the theme. 'I don't need to tell you . . . it's Dickens's Curiosity Shop, steep stairs, rickety buildings . . .'

'Tell me about it, with the rickety buildings,' interjected Adrian. 'Our shop's had a leaking roof on the frontage for four years. You don't see hide nor hair of our landlord then, of course. We just have to get the buckets out.'

'It is an amazing atmosphere though,' said Daniel. 'That's what Zoe and I always loved. Do you think the Harry Potter Diagon Alley was based on Christmas Steps? That weird diagonal thing has got to be reasonably unusual, to say nothing of the whole timeslip effect.'

'Might have been. Actually, that's not a bad idea. We could ask. It would be great publicity if J. K. Rowling said it was . . .'

'Aren't we getting a bit off the point,' pleaded Grace. 'The rates? Our landlord?'

'Landlord? Is there only one?'

'Looks like it,' said Grace, relieved they were back onto the issue at hand. 'I've been having a dig around. It turns out me, Adrian, Louise and Graham all have the same landlord, who is – as Adrian has mentioned – not around much. It's an offshore company called Kestrel Properties Limited. Also, we've all got the same lease agreement, more or less, which is not something we all realised before . . .'

Daniel's head had shot up. He was listening intently.

'And there's only two directors. The registered managing director and company secretary's a bloke called Samuel Bird. The other one's Desiree Bird. I'm guessing she's the trophy wife.'

His delightful client. Of course. He had forgotten to check, distracted by being sent on compulsory leave; but now he sighed and wondered whether to confess there was a connection.

'Okay, full disclosure time,' he admitted and then briefly explained his dilemma.

The group were silent for a moment.

'Well,' said Adrian, 'we've got nothing to lose talking to – and in front of – you, Daniel. Perhaps you can even help us. Talk to this Mr Bird . . .'

'As long as you understand I have to be able to demonstrate that I have acted in his best interest and not – well – yours,' said Daniel.

'Sure,' said Grace. 'Hopefully he – and you – will consider it in his best interest not to crush all his existing tenants with unreasonable rents because then it won't just be Noel's shop empty, it'll be all of them.'

'And no major retailer will want to take on these places anyway,' said Jenny earnestly, appealing directly to Daniel now. 'Think about it, you need to tell Mr Bird . . . the access is terrible. We're on a flight of steps, for goodness' sake. The disability access is non-existent.'

Didn't Daniel know it . . . he had had to leave Zoe's wheelchair at the bottom of the steps the last time they came. He had worried about it being nicked, until Zoe pointed out that heavy old dilapidated NHS wheelchairs were hardly sought-after items.

'And also,' Jenny continued, 'deliveries are tricky. I have to park at the top, bring in my stock down the steps and then move the van or I end up getting a ticket. And then, whenever I'm delivering flowers for a wedding or whatever, I have to go and fetch it again to load up. It's a major pain.'

'We all have to do that,' Louise told Daniel earnestly.

'And I take it your client will definitely use the rates rises to justify raising the rent in line with them?' asked Adrian.

'Well, he's not compelled to or anything,' said Daniel. 'There's nothing to say he should.' But he thought, given Mr Bird's inability to see the bigger picture, along with his and his wife's fondness for money, they probably would. 'Has anyone spoken to the council about the revaluations?' he asked. He could at least give them a bit of a steer. Nothing wrong with that, surely?

'I did speak to the valuations officer,' said Adrian. 'He told me all the commercial properties in Bristol were earmarked for a new valuation in a programme rolling out over the next three years. It was unfortunate for us that we were in pretty much the first tranche.'

'I'm sure other retailers in Bristol will be up in arms,' said Grace.

'Hmm, but they aren't yet,' said Adrian. 'Once the big boys with their lawyers and their chartered surveyors get involved they'll doubtless be fighting the City Council on it. But no one will bother with the issue until it affects them and by then, we could all be history.'

'Funny how they picked us first,' said Louise gloomily. 'We're easy prey.'

They all nodded in unison.

'So,' continued Adrian, 'I had a word with the valuations officer about whether the rateable value was wrong. He wasn't keen to suggest it was possible to challenge it, but I bet it is – if I only knew how to go about it. All he came up with was this taper relief thing.'

'What on earth is taper relief when it's at home?' asked Jenny.

'You don't have to pay the full rise straight away. If you're a small business – which I am sure we all qualify as – then you can gradually work up to the full amount over three years.'

'And when do the rents increase?' asked Graham.

'That's a matter for individual leases,' ventured Daniel, and Grace nodded.

'I've already checked that out,' she said. 'We're all in agreements where the rent can go up annually by as much as the landlord wants. It's a pretty crappy lease, actually, on several counts. The next rent review is in April.'

'We'd better make sure we've got a pretty good idea to meet the extra costs by then,' said Graham. 'That's when the rate rises start to kick in too. A double whammy.'

'I'll go back to them,' said Adrian, his chin jutting in determination, 'but I just don't know what to say.'

Daniel sighed. 'Tell you what,' he said, feeling guilty that it was his client signing the death warrants of these businesses, 'why don't I put a little exploratory call in to the valuations office myself and see what gives? I'm probably not going to be able to do anything, but there are a few questions I wouldn't mind asking.'

They all looked at him with hope in their eyes, which made him regret his offer instantly. 'I really don't think I can change anything but – like I said – I probably ought to do it for my client anyhow.'

'Your client Mr Kestrel whatsitsface?' asked Grace.

'Sam Bird. And Noel of course,' he said quickly. 'Clients'.

'Business gets quite good for us from April,' said Jenny, sounding a little more upbeat. 'It's the start of wedding season.'

'Talking of weddings,' said Grace. 'I've been thinking.'

They all turned to her expectantly.

'Look,' she went on, 'I have no magic solutions, but we need to think about how we can pull together. We are together anyway. We all support each other informally, that's why I love it here, the way we help each other out with loading and unloading, covering each other's opening hours when we need to and all that.'

''Course we do,' interrupted Graham. 'When we can. And I really appreciate it too. I appreciate all of you,' he said, unnecessarily ferociously to hide his emotion. 'We're like family.'

'Exactly,' Grace went on, her eyes shining with tears. 'Exactly. You're like my dad.'

'I think he was hoping he was more like your brother,' commented Adrian drily and they all laughed.

'Aaanyway,' Grace went on, grinning in spite of herself, 'as I was saying, like a family we all have different strengths, different skills to offer, and I just realised last night that actually we all cleverly manage to not step on each others' toes at the same time as – amazingly enough – having a rather large thing in common with one another.' She looked around the room expectantly, willing them on.

'We're all on Christmas Steps?' said Jenny, confused.

Grace looked frustrated. If she seemed like an earnest school teacher right now, they were a particularly dense class. 'Nooo, well, yes we are – but also . . .' she paused for effect and Graham jumped in.

'We all do weddings,' he said.

'Yes,' said Grace, triumphant. The class was not so thick after all. 'That's right. We all do weddings. At least we don't *all* do weddings but, when you think about it, we all have a little bit of our business that is, or could, contribute to the planning of a wedding.'

'I see what you mean,' said Louise excitedly. 'Obviously I'm doing wedding cakes – not just wedding cakes but, to be honest, they're the bit of my business that pays the best, especially since everyone started having piles of cupcakes or croquembouche instead of the tiered option, the profit margins on them are good . . .' She trailed off, and then brought herself back to the point. 'Anyway, so yes, obviously weddings are bit key for me; for Grace that's all she does; Graham, you said yourself just now you'd like to do catering for outside events . . .'

'Yes, but small ones,' he said. 'We're not kitted out for giving a four-course dinner to two hundred guests.'

'God forbid,' said Jenny, 'that's the last sort of wedding event you'd want. Nightmare. Anyway all the big hotels that cater for those sorts of numbers have their own in-house catering. What you'd be brilliant at is the quirky, smaller events where people hire unusual venues and have boutique-type affairs: afternoon tea for sixty people, that sort of thing.'

'That would be brilliant,' said Graham. 'I could do a Champagne tea, with sandwiches, savouries, little meringues. I wouldn't want to do the main cake though.'

'I should hope not,' said Louise, mock sternly. 'That's my department.'

'And I especially love doing the flowers for those sorts of things,' interjected Jenny, enthusiastically. 'You can get a license to get married more or less anywhere nowadays. I did the flowers for the most glorious wedding in the physic garden by the ruins at St Peter's in Castle Park last summer. It was really beautiful.'

'I'd love to do that. What about if it rained?'

'Buy some canopies, a marquee or something,' suggested Adrian, totally entering into the brainstorm. He thought his role in the wedding theme was probably marginal, but Grace had other ideas.

'Adrian, you should be providing a service for the grooms,' she said. 'Even if they're hiring their own morning coats, or if they've got them anyhow, you should be working with me and Jenny and the bride because, let's face it, she's the one making the decisions – her and her mum usually. The bride tends to want to know that the groom and his team are going to fit in with the theme. You should be providing cravats and handkerchiefs.'

'Brilliant!' said Adrian. 'And I sort of already do. I think I mentioned to you,' he said to Grace, 'that a couple of your clients came into my shop last month and gave me one of the best day's sales that I've had in a while.'

'There you go,' said Grace. 'And socks.'

'Socks,' he said, picking up instantly. 'Socks are a big thing. I've found an amazing new sock supplier who will dye socks to any colour out of about, I dunno, fifty shades.'

'Excellent,' said Jenny. 'I'll recommend they come to you as well, to get accessories that match the flowers.'

'So, there we are,' said Grace. 'We boost each other. We maybe even do one of those wedding shows, the exhibitions. They're usually early spring because so many people get engaged over Christmas and Valentine's Day.'

'They're expensive though,' said Louise doubtfully. 'I looked at doing the biggest Bristol one last year, in a fancy hotel out of town, but even a tiny stand was a huge price.'

'Sure, I know. I've looked at it too,' said Grace. 'But we've never looked at doing it together, sharing costs . . . persuading brides that Christmas Steps is the only boutique, exclusive, one-stop wedding shop in the city.' She held her hands out wide. 'Whaddayathink?'

Daniel realised after he got back to the boat that he hadn't asked the Christmas Steps crew for their advice about Noel's shop. It was clear though that it was going to take a very special person to take it on. Now he understood. They were a family. His job was to find the missing part of that family, so they could all work together. The wedding idea was a brilliant one, he thought. Not being an avid shopper and reacting in horror to the thought of having to shop for some girlie wedding plan made his heart sink but he could see how having everything together could work. An integrated, bespoke, boutique service. It was a winner. So, that meant he was looking for someone who filled a gap in that service.

But what? He might need to ask Cara. She was a girl *and* she was planning her wedding to Paul. She would know.

Kate, like Daniel, was also in reflective mood. Seema had been an absolute pain but she thought her friend would be proud that she had witnessed her doing something silly, joyful and Christmassy. With a gorgeous man in tow, too! That should get her off her back a bit. She relived the moment when Daniel had pulled her back against him on the sledge. That had been delicious, and she had been touched almost to the point of tears seeing him so easily and naturally interacting with the boys. How amazing it would be to have someone to share the ups and downs of life with. She could see that, but could she ever replace Tom? She had always been proud to say he was the love of her life, but proudness could be stubbornness too, couldn't it? Sometimes, just recently, she had been wondering whether the true point of this ridiculous Christmas exercise was to loosen up enough to realise that there was a life beyond her marriage to Tom. Maybe.

Jack, tired out from the sledging and the running around with Daniel and Krishna, had been fractious and argumentative that evening. Soothed, eventually, by the routine of supper, advent calendar and bedtime, he had been heavy-eyed and potentially tearful by the time she had tucked him up in bed.

'I like Daniel,' he said, sleepily. 'He's nice. Can we see him again?'

'He is nice, monkey boy. There are lots of nice people like Daniel. We can have them all in our lives, can't we? Seema is nice. Helen is nice. Mrs Akintola is nice, isn't she? She's going to be babysitting you in a couple of days, so I can go to my Christmas party at work. You like her too, don't you?'

'Yeah,' said Jack, uncertainly. He definitely did like Mrs Akintola, although she was sometimes a bit too keen on big hugs. Being engulfed into her vast, cushiony chest while she exclaimed over his gorgeousness was an acquired taste.

'She's not a daddy, though is she?'

Kate paused, and thought carefully. 'Daniel isn't a daddy, sweetheart,' she said. 'You only have one daddy, don't you?'

'But he's nice though,' Jack insisted.

Once Jack was asleep, Kate turned on the radio and immersed herself in her jewellery-making. She had enough stock, hopefully, to satisfy Anastasia and her friends, but it wasn't just about having enough. She knew from experience it was about having more than enough so that people felt they were choosing their favourite thing. Over the last few nights she had concentrated on the cheaper items such as the friendship bracelets with a single semi-precious stone, along with labels explaining what each of the stones represented. There was beautiful striped green malachite for confidence – she could probably do with more of that – and then there was moonstone for intuition and patience, pretty pink rose quartz for love and trust, and so on . . . Actually, she thought as she worked, the friendship bracelets, with their coloured cords to match or contrast with the stones, could be the little project Anastasia wanted her to let her friends do.

Talking of which, she should stand up for herself more. Maybe that should be her new year resolution: to say what she felt and not take any crap. Taking crap had been a bit of a theme over the last four years. Where was the old, confident Kate, whose passion and energy had made Tom laugh, marvelling at her determination. 'You'll always achieve whatever you set your mind to, girl,' he would say fondly. 'I pity the man who gets on the wrong side of you. Never mind our semi-automatics, if we had you in Afghan the dissidents would run away screaming . . .'

'Thanks,' Kate had said wryly at the time, but she dared herself to wonder what Tom would make of her efforts now.

That night she dreamed more vividly than she had done for months. She and Jack were in a house she didn't recognise, but somehow she knew it was their home. She was in the kitchen preparing salads for a barbecue. The sun was shining in through the open French windows into the garden. It had a stone-flagged patio leading to a wide lawn with a football goal on one side and a discarded boy's bicycle. There was a deep bed of flowers on the other side against the brick garden wall. In it she could see lavender, blowsy roses, tumbling honeysuckle and other plants Kate didn't know. She could even smell the cut grass warmed in the hot summer sun. There was a barbecue on the patio and a man in a striped apron, like the one Tom used to wear. But it wasn't him. She couldn't see the man's face, but Jack was laughing and messing around with him and a shaggy brown dog, who was barking excitedly. Kate smiled in her dream. This was the life she wanted. Simple things. And then there was an insistent thrumming noise, a rushing sound, like a shower. She looked up to the ceiling in this mysterious house she was in but then realised the noise was from outside. She looked back into the sunny garden and was dismayed. Rain was falling, blurring the garden into grey. The sky was dark, like evening, the water was pelting the rose bushes, ripping off the petals as she watched. The stone patio was now dark and slick and there was nobody there – no dog, no man, no Jack.

17th December

Kate woke with a lurch of dread. The rain which had invaded her intriguing new dream was real. It was sluicing down her window, washing away the grime from the street and darkening the dawn sky as if it were still night time. The snow had disappeared, save for mounds of brown slush in the gutters, even that fast disappearing as the cars swished down the street.

School would be open. Jack would be devastated.

'But it's your nativity today,' she cajoled.

'Oh yeah . . . the camel thing.' He thought. 'I don't know my lines! Mrs Chandler will tell me off. She always tells me off.'

'You have lines? But you're a camel! Why didn't you tell me? What lines?'

'They're at school,' Jack admitted. 'In my drawer.'

'Well, they're no good there are they? Never mind. I am sure Mrs Chandler will let you practice today. I'm really excited about seeing you.'

Jack drank his milk unenthusiastically.

'Anyhow, what do you mean Mrs Chandler always tells you off? I didn't think there had been anything recently . . . has there?'

'She keeps putting me outside,' he complained. 'And I haven't done anything.'

'She puts you outside the classroom?' said Kate, her anger with Mrs Chandler gathering strength. 'Does she now?' Clearly Kate would need to have a word with Jack's class teacher about that.

'Come on monkey boy. We've got to go. You're at Helen's after school too, remember?'

'Can't I go to Krish's house?'

'Nope. You've got to go to Helen's. You like Helen's.'

'Awwww.' Jack dragged his feet and swung his arms, but Kate ignored him carefully. 'What's my Christmas thing today?' he said, distracted by the lack of response.

'You saw it last night, silly. It's your nativity play. Doesn't get much more Christmassy than that.'

'What is it tomorrow?'

'Oi, that's not the deal. You find out about tomorrow before you go to bed, don't you? Not now.' Damn, that was another thing. What was his Christmas treat tomorrow? She would have to have a look at the dwindling list. Hopefully something would pop up today and she could slip it into the advent calendar tonight.

Daniel was feeling flat. He stared at his computer screen unseeing, his coffee growing cold beside him. She hadn't been there when he walked down the street that morning. Instead, there was a large young man with short-cropped ginger hair, hefting the eight-foot trees around as if they were cocktail umbrellas. He was no substitute and Daniel was missing his little daily dose of Kate; not Christmas Tree Girl any longer, but a living, breathing woman with a name. Paul was going to be proud of him. That said, when he had dropped Kate and Jack at home the day before, he had flaked out of asking her when he would see her again. Paul wouldn't be proud of that. Maybe Daniel wouldn't mention that bit.

He cast around for something useful to do that didn't require concentration he didn't have. Remembering his meeting with the Christmas Steps crowd last night he picked up the phone to his contact in the City Council valuations office.

'Geezer!' said Gideon when Daniel announced himself. 'What can I do you for?'

'I suspect, and sincerely hope, that you can't "do me" at all,' said Daniel and briefly explained.

'Ah yeah, bigger than me, this revaluation thing. The councillors have got it into their heads there's "gold in them thar hills" and they're determined. It's a whole City business rates review. A huge amount of work . . . I don't expect any sympathy but I'm working my knackers off here, for no more money, and – as an added bonus – everyone hates me.'

'They hated you before, to be fair,' Daniel teased, 'I'm sorry to break it to you but it's your job. On the "most hated" list you're kind of up there with politicians and estate agents. I sympathise, though. I'm nearly an estate agent so I get a bit of that myself sometimes. Was it you that did the work on Christmas Steps review?'

'It was, as it happens,' Gideon admitted. 'They don't fit the criteria, I grant you. Such a strange little place to value. Square peg, round hole . . . I wasn't overly impressed with the maintenance on a couple of the properties. I gather the landlord isn't keen on keeping repairs up to date, which is a bit short-sighted if you ask me . . . If I was looking at the quality of the space, not just the size and location, I might have come up with a different result. So, yeah, funny place: on the one hand terrible access, tiny units, crappy buildings, on the other hand amazingly close to the town centre. I've got to tell you I could have landed them with an even worse result. If I valued them on Cabot Circus rates per square metre, they'd really have something to complain about.'

'I think they feel they already do,' said Daniel. 'Thanks, though mate. I appreciate it's not down to you.'

Next, Daniel put a call in to his client Samuel Bird:

'Mr Bird,' he said, once they had got the usual niceties out of the way, 'I have been studying your portfolio and I think I may have spotted an opportunity that might be of interest to you.'

'Go on, son, spit it out. I'm a busy man.'

Daniel started with the rateable value changes in Christmas Steps properties and before he got any further, Mr Bird interrupted.

'There you go, son, the intuition never fails. I don't mind telling you, I snapped up the freehold on those units for a song. I was clearly right about them being a bargain. Well, you know the drill, roll out rent rises on the next renewal date. I'll have the full amount they're worth, thank you very much, the rateable value is the peg.'

'Or . . .' said Daniel, when he could get a word in edgeways, 'as the canny businessman you are, I am sure you would be prepared to consider other ways to optimise your investments – ways that may well pay even better dividends in the long run. I mean,' he gambled on Mr Bird's ego getting the better of him, 'I wouldn't suggest this to all my clients. With the majority of them you just have to keep things simple, if you know what I mean. They don't have the business acumen you have . . .'

'All right, all right, flattery will get you everywhere. What are you actually suggesting? To beat a frank rent rise it's goin' to 'ave to be bloody good, young man . . .'

Daniel explained the boutique wedding service concept, dropping in the idea that holding the rents down for now could net him a better return in the long run. He also hinted at the possibility that Mr Bird could be the *Dragon's Den* benefactor who would cannily see the opportunities and get the credit, as well as the payback, when the idea took off. He wasn't entitled to suggest anything of the sort without Grace's and the other shop owners' permission, but he was sure they would agree if the deal was right. There was a price tag on the branding and marketing proposal she was proposing, and the money was going to have to come from somewhere.

'All right laddie, I'll admit, I'm interested enough . . . but I was only with you a couple of days ago. Why didn't you mention it then?'

'I didn't know,' Daniel explained. 'It's all for the taking at the moment – a fresh idea – but I don't think the opportunity will be around for long once other investors get to hear about it.' In for a penny, in for a pound, thought Daniel. God knows he had stuck his neck out just as far as he was able without breaching the chartered surveyors' rule book. From his own point of view, he really didn't fancy having to find a whole new set of tenants for his client once he had ruined and bankrupted the ones Mr Bird already had. It wouldn't help anyone if that happened, including poor Noel.

'All right, I'm interested,' Mr Bird said, with no warmth. 'I'd better meet these idiots then, hadn't I? And soon too, if you're suggesting someone else will step in.'

Kate had had to rush to the Apple Café because she had been late leaving work. Mr Wilkins had grabbed her as she was gathering herself up to leave. He wanted to tell her she wasn't selling enough trees that week, which seemed unfair as sales always tapered off this close to Christmas. Most people had theirs by now – though not she and Jack, admittedly. Her boss's narrow grey eyes glinted meanly in his fat, red face – his skin like corned beef from too much alcohol and rich food. 'Remember your contract renewal,' he said, scanning her up and down appraisingly, 'I think you definitely need to make yourself more amenable, young lady. Yes, more amenable.' He half-closed his eyes and leaned his head back. 'To customers as well.'

Kate shuddered as she relived the conversation. She was half running along the street to the café, feeling the water from the puddles seeping through her shoes.

She burst into the shop. 'Sorry! I'm here at last . . . I couldn't get away . . .'

Brian was sitting at one of the little tables, like a bear at a dolls' tea party, overspilling from the dainty little chair on all sides. Kate was astonished it would hold his weight. She was so preoccupied with this thought, with her lateness, with the cold, that she barely registered the broad back of the man sitting opposite him. But then she clocked the brown wavy hair curling onto the collar.

When he turned it was like coming home. She met his smiling hazel eyes with her own.

'Hello stranger,' he said. 'Fancy meeting you here.'

'You know each other?' said Brian, in surprise.

'Sort of,' explained Kate. 'I might have guessed though. Did Zoe work here?'

Daniel nodded. 'I've not been back much. At all. It's a bit weird. Brian thought I might be useful with this fundraising thing, but I don't know . . .'

'What, you mean "We've got a crisis quick, call a chartered surveyor",' she joked.

'Yeah, exactly.'

'Beth's coming in soon,' said Brian to Daniel. 'I thought I'd better warn you.'

'Ah. Thanks. It'll be good to see her, but . . .'

'Weird?' suggested Brian. 'It's been long enough. You've both got to get on with it. Speak of the devil,' he added as they heard a door at the back of the shop close with a distinctive thunk.

They waited, listening to chatter they couldn't quite distinguish, and then the young woman that Pat and Kate had met the other day came through into the café area.

'Beth,' said Daniel, standing up. 'I know . . .' he added as he saw the tears springing from her eyes.

Her face crumpled as he spoke, her mouth making an upside-down smile of misery.

'Come here,' he said, holding out his arms.

She went towards him and the two of them folded together into a hug. Beth barely came up to his chest. Her arms, wrapped around his body, could not quite meet behind him.

He spoke softly into the top of her head and they rocked gently together for long seconds, the silence broken only by the young woman's sobs.

Kate felt herself welling up as she watched.

'Beth and Zoe were really good friends,' Brian explained. 'It's been hard for her.'

'I really miss her,' Beth wailed, pulling away a little so she could see Daniel's face.

'Me too,' said Daniel, wrapping her tighter. 'Me too . . .'

Eventually, gradually, Beth's sobs abated and Daniel let her go, handing her a napkin to dry her tears. 'Where have you been?' she demanded in her gruff voice, mopping her face.

'I know. I should have come sooner,' he said, sitting back down and gazing after her as Beth returned to the back of the shop, muttering that she had cooking to do.

'Yeah,' said Brian. 'You should. So anyway, now you're here you can make yourself useful. Kate, what do you need us to do?'

'Well, it's just to follow up on the conversations you had with Pat the other day, Brian.'

'Wonderful woman, that Pat,' acknowledged Brian, stroking his beard.

Daniel and Kate exchanged a smile.

'She certainly is,' said Kate. 'So, there's the bake-off and the mince pie giveaway . . .'

'Giveaway?' interrupted Brian. 'Can't we sell them?'

Kate shook her head, regretfully. 'No, I double-checked with the legal guys and it's tricky. But we can ask for donations. The main thing is to get the team here, along with Portman Brothers staff, to give away the mince pies outside the store and to get these flyers into people's hands, showing them where you are, your offer, your opening hours, that kind of thing.'

'Flyers,' said Brian. 'That's the thing . . .'

'That might be something for me,' interjected Daniel. 'If it's a simple design – what? – one third of A4, something colourful, visuals and a grabby headline on one side, map and opening hours on the other.'

'Sounds perfect,' said Brian. 'And we'd need perhaps a thousand?' he looked at Daniel apologetically.

'I think two thousand,' said Daniel. 'No harm in having some left over. I am sure they'll come in useful.'

'Also, don't underestimate how many people we could reach,' said Kate. 'Honestly, on a Saturday morning leading up to Christmas, you can barely move for bodies outside the store. I should have thought two thousand was definitely more like it.'

'I reckon you need five thousand then,' said Daniel. 'My firm will cover the costs. I'll have a word with our directors. Maybe we could have our logo on the bottom somewhere?'

'Done,' said Brian and Kate simultaneously.

'And you mentioned Saturday, so I assume you mean this Saturday?' he said, getting out his phone and tapping in a note to himself. 'That's not long.'

'Last Saturday before Christmas, so that'll be the one,' said Brian.

'Sorry,' said Kate. 'It's all been a bit last minute. Is that going to be okay?'

'Three days? I'll make it work,' said Daniel. 'Blimey, it's less than a week 'til Christmas then, you know.'

'I do,' said Brian. 'You can come and help. Beth would love to have you there. If you still need to do Christmas shopping, and I bet you do, we might let you sneak off and do it.'

'I've not really got anyone to buy for this year,' said Daniel. 'I'd better get something for Paul and Cara. They're getting married, did you know?'

'I didn't,' said Brian. 'Congratulate them for me, could you?'

'Brilliant, so that's the mince pie giveaway. I was thinking about maybe carol singing too, but that might be complicating things unnecessarily.'

'Agreed. It's better that the public has a chance to chat with staff rather than hear them sing, although Beth, for one, has got a sweet little singing voice, when she gets over her shyness. You don't want to hear this one giving it "Good King Wenceslas", though, I can assure you,' he added, indicating Daniel with an inclination of his head.

Kate giggled. 'No singing then. And the next thing is the bake-off competition,' she said, scribbling a note on her notebook.

'Logistically, it's better our staff do their baking for entries here. And perhaps Portman Brothers staff could do theirs at home. We just need to sort out the categories, and actually . . . he reached into his pocket and extracted a folded piece of paper, 'I just put this down,' he said, spreading the paper on the table for them all to read.

'Five categories,' read Kate. 'Christmas cake, mince pies, stollen, raised game pie, signature bake. Cool.'

'Pat and I decided there would be no entry fee; we don't want to put people off. But they have to donate everything they submit for judging, and we'll raffle it all off afterwards.'

'How about an auction? Better than a raffle, surely?' said Daniel. 'I've got a friend who's an auctioneer. I'll get her to come with her gavel. We'll do it in the store?' he looked enquiringly at Kate.

'I think the Board would love that. They're the ones with the deep pockets. I'll make sure they're all there. It'll create a bit of a buzz in store too.' Kate was scribbling it all down, then she had a thought. 'We need to let the local media know.'

'I'll do that,' said Brian. 'I'm onto them often enough about other bits and bobs, usually to no avail,' he admitted. 'You grow a thick skin running a charity. But I think they'll like this.'

Kate was glancing anxiously at her watch, hoping the two men wouldn't notice. She had to get home and get changed, then get to Jack's school in time for the nativity. The last thing Jack wanted was his mum turning up in an elf costume. She felt enough of a tit having to wear it to the café because she hadn't had enough time to change.

'So, we're pretty much done, aren't we?' said Daniel, noticing her anxiety. 'I should maybe get together a quick poster for the bake-off competition entries too. For the staff here and the staffroom at Portman Brothers?'

'Brilliant,' said Kate, getting to her feet. 'That would be fab. Thank you.'

'I'll do it tonight. I could drop it off with you tomorrow morning? I'm not supposed to be at work – enforced holiday – but I've been "allowed" to come in for the monthly staff meeting at nine.'

'I won't be there when you come past,' said Kate, regretfully. 'My shift starts at ten tomorrow.'

Neither of them wanted to suggest he drop them with Pat, or just into the store. Daniel thought for a beat.

'Jack wants to come and see the boat,' he said. 'Why don't you both come after school tomorrow? I'll be there, wondering what to do with my time . . .'

Kate sighed and the tension in her shoulders fell away. 'Perfect,' she said. 'I'd like that.' The thought that it would be only a day until she saw Daniel again filled her with a sense of relief. Again, there was that feeling: the one that made her daydream about how lovely it would be to have someone in her life. A grown-up someone, as obviously she had Jack.

But then, instantly, there was a feeling of guilt that she was allowing herself the possibility of replacing Tom. She never could. It was as simple as that. Best to weather life alone than face that possibility of devastating loss again, surely?

She barely had time to get back to the flat to change, but she did it anyway because going straight to the school would make her early and it wasn't her favourite place to hang around at the moment. A quick shower and change, putting on warmer clothes, and she was back out of the door, checking her watch anxiously. Just let there be a bus . . .

*

236

Anastasia and her cronies were giving Kate a wide berth. It puzzled her slightly, but she didn't care. Instead, she waved back at Seema, who was indicating through extravagant gestures that she had saved Kate a place. It was the front row, in the already steamy and hot assembly hall that doubled as the school dining room and still smelt of cabbage and mince from lunchtime. At least the children were too young to make it smell of sweat too, Kate always thought when she was in there: it was the school's gym too. She was sure Greystone Manor didn't have to overuse its spaces in that way.

'Check out the school gate mafia,' said Seema as Kate sat down. 'What gives?'

'You noticed too? I dunno . . . I thought I was just being paranoid.'

'Yeah, you probably are. They can have that effect on a girl after a time. I can't believe you're doing that jewellery party for the old witch and her coven.'

'Shush! I just want to make some money from them, that's all. I'm not exactly doing it for love. Have you been invited.'

Seema gave her a beady look. 'What do you think?'

'Pole position, eh?' Said Kate, changing the subject. 'You must have been here very early. Well done.'

'What, this? Far from it. I've only been here five minutes, but I fought my way to the front. There was violence involved and some lives lost but it can't be helped. Needs must.'

'You didn't,' said Kate with a grin.

'No, I didn't,' Seema admitted. 'Krish was a bit anxious about being late. They both were, so I've been here for absolutely bloody ages. I've rehearsed Jack's lines with him too. I can't promise he'll say the right words but – let's face it – a talking camel's pretty memorable whatever it comes out with.'

'He was a bit nervous. Thanks.'

'You're welcome. Look,' she said, pointing to the classroom window. 'I just saw one of them.'

Kate waved, and a little hand waved back. It was Jack, his entire head encased in her excuse for a costume.

'Good effort again with the costume,' said Seema, mind-reading.

'I try.'

'You're a good mum.'

'Do any of us actually think that?' asked Kate, genuinely. 'Do we all think we're crap mums where actually we're good? Or at least okay? Not "good": let's be realistic.'

'Hey, hey!' said Seema, deep concern in her eyes. 'You've never been a crap mum. You're the best. Where is this coming from?'

Kate sighed, and wiped away the sudden tears. 'Nothing. I'm fine.' She looked at Seema. 'I'm fine,' she repeated.

The nativity play was enchanting. Or at least Kate thought it was. You probably had to be a parent or grandparent to enjoy it. The old tale, comforting in its familiarity, was played out with the usual clunky mishaps and errors. The set threatened to topple over, the innkeepers forgot their lines, little Mary – in her flowing blue gown and looking like butter wouldn't melt – had no discernible maternal skills, picking up the Jesus doll by one leg and then plonking it back in the manger to the hilarity of the audience. Jack and Krishna, being with the wise men, didn't turn up until near the end, but once they were there, all eyes were on them, or so Kate and Seema imagined. They stole the show with their special, loping camel walk and their heads weaving in an exaggerated camel-like manner when all the other actors were obediently standing still. They were especially animated during 'We Three Kings of Orient Are', where they gave it their all, to everyone's amusement. Kate actually got to hear Jack say his lines twice, because he initially did them too soon, and then just repeated himself when the correct cue came along.

And then Mrs Marshall arrived on stage and they all had to sit through the interminable thank yous for absolutely every member of staff who had contributed in the slightest possible way and – almost as an afterthought – a thank you for the children. That got the biggest cheer of all, partly because the audience knew it was the last one.

'Forty-five minutes,' said Seema, checking her watch.

'Felt like longer,' commented Kate, thinking of the unappealing bus ride home.

'I'll drop you both off,' said Seema.

'It's not on your way.'

'I'll drop you,' she said firmly. 'You look exhausted. I hope you're taking some time off over Christmas. Proper time off, that is.'

'I might be taking more than I'd like,' admitted Kate, briefly telling Seema about Mr Wilkins's comments on the matter earlier that day.

'That's disgusting,' Seema said. 'He can't go around saying things like that.'

'As long as no one hears him, he absolutely can,' said Kate. 'It's his word against mine . . . and anyway he hasn't actually done anything. It's just talk.'

'I don't like the direction it's heading in,' said Seema. 'I think you should look elsewhere.'

'Easier said than done,' said Kate, in despair. 'It took me weeks to find that job.'

'It was the right job at the time. Maybe now it's time to start setting your sights a little higher?'

'Maybe,' said Kate, glumly. 'It would be nice to think I have a choice.' Seema was right, though. She should be looking for another job right now but she had her head in the sand. They couldn't sack her, surely? She had been a perfect employee. She would keep her head down and it would be all right. It had to be. She had too much else to think about at the moment, with Jack's schooling, her jewellery, the care home . . . Kate groaned aloud and then saw her friend looking at her, concerned.

'How's the Christmas miracle project going,' she asked gently.

'Not well,' admitted Kate. 'Not well at all.'

18th December

'Cooee,' came the shout, as Kate was giving Jack a big cuddle, prior to pushing him in through the door of the classroom. It had taken all of her strategies to get him dressed, fed and in through the school gates with her. She was propelling him forward both physically and mentally with every ounce of her being. It could go either way.

'Cooee, Kate,' came the shout again. Jack gave her one last clinging, intense hug and went inside, encouraged – thankfully – by the realisation that Krishna was already there and waiting for him.

Kate straightened reluctantly and turned.

'Anastasia!' she said. 'Sorry, I was distracted, just getting Jack in, with all his stuff, crucial moment, you know how it is . . .'

'Yah, yah,' said Anastasia, 'mine don't make a fuss, I'm lucky.' Her tone clearly indicated that she didn't think herself lucky. Her children were superior. That was why. And so was she. 'I was trying to grab you last night . . .'

No you weren't, thought Kate.

'. . . just to say I don't need you after all for the jewellery party.'

Her heart sank, but she wasn't going to show Anastasia her disappointment. 'Really?' coolly. 'It's quite short notice.'

Anastasia's face hardened. 'You say that, but it's just a casual arrangement between friends and I imagine you've got a lot of other things to think about what with Christmas, and Jack's, well, Jack's "issues". So, I had a call from a company who send people out to run chocolate parties. You know, you can buy chocolate gifts at really good prices. Very good quality stuff. Lots of samples obviously. I mean, you can see the attraction, can't you? Who doesn't like chocolate?' she gave a high-pitched giggle. 'Anyway, I just couldn't get a date when all the other girls could make it. We're all sooo busy, with all the Christmas parties,' she rolled her eyes, 'so I gave them your date.' She examined Kate's face again dispassionately. 'You should come.'

'I won't, thanks,' Kate ground out through gritted teeth. 'Like you said, lots of preparation to do. Christmas coming and all that.' Not that she could afford Christmas now, mind you. Not now she had tied up whatever spare money she had possessed in the materials for stock she no longer had the opportunity to sell.

'Suit yourself,' said Anastasia, with a cruel little twisty smile and turned on her heel, going back to join the group at the gate. Kate thought the cold might cause them to disperse a little earlier than usual, to retire to their coffee shop where they would generally gossip the morning away before whisking off to their gym class or manicure, or whatever else they did to amuse themselves on the average Thursday morning. Doubtless they were making the most of their last days of freedom before the school term ended tomorrow.

They all turned to look over at her. She stared brazenly back. What did she have to lose? She had taken a lot of crap at the school gates for Jack's sake. And now they were kicking him out anyway. Which reminded her of another thing. After her altercation with Anastasia she was up for a punch-up and she was keen to find out exactly what Jack was referring to in his frequent exclusions from the classroom.

'So, Mrs Chandler *is* sending him out of class. It's true,' stated Kate.

Mrs Marshall wasn't quite so keen on such unequivocal statements. 'It is true that – according to our records – Jack has been removed, briefly, on occasion. I am sure this can be no surprise to you given our recent discussions over Jack's needs,' she said. 'I think it is indicative of the question over how suitable the school is to meet those needs that we find ourselves resorting to those measures.'

Kate regarded her thoughtfully. 'Would you say Jack's "needs"' – she even made the air quote gesture, in defiance – 'have grown since, say, the beginning of this term?'

'I . . . no, I don't think so,' said Mrs Marshall, not quite knowing where the conversation was going.

'No, nor would I,' said Kate. 'I mean, these sudden discussions brought to me over his apparent unsuitability for the school have started this term, even though he's been at the school for more than two years already. But, as you say, he hasn't suddenly become a different child. In fact, if anything, Jack is coping better emotionally as time has gone on. Wouldn't you say?'

'Yes,' agreed Mrs Marshall sulkily. 'I suppose you could say that, although I would return to the previous point, which is the policy for schools to wait until year two to see how children with different needs are faring in the classroom. In Jack's case, his issues have not resolved sufficiently and that is why we feel his needs are best met within the framework of an EHCP.' She dredged up her reassuring professional smile with difficulty.

Kate counted to ten. 'Right,' she said. 'Please will you look in your funny little naughty book' – she indicated the register on Mrs Marshall's desk – 'and tell me the total number of times Jack has been sent out of class this term in comparison with an average term during the previous two years.' She paused. 'Actually, don't even do that,' she amended. 'You're bound to say different class teachers have different styles and all that bollocks, in which case I would remind you this is Jack's second year with Mrs Chandler, because she had him in reception too.'

Mrs Marshall blinked, surprised, at Kate's more than usually robust language.

'So,' Kate continued, 'what I want you to do is compare and contrast an average half term's worth of exclusions from the classroom in the past with how many times he's been sent out in the last six weeks. Bearing in mind,' she held up an admonishing finger, 'you have just specifically told me you agree his behaviour has not deteriorated recently. In fact, it's probably got better. You said so yourself.'

By this time Mrs Marshall had gone noticeably pink. She bent her head to her records and using a biro, totted up the numbers.

By the time she finished, she had gone even pinker. 'I really don't think this is a particularly illuminating exercise, but it would seem,' she admitted, 'that the number of *brief*' – she stressed the word – 'classroom exclusions have increased during this half of the term.'

'By how much? Give me specifics?'

Mrs Marshall cleared her throat. 'He's been sent out most days,' she admitted. 'Sometimes twice.'

'And before?'

'Fewer, I'll grant you . . .'

'You've been trying to set him up as a bad child,' said Kate, tears of rage barely contained. 'You can't wait to get rid of him – probably because he's stuffing up some poxy flipping league-table aspiration of yours – and so . . .' she stumbled, pressing her hand to her lips to stem the furious flow of words, 'so, you are all racking up disciplinaries to support your random contention that he should go to the PRU. Because you don't want my boy, and you're prepared to go to any lengths . . .'

By this point, Kate's heart was hammering so hard she thought it might burst out of her chest. She was filled with a rage so elemental, so overpowering, all she knew was that she had to get out of there. Out of the office, the building, away from Mrs Marshall's simultaneously obsequious and disapproving face. She got up, grabbed her rucksack and left.

Thank goodness the school-gate posse had dispersed during her all-too brief meeting inside. It was only when she was marching down the street that her heart began to settle a little. She felt lighter the further she got from the school but had to resist the urge to run back to him and scoop up Jack. How could they reject him in such a cold, devious, underhand way? Her boy . . . whom she loved, and would crawl over broken glass for, who had already had such sadness in his life, such trauma . . . Hot tears streamed down her cheeks as she walked, or marched, along streets she didn't know. Gradually her walking slowed, and her tears dried. She must look a fright. She was in a mean, shabby neighbourhood now. People stared at her oddly. Three men in hoodies loped towards her, staring as they passed. But at least they passed. She took a deep, shuddering breath. Right. What would Tom do? She went into a greasy café on the corner of the street and ordered a cup of tea. While she was waiting she went into the rank-smelling customer toilet, with a grimy basin and a toilet with a missing lid, to wash her face.

Back where her tea was waiting, she placed her hands on the table top and thought. One thing at a time, that was what Tom had taught her. Pick your battles. Know your enemy. So, Jack was clearly going to be leaving his school. She would kick the arses of those who had behaved appallingly later, when she was stronger. At the moment, the priority was to find him a new school. Somewhere that would care for him and nurture him. She had not given up on Greystone Manor but was still waiting for the LEA to pronounce on whether it was prepared to fund it or argue that the PRU met his needs. Thoughts of Jack in a Pupil Referral Unit made Kate want to sob all over again, but she pulled herself upright. As Mrs Marshall – or someone – had said in that meeting, the PRU was remarkably well resourced. They had been positive. Given that it might well be where Jack ended up, she should at least see it. Maybe it wouldn't be so bad.

She googled the number and called.

'Of course, Mrs Thompson, I believe we have been sent some information about Jack. We look forward to meeting him . . .'

'I'm not saying you will.'

The lady paused. 'Perhaps you should bring him here, so you can both see . . .?'

'He's not coming,' said Kate, decisively. 'Not unless he has to. But I will.'

'Good!'

'Can I come now? Please?'

The PRU was a series of low, flat-roofed buildings – sixties architecture – in the midst of a housing estate.

She followed the signs to reception, taking the opportunity to peer in through windows as she went. She saw no children, oddly; just bare rooms with lino floors and minimal furniture, extremely neatly arranged. And then she looked more closely. Chairs and tables were bolted to the floor. So that was why. Nice.

An intercom on the external door was answered after a delay. She couldn't understand what the person was saying, but she announced herself and that seemed to do the trick. Buzzed inside, she found herself in a vestibule, but still blocked from entering the school by another locked door. To the left, a hard-faced woman was sitting behind a reinforced glass screen, with holes punched in it at face height, like a ticket booth in a railway station. When staff are the bearers of bad news or bad attitudes or the purveyors of bad service, Kate reflected, a physical barrier to offer protection from the general public becomes a health and safety necessity. This woman had the kind of face a few people would take exception to.

'I'm here to look around. I'm a parent.'

'Well, you're not a pupil,' said the woman, rudely. 'Wait there. I'll send someone out.'

The 'someone' was the headteacher herself, introducing herself as Ruth and providing a firm handshake.

'Thanks for calling. I've read Jack's report. I can understand why you are nervous. I hope I can set your mind at rest. Let me show you what we do.'

The school looked much like any other, but smaller. The institutional smell of cabbage and overcooked mince was present and correct. There was a library just off the main atrium. There was also a small room – a pod with curved walls – sitting in the centre. It had bright pink painted walls and piles of brightly coloured cushions. No furniture. There was a lock on the door. A padded cell, essentially, Kate thought. She wondered how often it was used and why.

There were lines of classrooms either side. The explanation for the absent children was that they were all having lunch in the dining hall. Kate peered in, with Ruth at her shoulder. The children were lining up, choosing their food, finding places to sit. So far so normal. The most notable thing about it all was the number of adults who were dotted around the room, sitting beside the children.

'You're looking at all the staff,' commented Ruth. 'That's the one biggest difference between us and other schools,' she said. 'We have a fantastic staff-to-pupil ratio. About one to three, actually, or four . . .'

Suddenly, there was a commotion at one end of the room. A tray went flying, a chair was tipped over and there was a scream, a long-drawn out bellow of rage, frustration and pain. A pale child with a shaved head and drawn features was standing by the window, swearing with a fluidity and imagination that belied his tender years. Quickly he was surrounded by staff making pacifying gestures with their hands. They were guarded and watchful, gauging the situation second by second. This lack of action and overbearing adult presence seemed to enrage the little boy even more and his face became a contorted, red mask of misery, screaming so loudly Kate could barely hear the voice of the male teacher who had appointed himself chief envoy. Several seconds past and then – as if there had been a signal between the staff, which there probably had – three of them moved in on the boy, pinning him and lifting him from the ground. They travelled together across the room, the boy in their midst, still screaming. Ruth and Kate stood to one side as they bundled him into the pod. By the time they had done this, he was less being contained by them and more clinging to them. But they peeled him off, dumped him on the floor and swiftly exited, slamming and locking the door behind them. Two of the staff then took up a vigil, standing either side and intermittently looking through the glass at him.

'Sorry about that,' said Ruth, who was clearly unmoved. 'This is a boy who hasn't been with us very long. He has, as you can see, quite severe emotional and behavioural issues. Shall we . . .?' she added, gesturing with her hand to the classroom nearest where they stood.

For the rest of the tour, Kate was distracted. She vaguely took in the well-appointed computer room, the library, the outside space with play equipment and the gym, which was also, Ruth explained, a good, secure space for children who needed to work off excess energy. 'The staff can bring the children in here at any time during the day, if that's what they need. We find it a useful outlet for aggressive and destructive behaviours. Very valuable.'

Kate peeked into the little secure pod room as they went back past on the way to reception. The little boy was now curled up on a pile of cushions, his face streaked with tears and snot. He was alone.

'So,' said Ruth, as they went back through the security lock to the holding cell that was the reception area, where the sour-faced woman behind the grille was temporarily absent. 'What do you think? Can you see Jack thriving here?'

Kate thought about the little boy in the pod. Whatever the psychoanalysts' theories said about helping boys with his issues, as a mother she knew what she wanted. She wanted to go into that room and hug him, comfort him, wipe his face, blow his nose and care for him like the little boy he was. He couldn't be more than two years older than Jack, although she had seen a look in his eyes that wouldn't be out of place on a person three times his age.

'No,' she said. 'I don't see my Jack here. I don't see him staying at his old school either.' She raised her hands in a helpless gesture and let them fall again to her sides.

Ruth stood regarding Kate in silence for several long seconds: 'Mrs Thompson,' she said, 'I feel for you. And I agree with you. And let me tell you this,' the older woman held her gaze and continued: 'As a parent you know your child. Don't let anyone bamboozle you to thinking otherwise. The authorities will do the least they can, as cheaply as they can, to make a pretence of meeting your child's needs. They have an obligation to do that, you know. A legal obligation. Parents' opinions don't count for much in all that, but I see something in you that tells me your opinion should be valued. That puts Jack at an advantage over most of the children here.'

She turned to the keypad by the door and punched in a code. The door opened and she stood to one side.

'And don't quote me on that,' she added, as Kate left.

'Will we ever live on a boat?' asked Jack as they walked down the wooden jetty towards Daniel's narrowboat. Kate was holding his hand tightly as he skipped along. The water seemed far too close and accessible for her liking, the grey-brown river surging powerfully below and around them like the rippling muscles of a sleeping leviathan.

'I don't know, darling. We might do one day. We might sail away somewhere wonderful, where it's always sunny and warm.'

'Where there are palm trees!' said Jack.

'Yeah . . . And monkeys – lots of monkeys . . .'

That would be nice, she thought, shivering in her thin coat. She had brought Jack straight from school and the temperature was dropping as night got ready to fall, the light already dimming into dusk though it wasn't even four o'clock.

The row of windows down the side of *Wonderland* glowed invitingly. He was in. She sighed in relief and relaxed her clenched jaw just a little.

'Ahoy there,' she called as she lifted Jack carefully onto the little fore deck and stepped down gingerly herself. Beneath her the boat barely moved, just rocking gently, almost imperceptibly . . . a soothing lullaby. She imagined curling up in Daniel's bed at the front of the boat and being rocked gently to sleep for years and years.

She shook herself. And then he was there, reaching up to lift Jack into the cabin and then turning to help her down the steep, wooden steps.

They were inches apart – there wasn't much choice in the tiny cabin – and he leaned over to kiss her cheek as if it was the most natural thing in the world.

'Wow, you're cold,' he said.

'It's just my face,' she replied, but then gave away her lie with a convulsive shiver. 'I'm fine, really.'

'You sit closest to the stove,' he said, leading her by the hand. 'Jack, you need to make sure you don't touch this, okay?' he said gesturing to the little black stove. 'It's really hot, like a radiator only much hotter.'

'It's got fire,' said Jack delightedly. 'It's like a fire in a box. I love your house, it's really cool.'

'It is really cool,' agreed Daniel.

He was smiling delightedly at Jack as he explored the cabin, marvelling at the tiny kitchen, the neat little bedroom at the end, the way the toilet and shower were tucked in, looking as if they were just cupboards, leading off the narrow corridor. Daniel was so absorbed it gave a chance for Kate to observe him. He had a childlike joy in sharing his world. He was patient, encouraging and sweet with Jack. It reminded Kate of Tom. But he wasn't Tom. There was a softer, more emotionally available vibe about Daniel. It was impressive. And attractive. She allowed herself another little daydream, a gentle prod of her psyche to explore the possibility that she was able to soften and yield enough to allow the idea of a romantic relationship with a man who wasn't Tom. Who wasn't the love of her life. Could it ever work?

'Penny for them?' asked Daniel, turning, smiling to see her gazing at him.

'Sorry. I was staring . . . You remind me of someone I used to know.'

'Someone you liked, I hope.'

'Yeah,' she said quietly. 'Someone I liked.'

'Tom?'

'Yeah.'

'I'm honoured.'

'You're not the same.'

'You will never find someone who cares about you the way Tom did,' he ventured.

'No.'

'But what about someone who cares about you as much as Tom did,' he said, watching her face intensely for her reaction. 'That could work, couldn't it?'

Kate was stricken. She squeezed her aching head with both hands. 'I don't know,' she said.

He nodded. 'Okay, look, I need to show you these flyers. I hope they're okay, I got the Portman Brothers logo from your marketing department and I ran it by them too.'

'Perfect,' said Kate, relieved at the change of subject and looking at the flyer he handed her from the top of the box on the little table.

She felt warm now, and as she relaxed she sank into the little sofa, and a deep weariness flooded over her. Daniel noticed.

'You look like you need a good night's sleep.'

'Ah, sleep, what's that?'

'You and Jack should stay here one night,' he said, tentatively, determined to return to his earlier theme. 'You could both take the big bedroom. I could sleep on the sofa here. Why not come when I'm moving the boat? I do that for a couple of months in the summer, usually, I go down river to this place that's a bit quieter. Things get a bit hectic here in the middle of town during tourist season. I prefer to avoid it.'

'Jack would love that. So would I.'

'Kate?' Daniel looked at her, his eyes softening. He didn't need to say anymore.

'I know. I just . . . I don't know whether I can.'

'No pressure. We could take it slow.'

She sighed, a deep, weary sigh, breathing out all the tension and pain and misery of the past four years. Looking at this lovely, kind, gentle man, who was gazing at her with such tenderness. It made her want to cry.

'Not now . . .' she said at last. 'I can't do it now. I'm sorry.'

Daniel hung his head. 'That's what I thought you'd say.' He smiled. 'I'll stick around though, Kate. You're not getting rid of me.'

'Mummy! Look at the toilet!' exclaimed Jack. 'It's metal.'

'Well that certainly breaks the mood,' he said, turning away.

'We should go.'

'What are you doing tonight?'

'Ah, well, I was supposed to be doing a party at another school mum's house,' said Kate, briefly explaining the last-minute cancellation.

'She sounds like a horrible woman,' said Daniel, in wonder. 'So, you have all this jewellery stock and nowhere to sell it.'

'That's about it,' admitted Kate. 'All my money tied up in jewellery I have no way to sell, so Christmas just got even harder.'

'That's awful,' said Daniel, his mind churning, looking for possible solutions. 'At least that means you're free this evening after all.' He brightened. 'I'm meeting friends for supper. They're really nice. You should come.' He ducked his head, tentatively, nervous for her reaction.

'Won't that be the exact thing I've just said we're not doing?' asked Kate. 'Acting like we're . . .' she hesitated over the word, 'together?'

'No, okay, stupid idea.'

'It really isn't. Wasn't,' she insisted. 'It was kind. But I can't, not least because I would need someone to look after Jack. I've got my landlady babysitting him on Saturday so I can go to my work Christmas party.'

'Always a joy, those things,' he grimaced.

'It's politically necessary,' agreed Kate. 'I need to be seen.'

'We'll do something though,' said Daniel, meaning it. 'You, me and Jack. What about getting a Christmas tree? You'll need a hand, with no car.'

'Yay! Christmas tree,' said Jack, who had previously been ignoring their boring adult conversation. 'We haven't got our one yet, have we Mummy?'

Kate pulled a comedy face, relieved the intense mood had been broken, for now at least. 'Thanks for that,' she said with a hint of sarcasm. 'That's another thing . . .'

'Offer her the empty shop unit, you idiot,' said Cara, once Daniel had brought them up to date on his complicated week, 'The Olde Sweet Shoppe, durr brain. It can be a bespoke jewellers.'

'What, jewellery? Really?'

'It's weddings, isn't it, dumbo?' she went on. 'God, you boys, you need telling everything.'

'Lucky we've got you then,' said Paul, amused. 'Don't savage him too viciously. He's in lurrrve. It's addled his brain.'

She sighed, gathering her patience noticeably. 'As you've just explained, the shop owners surrounding it are offering a one-stop wedding service. You have a florist, a dress shop, a cake shop . . . yada, yada . . . Nowhere in your story have you mentioned a jeweller, and yet how can it be a complete service without engagement rings, wedding rings, presents for bridesmaids . . .'

'What?' asked Paul. 'Presents for the bridesmaids? Is that a thing?'

'Obviously.'

'Yes, but jewellery-type presents? I mean . . . that sounds expensive.'

'It's the norm.'

'So, are we . . .?'

She dismissed him with a crushing look. 'Aaanyway, obviously,' she said to Daniel as she held up one finger, 'they're going to need a jeweller.' She held up two fingers. 'You know a jeweller.' She added a third finger. 'Your client needs a tenant.'

Daniel pulled an 'oh yeah' face of dawning clarity. 'She's quite good, really, isn't she?' he said to Paul.

'She has her moments.'

Cara took a swig of wine and plonked her glass back on the table decisively. She had one more message to deliver. 'And tell her I'll get my friends together for a jewellery party.'

'What? Like the one her delightful school gate "friend" flaked on?'

'The very thing,' said Cara. 'Wine, chat, buying stuff . . . usual format. Tell her I'm in. I'll get texting. It needs to be before Christmas, though; no point otherwise. Gosh, it nearly *is* Christmas, isn't it? Ask her if she can do it.'

She got out her phone and tapped the screen a few times. 'It's going to have to be Tuesday. That's okay, my lot are hard-arse, they can drink Prosecco any night. Most of us are on our Christmas holidays by then anyway.'

'This is a "girls only" thing, isn't it?' Asked Paul nervously.

'Yeah, don't worry, I won't let them loose on you. You and Daniel can keep your heads down. Why don't you both go out and do some late-night Christmas shopping or something? I know for a fact you still need to buy my present.'

'I do,' admitted Paul, looking at Daniel with relief. 'We're sprung, mate, do you fancy it? We can get the present-buying done and reward ourselves with a bevvy.'

'That would be brilliant,' said Daniel, relieved that he wouldn't have to help or anything. He suspected the emotionally unstable dipsomaniac Hayley might be there, and he wasn't sure he had the energy for that again. There was only one emotionally unstable woman he felt he had the energy for, and that was Kate.

'So, wake up! When are you going to tell her you've done a blinding knight-in-shining-armour number? That'll seal the deal, won't it? Me and Cara are fed up with you mooning around after her. Get in there.' He made an unmistakable gesture to illustrate his point.

'Idiot,' said Daniel, without heat. 'I'm not at all sure I'm handling this thing right, but I'll ask her to meet me tomorrow.' He brightened at the thought. They would talk. He would apologise for being a numpty – for pushing her to give him an answer too soon. Then, he would transform her immediate prospects by telling her about the jewellery party. Then, he could see about transforming her entire life forever by telling her about the shop. He was pretty confident Noel would love her, and she would love Noel. So . . . big plans.

19th December

It had been a while since she had had the dream. She had missed it, even tried to will herself into having it again, desperate to immerse herself in those moments of happiness and warmth, seeing his face, feeling his love. Like crack cocaine she wanted it, even though the shock and pain of awakening was all the more painful for the moments of bliss that preceded it.

This was not the one about the barbecue on the patio that had dissolved, so recently, into rain. The dream was the one she had had a hundred times about Tom's last day before leaving for the last time, with the bright sunshine sharpening the shadows and bleaching out the colour of the roses Kate had planted in the front garden. Even though they never stayed anywhere longer than two years in a succession of services quarters, she had always planted roses.

'I'll bring you back some camel shit from Afghan,' he had joked. 'Apparently, it's rocket fuel for roses, camel dung is. Hopefully then we'll actually see some flowers before we move on to the next house.'

'I don't mind,' Kate had said, smiling at his teasing. 'Jack and I like gardening, and I like the thought we are giving something lovely to the next family who live here. Army quarters' houses would never have nice gardens if people didn't take that attitude.'

'People don't take that attitude. Only you do. That's why the gardens we move to are always so crap.'

'One day,' said Kate, shyly. 'We'll have our own house one day, won't we? With our own garden? I want Jack to grow up with a garden.'

'We'll plant an apple tree,' said Tom, slipping his hand around her waist. 'Better still, we'll find a garden with an apple tree already in it. For the tree house.'

'The tree house?'

'Like the one I had,' he said. 'Before we moved out of our old house. You never saw . . . it was brilliant. All boys should have a tree house,' he said, taking Jack from her arms and spinning him around until he squealed, 'shouldn't they, Jacko?'

'We've just had lunch,' she protested. 'You'll make him sick.'

There had always been a sense of unreality on the leaving days. They generally woke up early. Kate, trembling with nerves, had usually lain with her eyes pinned open for hours anyway by the time Tom would bring them both a cup of tea to drink in bed. Jack was invariably in the bed with them by then, squirming, pulling hair and inadvertently poking them both in the eye. His antics were a welcome distraction from what was to come.

The commanding officers were kind on leaving days. Generally, the troops wouldn't have to report to barracks until a little later than normal. Most of them were family men, leaving young wives and children; some were younger still, barely out of school themselves. If it was their first tour, Tom and the more experienced soldiers would work hard to support them, subjecting them to even more brutal and relentless banter than usual, carrying the frightened young men along with them on a wave of positivity and energy so they had no time to crumble or doubt.

She hated the round black clock in the kitchen on those days. There it was, implacably marking out the minutes, as he shaved, showered, packed his bag, checked his kit, all the seconds ticking away until he hoisted his pack onto his shoulders, put on his cap and walked out of the door, giving Kate and Jack one last fierce hug before turning away. That last time, on that seeringly bright summer's day, he had stood, frozen for a moment in the doorway, his big frame and broad shoulders silhouetted against the light. She had held her breath. Clenched her fists. And then he was gone, marching down the little pathway with a bouncing athletic stride. The possibility he might not return had barely ever been discussed, but that time, on that fiercely hot day, it had been true.

Her leaving date had been negotiated with reasonable tact. The Army was keen to ensure she felt well-enough supported by them, as an army widow; that she would not complain afterwards. Not publicly anyhow. As always, when she left the quarters, on checking-out day, the officer came with his clipboard to make sure she had not stolen anything or damaged the property. He had seen the round, black clock sticking out of a bin bag and asked about it.

'Is it broken?'

Kate shook her head.

'Shall I take it then? Give it to someone else?'

She nodded, but seeing the silent anguish on her face, he had left it there, untouched.

Her dream always ended the same way, those final moments, when Tom paused in the doorway and then turned away. Up until that point, the story varied. Sometimes they were having breakfast together, the three of them; sometimes, in her dream, the garden in the quarters was magical in the way dreams can make it: a whole acre of garden, rather than the mean, scrubby rectangle . . . flowerbeds, vegetable patch, rough grass dotted with wildflowers and, at the far end, a wide, low, gnarly old apple tree, with a platform of wood offcuts forming a rough treehouse. Cradled in its branches, a rope ladder swayed from its fixings, moving gently in the breeze. That was the version of the dream she liked best. This time, when the story played out its ending – when Tom lifted his kit bag, opened the front door, stood on the top step, framed against the light – she braced herself to wake as she always did, and he turned to face her as he always did.

This time it was Daniel.

The text from him came in just as she was kissing Jack and posting him in through the classroom door, keen to get away from the mummy clan without making eye contact. Putting her hand into her coat pocket to fish out her phone, she also encountered the wodge of post she had grabbed from the mat on the way out of the door that morning.

First, she read the text. It was Daniel: *I've got an idea. Come to Christmas Steps this afternoon at 1.00 p.m.? Purely business, no funny stuff, I promise. Daniel (no kisses as unprofessional, but would otherwise, despite our discussion).*

She was intrigued. At least he was still speaking to her, not put off by her rejection of romantic entanglement yesterday. She put the phone back and yanked out the fistful of mail, standing next to the rubbish bin by the bus stop where she now stood so she could get shot of the rubbish. Which was probably all of it.

There were two invitations to apply for a credit card she couldn't afford to take out, and one for payday loans that she probably – at this rate – couldn't afford *not* to take out. They went in the bin along with an advert for a local pizza and kebab shop. Then Kate was left with a slim, white envelope, franked rather than stamped, with *Private and Confidential* printed on the front in red.

FAO: The Parent or Carer of Jack Thompson, it read.

On the reverse, the sender was identified as *City Hall, Bristol.* With trembling fingers, and with a swift look left and right to ensure her pain or her triumph were not witnessed by any of the toxic mums, she slit it open.

Dear Mrs Thompson, we are writing to inform you that – further to our evaluation of the educational needs of Jack – we have declined your request for this child to attend Greystone Manor on the grounds his needs are met at Peartree Pupil Referral Unit. We are therefore able to confirm that a place will be made available at Peartree PRU from the beginning of the Spring Term . . .

It was signed Lorna Evershed, Head of Educational Special Needs Resource.

Words burst from her. 'Bloody civil servants, fat salaries, tiny brains, non-existent hearts,' Kate railed aloud, not caring now who heard her. 'My boy . . .' she said, her diatribe interrupted by a sob.

She looked at the letter again. Who was this Lorna Evershed woman? Wasn't that Sheepface from the meeting at the school? Her name began with an L, definitely. Kate read the whole letter again. The paper was shaking in her hand, whether with cold, anger or fear she couldn't tell. She scrunched it furiously, pulling back her arm to hurl it into the bin with the rest of the rubbish but then she took a deep breath and dropped her arm. It was as if she could feel Tom standing beside her. 'You end it now, and they've won,' she could hear him saying. 'Fight.'

She pulled the scrumpled up paper straight, tearing it a little, the signature of this Lorna woman jumping out at her. There was a telephone number there too. A direct line, or so it claimed. Expecting a voicemail, Kate tapped the number into her phone.

'Hello? Lorna Evershed speaking. How can I help?'

Kate nearly dropped her mobile. Damn. She had no clue what she was going to say. It was definitely Sheepface though, the dreary, monotonous voice was unmistakable.

'I think you are wrong,' she blurted. 'My son Jack. He needs your help and you are . . .' She searched desperately for the words; tried even more desperately not to cry. She took a deep, shuddering breath. 'You can't send him to the PRU,' she said, hating the pleading note in her voice. 'You don't know him. He won't survive there. I need him to go to Greystones, he needs to go there. Why won't you help?'

'Mrs Thompson,' said Sheepface heavily, 'we *are* trying to help. We have assessed Jack's needs, we have evaluated the options, and we have allocated a place in a suitable setting . . .'

'But the most suitable setting is Greystones and you are supposed to have a legal obligation – I thought you did . . .'

'We don't have to provide "the most suitable" setting, we only have to provide "*a* suitable setting" and we have determined the PRU to be suitable.'

'So, what would it take to get Greystones? You fund children to go there; who are these children?'

'I believe the local authority funds a tiny number of children at Greystones. I personally have not done so.'

'I bet that makes you popular. If there's some kind of bonus system for saving the authority money I reckon you win it every time . . .'

'I will ignore that remark.'

'I apologise, that was rude,' Kate said with gargantuan restraint. 'But please tell me – what have these children got that Jack doesn't?'

'It is likely the children have similar educational needs,' admitted Sheepface. 'But you have to understand, some of these children also have additional challenges that Jack certainly doesn't have. They may, for example, be "looked after" children . . .'

'"Looked after"?' said Kate, incredulously. 'Jack's "looked after", for heaven's sake! What on earth do you mean?'

'Mrs Thompson, of course you look after Jack,' she said with studied patience. She even had a slight bleat to her voice now she was getting nervous, a vibration that added even more to the sheeplike qualities. 'It is the very fact you look after Jack that means he is not a "looked after" child. These are children who have either lost their parents or been taken away from their parents. I am sure you can appreciate these children require and deserve additional care. I gather there is a tiny handful of children at Greystones who are in this category and they are, therefore, fully funded by the local authority. Naturally.'

Kate hung her head, her phone still clamped to her ear. So, it was her very presence as Jack's mother that was the hurdle between him and a place at the only school where he felt he belonged, the only school where they seemed to instantly know how to tap into the mind of her beautiful boy . . .

'Okay,' she said at last. 'Thank you. I understand.'

'How ridiculous,' exploded Pat, when she heard. 'What absolute nonsense, to think they are weaselling out of their legal responsibilities on a ridiculous sleight of words. "*Most* suitable" and "*a* suitable"! It makes my blood boil. I would go and see our MP if I were you.'

'I could make a fuss,' said Kate, listlessly, 'but I don't think that would help Jack, and there's no getting away from it

. . . he has – well – not "parents", but at least a "parent" and that means he doesn't take priority.'

'I'm going to contact Ursula, that's what I'm going to do,' she continued. Kate's blank acceptance and lack of fight concerned her. She had never seen her friend so limp and defeated.

'I don't think there's any point . . .' she began, but then she was distracted by a buzz from her mobile in her pocket. She fished it out.

You didn't reply. Don't forget, it's Christmas Steps at 1.00 p.m. This is not a date, I promise. Daniel. X

There was a rueful smiley face emoticon too.

'Are you all right, dear,' said Pat.

'Yeah, yeah I'm fine. It's from Daniel.'

'I hope he's asking you out.'

'He's texted to say he's not asking me out, actually.'

'How odd. Well, I think it's a shame. He's a lovely young man, from what I've seen. Was he really just texting to say that?'

'No, he says he can help with something.'

'Then let him.'

He accepted her point about no romance – he really did – but just being around Kate felt great. And Jack was great. And anyway, one day she would be ready for a new relationship and, when she was, he would be there. So that was great too.

As he walked down Broadway to Christmas Steps, he allowed himself to drink in the holiday atmosphere. For the first time that month, the idea of Christmas didn't fill him with black despair. Instead, the twinkling lights, the comical penguins and snow slides in the window of Portman Brothers, with the animated snowball fight – who even knew penguins could throw snowballs with their funny little short flipper arms – made him smile, just a little bit. Zoe would have loved it. For the first time he began to see that 'would have loved' was enough, that it might one day be okay to allow your mind to remember someone who was gone and that the sadness could perhaps be bittersweet, rather than annihilating, a heartfelt nod in honour of moments much missed.

What did he always say to the people he spoke to on the hotline? These were the people who could not see a way out of a pain so overwhelming that permanent oblivion started to look like an attractive alternative. He would tell them to stick with it, and that things would eventually get better. That's what he always said. Maybe he wasn't talking complete bollocks after all.

And there was Grace, coming out of the wedding dress shop, as if on cue to meet him.

She was crying.

'It's Noel,' she said as Daniel raced up the steps towards her. 'He's in hospital. I found him this morning. He'd been lying on the floor all night.' Her face crumpled, and tears sprang anew. 'In the cold,' she sobbed. 'I thought he was dead.'

Daniel gathered her into his arms. She was tall, only a couple of inches shorter than him, but he hugged her, holding her tightly for fear she might sway and fall down the steps.

'They think he might have had a stroke,' she wailed, freeing a hand from his embrace so she could fumble a tissue up to her streaming nose and eyes.

'Thank goodness you checked on him.'

'I know! I don't usually . . . I just had a feeling . . . I generally glance in, just through the door, to make sure nothing's happened, that it hasn't been broken into or anything.

You never know, when places are empty, squatters can go in and set fires or whatever . . . But I just saw his foot sticking out from the kitchen at the back. I so nearly overlooked it. He would have just laid there alone . . .'

'But you found him,' Daniel said, rocking her gently. 'Where's your partner?'

'Megan? She's gone off to a wedding supplies trade fair. Won't be back until late tonight. I wanted to go up to the hospital with him, but I have to keep the shop open. I'm expecting a couple of clients to drop in and collect things.'

'I can go up,' he said. 'Not straight away. I'm meeting Kate here and then I've got your landlord Sam Bird coming around with – well – with his bird.'

Grace smiled at the weak joke.

'Let's hope his bird's into weddings.'

'I assume they're already married,' said Daniel regretfully. 'Her name's on the limited company information as director. It's a tax dodge, I imagine. I can't think he lets her actually have any control,' he chatted on aimlessly, distracting her as he led her back into the shop.

'Who's Kate?' she said.

Daniel thought. 'In this context,' he said slowly, 'she's a potential tenant for Noel's shop. And . . .' he paused for effect, 'she's a jeweller.'

'Fab! Perfect! I can't wait . . . Where is she then?'

Kate didn't come. Daniel was checking his watch anxiously while he and Grace had coffee from the café. She positioned him behind the counter with his paper cup, as far away as possible from the white clouds of dresses on the rack. 'You can't be too careful,' she explained apologetically. 'A customer brought a child in with a Magnum ice cream once. It cost a fortune in dry-cleaning . . .'

'You definitely can't trust me with a chocolate ice cream,' agreed Daniel, sipping his coffee and placing it down with emphatic caution onto the countertop.

'So, tell me more, who's this Kate then?'

'You'll see. You'll like her. But I'm worried I've messed up the arrangements,' he said, checking his phone for the umpteenth time in case he had missed a text from her. Nothing. No reply to either.

'Mr Bird is going to be here soon. Then I won't get time to look after Kate. I've tried too hard to multitask.'

Grace tutted. 'You don't want to do that multitasking thing,' she said. 'You being a man, and all. You can always hand her over to me. Noel gave me the keys. I'll show her around and we can talk about the wedding group plan.'

Daniel spun around as he heard the shop door clunk open, thinking it must be Kate at last, but through it came Mr Bird and his companion, who was tottering on the highest of high platforms, with laces crossed all the way up her perma-tanned legs to the knee. Above them was an alarmingly brief skirt and then Daniel, allowing his eyes upwards only reluctantly for fear of what he would see, encountered a pair of breasts that only just spared onlookers a sight of the nipples. Realising he had been openly scanning her bare essentials, he swiftly looked away without meeting her eye, but gained a general impression of thick black lashes, full, shiny lips, and a quantity of blonde hair that was unlikely to be natural on grounds of both colour and quantity.

'Eying up Bird's bird, I see,' guffawed Mr Bird, slapping Daniel on the arm with painful enthusiasm.

'Sorry,' said Daniel, shaking his head vigorously to dispel the horror of the image of him and Mr Bird having sex with the same woman. 'You must be Desiree,' he added, holding out his hand. 'I mean, Mrs Bird. Sorry.'

'Is she like as 'eck,' said Mr Bird loudly, laughing even harder. 'She wants to be, ah don't doubt, but I've barely recovered from paying off my last wife. I can't afford another divorce just yet, young man.'

Daniel blushed. 'God, sorry,' he muttered to the woman, meeting her eye at last in apology.

She gave him an embittered look and turned away dismissively. 'You know I'd love to, Birdy-wordy,' she simpered, stroking Mr Bird's arm, her long, red talons threatening to rake his abundant flesh. Actually, she might have just been grasping his arm for support. Even in the shop on a level floor she seemed to be teetering. Perhaps they had both had a liquid lunch, he thought.

Grace caught his eye, and turned away, bowing her head as she did so. He wondered if she was crying again, seeing her shoulders shaking, but then realised she was barely managing to stifle her mirth.

'I'm Cheryl,' said the woman crossly to Daniel. 'Desiree's his *ex*-wife. I don't look anything like 'er. She's about sixty for a start.' Cheryl looked hugely put out.

'So, go on then, lad, what's the big idea,' said Mr Bird.

Daniel briefly explained but then handed over to Grace, who quickly overcame Mr Bird's incredulity that someone so young, so female and with such extraordinarily coloured hair should know something about business.

'That's impressive, lass,' he said at last. 'I like your thinking. So, what do you want from me, exactly?'

She faltered, glancing at Daniel for support. 'Well, money I suppose,' she said at last. 'At least not straight away. What we really need from you now is a stay of execution on the rent rises.'

'I'll hold down your rent for two years, young lady, but no longer,' said Mr Bird. 'After that, we'll see.'

Grace nodded gratefully, sagging with intense relief. 'And that's for all the units you own here?' she added, suddenly remembering.

'I'm not sure my other tenants are quite as persuasive as you, but – yes – go on then. How many have I got here?' he asked Daniel.

'Four,' said Daniel. 'You own four out of the six shops involved in the wedding team.'

'Fine,' he said, heavily, 'but I'll want something else from you all too.'

Grace raised her eyebrows expectantly.

'In return for a twenty per cent share of your profits for the next five years, I'll fund your first year's marketing plans.'

'What, totally?' said Grace, astonished. 'The rebranding? The printing? The wedding fair?'

'Everything you've just told me about, lass,' he confirmed.

'I don't know if the others will agree,' she said doubtfully.

'Ask 'em. And we'll see. It's all or nothing because I'm not interested in buying into some half-arsed underfunded pie-in-the-sky scheme. I've not made my money from that over the years, and things aren't going to change now.'

'Birdy,' said Cheryl, stroking his arm and tilting her head appealingly, 'this is all lush. This is class, this is . . .'

'Your point being?'

'Well, if we were to . . .' she cocked her head at the wedding dress rail, smiling in what she presumably thought was a beguiling way.

'Now look what you've started,' he accused Grace, who gave him an artless grin.

'What sort of shape were you thinking?' she said, addressing Cheryl alone and throwing Daniel a naughty look which lasted a micro-second, so Mr Bird couldn't see. 'Are you after a princess dress with a full skirt? Like Jordan's one when she married Peter Andre, do you remember? Only maybe not pink . . .'

'Yeah, no, definitely,' said Cheryl. 'I loved the pink, it was gorge . . .'

'Okay,' said Grace, blinking, 'or we could do a mermaid with a fishtail, that's really elegant . . . with your figure you could carry anything off. How about a sheath dress, dead simple and classy?'

The two men looked at each other helplessly. 'Get me out of here, lad,' said Mr Bird.

'Looks like the wedding group have found their first clients,' Daniel replied, trying and failing to keep a straight face.

Kate was relieved when her shift ended. She didn't stop to have lunch like she normally would – Marmite sandwiches from home to save money. Instead, she changed out of her elf costume, grabbed her rucksack and decided to head over to Christmas Steps early. Maybe Daniel was already there. She was so glad and relieved he had not taken offence at her saying she didn't want romance. Telling Pat about the latest disaster over Jack's school hadn't made her feel better. She needed to tell Daniel.

She was walking so fast it was only ten minutes to one o'clock when she turned the corner into the funny little street. She looked up the steps and was touched to see a couple embracing at the top, silhouetted against the grey, wintry sky. They looked so sweet, so together, wouldn't it be nice if – one day – she and someone, maybe Daniel . . .

She stopped dead. It *was* Daniel.

She recognised the coat, its collar turned up against the cold. And how could she have overlooked that wavy brown hair, the chiselled jawline. He drew back his head, and the willowy, slender woman he was embracing turned to him, both of their handsome profiles perfectly framed against the light. They looked great together.

'And that's fine,' thought Kate, her heart pounding, as she scuttled out of sight before he looked down. Before they kissed. Which they were absolutely just about to do. She didn't need to see that. Not that she cared. Obviously, he was completely free to snog anyone he liked. As a friend, she would positively encourage it, in fact. He was clearly up for a relationship. She had thought he was interested in her, but it turned out anyone would do. And it had to be acknowledged, the woman he was embracing at the top of those steps was a darned sight more glamorous than a world-weary single mum in a gnome costume. Elf costume, she self-corrected. And that was fine too. Perhaps they could still be friends. Of course, they could still be friends. And then she realised a tear had stolen down her cheek. She brushed it away, irritated

Thinking of Jack gave her some comfort as she walked to the bus stop, but then she remembered how he was just about to be chucked out of the only school he had ever known, where all his friends were. She was sobbing openly as she walked through the teeming crowds on the pavement. People stared; an older woman looked concerned. But nobody approached her, and she was glad.

She was on her own again. Just her and Jack against the world.

20ᵗʰ December

'What are you wearing?' asked Pat as she supervised Kate and Wayne carrying the folding tables outside.

'This?' said Kate, puzzled. She was wearing her usual elf costume as she had been selling the last of the Christmas trees minutes earlier.

'What? Really? I thought you might want to wear a pretty dress – get out of that tunic for a change,' said Pat, puzzled.

'Sorry, what are we talking about? Selling mince pies?'

'No, silly, the staff party tonight. You are coming?'

'I was tempted to skive,' she admitted, 'but then I thought I'd better come: I might have a chance to chat with Mr Wilkins when he's relaxed. Put in a good word for myself.'

Pat chewed her lip. 'I'm sure you're right. I'm glad you're going to be there. I'm not looking forward to it much myself.'

'What's the matter with it?' asked Wayne, coming late to the conversation because his language processing was a bit slow. 'There's dinner plus beer you don't have to pay for. What's not to like?'

'All the dad dancing for one thing,' muttered Kate, knowing she was sounding like a bore. It wasn't her. She was struggling to find her joy at the moment. 'And the warm white wine. I'd pay good money not to drink that.'

'And the dinner's not all that, is it really, dear?' asked Pat.

'I like a turkey dinner,' said Wayne. 'Wosser matter with it?'

'I'm happy to eat it once, on Christmas Day, and that's about my limit with dry turkey and overcooked sprouts.'

'I'm not eating the sprouts,' said Wayne, in faint horror. 'I don't do veg.'

'Goodness knows how you grew up to be so strong,' said Pat, watching him cart and then set up a heavy folding table with the greatest of ease. 'Anyway, back to the important stuff,' she said, raising an eyebrow at Kate.

'My black dress I suppose. The usual.'

'I'm sure you'll look very pretty – if not particularly festive.'

'I'm not sure I want to look festive,' said Kate. 'I think I'd like to have people notice I'm there and then slip away for an early night.'

But Pat wasn't listening. She was looking over Kate's shoulder and flushing pink in a way Kate had begun to recognise in her old friend.

'That'll be our Brian,' mouthed Kate, to Wayne. She turned and there he was, several inches taller than the three people walking with him, each carrying a large Tupperware box.

'Pat,' he said gruffly, clearly delighted. 'And Kate . . . hello . . . I'm Brian,' he said to Wayne, holding out a hand.

'Here's the team,' he added, pointing in turn, 'Beth and Will, you two have already met, and then this is Joe,' he said, indicating the dark-haired young man on the end who had the worst acne Kate had ever seen, along with bottle-bottom glasses and protruding ears.

'Joe,' she said, holding out her hand. 'Hi, it's nice to meet you, and lovely to see you both again,' she added to Beth and Will. 'Are these the mince pies?'

'Three hundred of them altogether,' said Brian. 'We've worked pretty hard, haven't we, team?'

They all nodded. 'I did the tops,' said Joe. 'The tops are quite hard.'

'They are,' agreed Kate. 'Sometimes they don't stick on properly do they?'

Joe looked perturbed. 'I think they're stuck,' he said, frowning anxiously.

'I'm sure they are,' Pat reassured him. 'Do you know? I can smell them . . . delicious! I'm sure people will love them.'

'And here are the flyers,' said Kate. 'Look, aren't they amazing? They've got the map to the café, plus the details of the auction this afternoon. There wasn't time to promote entries for the bake-off but that's more of an "Apple Café employees versus Portman Brothers" thing, isn't it?'

'Cool,' said Beth, shyly. 'I can give them out, can't I?'

'You can,' said Pat.

'Let battle commence,' said Brian, giving her a smile.

Just as Wayne was sticking the last bit of tinsel to the edge of the tablecloth and the team from the Apple Café were marshalling their towers of mince pies for Brian to dust with icing sugar, Daniel arrived.

'Dan!' said Beth, running to him for a hug.

He greeted Beth enthusiastically, but his eyes were fixed on Kate. Thank goodness she was there, safe and sound. He had begun to wonder if something awful had prevented her from meeting him the previous day.

By the time he had embraced Beth and said hello to the rest of the team, including Brian, he looked around for Kate. But she had slipped away.

Catching her breath in the staff storeroom, the furthest place she could go to get away from him without leaving work altogether, she put her hand on her chest to steady herself. She could feel her heart pounding. Why on earth could she not bear to be with him? The unexpectedness of his arrival had unnerved her. He never told her he was coming to help.

But then he was probably going to mention it during their failed meeting yesterday. What was she telling herself about them being friends? No chance. It was best for her to keep out of his way, for his sake. She had a knack for casting a dark pall on everything she got involved in, she realised now. She should back off. It was far too painful to see him with another woman anyhow. It was time for her to admit to herself she thought he might have been the next man in her life. At last. She was wrong. There was going to be no Christmas miracle for her.

'Where have you been?' said Pat, coming into the staffroom to put the kettle on, just as Kate was reappearing, wiping the mascara from under her eyes to hide the recent tears.

'You've missed that nice Daniel,' she said. 'He's gone off to talk to the management team about the cake auction this afternoon. You'll never guess! He's managed to get that auctioneer from Messam's auction house – you know, the one who's on the telly doing that show about stuff people have in their attics that's worth a fortune.'

'Oh God, the auction,' said Kate, weary to the bone.

'Did you bake something?'

'I didn't, I confess. I feel bad, it was supposed to be me running all this.'

'Don't worry,' said Pat kindly. 'You've had other things to worry about. Anyhow, Brian and I,' she paused, reflecting on the words, before continuing with a contented sigh, 'Brian and I have had a lovely time sorting stuff out. And that lovely Daniel's done loads too, what with the flyers, and the auction.'

'Have you baked for it?'

Pat bridled. 'I might have had a bit of a crack at it,' she said. 'I told Brian I wasn't going to do anything. He's a master – how can I compete?' she didn't look as if she minded. 'But I did do a Yule log, I confess. Well, I was baking one anyway; I just did two. It's for a good cause.'

'So, come on, 'fess up, are you and Brian a "thing"?' asked Kate, managing with superhuman strength to dredge up a weak smile.

'We're spending Christmas Day together,' she said in a rush. 'And I know what you're thinking . . .'

'You do?'

'That we're ridiculous old farts who should know better at our age, and we're moving too fast, and it'll all be a disaster, and what on earth are we thinking . . .'

'Wait, wait!' This time Kate had no trouble finding a smile. She had never seen her old friend like this before. 'I'm not thinking any of those things. I think it's lovely. You're great together. I couldn't be more delighted for you both. Am I buying a hat?'

'Now *you're* being ridiculous,' scolded Pat, but she was mollified, patting her hair as she told Kate more. 'We're going to Ursula's, so *that'll* be fun,' she sniffed. 'Brian's bringing one of his Christmas puddings and she'll not have had one as good as that before.'

She smiled a secret smile, smoothing her skirt even though it didn't need smoothing. 'And, talking of which, I must get back and sort out all the entries for the competition.'

'I hope we got enough, did we?'

'I should say,' said Pat. 'Wayne's done something for every category. He's let me have a peek at his raised pie. It's pretty impressive, I can tell you.'

'God, I hope that's not a euphemism,' muttered Kate to herself. She wasn't sure she wanted to see Wayne's 'raised pie' or his raised anything, come to that.

There was still a lot to do and everything to play for with her fundraising target. And her job. There were the mince pies to give away to the public – she must go out and help now she knew Daniel was elsewhere – and then there was the auction. She had been told the Managing Director wanted to give a speech – he rarely missed an opportunity to hold forth – and she still needed to put a final call in to the media, making sure the paper was sending a photographer and the marketing department were giving it their all with social media. After that, she was collecting Jack from Helen's, taking him home, getting dressed for the staff party . . . It was enough for a week, never mind a day.

'Penny for them?'

'I wouldn't burden you. I must go and give them a hand outside,' said Kate, brushing past her friend without meeting her eye. If she started to tell Pat all her worries she was afraid she would never stop.

There was a carnival atmosphere in the street. Brian was standing back just keeping an eye as Joe, Will and Beth handed out mince pies and flyers. Kate was thrilled to see that people – initially wary – were quickly beguiled, stopping to chat and to compliment the team on their baking. Kate was touched to see how patient most people were with Will, whose stammer seemed a little worse when talking to strangers. They were generally happy to allow him to take his time, gently encouraging him and praising his pastry. Joe was repeatedly explaining how difficult it was to get the tops of the mince pies on really well and Beth was accepting compliments bashfully for the mincemeat which, she was explaining, contained lots of apple and cinnamon – her two favourite things.

Kate saw Beth gazing admiringly at Will when his back was turned, taking more mince pies out of the boxes to put on the tray.

'He's nice, Will, isn't he?' she said.

Beth didn't reply but her secret smile as she gazed at her shoes told the story.

'I think you two would make a lovely couple,' she went on, but Beth shook her head.

'Zoe liked Will,' she said, in her charming hoarse voice. 'She liked him, so . . .'

'I think Zoe would love you and Will to get together,' encouraged Kate. 'If she loved you both she would want you both to be happy, wouldn't she?'

Beth's face registered the possibilities with growing awe. 'I will tell him,' she said to Kate and went off to help him, just as Brian arrived at her shoulder.

'I've been matchmaking,' she admitted proudly to Brian.

'They'd make a good couple,' he said, seeing the two of them, heads bent over the mince pie boxes, giggling at some private joke. 'I think a chat about the birds and the bees might be in order,' he added mock sternly. 'I'll have to take them to one side.'

'Talking about birds and bees,' Kate added mischievously, 'what are your intentions towards my lovely friend Pat.'

'Ah yes, that was you too, wasn't it?' he smiled broadly. 'You've got quite the matchmaking knack. Well, since you're cheeky enough to ask, my intentions are serious. And,' he added hastily, 'entirely respectful and honourable of course.'

'Of course,' said Kate, feeling a little less bleak for a moment, before a flashback to seeing Daniel at Christmas Steps reminded her about her last contact with him. He appeared to have demonstrated that his intentions towards her were considerably less serious, respectful and honourable than she had thought. It served her right for keeping him dangling. 'You snooze, you lose,' Tom had always said.

*

Looking back at the crowds as the mince pie giveaway recommenced, it was encouraging to see the flyers were being carefully folded and stored away in pockets and shopping bags, with people promising to make visits to the café soon in the new year. Better still, many of them were happy to return for the auction in the store after lunch.

'It seems to be going pretty well,' said Daniel in Kate's ear, making her jump. She shot sideways, colliding with a shopper, with multiple bags in each hand, looking grumpy and puffing behind a formidable woman who might be his wife.

'Look out,' the man said tetchily.

'Sorry,' said Daniel, offering him a mince pie.

'Oh, go on then,' he said, stopping and softening. 'She's not let me have any lunch,' he complained, gesturing at the woman who was steaming ahead, oblivious to his mutiny.

'Good, eh?' said Kate, watching him chew.

'Best I've ever had,' he said, around a large mouthful. 'What's all this in aid of?'

Daniel briefly explained.

'Where's the collecting tins then?' the man said, fishing a tenner out of his wallet.

'We didn't think, did we?' said Kate to Daniel, stricken. 'We should have had tins for donations.'

'I'll make sure it gets to the right place, thanks,' said Daniel to the man as he walked off. He didn't remind Kate that, in their planning meeting, she was the one who had been delegated to find collecting tins. Clearly she had no memory of it and he wasn't going to undermine her confidence by pointing it out. 'We'll make plenty with the auction this afternoon,' he reassured her. 'Where were you yesterday?'

'Sorry, I got held up,' she replied, daring him to press her further with a blank stare.

'No problem, but we need to catch up.'

'No, we don't,' said Kate, firmly. 'We don't. It's fine.' With that, she walked off, Daniel staring after her in amazement.

Kate needn't have worried. The entries for the bake-off were stupendous. The café in the basement of the store, where they were holding it, had tables roped off so they could lay everything out. It was packed shoulder to shoulder. Lots of shoppers and all the employees, including those who had not entered, were gathered around. Through the crowds Kate could see Sarah from Human Resources chatting with Mr Englebert, the oldest member of the board. He should have been pensioned off years ago, but he seemed reluctant to leave and the rumour was his wife didn't want him at home under her feet. Sarah seemed so nice from a distance, and Kate remembered with gratitude how she had encouraged her to bunk off when it snowed. She supposed hiding a ruthless core with a friendly exterior was a prerequisite for working in HR. She had seen the woman's steely side and didn't reckon on her own chances if they ever went head to head.

At least she had plenty to take her mind off things. She made sure the photographer got good shots of the cakes, pulling Beth into the frame by getting her to stand next to her own entry, which was an elaborate triumph of royal icing and a fondant holly wreath. Then she persuaded the Managing Director, Leonard Hill – it didn't take much – to say a few words. Quite a few words. Yawns were being stifled and watches surreptitiously checked by the time he got to the end of his yarns about Portman Brothers' proud history of altruism, its rise and rise, the tradition, the forward-thinking attitude, the bright young staff, the old, loyal staff . . . it went on and on. Eventually he got to reading out who had won each of the six classes. Wayne was pink in the face when he took first place for his raised pie. Shy Will was lauded for his salted caramel brownies, which went straight to the cake counter to be sold to shoppers that day, with all resulting funds going to the Apple Café. The final category, the Christmas cakes, was hotly contested between Wayne, Pat, Beth, Brian and several others. When Beth won, she was ecstatic, giving a little jump on the spot and clutching her hands together in glee.

Eventually, it was the auctioneer, a slim, glamorous woman in her forties who had been signing autographs all the while, who slid in next to the Managing Director with a beaming smile and pointedly started the applause to thank him for his efforts before apologising for being in a hurry and starting the bidding at a frantic pace.

Kate was worried. How would they make a thousand pounds just from cake? Perhaps they should have found a way of selling the mince pies rather than giving them away, she fretted. She kicked herself again for not thinking of collecting tins. What was the matter with her? She had reached a point where – every day – she did something to mess up. That was no good for Jack. She was a failure as a mother and a human being. And so the vicious inner voice continued as – on the outside – Kate smiled and clapped politely. That did it. They must only have raised about five hundred pounds at the most and there were only the Christmas cakes to auction now. People were being generous – Wayne's pie had made an astonishing fifty pounds – but she would be held responsible for the one performance measure on which the management team would use for this task: the money. And that would be that. Job gone. Game over.

An unattractive thought of Mr Wilkins popped into her mind, rudely interrupting her spiralling negative thoughts.

And then she realised why; his aftershave, a miasma of grubbiness and cloying musk, had filled her nostrils. And there he was, beside her. She looked up and gave him a rictus smile. He grinned back, smugly and smoothed his thinning and greasy hair back from his forehead with a habitual swipe of his hand.

Sandra, the auctioneer, had left Beth's cake until last.

'And now,' she announced, holding the cake up triumphantly, 'the winning cake from the most prestigious category in this competition, ladies and gentleman, the most succulent, the most elegantly decorated, the *pièce de résistance*, the – if you will allow me –' she winked confidingly at the smiling crowd, 'the icing on the cake . . .'

There were a few groans, but largely the amiable gathering was amused and entertained. Beth, Kate noticed, was standing next to Will. They were holding hands and he was gazing at his new girlfriend admiringly in her big moment, as if he could hardly believe his luck at the fortunate turn of events.

Kate forced herself to smile encouragingly at Mr Wilkins. 'Will you be bidding?' she said.

'I did say to the missus I'd sort out the cake,' he admitted, looking anxious, as he generally did when his wife came, however briefly, into the conversation.

'Here's your chance, then . . .'

'Do I hear fifty pounds,' said Sandra in ringing tones.

Daniel put up his hand.

'Thank you, sir,' she nodded at him approvingly, but he wasn't looking at her. Instead, through a gap in the crowd, he looked straight at Kate, giving her a sharp head jerk of command. She frowned at him, and he flicked his head slightly toward Mr Wilkins again in silent instruction. She nodded back.

'You're not going to let him get it are you?' she asked Mr Wilkins. 'He's not even staff. I think the board would be awfully impressed if you got it instead, don't you?'

Mr Wilkins shuffled nervously and then stiffened with resolve. 'I will,' he said suddenly, shooting up his hand, just as Sandra cried, 'Do I hear seventy-five?'

'Here!' shouted Kate, just to make sure Sandra noticed, but she had, of course and immediately took on an expression like the cat that got the cream. Competition. An auctioneer's dream.

'So, which of you lovely gentlemen are going to take this cake home to the wife for Christmas?' Sandra said. 'She could only be grateful . . . the quality, the taste, the look of it. This cake is set to be the centrepiece of the Christmas tea table and you – gentlemen – have the priceless opportunity to put yourself in your wife's good books . . . I firmly believe a cake like this gets you off the washing up until at least the new year. Do I hear a hundred?'

Daniel immediately shot up his hand, and so did Mr Wilkins. 'Bidding against yourself there, sir,' Sandra joshed to Mr Wilkins, who blushed.

'Do I hear one-fifty?'

Whenever an increasingly nervous Mr Wilkins agreed to a bid, Daniel's hand immediately shot up again. Quickly, and almost unbelievably, the bidding rose to four hundred pounds, the crowd gasping and laughing in amazement. Beth's eyes were like saucers as she bounced up and down in excitement, still with her hand in Will's.

Kate did a swift calculation. If the price went to five hundred pounds she was sure she would have made her one-thousand-pound target. The local papers would love it, and her appraisal over her future employment would definitely go better. Daniel was an idiot. She was sure he told her he didn't even like fruit cake the other day . . .

Daniel shot her another significant look and put his hand up again. The bid stood at four hundred and seventy-five pounds. In response, Kate put her hand on Mr Wilkins's arm and breathed, 'Wow, Mr Wilkins, this is so amazing of you. I reckon five hundred pounds would seal the deal.'

Mr Wilkins puffed his chest out a little more and raised his hand.

'Five hundred pounds!' crowed Sandra triumphantly. 'Do I have any more bids at five hundred pounds? Going, going, gone – to the gentleman at the back of the room standing next to the elf.'

As Mr Wilkins, looking slightly green at what he had done, went up to pay and to claim his cake, Daniel worked his way through the crowds to Kate's side.

'That was daft,' she said, when he got to her. 'What if he'd let you outbid him?'

'I did get a bit worried at the end,' he admitted. 'I thought I'd pushed him too far.'

'What would you have done?'

'Coughed up, I suppose.'

'You told me you don't even like fruit cake.'

'Hate it,' he agreed. 'Now, I'm glad I caught you . . .'

Just then, visions of Daniel with the girl with the pink hair flooded into her mind again. What was the point? She knew now their easy friendship was over. She wanted more. She couldn't have it. Being around him was therefore too painful to bear. 'Sorry,' she said. 'I've really got to go.' She didn't want him to see her with tears in her eyes. Again, she fled.

*

By the time she had ensured the local paper had its photos and she had caught up with Brian on the amount raised, what to do with the money from the cakes sold in the café and how soon she was going to call in with Jack, Kate barely had time to get home, sort out some supper for her son and get changed for the staff party.

Pat had been right; her black dress was not festive. It was boring, she realised, looking at herself in dismay. If she had to find a dress that summed up her failure to find the joy she was determined to rediscover this Christmas, this was it. It had been her go-to dress for years. She and Tom had bought it together. He hated shopping, but when he saw her in it – a structured, curvy number, demurely on the knee but sexy in the way it clung to her body – he insisted on paying for it, even though it was the most expensive item of clothing she had ever owned.

She would never get rid of it. She just needed to fill out a bit – reacquaint herself with her boobs, which seemed to have disappeared. She rummaged in the drawer where she kept her make-up and bunged on some scarlet lipstick. Worse. Now she looked like a recently exhumed corpse that an undertaker has laboured to present in a positive light. It was like putting a cherry on a turd, but it would have to do. She grabbed a silver scarf, one of her favourites, and wound it around her neck. That would help. At least it partly hid the gaping neckline where her tits used to be.

Mrs Akintola was already there, and she could hear the older woman and Jack chatting as she fixed his tea.

'My Daryl still loves my sweet potato fries,' Mrs Akintola told Kate as she took a delicious-smelling tray out of the oven. 'It's the thing that keeps bringing him home to his Mama.'

'They look delicious,' she told her. 'Thank you so much for this.'

'You're welcome, my darling, now you have a lovely time and don't worry about a thing. Don't rush back either. You don't get out often enough. I want you to make the most of it.'

'I really won't be late,' said Kate, dropping a kiss on the top of Jack's head. 'Now don't let this one tell you he's allowed to stay up 'til God knows when,' she said. 'He's had a few late nights recently. I want him in bed asleep by eight o'clock. You hear?' she added, catching Jack's eye.

'Go,' said Mrs Akintola firmly, shooing her out of the door.

To a hard core of Portman Brothers staff, the Christmas party was a key event in the social calendar. Most of the women were dressed up to the nines, some with comedy Christmas earrings complete with little snowman baubles and flashing lights. Spirits were high by the time Kate got there.

Standing around clutching a glass of warm white wine that smelled of armpits, Kate felt her head swimming a little. The noise from the conversations seemed to come from far away and yet to pound painfully into her head like a jackhammer.

She surveyed the room. Mr Wilkins had already got rid of his suit jacket and had large patches of sweat under his arms. He was swigging from a pint of beer, his full lips folding around the edge of the glass and coming away wet and shiny. Kate watched him with horrified fascination. He noticed and fixed her with a stare and a wink. She looked away, trying not to allow her face to contort into the disgust she felt.

Wayne was there, with too much hair gel and a close-fitting shirt that showed off his bulky, weightlifter arms. He seemed in high spirits, doubtless buoyed by his success in the baking competition. Amused, Kate watched him scanning the room, his eyes resting on a young woman from Accounts – Jessica, Kate thought she might be called – who had all her fixed assets on display, along with a few of her variable ones.

Weary of standing, Kate took her seat at the long tables laid for dinner. The canteen staff had done their best with the Christmas decorations. Swags of tinsel lined the walls and each place setting had a folded paper napkin with robins and holly on it. She looked at the place settings opposite and beside her. There was Pat's name, thank goodness, and a girl from the Food Hall on her left whom she didn't know well but who seemed sweet. Then, to her horror, she checked the place on her right. Malcolm Wilkins. The very smell of the man would make it impossible for her to eat. She already felt sick. It was probably the wine. She had just reached out to swap his card with someone else's – anyone would do – when his fat, hairy hand appeared on the back of the chair next to her, his wedding ring looking uncomfortably tight on his sausage-like fingers.

'This is me,' he announced. 'How nice. We can talk about the Apple Café project. A good result, I felt.'

'Thank you,' said Kate, faintly, accepting her fate with resignation. 'You were really generous, and it is a good cause.'

'Aren't you too hot with that scarf on?' he asked as he sat down, taking the opportunity to have a good look down the front of her dress as he did so. 'Shall I help you take it off?'

'I'm fine thanks, Mr Wilkins,' said Kate, trying to smile. 'I'd prefer to keep it on.'

'Pity,' he said, with a lick of his lips. 'And do call me Malcolm,' he added. 'No need to stand on ceremony – it is Christmas after all.'

*

Thankfully, Mr Wilkins was distracted for much of the meal by a pretty girl on his right who looked terrified at being noticed by someone so senior.

Kate began to relax but then, as pudding was cleared away – a solid and bitterly curranted Christmas pudding with lumpy white sauce which was not nearly as delicious as the Apple Café one would be – Malcolm turned back to her with a glint in his eye.

'Let's dance,' he said, holding out a hand glistening with sweat. Slade was playing now, the music growing insidiously louder as the evening progressed, and a few other – quite drunk – employees were venturing onto the temporary dance floor.

'I don't really . . .'

His gaze hardened. 'I think we have to set an example, don't you?'

Kate wasn't sure what positive example was being set by seeing senior managers pawing junior staff on the dance floor, but she accepted her fate.

Malcolm was immediately handsy, grabbing her around the waist and holding her so tight she could feel him squeezing her rib cage.

'There's not much of you, is there?' he murmured in her ear as they jigged from side to side, more or less in tandem. 'You need feeding up.'

'A few more Christmas dinners like that, and I'll be the size of a house,' countered Kate.

'Like my wife,' he said. 'She's a well-built woman.' He shook his head, clearly keen to shake off the thought, but Kate was happy to keep his mind on his wife by way of distraction.

'What does she do, your wife?'

'Spends my money. And eats,' he replied. 'But let's talk about you . . .'

He then proceeded to talk about himself, bellowing in her ear as someone turned the music up even higher. She could feel flecks of spit hitting the side of her face. His voice was now difficult to distinguish from all the other noise around her. The fluorescent ceiling lights were turned off. The only illumination came from the candles on the tables and the swirling, multi-coloured disco lights that throbbed and spun, catching sweaty, laughing faces and jerking limbs as even the older staff, emboldened by free alcohol, strutted their stuff.

Kate wondered how soon she could slip away. She longed desperately to be curled up on the sofa in her pyjamas with Jack snuggled under her arm and the duvet on, watching Christmas movies.

'I must just . . .' she bellowed, thinking desperately of an excuse, 'I must just go for a wee.'

'I'll come with you,' he said immediately.

'I don't think you're allowed into the ladies.'

'I want to talk to you,' he said, nodding portentously. 'There's something we need to discuss.'

God, he was really drunk, she realised, horrified. When he nodded, his entire body moved to counterbalance his head. Even with this precaution, he nearly lost his equilibrium and would have fallen if she hadn't reached out to steady him.

He looked at her hand on his arm delightedly. 'Can't keep your hands off me, eh?' he slurred. 'That's understandable . . . c'm 'ere gorgeous,' he added, grabbing her around the waist and more or less frogmarching her out of the canteen. In the corridor, she quickly discovered that manoeuvring him nearer to the wall seemed to steady him in a way that allowed her to detach herself slightly. She could feel a cool draught where his sweaty hand had made her dress damp around her waist. She shuddered, which was a mistake.

'You're cold, my gorgeous,' he said, noticing, and wrapping his arm around her again. 'I'll keep you warm.'

And so, they staggered down the corridor as far as the stock room.

'It's in here,' he said, suddenly veering off and pulling open the door. They fell into the room, which was dark, and Malcolm let go, turning his back.

Kate sighed with relief and stepped back towards the doorway, grateful for the light from the corridor at least. She had better play out this ridiculous charade with him. He wasn't going to be dissuaded, but she was dying to get to the loo, not just because she needed a wee but also because the leaden Christmas pudding, a world away from the one she had tasted at the Apple Café, was threatening to make a reappearance.

Malcolm fumbled with his trousers and then turned. 'Ta da!' he said, his face shining red and sweaty in the light filtering in from the corridor.

Kate's face must have shown her confusion. A moment passed and then Malcolm looked down at himself. Kate followed his gaze.

'Mr Wilkins!' she said, in horror.

'Come on darlin',' he leered. 'You know you want to.'

At that, he lunged forward, his hands outstretched. 'Just let me have a little feel,' he muttered, reaching for her.

She sidestepped him and rapidly backed towards the door. 'Mr Wilkins, no,' she said firmly, like you would to a dog about to steal a packet of sausages.

He reacted to her words as if he had been slapped, stopping dead in his tracks for a moment, which was a mistake. At the sudden change in trajectory, he overbalanced, nearly recovered himself and then – gravity and alcohol getting the better of him – he fell backwards, heavily, with a crump sound, onto a head-high pile of cardboard boxes. The top two fell onto the floor between them, blocking his way. She didn't wait for a second chance. She ran.

She suppressed her desperate urge to run outside and not look back. To get home to Jack, she would need to grab her bag from the table where she had left it. She forced herself to walk to the table, head down, and was nearly out of the door with her bag in her hand, when Pat intercepted her. 'Kate! Whatever has happened to you?'

'I have to get back to Jack,' shouted Kate, in Pat's ear, over the thumping music.

She summoned an Uber, but remembered little about the ride home, except the sense of relief she felt when the door of the car slammed shut, and as it pulled away, turning to look behind her, still petrified that Mr Wilkins would come running out. She swallowed deliberately, breathing deeply to calm herself. The last thing she needed was the cost of the cab – so much more than the night bus she intended to take – but never mind that.

The sound of her pounding up the stairs to the flat must have roused Mrs Akintola who was right on the other side of the door, when Kate opened it, her hand shaking as she put the key in the lock.

'Whatever is the matter, chil'?' she exclaimed.

'I need to get to Jack,' said Kate, desperately.

'No, you don't,' said Mrs Akintola. 'Not in the state you're in . . . he fast asleep and dreamin' sweet dreams about Christmas. Don't you go in there disturbin' him.'

Kate calmed herself and quickly dispatched Mrs Akintola into the night, thanking her profusely but shutting down her questions with an averted gaze. 'I'm fine,' she said. 'I'm fine, I'm fine . . .'

She stared at herself in the hall mirror. 'I'm fine,' she repeated, tracing the moving mouth of her reflection with her finger. This pale, hollow-eyed creature wasn't her.

Risking waking Jack, she ran a hot bath, damn the cost, and sat, hunched and shuddering in the steaming water, trying and failing to get warm. Eventually she couldn't stay still any longer. She got out, dried herself and quickly climbed into as many layers of clothes as she could find – pyjamas, socks, a fleece, even a woolly scarf of Jack's that was hanging on the peg in the hallway. Nothing she did seemed able to transfer any warmth into her body. She was too cold to sleep. She tried it but gave up after minutes. Her body felt heavy, her eyes pinned open and sandpapery, her head pounding so hard she found herself with a hand on the side of her head, almost as if she was trying to keep it attached to her body.

21ˢᵗ December

She huddled on the sofa and must have eventually slept, because Jack woke her.

'Mummy, Mummy, Mummy!' he cried. 'Why are you here? Can I have breakfast? Can it be pancakes? Can I watch telly? It is still the weekend, isn't it? There's cartoons . . .'

Kate got him some breakfast, but her brain was fogged, her movements slow . . . to save her life she couldn't seem to function normally.

'Mummy,' said Jack, in a tiny voice. 'Why are you crying?'

She realised she was standing, staring at nothing, slow tears coursing down her face.

'Nothing, darling,' she said, but it felt like it came out slowly and heavily, like a record on the wrong speed.

She tried again. 'I'm fine. I've just got a sore head from too much wine. That silly thing grown-ups do . . .'

'Silly grown-ups,' echoed Jack, slightly reassured.

It was another raw, rainy day, the skies heavy and the cold viciously reaching into the little flat, making Kate shiver.

'Christmas telly,' she said brightly. 'With popcorn.'

'Yay!'

'But first . . .' she said, inviting Jack to fill in the gaps.

'Yeah, I know, cleaning,' he said, pulling a face. 'Boooring . . .'

'But then . . . we put our Christmas decorations up.'

'Yay! Have we got a tree?'

Kate sighed. 'Does it look like we've got a tree?' she snapped, and then instantly felt ashamed.

'Sorry, monkey boy. I'm like a bear with a sore head today. We don't really have room, do we? But I've got a cool set of lights we could put around the windows, and . . .' she paused for effect, 'I've got some glue and old wrapping paper, and I thought we'd make some paper chains while we watch Christmas telly. How about that?'

The day wore on, and Kate found herself frequently zoning out. Memories of last night kept crowding into her consciousness, so vividly that she was being assaulted by bouts of nausea, her heart racing, her head totally back in the store room, in the dark, Malcolm staggering towards her . . .

In the end she called Seema.

'Look at the state of you,' Seema whispered fiercely, glancing at the two boys, who were happily charging around the tiny sitting room chasing one another. Kate was wandering around the kitchen with the empty kettle in her hand. Seema took it off her and filled it from the tap.

'What the hell happened last night? Tell me,' she said as she flipped it on and reached for the tea bags.

Kate looked at her friend desperately and haltingly put it into words:

'It's just so ridiculous . . .' she said, when she finished. 'He's just a nasty, slimy little man, I can't believe I'm letting it knock me like this . . .'

'It was assault. You should call the police.'

'God no, I'd get nowhere with that. What would it achieve? And he didn't actually touch me.'

'It's still assault. It would protect other women from the same thing.'

Kate bristled. 'Oh, for heaven's sake,' she said. 'Don't lay that one on me, on top of everything else, this idea I've got to single-handedly stop other women being abused.'

'I didn't mean that. But – look – how do you feel about going back into work and being around this man.'

Tears sprang to Kate's eyes.

'There you go,' said Seema. 'You've got to do something . . . at least report it to your HR department. You've got one, I presume?'

Kate thought of Sarah, and how she had encouraged her to take time off for childcare when it snowed.

'I'll go in first thing tomorrow,' she said, sitting straighter. 'That's what I'll do.'

'Why don't you let me take Jack for you,' Seema went on. 'You're exhausted. He can pack his school uniform; I'll take him in tomorrow. You collect on a Monday afternoon, don't you?'

'I'll miss him . . .'

'Relax. You need to look after yourself.' Seema suddenly had a thought. 'Why don't you come too? I can only offer a sofa to sleep on tonight.'

'It's fine,' Kate gave her a watery smile. 'You're right. Jack's better off with you . . .'

'That's not what I said,' Seema corrected her. 'What I said was you need to rest, eat something, get some sleep . . . just take a bit of time for yourself.'

Once they had all gone, the flat echoed with silence and loneliness. The launderette was closed on Sundays so there wasn't even the hum of the machines and the smell of the soap – humanity, close by, within touching distance. Kate could have been on the moon, she was so isolated.

Eventually she took herself to bed where she remained, staring, wide-eyed into the darkness until dawn.

22nd December

By the time she dragged herself into work the next morning, she had a sense of unreality. Her feet seemed barely to register touching the ground. People's voices were coming from far, far away.

'Good grief,' said Pat when she saw her. 'What on earth has happened to you, pet? Why did you rush off on Saturday night?'

'I need to go to HR,' Kate muttered. It felt like such an effort to speak. 'Something happened . . .'

'I'll come with you?'

'No. It's fine. It's nothing, I can handle it.'

Sarah was in her office. When she saw Kate, her expression was unreadable.

'Come in,' she said, putting a hand on Kate's shoulder and leading her to a chair. She put a glass of water in front of her without being asked.

'He's already been in,' she went on, sitting beside Kate, her chair angled toward her. 'It's not looking good . . . you have to appreciate, I'm in a difficult position and it's so blindingly obvious it's not true, but . . .'

Kate was perplexed. She had barely had time to wonder what on earth was going on, when Malcolm Wilkins entered, looking smug and belligerent. Behind him was a narrow, mean-looking man whom Kate vaguely recognised.

'So,' said the man, 'here we all are.' He looked at Sarah for permission to continue. Sarah nodded, curtly, without meeting the man's eye.

'It would appear there was an incident of the gravest nature at the staff party this weekend which needs to be looked at carefully in light of this and other, ahem, "issues"' – he all but put up the air-quotes – 'concerning the same employee. I gather you are Kate Thompson?' he added, looking at Kate for the first time.

Kate nodded, dumbly. If this was a judge and jury examination of Malcolm's appalling behaviour this weekend, he was looking mighty pleased with himself. Then the reason for his confidence became clear.

'Mr Wilkins tells me you acted in the most extraordinarily inappropriate way towards him,' he accused Kate, with a note of utter disgust in his voice.

Her heart quickened.

'I don't believe we've been introduced,' she said, coolly, holding out her hand. 'And you are?'

'Bruce Holden,' he admitted reluctantly, twitching his hand but then deciding against offering it to be shaken. 'Legal.'

'Nice to meet you, Bruce Holden-Legal. Unusual name. Do tell me what I'm supposed to have done.'

'Well, I'm not surprised you don't remember, Kate,' interrupted Malcolm waspishly. 'You seemed awfully drunk, not that it's any excuse . . .'

'Detail please,' interrupted Kate. 'Graphic detail, why not, eh? I like a bit of imagination. Story-telling.'

'Well,' he said, blushing, 'as I was explaining to Bruce and to Sarah earlier . . .'

Aha, thought Kate. You had to hand it to him. The early bird catches the worm, and all that. No wonder Sarah was looking so grim.

'. . . So, I was forced to explain how you got me to go with you to the store room on a false pretence. I felt I had to accompany you as you were so insistent. I was worried about your welfare because you were so drunk . . .'

'Get to the point, Malcolm. Dish the dirt. Personally, I'm dying to hear what I did next.'

'So,' he threw her a triumphant look, 'then I was compelled to share with the team how you physically abused me, in a – well, in a sexual manner, if I must – and then, when I did my best to restrain you, for your own welfare – you struck me, in the face, with your hand.'

There was a peculiar sound. Kate was pretty sure it wasn't her. She looked at Sarah who met her gaze before looking away, wiping away all emotion and replacing it with a blank, professional demeanour.

'You. Are. Kidding,' Kate said, to the room in general.

'And it might have been possible to overlook this one occasion if it weren't for your general attitude recently,' said Malcolm, gaining impetus from the nod of approval and shared distaste he got from Mr Holden-Legal, who sat, with his notebook and pen, impassively by his side. He had written no more than a couple of words on the page. Kate craned to see.

Sexual, it said. And then, *Attitude*, with an underline.

'Yes,' said Malcolm, bossily, 'I mean, I wouldn't mind – well, I did mind, obviously, I'm a happily married man – but in light of the poor sales of Christmas trees this year, your tardiness, time taken off for supposed illness . . . all in all, this is not the behaviour we want to see when we are considering the bigger picture.'

'Just one small thing,' Kate interjected, holding a finger in the air to stop him.

He looked amazed and stopped talking, his mouth hanging open.

'What?' he said, irritably.

'This whole thing about *me* sexually abusing *you?*'

'Yeah?'

'Well,' she said, using both hands to gesture towards him, then looking at Bruce and Sarah in turn. 'It's just not very likely is it?'

There was another sound – this time very obviously a snort, from Sarah, before she regained her composure with visible effort.

'Not very likely?' Malcolm repeated, looking confused. Clearly in his universe it was entirely understandable that women like Kate should be unable to keep their hands to themselves in his presence.

'Look at him,' Kate appealed to Bruce Holden-Legal, who had developed a twitch. 'I may be single, and I may be desperate to hang onto my job, but I'm not that bleeding desperate . . .' Kate made as if to go on, but Sarah waggled her eyebrows fiercely at her in some secret signal she struggled to interpret. Luckily the diverting sight of the other woman's vigorous communication was enough in itself to silence her.

Sarah cleared her throat vigorously, shuffled some papers together and stood up.

'I think we've heard enough,' she said throwing Malcolm a filthy look. 'Absolutely,' said Kate, sitting back in her chair and throwing up her hands. '*I've* sure as hell heard enough.'

Bruce Holden-Legal looked disappointed. He was clearly dying to see what happened next.

'I have been instructed to inform you,' Sarah told Kate apologetically, 'that the board will be considering the evidence with a view to terminating your contract on grounds of alleged gross misconduct, but that you might prefer to consider your position prior to them making their decision, which will be by the end of this week.'

'The end of this week? So, Christmas Eve, presumably,' said Kate. 'They want me to resign or I'll be sacked. On Christmas Eve. Nice one.'

Sarah said nothing, but once she had ushered Malcolm and Bruce out of the room, checking to make sure they had gone, she turned back to Kate and shut the meeting room door.

'This is shit,' she said.

'Yeah, I was thinking that,' said Kate. She and Sarah could have been friends in another life, she thought.

'I didn't say this, and don't quote me on it, but this is absolutely bollocks. My advice to you would be to totally walk out of this building right now and consult an employment lawyer. Explain what's just happened, and show them this,' she went on, pressing a slim wodge of A4 paper into Kate's hand.

'What's this?'

'It's a photocopy of your employment contract. I thought I'd better get one done for you, in case you couldn't find your own. It's pretty standard stuff. There's our bullying and harassment policy in there too. The bottom line is – they shouldn't be able to do what they're trying to do.'

'And yet they plan to,' said Kate, sadly. 'And – let's face it – they probably will, won't they?'

Sarah sighed. 'I can't say any more. It's more than my job's worth.'

'You might want to keep away from Malcolm on a dark night, then,' advised Kate. 'If you're planning to stay and you value your job, that is . . . to say nothing of your sanity.'

Kate would have liked to have seen Pat but equally she was keen to get out of the building and away before anything else happened. Sarah informed her, walking her to the back door, that the day would count as sick leave paid only at the statutory minimum rate. Of course. She would not be expected back into work that side of Christmas.

'But that'll cause problems for everyone,' said Kate.

'Not for you, it won't,' said Sarah. 'For you there's nothing to lose, and who gives a shit who else you put out, under the circumstances.'

She had a point.

'Were you told to "escort me from the building"?' said Kate, as it occurred to her. 'I've been thrown out of better places than this, you know,' she joked, weakly.

Sarah ignored her attempt at humour. 'Get legal advice,' she said, her hand on Kate's shoulder. 'Promise?'

It was weird being back at the flat on a Monday afternoon. She felt she was intruding on a life she should not be seeing: a dull, monotonous life, with the machines churning downstairs. Mrs Akintola did her laundry service on Mondays: the napkins for restaurants, sheets for hotels and towels for the hairdresser down the road. Kate could hear her below and felt a yearning just to sit with the woman and take comfort from her presence, the orderly routine, the hum of the tumble dryer. But if she went downstairs looking the way she did, she knew Mrs Akintola would fuss.

Instead, she picked up the small pile of post on the doormat and sat on the sofa, holding the letters and flyers in her hand. After an age – she didn't know how long – she flipped through it. Junk, junk, junk, and then an official letter with a Yeovil postmark. It was from the funding authority for Somerset, which was the county council responsible for Maureen's care home.

She skimmed the letter inside: . . . *following assessment of needs . . . found to be of social rather than healthcare . . . funding withdrawn . . . government guidelines . . .* And then there was something about appealing the decision, but she knew there was no point. She really must stop opening her post.

She phoned Carol.

'I know,' she said. 'I was copied in. I got mine yesterday actually; I was going to give you a call. It's not just you. Several of my residents' families are facing the same thing, if that's any consolation.'

'Not really, no.'

'So, I'm afraid we are in dire straits, Mrs Thompson,' she went on. 'The funding is to be withdrawn immediately and that means there is a considerable liability to be covered for the January bill.'

'How much?'

'Five thousand, four hundred and forty-three pounds.'

Kate gave a gasping laugh. 'That's everything we have left in her account. A bit more, actually. It was supposed to last another six months, but it won't without the council funding. What about her pension?'

'Assuming we are able to use all of that, it's nearer five thousand that's owed. I'll get you the exact figure if you like.'

'I wouldn't bother,' said Kate. 'And what happens if . . .'

'Mrs Thompson, we care deeply for Maureen, and the last thing we want to do is cause extra stress for you, but we are running a business here.'

'But she's so unwell,' gasped Kate, struggling for the breath to even make a noise. 'She just needs to be looked after until the end. You said yourself, it's not long. Within six months, you said.'

'Even if it's that,' said Carol, 'we provide an expensive service with considerable overheads. We can't afford to just lose that contribution. If it's six months without the council contribution then we're talking five thousand, more or less, every month.'

'Thirty thousand pounds,' said Kate, faintly, doing the maths.

She didn't know how much longer she stared into space after she put down the phone. Slowly it dawned on her she was still holding some paperwork. She scanned it listlessly. There was the 'thirty thousand pounds' jumping out at her, halfway through a paragraph, but why was the Portman Brothers logo on the top? She sat up straighter and looked properly. It wasn't anything to do with the care home; it was her employment contract, the copy Sarah had given her. She read it properly. There were no surprises on the first page, just a description of her job, including the usual 'anything else we can think of to make you do' clause, along with the dreadful rate of pay. There was some impenetrable stuff about holiday allowance and then, that thirty-thousand-pound figure. It was a paragraph about death in service. Kate read it. And then she read it again. And then she picked up the phone:

'Sarah, this contract you gave me? Am I still employed?'

'Yes. Until the board says otherwise, or until you resign, you're still employed.'

'And all the rights I have in the contract are therefore still in place?'

'For now . . .'

'You know the death in service bit?'

'Yeees . . .'

'Do I have to die at work?'

'What do you mean by that?' asked Sarah, sharply.

'I don't know,' said Kate, and she truly didn't. 'But do I?'

'No, you just have to die during your employment. Hang on . . . Kate? Wait a minute –'

Kate had already hung up.

It was all too much to take in. All her problems were tangled around each other in her head like a nightmare piece of knitting. They were separate, but interlinked in a hopeless circle: the care home, the school for Jack, her work – or lack of it . . .

She needed time. She needed to think. What she didn't need was to have to pretend to Jack that everything was all right. Not at the moment.

She texted Seema, asking her to take Jack home with her after school. Seema replied immediately, agreeing and asking how Kate was.

She didn't answer.

She sat, right in the middle of the sofa, perched on the edge of the seat, staring out of the window. Time passed. At last she stirred, realising how stiff and cold she had become. Outside it was dark. She must have been sitting there for hours, her thoughts chasing round and round in her head. With half an idea about a cup of tea to warm her, she went to the kitchen. The milk was still out on the worktop from breakfast. She sniffed it. Off, and she had no money to buy more . . . Tipping it down the sink, she stared sightlessly at the board she and Seema had made. Twenty-five days 'til Christmas. A new, happy, positive celebration of life for her and Jack. Let's face it, things weren't going to plan.

Suddenly, it was as if the problems in her mind, so numerous and huge, seemed to fill the little flat to bursting, pushing at the walls and windows, seeking the space to be seen clearly. Nervous energy surged through her body.

What was it Tom always said? 'When the going gets tough, the tough get going.' That was him. He would square his shoulders and face down the enemy; that was what he would have expected her to do now. She didn't know how, but she did know the answers didn't lie in sitting on the sofa staring into space.

She quickly put on her coat and then pulled on the green woolly hat Daniel had given her. Seeing it gave her a pang of regret, remembering him embracing the pink-haired girl. She missed her chance with him and she was painfully, desperately sorry for it . . .

Tough. It was just her and Jack now.

The street was full of happy Christmas drunks, even though it was a Monday evening. People were demob happy, looking forward to their several days of eating, drinking and catching up with friends and family.

Sidestepping the drunks and merrymakers, she walked west – along the length of St Paul's Road – passing all the bars and restaurants, the charity shops in the poorer areas, the sad bundles of bedding in shop doorways, the grand university buildings lit up like Christmas trees – and she kept walking, without purpose, driven by her demons. She was in a more suburban area now. The houses were filled with happy families, preparing for Christmas, with packed fridges and twinkling decorations, wine at the ready for guests and family, presents piled up at the foot of trees too big for the sitting rooms. Despite the dark, many of the windows had curtains still open, giving Kate a glimpse into other lives – vivid tableaux of the life she was trying so hard to build for Jack. And look at where she was now. No job, no school, no money to help Maureen, not even the jewellery sale evening to bring in extra cash and launch some sort of business. Nothing.

The street she was walking down turned into a shopping area again. There were sweet, bijoux shops . . . one selling flowers, another selling nothing but macaroons, stacked in pyramids on glass cake stands . . . beautiful shops, pretty things, a charmed life, but not for her and Jack. There were tall, Regency houses now, hugging the hillside, overlooking the Avon Gorge. She had never walked this far with Jack. They got the bus here as a weekend outing in the summer, when she could spare the fare. And there she was, walking up the grass bank that led to the bridge. She remembered Jack rolling down the hill repeatedly in the sunshine. They both had, arriving at the bottom laughing, out of breath and covered in grass. This evening it took all the strength she had to get up there, fixing her eyes on the little brick shelter by the bridge. She was cold now and could at least go in there to escape the bitter wind.

Daniel had had a stressful and boring day, which was a bad combination by anyone's reckoning. It felt as if all his clients had suddenly realised it was nearly Christmas and were quite unnecessarily using the holiday as a benchmark for getting things done. It meant Daniel had spent the day chasing ongoing deals to completion, struggling with not being able to contact the necessary people either because they were super-busy themselves, for the same silly reason, or because they had already clocked off for Christmas. He had had no time for lunch and was starving. His shift started at eight o'clock, and he would have to go straight there. He could only hope one of the shops on his route was going to be able to sell him a sandwich and a strong coffee.

He shut down his computer and thought about trying to spend a few moments getting in touch with Kate. He had been meaning to all day. There was still the good news to tell about Cara hosting the jewellery party for her tomorrow night. Of course there was the shop at Christmas Steps and the wedding group too. And he needed to go and see Noel in hospital; that was another thing work had prevented him doing today. He wished, for a moment, he wasn't on the helpline tonight but then he straightened and took a deep breath. At this time of year, the Crisisline was crucial. Suicides soared around Christmas, when people realised how alone they were, or when they fell out with family at tense Christmas get-togethers. He wondered whose life he would end up dropping into tonight – spending time with strangers at their saddest and their most vulnerable was what it was all about.

He checked his phone again. Nothing from Kate. He bashed out a quick text, asking her to give him a call. Urgently.

In the helpline office, he was amused to see Barbara had been putting up some decorations.

'These are rejects from the box at home. My daughter's decided she wants to be an interior designer,' she explained. 'It makes her ever so snobby about what we have. It's all teal and copper this year, apparently . . .'

The office had sprouted a random selection of dangling tinsel balls, along with paper chains, and some dodgy looking blow-up decorations including an obese, inflatable snowman that yawed gently in the corner at an angle that suggested it might have had one or two.

'I'm not an interior designer myself, but I suggest hell might freeze over before your daughter announces there's a trend for fat, drunk, inflatable snowmen,' agreed Daniel. 'How's it been today?'

'Oh, you know . . . a big influx of daughters dreading spending Christmas with their mothers who never tell them they're good enough. Fewer men complaining about mother-in-laws, but that's more about men not talking rather than mothers-in-law being not a problem.'

'I bet you're a lovely mother-in-law,' said Daniel sincerely.

'It's easy to be, if I am,' she agreed. 'He's brilliant. Far too good for my daughter.'

23rd December

It was past midnight now, but there was still a fair amount of traffic going over the bridge, people still out and about, despite the late hour and the cold. It would stop soon. She wandered up to the bit where the bridge began, the first tower. It was beautiful. The bridge was lit with cascades of twinkling white lights that marked out its elegant curves, shining like a vast diamond tiara against the rugged landscape.

At the base of the tower, there was a sign. 'Need to talk?' it said. 'Call us.' And then there was a phone number. A strange, short one; they must have a special arrangement with the phone company. Presumably people who were just about to kill themselves didn't have the focus to remember a long one. Kate wondered if it was the charity Daniel volunteered for. She wished she had asked more about it now, and she wondered what he was doing at that moment – out with the pink-haired girl, probably, at some glamorous party.

Hugging herself to ward off the cold, Kate walked, as if compelled by hypnosis, to the very centre of the bridge, where the sweeping curves reached their lowest point. She stood there, not moving, a lonely figure, gazing out over the city.

She really should go back to the flat – home – and get some sleep. But it wasn't home, was it? When she and Jack had blown into town nearly four years ago, the flat, the job and the school were all the trappings of a life she had hurriedly put together. They would do, until she found something better for them both. But then she had got stuck there. And now even these thin, unsatisfactory solutions were slipping through her fingers and she was back to square one. She stared, unseeing, down to the river far, far below at the bottom of the Gorge. Even in the dark, she could see it seething, the current eddying and pulling at the waters, full of endless and implacable forces as the river was drawn out towards the sea.

She and Jack could just go. Anywhere. Start again in a new place, and this time perhaps the dice would fall more favourably for them both. In the West Country, perhaps Cornwall where she and Tom had taken Jack for a beach holiday when he was a baby. They had stayed at a little B & B by the beach, with a kindly lady who adored Jack and babysat him one night so she and Tom could go out for dinner together. People were kind there. The communities were small and close-knit. A village school might suit Jack better – somewhere with mixed-age classes, where a child was an individual, not a number in the league table data, required to fit into a mould pre-destined for him by an ambitious headteacher driven by national initiatives. Yes, that could work. There was employment in Cornwall too. From what she understood there was seasonal farm work, picking flowers and soft fruit . . . the work was hard and the pay was poor, but the idea of tough physical labour, making her so tired at night she could no longer think, felt like what she needed. The jewellery-making as a full-time career was a silly pipe-dream. She saw that now. Perhaps in Cornwall, when the seasonal work was thin, she could supplement their income with something along those lines, making something simple and cheap to sell to holiday-makers. That was all the jewellery could ever be.

She straightened. Why not act now? She would go back and pack immediately. Once she had the energy for the walk, at least. Maybe she would rest there for a few minutes more. Plus, there were goodbyes, which she preferred to keep to a minimum. Best not to make a big deal of it, just to slip away and keep on moving, that was what Tom would have done. She got out her phone, noticing the battery was on just eight per cent. Damn, normally by now it was sitting on the kitchen counter, charging. She noticed a text from Daniel asking her to call. She owed him a response at least, so she tapped out a brief text. Her finger hovered over the 'x'. Should she do a kiss? Thinking of it reminded her vividly and painfully of the pink-haired girl in his arms. Maybe no kiss then. But it would be lovely to talk to someone. Someone who wouldn't judge, or try to persuade her not to go. Someone who could salve her loneliness and soothe the pain of this new loss in the middle of all her other troubles. This was not only the loss of her life in Bristol with Jack but the loss of the new, desperately tender but hopeful possibility of a relationship with Daniel which she had tentatively allowed herself but which was now – she accepted – never going to happen.

Daniel had just managed to grab himself an instant coffee between calls. He was already exhausted. Two more hours to go on his shift and then bed, thank heaven, for a horribly short time before he went to work for his last day before Christmas and then – on the day itself – he would be back here. Tomorrow was just two days 'til Christmas and he could hardly believe it – after dreading the run-up to Christmas, the pain of being reminded constantly that Zoe wasn't with him, it had snuck up on him. It had been okay, and Kate was partly to credit for that. His blossoming friendship with her had smoothed the way, salved his pain.

But where was she?

His phone was ringing as he got back to his desk. He nodded to Barbara and picked it up, sliding back into his seat with his mug carefully poised as he did so.

'Crisisline,' he said. 'Jonathan speaking. I'm listening . . .'

'My name's Kate,' said a hauntingly familiar voice.

Daniel froze. 'Hello, Kate, how are you?' he said at last.

'I just wanted to hear a friendly voice.'

'It's nice to talk to you. Would you like to tell me how you're feeling?' he asked. He could hear his heart pounding in his ears. Should he tell her it was him?

'I'm okay now, actually. I've been really sad, really worried, but I've decided now.'

'What have you decided, Kate?'

'I've decided the answer is to just go.'

Daniel froze, and dread flooded through his body like a tidal wave of freezing water.

'Kate,' he said carefully, thinking fast, 'I can get you help. I can get someone to come to you. Would you like me to do that?'

'No, I'll be fine thanks,' she said. Gosh, she wasn't expecting that level of service. Although a lift back to the flat would be fab, she was sure that wasn't what this man was offering. 'I just want to talk,' she said.

Daniel thought again, frantically. 'That's okay, we can just talk. We've got as much time as you need. There's no rush. Do you have children, Kate?'

'I've got a little boy.'

'Would you like to tell me about him?'

'He's called Jack.'

Daniel shook his head in silent anguish. It was definitely her. No doubt about that now. 'Where are you, Kate?' he said, trying with all his might to keep his voice even and relaxed.

'I'm on the bridge,' she said. 'It's really beautiful. What did you say your name was?'

'Jonathan.'

'You sound like someone I know,' she said.

'Do I?' he hazarded. Now wasn't the time . . . 'Yeah, I get that a lot.'

'He's lovely. He's sad too, like me . . . but he'll be all right. I've wanted to say things to him and – well – I know now, I've missed my chance. It's never going to happen, so I've decided it's right to just leave everything behind.'

'How about Jack. Will Jack be all right? If you do this, who will look after him?'

'I'm doing it for him. He'll be fine. It's important that I do this because when I do, everything will be all right.'

Daniel thought frantically. She said she was at the bridge so it had to be the suspension bridge. There was no other bridge she could have got to without a car. It went against every policy for him to do what he was just about to do, but he would worry about that later.

There was a beep.

'Was that your phone?'

'Yeah, the battery's nearly dead. Doesn't matter. It's been nice talking to you. I think it's because you sound like my friend. I thought . . . we nearly got it together – me and him – but I said "no" and I should have said "yes". I've made lots of mistakes, you know. Lots of mistakes.'

Daniel had a thought. 'Maybe you haven't. Why don't you call him?' he said. 'I am sure he would want to help if he knew how you were feeling.'

'I think it's best if I don't,' said Kate. 'I don't want to get in the way. I've sent him a text.'

'Really?' said Daniel, his voice cracking. 'Are you sure he's received it?' As he spoke, he grabbed his phone, checking the screen for text notifications. Nothing. 'I mean . . . he might not have received it.'

Kate was unperturbed, although a little puzzled at Jonathan's urgency on the issue. 'Well, no,' she said. 'They can be delayed, but that doesn't matter does it? He'll get it in the morning. I expect he's asleep in bed.' Another agonising image of Daniel with pink-haired girl popped, uninvited, into her mind, this time both of them sleeping, draped around each other in Daniel's compact cabin bedroom.

The beep came again.

'Oops,' said Kate. 'That's me gone, I think. Thanks anyway. It's been nice talking to you.'

'No! Don't go, Kate . . .'

But the line went dead.

'Kate!' exclaimed Daniel in anguish, his agonised tone making Barbara jump up and come over to him.

'What?'

Daniel was fumbling with his phone, his fingers shaking and slowing him down. He held it to his ear expectantly, staring at Barbara as he listened.

'This number is currently unavailable,' the recorded voice of a woman announced calmly, oblivious to the gravity of the situation.

'Shall I call for backup?' she asked.

'I'm on it,' said Daniel. 'Explain later,' he added as he grabbed his car keys and jacket, leaving Barbara staring after him, astonished.

He thanked fate he had managed to park his car reasonably close. In seconds he was on the road, heading for the bridge, his phone on the seat next to him. It was just gone two in the morning. The streets were empty, the street lamps were off. His phone beeped the arrival of a text. There was a law against using a mobile on the move, but then racing at twice the speed limit was frowned upon too. There was a time and a place for disregarding the law – and this was it. He flipped open his phone case and glanced at the screen.

It was from Kate. He opened it, alternating his gaze from the screen to the road. In snatches, he read: *Daniel . . . Thank you for trying to help me. I am so grateful to you for being a good friend but I've decided I need to go now. Goodbye, and take care of yourself.*

Shit. He groaned, pressing his foot down on the accelerator a little further.

At the approach, he debated driving right onto the bridge and decided against. Better to cover the last stretch on foot. He screeched to a halt, leaving the car at an angle just at the toll booth, and jumped out. It was blocking the road, but that was just tough. He grabbed his phone, opening Kate's text and stabbing the return call button. Where the hell was she? He peered onto the bridge, the spitefully cold wind cutting through his thin shirt like a knife. He cursed the lights on the bridge. They dazzled rather than illuminated. He couldn't see.

Daniel groaned again in despair. He was too late. Then he saw something. First, he thought it was a bird wing, a flash of white, whipping briefly across the corner of his eye, and then he looked more closely. It was her. It must be. A tiny figure, right in the centre of the bridge, at the lowest point of the elegant inverted curve of its supporting cables.

'Kate,' he called, and then regretted it. He should approach her quietly. Not startle her. She was still on the pavement, pressed against the anti-suicide barrier, the top of which curved inwards to prevent all but the most agile and determined jumpers.

He jogged towards her. She showed no sign of having seen him, resting motionless against the metal grille, just staring into the water far below.

'Kate,' he called again, more gently, when he was just a few yards away.

She turned, her face a pale blank, and then – when she saw him – a sad smile spread slowly across her face. She was astonishingly relaxed, seemingly impervious to the cold now, he noticed. He was reminded of the paradoxical effects of hyperthermia, how the shivering stopped and casualties thought they were warm, stripping off their clothes and lying down to sleep.

'Daniel!' she said, with incongruous delight, as if she had unexpectedly bumped into him in the street on a sunny day. 'How did you know I was here?'

He put his head on one side, his arms slightly raised with hands turned out, and walked slowly towards her.

'It was you on the phone, wasn't it?'

He nodded.

'What are the chances, eh?'

'Kind of like fate intervened, don't you think?'

'I'm glad I have a chance to say goodbye to you properly.'

'Don't go.'

'It's the best thing.'

'It can't be. What about Jack?'

'Well, I'm taking him with me, obviously . . .'

'That's not right, and you know it,' he said, puzzled but relieved. Jack evidently wasn't there, which meant that at least she didn't plan on doing anything irreversible in the next couple of seconds.

'Er, excuse me, you have to let me decide what's right for my child. He needs a fresh start. A new school where they don't mind him being not like the other kids . . .' she explained. As she did so, watching Daniel's face change, the realisation dawned.

'What?' she exclaimed. 'You didn't seriously think . . .' she waved a hand at the seething waters hundreds of yards below them.

Daniel nodded apologetically. 'You have to see how it looked,' he said in his defence. 'And you sent me a text.'

'Yes, sorry, I just thought well, if we're going, we're going . . . it was a cop-out not to say it face to face.'

'Don't go.'

'I have to.'

'You don't.'

'It's been lovely,' said Kate, despairingly, 'but there's just too much difficult stuff here, the school, the job. It's all a mess . . .'

'But there's us,' said Daniel tentatively, closing the gap between them hesitantly, gauging her reaction with every step, as if she were a horse that might bolt.

'Us? I don't think so,' said Kate, taking a step back. 'Listen, I appreciate there was nothing agreed between us, but if you think there's an "us" and you're off kissing girls with pink hair . . .'

'What?' Now it was Daniel's turn to be astonished.

'It's totally fine,' Kate said. 'No reason why not. She looks really nice. Obviously I can't tell. I like the hair, it's cool. Plus she's tall, which is obviously a draw . . .'

Daniel was perplexed. 'Hang on,' he said, feeling a growing sense of unreality. It was bad enough he was on a bridge in the freezing cold in the middle of the night, trying to save someone's life – not just 'someone' actually – Kate's life, or at least he thought he was, and now, suddenly they were talking about someone's hair.

'Who's hair? Who's tall?'

'That girl with pink hair who you were kissing. You were in each other's arms. At Christmas Steps.'

'Grace,' he said, realising. 'You saw that.'

'It's not a problem . . .'

'It *is* a problem. Huge. And we weren't kissing. She was crying because of Noel and I was hugging her . . . She's gay, by the way. She's got a girlfriend.'

'Oh.' Kate's world shifted a little. A bubble of happiness formed somewhere deep in her chest. She gazed at him, perplexed.

'And I wondered where you'd got to,' he went on. 'I had some important things to tell you. I *have* important things to tell you. Things that might make a difference to – well – you leaving everything.'

'Listen, you actually make a fair point with the dying thing,' Kate explained. 'I'm worth a darned sight more dead than alive,' she said, remembering the death-benefit clause in the contract. It was more than enough to cover the care home fee, plus Jack would automatically get a place in Greystone Manor as a 'looked after' child. But of course she would never leave him. The though he might lose her after having to cope with losing his father made Kate cry tears she wouldn't allow herself to cry for her own grief.

She wiped her nose and eyes unselfconsciously, drying her hand on her jeans. 'Look,' she said, pushing her hair back where it was being whipped across her face by the cruel wind. 'I've got a lot of complicated stuff that I have to solve. And I have to do it for myself. No one else is going to sweep in and rescue us. Not even you. You might think

I'm running away, and I am, but I'm running to build a better life for Jack.'

'Don't go,' he said, more softly, catching her hands in his own, warming them.'You have a wonderful life here, you and Jack. There's nothing we can't fix. Let's give ourselves a chance to be happy together.' He reached out, hyper-alert for her reaction, and gently rested his hand on her arm.

She stiffened. 'I love the thought,' she said, sadly. 'But there's just too much. I have to be strong. Doing this solves problems. It's the only way . . .'

'I have so much to tell you. What do you need?'

'Money for Maureen's nursing home.'

'Done.'

'A career.'

'Done.'

'A school for Jack.'

'Okay, erm, done. Somehow.'

Kate paused. She looked at Daniel, gazed at a point in the distance and then back at his dear, kind face, that she had known for such a short time and yet felt she had known for ever.

'You?' she smiled a cautious, sweet smile.

'Done.'

Kate shivered. It was a shudder that ran through her body so violently it made her sway. It was like watching the life course through a newly delivered foal as it staggered to its feet.

He let go of her hands and embraced her, pressing his body against her. He brought around the jacket he still held in his hand, covering her back with it, hooking it onto her shoulders and holding it there as he rocked her gently in his arms. Slowly he felt her relax against him.

'Let's go home,' he said in her ear. 'It's bloody cold here and I reckon you need one of my green slime matcha tea specials inside you.'

'Is everything really going to be okay?' she said, pushing herself away just a little so she could look up into his face. Her face was as open and innocent as a baby's.

He smiled down at her. 'Yes,' he said. 'It really is. Trust me.'

He had whacked up the heater to full blast as soon as they got into his car. By the time they got back to the houseboat, Kate was so profoundly lulled by the heat and the release of tension, she was nearly asleep.

She felt him open the passenger door and allowed him to help her to her feet. She shivered again in response to the biting wind but soon, barely registering the walk to the boat, she found herself in the tiny cabin. He ushered her straight into the bedroom at the prow of the boat and – without words – got her to get under the duvet, fully dressed.

When he came back with two mugs of strong tea, she was asleep, curled up on her side with tremors of cold still sporadically coursing through her. He put the mugs on the bedside table and climbed in next to her, spooning into her back and taking her still freezing hands in his own.

'Tea or coffee?' he asked, as she clambered out of the little bedroom the next morning, rubbing her eyes with her fists like a child.

'What time is it?'

'Nearly eleven.'

'What day is it?'

'The first day of the rest of your life,' he said grinning, handing her a plate with a doorstep bacon and egg sandwich on it. 'Tomato sauce?'

'Go on then,' she said, holding out her hand for the squeezy bottle. 'I've still got problems.'

'Haven't we all? The good news is, you've got me on the case now.'

'We didn't?' she gestured to the little bedroom. The previous night felt so muddled in her mind she wasn't sure.

'Of course we bloody didn't. What kind of a man do you think I am?'

'A good one,' she said, sliding onto the bench, and sinking her teeth into the sandwich. 'I'm glad I'm not dead.'

'So am I.'

'I can't believe you thought I would.'

'It's the company I keep. Where is Jack, by the way?'

'Having a whale of a time with Krishna,' she said, her face clouding over again, and her body drooping under the weight of remembering a sadness that still threatened to overwhelm her.

'Tell me,' he said.

And she did.

'Okay, well, I admit that's quite a lot . . .' conceded Daniel. 'Let's start with the stuff I was trying to tell you about when you were avoiding me because you decided I was snogging a lesbian. For a start, and I grant you this is quite a small point, my friend's fiancée Cara is having the girls around this lunchtime for a pre-Christmas drink, and she's expecting you to turn up with all that jewellery you made for the school-gate nightmare mum's party. Give 'em a glass or two of Prosecco and they'll bite your hands off for whatever you've got, I reckon.'

'Hopefully they don't have to be drunk to like my jewellery,' protested Kate, but she was smiling. 'And it's great, but you're right: that is the least of my problems.'

'Okay, try this. When we go to your flat to collect the jewellery, you need to pick up your employment contract, because it just so happens Cara is a shit-hot employment lawyer who hangs, draws and quarters sex-pest managers for kicks. In fact,' he said, looking at his watch, 'we should get cracking. One thing at a time, that's what I tell the people on the hotline. Just deal with one thing at a time.'

After Cara had introduced Kate to her half-dozen, half-cut mates, who fell upon Kate's jewellery with cries of delight, she took her into the kitchen and grilled her on the lead up to her extraordinary meeting the day before with Malcolm, Bruce Holden-Legal and Sarah.

'And then they said what? . . . And then what happened?' she prompted. 'You're joking!' she exclaimed at one point and then, when Kate more or less got to the end, she reached for the bottle and topped up Kate's glass.

'Oh dear, oh dear, oh dear,' she said heavily, as she slowly shook her head.

'Is it bad?'

'Oh yes, very bad.'

'Okay,' Kate said, shrugging, 'I just thought maybe . . .' she trailed off, smiling in defeat.

'No, no,' said Cara, realising she had been misunderstood. 'I mean this is very, *very* bad for Portman Brothers. The terms and conditions changes, the bullying, the refusal to accept reasonable request, the flipping SEXUAL ASSAULT,' she shouted, making Kate jump.

'He didn't actually – you know . . .' said Kate, in his half-hearted defence.

'It was assault,' Cara insisted, 'and failure to take disciplinary action against this bloke . . .' She let the consequences linger unspoken. 'We're talking five-figure-pay-outs bad;

six-figure, even. We're talking sackings, fines, reputational damage. We're talking –'

'Six-figure payouts? What? To me?'

'Yes, to you,' said Cara. 'If I don't justify my fee with a damages award exceeding fifty thousand pounds, then I'll never offer a no-win, no-fee ball-breaking service ever again.'

Kate sighed, a deep sigh that left her slumped at the kitchen table, her hand curved around her wine glass, too weary to lift it to her lips. This drinking at lunchtime thing was interesting, she thought. Especially after minimal food and sleep. 'I dunno,' she said. 'It doesn't feel right to be turning the whole revolting episode into an opportunity to make money.'

Now it was Cara's turn to sigh. She got this a lot. Clients wanted her to somehow right wrongs, not to extract lucrative payouts, but – as she had to explain – there was a price to pay for every sin, and the common measure of the size of the wrong, when it came down to it, was money. Apologies were possible too, if that's what the client really wanted, but words were cheap and Cara was hardbitten nowadays. Words didn't pay her salary.

'If you want to protect other women from this tosser you need to take action. This is the action they will pay attention to. The sad thing is, they essentially don't care about bad behaviour. What they care about is their bottom line. You hit that, you've got their attention. You get their attention, they will be keen to ensure they don't get hit for it again and they'll do a lot to make it all go away. This is your power, girl. This is how you do it.'

Kate looked at Cara and recoiled slightly at the blazing zeal in the other woman's eyes. 'I see your point,' she said reluctantly. 'And if I'm using the money for good . . .'

'Exactly.'

'Are you offering to deal with it for me?'

'I certainly am,' she said, folding Kate's employment contract and sticking it in her bag. 'In fact, leave it totally to me.'

'No win, no fee?'

Cara nodded.

'You need to speak to Sarah in HR,' Kate told her. 'I think she'll be secretly pleased.'

'So that's that,' said Daniel, briskly. 'Another problem ticked off the list, and I do believe the immediate cashflow issue has been considerably eased by those scary women in there.'

'Have they bought stuff?'

'Have they bought stuff?' Daniel pretended to think: 'It would be fair to say they like your shit. There's not a lot left, but there's a pile of paper money on the table where it was . . . enough to buy Jack a decent Christmas tree and the rest.'

'I can't thank you enough,' said Kate tearfully, and the tears were spurred by mixed emotions. Maureen's care-home fees could be funded by any employment pay-out Cara might wangle – she was sure Carol would be prepared to wait for that. And the jewellery sales would help with Christmas. But there would still not be enough for the school fees she needed to help Jack.

'You had better go and meet your fans,' said Daniel, bowing and sweeping an arm in the direction of the living room. 'Watch out for that Hayley, she's bought a lot, and drunk a lot. She's likely to be over-emotional.'

Kate was shy. All these women telling her how much they liked her stuff were more than she could cope with. Cara was grinning too . . . 'And they all love the wedding group idea,' she told Kate to her confusion.

'What's the wedding group idea?'

Cara gave Daniel a questioning look and he shook his head. 'I haven't got to that bit yet,' he explained. 'Give us a chance . . .'

Cara shook her head in frustration at him but turned to Kate. 'There's a cunning plan that Daniel will explain to you when he can be arsed; personally I can't think what he's been doing with his time. It's just . . . have you ever thought about offering a jewellery design service for weddings?'

Kate did a little excited jump. 'Absolutely!' she said. 'I've always thought . . . I haven't quite managed to get it going, but hang on,' she fumbled for her phone, 'the thing is, you want to offer something really personal, don't you? And also, something where the brides' rings go with the grooms', and you can do loads with all the different colours of gold and silver – look . . .'

Cara came around to stand next to her, peering at the little screen. 'And these are just ones you've done on spec?' she said, looking on in wonder as Kate scrolled through the photos. 'These are amazing, you are going to do soooo well with this, the Christmas Steps lot are going to love you,'

'And then – hang on, where are they? Oh yes here – there's these pendants for the bridesmaids . . .'

'Bridesmaid presents!' exclaimed Cara, looking triumphantly at Paul. 'Now there's a thing.'

'We'll leave them to it,' said Paul, ushering Daniel out of the room.

'Daniel!' came a cry, followed by Hayley swaying precariously down the hallway towards him, tottering on her platform heels.

He winced, before putting on a polite smile. 'Hayley, how are you?'

'A bit drunk,' she admitted, giving him a smacking kiss on both cheeks.

'No! Really?'

'That girl,' she said, ignoring his gentle sarcasm and pointing into the kitchen at Kate. 'She's special.'

'I know.'

'She's the one for you,' she continued, staring at him owlishly. 'I wish I was. But she is,' she said, regretfully. 'Be nice.'

'I will be,' he said, his polite smile replaced with a genuine one. 'I fully intend to be.'

'Good,' she said, dismissing him and reeling away, bouncing off the wall. 'I'm dying for a wee . . .'

Kate was just putting her phone away when it rang. 'Go ahead,' said Cara. 'I must get some more wine for this lot. Daniel, Christmas Steps thing, remember?' she added, as he came back into the room.

Kate was staring at her phone as it rang.

'Who is it?' he asked.

She turned the screen towards him. *Greystone Manor*, it declared.

'Aren't you going to answer it?'

She looked anguished. 'I can't,' she said, holding it out to him. 'I can't cope with any more . . .'

He gave her a concerned look and held it to his ear.

'Hi, this is Daniel,' he said. 'I'm with Kate, but she can't answer at the moment.'

He listened and then smiled.

'It's Ursula Moore. And she says it's good,' he told Kate, holding the phone out toward her. She took it, cautiously, as if it would bite.

'Kate,' said Ursula. 'It's all going to be fine.'

'How can it be? The local authority has told me . . .'

'I know.' In those two words Ursula communicated exactly what she thought of the local authority. 'So, I've been thinking hard about Jack,' she went on. 'To be honest I've struggled to think of anything else. You and I both know that Jack needs to be with us and – let me be quite clear – as a school we need Jack too.'

'But how . . .'

'Ways and means. I can't say it's been easy. I had to call our governors and trustees together for an extraordinary meeting last night. They weren't thrilled about it but as a registered charity we have a duty to provide bursaries for students who can't afford the fees.'

'You are so kind,' interrupted Kate, 'but – even with a bursary – I've got to somehow pay the rest, plus care-home fees for my mother-in-law too, I've got no job . . .'

'No, I really do think I can help you with Jack, at the very least,' she interjected. 'What I meant to say is that they have approved a full bursary for Jack. These things are rare. Rarer than they darned well should be, in my view. Too many schools just offer a few per cent discount on fees to lots of parents so they can say they are meeting their obligations . . .'

'Sorry, did you say a "full bursary"?' interrupted Kate belatedly, this fresh surprise having to shoulder its way through so many earlier ones before it began to make any sense to her. 'I just thought I heard you say you were offering a "full bursary" . . .'

'I did.'

'So, yeah, so . . .' Kate was still floundering, 'what does that actually mean? When you say "full" does it mean the fees get paid – well – fully?'

'Jack's fees will be totally paid by the bursary. Also, I don't want you to worry about the uniform. It can cost quite a bit to kit the boys out when they first start – everything at once – and I appreciate that's daunting, but I am pleased to say there is a small discretionary fund for that too. Bring him in so we can take a look at sizes, there's an excellent second-hand uniform cupboard run by the PTA. I know what you're thinking, you don't want him in rags; but honestly, this is really good stuff. God knows, the boys grow so quickly, they don't get time to wear things out . . . Kate?' she added, realising she had heard nothing from the other end for a while.

Kate, now sobbing, handed the phone back to Daniel wordlessly.

'I think she's pleased,' he said to a concerned Ursula. 'Yeah, it's definitely joy,' he added, as Kate slid down the wall and sat on the floor, her head on her knees, sobbing. 'Will you please quickly tell me what you just told her?'

'So,' said Daniel, 'I think you've had enough excitement for one day, don't you? Would you like me to take you home? Pick up Jack on the way?'

'No! I'm fine. I can't remember the last time I felt this energetic,' crowed Kate, folding the thick wodge of cash Cara had just handed her and stowing it carefully in the inside pocket of her jacket. 'I'm dying to see Jack,' and she was, 'but I've finally got some money to go and get all the brilliant presents he deserves that I wasn't going to be able to afford. I need to do it in secret. I'll get him from Seema after that.'

'You've not slept for days. I think I'd better be your minder today. Plus, you'll need the car if this is the kind of major shopping I'm thinking it is.'

*

Jack was hugely curious about the mysterious parcels that had appeared in the back of Daniel's car. By the time Daniel took him and Kate back to the flat, everyone was flagging.

'Thank you,' she said, as Daniel brought up the last bag, this one full of the wrapping paper she would be using once Jack was safely in bed. She put her hands on his chest and leaned forward to give him a kiss. It was a gentle, tender, meaningful kiss. But it was on the cheek. As she did so, Daniel kept his arms rigidly at his side, though the urge to wrap them around her and draw her closer still was powerful. She dipped her head, and rested in briefly against him before drawing away with regret.

'First thing tomorrow,' he said. 'Back to Christmas Steps. And this time I'll take you there myself, to make sure you don't run away.'

'I know,' she said, blushing. 'Sorry. Ten o'clock tomorrow. Christmas Eve. Have a lie-in. You need sleep after all this too.'

Christmas Eve

Kate woke up with a start. She could hear Jack in the sitting room. He had taken it upon himself to switch the telly on, she noticed, but it was the Christmas holidays, so she would let him have that one. She had a moment of panic, thinking she had left unwrapped presents for him to find, but then she remembered: she had finished her marathon wrapping session before she went to bed, blearily putting away the scissors and Sellotape before falling into a deep sleep after midnight. Yikes, it was nine o'clock already. She didn't want Daniel turning up when she was still in her raggedy old pyjamas, the same ones she had had since Jack was born. She poked her head around the door to tell Jack to get himself some breakfast. She would then have a really speedy shower and chuck some warm clothes on.

'Off and get dressed, you,' she said, picking up his plate and mug. 'Warm clothes please, it's cold and I don't know what we're going to be getting up to today.'

'I do,' said Jack, slyly. 'Me and Daniel have a secret mission.'

'So, what's this secret mission,' teased Kate when Daniel turned up. He smiled at Jack conspiratorially.

'If I told you then it wouldn't be a secret mission, would it?' he said. 'Anyway, far more interesting for you is what you are going to be doing this morning.'

'Which is . . ?'

'You'll see.'

Daniel introduced Kate to Grace, who greeted her warmly. 'You're the one,' she cried. 'Daniel's told us all about you. We're all meeting up shortly, just needing to make sure we've got staff cover for all the last-minute Christmas shoppers. By which I mean the men,' she added, with a crooked smile.

'Oi,' said Daniel, 'that's not necessarily true, I think men are unfairly maligned.'

'Have you got all your presents?'

'Erm, no,' he admitted. 'That's why I've got Jack. He's my personal shopper for the morning.'

'Not just boring shopping,' protested Jack. 'There's the . . . *other thing*,' he said, without moving his lips and giving Kate an anxious look.

'Yeah, yeah, all good,' laughed Daniel. 'Come on, let's get going – busy day. There is just one other thing,' said Daniel to Kate. 'Once Grace and the team have finished with you, I need to go and see Noel in the hospital. I was trying to get to him yesterday but . . .'

'But it turned into a busy day,' admitted Kate.

'Yeah, and actually it's fine, because – really – I need to take you with me.'

'Ookay,' said Kate, puzzled. 'But you said he's terribly ill . . .'

'That's why he'll want to meet you. Trust me,' said Daniel. 'Grace will explain.'

Jack was delighted to go back to Krishna's for the afternoon and it gave Kate a chance to drop off the presents she had bought them the previous day.

'You shouldn't have,' said Seema, 'but I'm glad you did. We're going to have to drink this together,' she said, holding up the present Kate had given her, which was clearly a bottle. 'We've got lots of catching up to do, I gather.'

'It might be bath oil,' teased Kate.

'It isn't though.'

'No, I know you too well,' admitted Kate. 'We'll catch up.'

'But things are good?'

'Getting there.'

Seema gave Daniel a naughtily appraising look and said, 'I know what I'd really like for Christmas.'

'Yeah, well, he's not your Christmas present because (a) as you've said yourself, you're Hindu so you're not even supposed to get Christmas presents, technically, and (b) he's taken,' Kate shot back without thinking.

'Glad to hear it,' said Seema. 'About time.'

'I think I might have accidentally told Seema you and I are a thing,' admitted Kate as they walked to the hospital.

'Good,' said Daniel simply.

'Which, I suppose, we sort of are,' she went on, testing her soul tentatively for pain, as a tongue seeks out a mouth ulcer, expecting it to hurt. It didn't. Not now.

Ignoring this lukewarm assessment, he reached for her hand to cross the road, and when they got to the other side he didn't let go.

'It was amazing that I'd already seen the shop, though, wasn't it?' she asked as they walked. 'That I'd considered it, before I even knew you, or knew about the wedding group idea.'

'But did you think it was right for you then?'

'Totally. It was perfect. I just also knew that I wouldn't be able to afford the rent and rates, especially as I was getting started. It takes time to set up a business. Early cash flow and under-investment bury more new businesses than any other factor, even when there are amazing ideas that should do well.'

'You've done your research.'

'I have.' She had spent more time daydreaming about setting up a business of her own than she was prepared to admit. Even to herself.

'You don't recognise it, but you're pretty good at sorting out problems You're pretty impressive.'

'You say that, but the shop isn't a solution, although I'd love it. I still can't afford it,' she said, regretfully. 'I just can't.'

'Let's wait and see.'

'Are you sure I should be here?' she said again, hanging back as they got to the double doors leading to the ward. The nursing sister had given permission and confirmed that Noel was 'comfortable'.

'He knows you're coming,' said Daniel. 'He insisted.'

'This is her?' asked Noel, almost inaudibly, as Daniel and Kate sat themselves either side of the bed.

Daniel nodded, taking the frail old man's bony hand in his own strong, warm one.

'Thank you,' he said to Daniel before turning to smile at Kate.

She smiled back, unperturbed by his fragility. She had seen extreme age in other people at Maureen's nursing home, and in Noel she recognised the signs: the paper-thin skin barely covering a map of blue veins; faded, watery eyes; and just a few wisps of hair on his bony scalp.

'Tell me about yourself, my child,' he said, his voice faint, but gentle and kind.

*

'We didn't talk about terms and conditions,' said Kate anxiously as they left, nearly an hour later. Noel had fallen asleep, drifting serenely into slumber with each of his hands outstretched, one holding Daniel's and the other Kate's. Together, without a word, they had gently placed his hands on the covers and slipped away.

'Doesn't matter. I can sort that out with him later,' said Daniel. 'I was going to come in tomorrow once I've finished my helpline shift. I don't want him to be alone at Christmas and it's his birthday tomorrow too. The point is, he's taken to you. You're the one to take over the shop. The detail? We'll work it out.'

'I don't want you to be alone at Christmas either. Won't you come and spend it with us? Once you've seen Noel and said happy birthday?' said Kate. 'Nothing fancy, just me and Jack in our pyjamas?'

'Hmm. Maybe . . .' said Daniel, stopping in the street, and turning to face her. 'There's nothing I would like more, and don't get me wrong, but it seems to me like you and Jack need to be together, just the two of you, tomorrow. You've got the perfect Christmas lined up, more so than you know,' he gave a satisfied smile.

'What *were* you and Jack up to this morning,' she exclaimed, suspiciously.

'You'll see.'

They wandered through the streets from the hospital, down through Christmas Steps, where the team were making the most of the last few hours of trading before taking a few welcome days off over Christmas.

On the high street, the pavements were still bustling, but there was a sense of winding down. The light was fading, the Christmas lights were twinkling above, drunks were reeling out of pubs, well-refreshed from Christmas parties, saying extravagant goodbyes to workmates; excitement at the holidays tempered by drunken sentimentality at the thought of not seeing each other for a few days – even the people they usually did everything to avoid.

A deep peace spread through Kate's body and mind. As they wound their way down through St Nicholas's market, side-stepping last-minute shoppers in the narrow, stone-flagged corridors, the noise, the sights and the smells were like a cosy blanket, enveloping her and warming her.

As they went past St Stephen's Church, they had to flatten themselves against the wall to avoid getting in the way of an influx of people flowing through the double doors into the church.

'Shall we?' said Daniel, cocking his head in the direction of the entrance.

'Do you know what?' said Kate. 'Why not.' She had not been inside a church since Tom's funeral.

They joined the tail end of the crowds and found themselves right at the back. There was a hum of chatter, and laughter, the high ceilings and stone interiors turning the speech into a soothing white noise that surrounded them.

The candles were lit, casting a golden glow onto the children's excited faces, and casting the side aisles into deep shadow.

Then, as they waited, side by side, leaning against the back wall, the church fell quiet.

Kate looked around, confused, then a lone voice, in the flickering gloom, pierced the silence. There, slowly processing up the aisle, was a phalanx of angelic choirboys in their white cotton robes, a little boy at their head who couldn't have been much older than Jack, holding a candle that illuminated his bright blond hair.

'Once in Royal David's City,' he sang – pure, simple and crystal clear, as Kate's eyes welled up and spilled over.

The choir sang the second verse and by the time the congregation joined in thunderously with the third, Kate was sobbing.

'Are you okay,' said Daniel in her ear, his arm around her shoulders as he rummaged in his pocket for a tissue.

'I can *feel*,' she told him. 'I can really feel again. It's like I've been dead, and I've come back to life.'

By the time they left the church after the nine lessons and carols, Kate's eyes were pink and her nose was blocked, but she was elated. It was as if the cork which had been holding in all her emotions since Tom's death had finally become dislodged. She was exhausted, but filled with joy, for the first time in years.

And Christmas was real again. Like it had been in the past.

'One last surprise,' Daniel told her as they all arrived at the flat. Jack was so excited he was hopping from foot to foot.

'Me first, me first,' he said, as they opened the door to the flat. 'I want to see your face.'

She let him scamper ahead and then went in, Daniel behind, with a hint of nerves at what would be revealed.

When she first went into the sitting room, she thought there might be something the matter with her eyes, perhaps as a result of being dazzled by the street lights or from being made bleary by all the crying.

The cramped, ugly room had been rendered invisible because the only thing Kate's eyes would allow her to look at was the tree.

It was intensely over-decorated with baubles of all colours, sizes and shapes, competing for her attention with what must have been six sets of lights, some coloured, some just white, all twinkling on different settings. There were streams of multi-coloured tinsel, some arranged horizontally, some vertical and some just – well – 'random' was the only word for it.

'Me and Daniel did it,' squeaked Jack. 'We did it today, when you were out. D'ya like it? Do you? It's for you. Look, there's my salt-dough snowman on the top. I made it, and Daniel put it on the top. See?'

'You couldn't be Christmas Tree Girl and not have your own tree,' explained Daniel, a little sheepishly.

'I was "Christmas Tree Girl"?'

'Of course,' he admitted. 'I didn't know what else to call you. I thought about you all the time . . .'

'Thank you,' she said, reaching up and giving him a kiss on the cheek. 'Thank you for making Christmas matter again. For making me a better mother. For making me want to wake up and live fully again.'

'You did that yourself. You are the strongest woman I have ever met. I think you're amazing. I . . .' he paused, looking into her eyes, gauging whether he should say . . .

Kate put a finger on his lips. 'Nearly,' she said. 'Nearly, but not yet.'

Daniel looked at his watch. 'I,' he said, with infinite regret, 'now have to go and help sad, lonely people.'

Christmas Day

Poor Dorothy, thought Kate as she watched *The Wizard of Oz* for the umpteenth time. Kate felt like she had spent the last four years since Tom's horrific death trying to find a way back home, like Dorothy, only to discover that home was not a place, it was people and had been there all the time. All she had to do was to wake up.

She looked down and dropped a kiss onto Jack's head. He was slumped on the sofa beside her, tucked under her arm, still in his pyjamas even though it was evening. They were a new pair she had given him that morning amongst his other presents, along with a pair of warm furry slippers and a fleecy checked dressing gown, perfect for their chilly flat. He had no interest in sensible stuff though. The stand-out gifts for Jack were the Marvel figures – expensive luxuries she had only been able to afford because of the money from the jewellery sale. Money she had earned, fair and square, from her own talent, she remembered with quiet pride.

In contrast to Jack in his classic checked pyjamas, she was wearing a fetching reindeer onesie, complete with antlers, which Jack proudly announced he and Daniel had bought together before they got the tree. She would have to have words with that man. She looked a complete twit. It was even worse than the elf costume. Much more comfortable and cosy though, she had to admit.

It had been an amazing Christmas Day. They were both stuffed, from the pancakes with mincemeat at breakfast to the 'everything in a Christmas Dinner' sandwiches they made for lunch, because – let's face it – the turkey, cranberry and stuffing leftovers made such amazing sandwiches, why not just cut to the chase? The Christmas pudding from the Apple Café was unexpectedly delicious – much better than the black, heavy lump she had been given at the staff Christmas party, which felt like it had happened years ago. She and Jack had laughed, cooked, eaten, opened presents, played silly games and then – when Jack was exhausted – they had watched Christmas telly with a box of Quality Street until they were dazed and dozy with excess.

Kate scooped him up and carried him to bed. Toothbrushing could wait 'til morning, just for once. He barely stirred as she popped him under the duvet and pulled it up to his chin.

As she went back into the sitting room, her phone trilled its text signal.

'Is he in bed?' it asked.

'Yep,' she texted back.

'Fancy a Christmas toast?'

'Go on then.'

As soon as she texted, the doorbell rang, a short burst, so short she almost thought she had imagined it.

Surely not . . . She opened the door, and there he was, the melting snowflakes on his shoulders catching the light from the tree, more of them sparkling in his hair, his kind, lovely face breaking into a broad smile.

'There was one more thing I needed to make my Christmas miracle,' smiled Kate at the sight of him.

'This?' he asked holding out a bottle of chilled champagne.

'Okay, there were two more things I needed,' she amended, taking it from him.

'And what was the other one?' he asked, stepping inside and wrapping his arms around her, his hazel eyes dancing as he gazed down at her.

'This,' she said, standing on tiptoes and pressing her lips to his.

Acknowledgements

I am enormously grateful to the team at Orion for inviting me to write this book – who knew that it would end up being my personal air conditioning system? Writing about snowballs and mince pies during the hottest of hot summers since the last really hot summer feels like an elegant reversal of the Narnia stories where the White Queen made it 'always winter and never Christmas'.

The Bristol setting has also been a delight to write. I never knew so much about the city until now, and have blatantly set my story in real places, although – as always – real people are not included. I thank all the Bristolians who helped with my 'research'.

My agent Julia Silk is amazing and seems to dedicate her life to keeping me busy, which is just as well as who knows what mischief I would get up to if I didn't have enough to do. Grateful thanks to her and the whole team at MBA.

I also want to acknowledge the extraordinary support of all my family and friends, who provide gin and laughs and even take the trouble to read the damned thing – Alex, Claire, Clare, Kate, Nancy, Carolyn, Charlie, Catherine, Georgie, Sarah, Anna, Vicky, Kim, Helen, Sharon, Lisa et al – you know who you are. . . To say nothing of my stalwart husband and children, who have to endure all those late and hastily cooked suppers.

And finally, a million thanks to the lovely Laura Gerrard for instigating the project and to the delightful Clare Hey for picking it up with such enthusiasm. I also thank Olivia Barber, Brittany Sankey, Alex Layt and everyone at Orion for their hard work and expertise. Let's do this!

Credits

Poppy Alexander and Orion Fiction would like to thank everyone at Orion who worked on the publication of *25 Days in December* in the UK.

Editorial
Clare Hey
Laura Gerrard
Victoria Oundjian
Olivia Barber

Copy editor
John Garth

Proof reader
Laetitia Grant

Audio
Paul Stark
Amber Bates

Contracts
Anne Goddard
Paul Bulos
Jake Alderson

Design
Debbie Holmes
Joanna Ridley
Nick May
Helen Ewing

Editorial Management
Charlie Panayiotou
Jane Hughes
Alice Davis

Finance
Jasdip Nandra
Afeera Ahmed
Elizabeth Beaumont
Sue Baker

Marketing
Brittany Sankey
Tanjiah Islam

Production
Ruth Sharvell

Publicity
Alex Layt

Rights
Susan Howe
Krystyna Kujawinska
Jessica Purdue
Richard King
Louise Henderson

Sales
Jen Wilson
Esther Waters

Victoria Laws
Rachael Hum
Ellie Kyrke-Smith
Frances Doyle
Georgina Cutler

Operations
Jo Jacobs
Sharon Willis
Lisa Pryde
Lucy Brem